The Tapestries

ALSO BY KIEN NGUYEN

The Unwanted

The Tapestries

A NOVEL

Kien Nguyen

LITTLE, BROWN AND COMPANY
BOSTON NEW YORK LONDON

First Edition

The characters and events in this book are fictitious. Any similarity to real persons,
living or dead, is coincidental and not intended by the author.

The art on the title page of *The Tapestries* was taken from a tapestry
woven by the author's grandfather, who served as a professional embroiderer in the court of the last king of Vietnam in the early 1900s.

Library of Congress Cataloging-in-Publication Data
Nguyen, Kien.
    The tapestries : a novel / Kien Nguyen — 1st ed.
        p. cm.
    ISBN 0–316–28441–6
        1. Vietnam — Fiction. I. Title.
PS3614.G89 T37 2002
813'.54 — dc21   2002066092

10 9 8 7 6 5 4 3 2 1

Q-FF

Book design by Iris Weinstein

Printed in the United States of America

To my mother;
to my godfather, Frank Andrews;
and to my mentor, Nhat Tien

Part One

The Wedding

*D*uring the winter months, the Perfume River was chilly, especially at dawn. The morning of Dan Nguyen's first wedding was no exception. While the sun was still hidden, its early rays reached from behind the Ngu Binh Mountain, stretching pale-yellow fingers over the sky. Thin clouds wafted by, and the wind whipped up whirlpools of mist. Damp tendrils drifted over the jungle of oak trees that climbed the steep mountainside and were lost against the horizon.

Along the side of the river, a strip of land still lay in darkness. From afar, it looked like the back of a crocodile floating in the water. A few hundred feet away, a sampan moved slowly upstream. Both sides of the boat were painted with red resin from the lacquer tree and highlighted with gold trim in large rectangular patterns — the design reserved for weddings.

At the vessel's stern, a white-haired man with stooped shoulders sat on the floor. His gnarled hands clenched an oar, and he leaned heavily into its strokes. The man seemed lost in his own world. His eyes, hidden beneath the rim of a torn conical hat, focused on the water. The faded blue peasant shirt on his back was tattered, exposing his bony ribs. Next to him hung a red lantern that illuminated a short stretch of river ahead. The faint sound of the oar moving the water echoed against the silence.

Behind the old man, in the center of the sampan, was a small cabin with a roof built of red-lacquered bamboo stalks lashed together with palm fronds. Across its entrance hung a pink silk screen on which a canary-yellow dragon entwined with its feminine mate, an equally gracious phoenix. Custom dictated that the bride must be concealed from sight. She sat behind the silk barrier, careful not to make a sound while the boat rocked to the helmsman's gentle rhythm.

Just as the sun appeared from behind the purple mountain, the old man guided his bridal sampan toward land. Sunlight broke through the clouds into thousands of tiny golden pennies. The old man squinted, searching the shoreline for a place to dock. He did not have to look far.

Just ahead, where the ground extended into the water to form a long, narrow wharf, twenty people from the groom's family stood in a single file. Most of them wore the *ao dai*, the ceremonial garb reserved for festivities such as this. The costumes were similar for both men and women: a tunic, made out of silk or satin, with a long skirt separated at the waist into two panels, front and back. The men wore their robes over white pants, while the women wore theirs over black — a more subservient color.

The wedding party had prepared the landing site by hanging strings of firecrackers over the branches of the tamarind trees. Upon the arrival of the sampan, the two oldest men began the ceremony by burning purified joss sticks. Then they ignited the firecrackers. The red, petal-like missiles burst into the morning air, stirring flocks of sparrows from their sleep. They flapped their gray wings among the dark branches, adding their screeches to the din. The deafening sound of the explosives was believed to banish evil spirits as the groom's family prepared to accept their new daughter-in-law.

With the help of two young servants, the old man stepped off his boat. He took off his hat and bowed to the elders. His gesture was mechanical yet courteous. He focused his eyes on the crimson debris of the fireworks on the ground. After the last few scattered booms, silence returned to the riverbank, and even the fog seemed to settle back into its original pattern, draped over the oak trees.

From the greeting party, one man marched forward. He was about forty-five years old, and his deep-set eyes peered from beneath bushy eyebrows. His high cheekbones and the downward curve of his mouth made his features appear grim and darkly authoritative. He wore a headdress of black silk, folded into many layers, which framed the crown of his head like a halo. His *ao dai* was ocean blue, with a subtle, darker, dotted pattern of embroidery, representing the royal symbol of longevity. The fabric was handwoven from a superlative silk, made by the silkworms of the famous Phu Yen Village. Even a rich man could afford only a few such garments. He returned the old man's salutation with a slow bow, then knitted his hands together and faced his palms upward, placing them against his abdomen.

"Greetings," he said to the visitor. "My name is Tat Nguyen. I am the father of the groom. Welcome to our humble town."

The old man's head bowed lower, so that no one could see his lips moving as he spoke. "Thank you, but I am afraid that I can't accept your warm welcome, Master Nguyen. My job is to deliver my granddaughter to your home. It is now done, and so I must bid my farewell. Take her with you to the groom. From this moment on, she belongs in your household, sir."

He stepped aside, leaving room for the groom's family to approach the sampan. A pair of servants came forward and joined the other two on the boat. One stood at each corner of the bridal cabin. Then, with one synchronized movement, they hoisted the cubicle to their shoulders and carried it to the shore.

Master Nguyen lifted a corner of his robe and strode to the cabin. He parted the silk screen with the back of his hand to reveal its small interior. Looking back at him was a woman in her twenties. Dressed in a red wedding gown, she crouched with visible discomfort in the center of the cabin. The moment she saw his face, she recoiled farther into her cramped sanctuary. Her eyes, slanted and wide-set, darted as though she were searching for a way to flee. From years of working outdoors, her body had absorbed so much sunlight that a glow seemed to radiate from her skin. She had a big, flat nose, large mouth, and oversized teeth, which were stained black with the juice of betel nuts. He drew his eyebrows together disapprovingly.

"Master, do you like what you see, sir?" came a female voice from somewhere behind him.

He turned to see an elderly woman whose back was bent so close to the ground that she appeared to be crawling instead of walking. She was the matchmaker who was responsible for this arranged wedding. Trying to meet his stare, she looped her neck like a duck.

"How old is she?" he asked.

"Four and twenty, sir."

His frown deepened. "She is an old maid, isn't she?"

"She is very healthy," the matchmaker replied quickly. "She is as strong as a bull. And look at her breasts. They are heavy. You will be blessed with many grandchildren."

He relaxed his grimace, looked at the bride, and asked, "What is your name, daughter?"

Upon hearing this, the matchmaker turned happily to the others. "The master has approved. He called her 'daughter.' Bring in the musicians!"

A much louder noise from a turn of the street drowned out the old lady's excited cry — the pulsating sound of a drum. Within seconds, a dragon made of glossy painted wood, cardboard, and papier mâché, held up high on bamboo sticks, appeared at the opening of the wharf. From afar, it seemed to float through the village. Young men in white shirts and red pants danced under it to the beat of the drum. Lanterns, shaped like butterflies and fish, burned brightly under the early-morning sun. A soprano sang the ending verse from the famous opera *The King's Wedding*. Her voice glided to the highest note before it, too, blended with the sounds of revelry. More firecrackers soared through the air, and no one seemed to notice when the old man slipped away to his boat and turned it back downstream.

When the noisy celebration dimmed, the bride shyly answered her father-in-law's question. "My name is Ven, sir."

"Good." Master Nguyen nodded. It was a lowly name that one would give only to a dog, yet somehow it suited her, he thought.

The matchmaker handed him a red veil, which he hung over the bride's head, concealing her face. From that time on, all she could see were the ruby tips of her slippers, yet she was thankful. The sheer fabric became her protective shield. Alone in a strange town, she would rather be led through the ceremony like a blind woman, unaware of the disparaging looks, like the one she had just received from her husband's father. In the back of her mind, a pang of curiosity stirred up, as faint as smoke. What did he look like? She knew nothing about her bridegroom. What of his personality, his likes, his dislikes, even his name? And yet, these things mattered little at this juncture of her life. Like it or not, she was about to be a married woman.

The servants carried her through the streets. The farther they walked, the more vigorously the cabin rocked on their shoulders. She leaned back, closed her eyes, and let herself sway with its movement. The thought of becoming a fine woman in a rich man's home relaxed her aching muscles. The folds of her satin gown trapped her body heat, and she began perspiring. *"An elegant lady never sweats."* She dimly remembered an old saying she had heard as a child. She reached under the veil and wiped her forehead with the back of her hand.

At last, the bridal party stopped at what seemed to be the back entrance of a house. Someone swept aside the silk curtain of her cubicle and took her callused palm. She recognized the matchmaker's wrinkled hand as the old lady guided her down a muddy path that led to a wooden door.

At the entrance, a burning pot of red coals sat on the ground waiting for her. It was the custom for the bride to step over a blazing stove before setting foot in her new home. The fire would rid her soul of any evil spirits still clinging to it. The matchmaker explained that, according to the astrologer, Ven's unfortunate time of birth required her to enter through the back door and go straight to her honeymoon suite. The rest of the wedding celebration would continue without her.

Ven had to wait for her husband to come and lift her veil. This was another important tradition she had been told that she must follow if she ever hoped to have a long and happy life with this man. Seeing nothing but the tiles beneath her feet, Ven was led through unseen rooms and seated on her bridal bed, alone in the unfamiliar house.

*V*en lost count of how many hours she remained alone. From the fading of a few streaks of light on the floor, she could tell that the day had aged into night. Outside the window, the party seemed to be winding down. She could hear the laughter slowly diminish into the slurring of drunken guests. The ebullient opera had ended, and now there was a single, soporific moan of a lute. In the dark, her back throbbed, and the numbness in her buttocks spread down her legs. She was hungry and tired. The gown tightened around her bosom, making it difficult for her to breathe.

Just when she thought she could not wait any longer, Ven heard the squeaking noise of a door as it opened and shut. A small group of people tiptoed into the room. Their whispering sounded to her like the wind rasping against rice paper. The oil lamp on the nightstand by her side flickered into light. Moments later, she heard the intruders withdraw, carefully closing the door behind them.

But Ven could tell that she was not alone. The subtle movement of the furniture, the faint rustle of clothing, and the quiet footsteps moving back and forth kept her frozen in place. *It's him,* she thought. *It must be my husband. Who else could it be?* In seconds, her months of waiting would be over. Like a boiling pot of water, the anxiety rose up, and she could hardly control her composure. She sat tightly, watching her hands tremble. She could feel the heat from her husband's body as he approached her. She kept her eyes downcast. Touching the ruby tips of her slippers were two tiny bare feet, just half the size of hers. A small hand reached out and clumsily tugged the veil from her face.

Standing before her was a little boy wearing a groom's costume. He could not have been older than seven. She could see the wide gap of his missing front teeth as he grinned at her, and it came to her that this child was her husband.

She got up from the edge of the wedding bed and lowered the oil lamp until it emitted only a dot of light the size of a pea. Quietly, she took off her restrictive clothing. The boy sat on the bed and watched her with his large, almond-shaped eyes. He inserted his thumb into the gap in his teeth. Ven left her undergarments on and climbed into the bed, pulling the mosquito net over her. As she lay down, her husband snuggled into her outstretched arms. He buried his face in her armpit, sucking his thumb.

She took the boy's wrist and pulled the finger out of his mouth. With an effort, she made her voice low and reasonable. "Young master, you are too old for this habit." He lay still, looking at her. Then he closed his eyes and went to sleep. Ven struggled with an impulse to wipe the drool off his face.

In the dark, she began to understand what her position would be in this rich man's house. They did not marry her to make her a fine lady. They wanted her for slave labor. Yet, being a daughter-in-law, she was not entitled to the salary a servant would have been paid.

To her surprise, Ven found she could not cry. Soon exhaustion claimed her.

chapter two

Breakfast

Ven was awoken before dawn by a tapping on her shoulder. In the light of the oil lantern, she saw the shadowed face of a young woman leaning over her. At her side, still wrapped in her arms, her groom was asleep.

Ven pulled away from her husband gently, so as not to disturb him. His peaceful face, round with baby fat, pressed against the hard tatami surface. The oak bed creaked under her weight like the bones of an old person. Through the bedroom window the night seemed frozen in time, and the courtyard shimmered in an iridescent glow. Here and there, the moonlight lingered on a few rare orchids.

Beyond the high brick garden wall, she heard the lazy footsteps of a time-teller. In most communities, the task of telling time fell to the village idiot, since his duty was considered lowly in the extreme. Most often, he lived in a hut on the outskirts of town, far from any neighbors. Besides the clothes on his back, the time-teller typically owned only a small metal gong. Night after night, he wandered the streets, sounding the passage of time with his padded hammer. By counting the strokes he made, the villagers could approximate the hour. The night was divided into five intervals, each about two Western hours long, stretching from sunset to rooster's crow. Ven counted four strokes on the gong. Its hollow sound echoed through the stillness long after the man's shuffling footsteps had receded.

She dressed quickly in the dark, wearing the undergarments she had on from the day before. From the bundle of possessions she had brought with her, she chose a long-sleeved cotton blouse, as the sun would not come up for several more hours.

The young woman who had woken Ven up stood waiting by the doorway. She was dressed in servant's clothes — a faded brown uniform. She was about sixteen years old, and sleep still crusted her eyelids. With an impatient gesture, she beckoned for Ven to follow her. Ven took a lantern from the bamboo stick outside the bedroom door and watched the servant hurry ahead of her down the hall. The girl was heavy, and she waddled like a pregnant mare.

"What is your name?" Ven asked her.

"I am called Song," she said in a whisper.

"Where are we going?" Ven hastened to keep up as they walked down one of the manicured paths that cut across the garden, dividing it into rectangular beds of well-kept grasses and plants.

The maid stopped next to a plum tree and turned to look at Ven. "We are going to the kitchen, of course," she whispered. "First Mistress has ordered you to make breakfast and have it ready by the time the other mistresses wake up. Didn't the matchmaker tell you this would be your duty?"

"No," Ven replied. "When do the mistresses wake up?"

"As soon as the time-teller makes his last round. But if I were you, I would not rely on him. He drinks too much rice wine and is always late. You have about two hours to prepare the meal."

She resumed her swaying gait, and they walked in front of Master Nguyen's house. The mansion and its outlying buildings faced a white-brick path, about twenty feet wide and a hundred yards long, that led to the street. Three gates protected the compound from intruders. The middle and largest one was a solid piece of black granite, split in two. When closed, the two sides merged in a complicated carving that depicted a portion of the mystical world of Heaven — beautiful bodies of the immortals dancing in and out of the clouds. Through this elegant portal only family members and honored guests would pass. Servants and vendors used the two side doors, which were modest in size and made of simply carved wood.

Ven stopped to look at her new home. Under the indigo moonlight, its outline glinted as though made out of sapphire. Never in her life had she been in a place so magnificent. It was a miniature palace, from the golden roof, decorated with a bold ceramic dragon at each corner, to the red sliding panels of its doors. In front stood five massive granite columns, embossed with carved dragons. The veranda held an ornamental vase balanced on a wooden stand large enough to hide an adult. Inside grew a eucalyptus twisted into the shape of a phoenix, which reached its wings to the sky as if to take flight.

They turned onto a side path, and through a window of opaque parchment, Ven was surprised to see that the main living room was aglow. The light of oil lamps flickered on the silhouettes of two men. They leaned over a desk in serious discussion. Curious, Ven stepped closer. She could hear their urgent whispers, though she could not make out what they were saying.

Song slipped in next to her. "The master is meeting with Master Long, the town mayor."

"Did my father-in-law entertain a lot of overnight guests because of the wedding?" Ven asked.

The girl shook her head. "No, the master doesn't allow overnight guests, except for a few important people and, of course, his fishing crews. Master Long did not come for your wedding. He sometimes comes after dinner, and he and the master stay up talking until dawn."

"How often do they meet?"

"It varies," Song replied. "Our master and the first two mistresses are seldom home, but when they are, they entertain several guests. For example, Master Long was here four nights already this week. Occasionally, two other men accompany him."

"What do they talk about?" Ven asked. Her eyes were glued to the shadows on the screened window.

"I don't know. I assume it's about the master's business."

"What kind of business does he have?"

Song looked up at Ven with a fearful expression. "Please, Mistress —"

It was the first time that Song had addressed Ven with a title. She listened as the maid continued, "I beg you, don't ask me any more questions. Your in-laws would not hesitate to discipline me severely if they found out I was telling you these things." The girl turned away and hid behind the curtain of her hair.

Ven knew she should give up her prying and make herself sub-servient in the eyes of others. But inside she felt a touch of rebellion, and as isolated as she was in this strange house, she could not let go of the subject. She touched the girl's shoulder. "I am scared, too," she admitted. "You and I are of the same kind. We are both women. And we are slaves under this roof. But unlike you, I do not receive wages for my service, and to others I am still an outsider. For those reasons, I need your help. Please tell me about these people before I meet them, so that I can avoid mistakes. I promise I won't get you into trouble."

Song sighed. "I see that you know as little about them as they know about you," she said. "The master and his first two wives earn their living from the sea. Master is the captain of the largest fishing boat in this town. Most of the men in the village work for him as his sailors."

"What about Third Mistress? What does she do?"

"Third Mistress is like a water lily, beautiful but fragile. Before she was married to our master, she was an actress in a Chinese opera troupe, which performed in the big cities. She was sold into this house when she was fourteen. I learned this from Old Che, the family's cook. She was handed over to settle a debt the owner of the troupe had with the master. He loves her beyond reason. He treats her like a Buddha statue and never lets anyone or anything so much as touch her fingernails. Ever since she was blessed with a child, and nearly died giving birth to him, Master Nguyen has allowed her to handle the household while he is away at sea. That child is your new husband."

Ven ran her hand over the bars that protected the window. She knew it was dangerous to linger, but the voices from the other side of the parchment stirred her curiosity. "What could they possibly be talking about that would last all night? Surely it can't just be business."

Song's eyes took on a conspiratorial sparkle. "Do you want to find out?" Without waiting for an answer, she put a finger in her mouth and moistened it, then used it to poke a small hole through the parchment. Ven stepped closer and put her eye to the opening.

From her oblique angle, she could not see Master Nguyen's face. It was hidden behind a lantern, but she recognized his dark-blue robe with the sphere-shaped embroidered pattern. He was reading something to his guest out of a notebook. She had a direct view of the other man, who appeared to be in his early thirties. He had thick hair and wore thin-rimmed glasses. His delicate lips tightened to form a straight line across the lower half of his face. He appeared to be listening intently to Master Nguyen.

Song leaned close to Ven's ear. "Can you make out what they are saying, Mistress?" she murmured.

"Only a little," said Ven. "They seem to be discussing politics, not business."

"It's possible," the girl said. "Master Nguyen is passionate about political affairs. The royal palace once offered him a position, but he declined."

"Why?" To Ven, the idea of refusing the fame and fortune that came with a royal assignment was inconceivable.

"I don't know," Song said. "I once heard Third Mistress say that he isn't happy with the influence that the French government has over the court at Hue." The maid looked over her shoulder and seemed to grow worried. "Let's go," she said, pulling at Ven's arm. "Before someone sees us. Besides, I'm getting chilly, aren't you?"

Ven pulled herself away from the window and followed Song to the kitchen, a small building next to the living quarters. It was the dirtiest place she had ever seen. The original color of its walls had long been buried under a greasy coating of sticky black soot. A bitter smell of burned pork fat, mixed with the stench of singed feathers, formed a dark cloud under the low ceiling. Oversized pots and pans, some big enough to hold an entire potbellied pig, lay scattered on the damp cement floor. Ven could see the food encrusted around their edges. None of this surprised her.

Like most Vietnamese, her in-laws apparently believed that the kitchen was a place that generated fortune. The dirtier it got, the richer the owner would be. Anyone foolish enough to clean up his kitchen would soon find his fortunes wiped out. Ven's origins were humble. She never had a reason to follow this ancient custom.

"Where should I begin?" she asked, trying to hide her queasiness.

Song pointed to a small door behind the wooden cabinets. "All the dried food is in that pantry. First Mistress always has sweet rice with red beans wrapped in bamboo leaves and a bowl of sparrow's nest in shark-fin soup for breakfast. Second and Third Mistresses prefer black beans, not red ones. The master likes his sticky rice coated in mung-bean starch and steamed in coconut milk. The rest of the servants will have regular white rice and grilled chicken in lemongrass. Do you know how to make sparrow's nest soup?"

Ven nodded uncertainly. At home, her grandmother had taught her how to make many exotic and expensive meals in preparation for her married life. Yet she could learn only the principles of those recipes, for her family was too poor to buy the ingredients. But bird's nest soup was not her main dilemma. She was preoccupied with unanswered questions and impossible chores. She looked at the saucepans, cleared her throat, and asked Song, "How many people do I have to cook for?"

The maid replied, "It all depends. Today, because Master Nguyen and his crew are here, we will prepare food for everyone in the household, plus thirty fishermen. But usually, there are just the five of us. That includes you, the young master, Third Mistress, the gardener, and me. Today the matchmaker is also here."

"I was under the impression that there are lots of servants in this house. I saw so many at the riverbank yesterday."

Song laughed. "Those are Master Nguyen's crew. They were the ones who orchestrated your wedding yesterday. I am the only servant in this house."

"Who usually does the cooking?"

"Old Che was the cook until yesterday. First Mistress fired her just before the wedding."

Ven pushed up her sleeves. She regarded the young maid's ample curves and said, "You are very young and pretty. Why didn't the master marry his son to you?"

Song's cheek turned as red as the skin of a ripe Chinese plum. "Please, Mistress. Do not joke with me. A chicken cannot grow a peacock tail. I was a widow long before I came to work in this house. My husband was a fisherman who worked for Master Nguyen. He died from dysentery while at sea two years ago this full moon."

"I am sorry," Ven said, feeling foolish. "You look so young. Please forgive me."

Song waved her hands in front of her face. "It is quite all right, Mistress," she said. "Now you must hurry. There isn't much time left. You don't want to upset your in-laws on your first day."

"Will you help me make breakfast?" Ven asked.

Song nodded. "I am the kitchen assistant. Let me soak the bird's nest while you cook the sticky rice."

❧

Ven added the last threads of shark fin to the sparrow's nest soup just as the time-teller came around for his last trip. Song tasted the soup base and gave her approval. Outside, the sun sent golden rays into the dark kitchen to heat the cool air.

Song handed Ven a set of china soup bowls that were as thin and delicate as a sheet of paper, and just as white. The dishes nestled into her hand as though designed for it. To Ven's amazement, when she poured the soup into the bowls, they instantly turned a bright shade of jade green. There was no table in the kitchen, so Ven arranged everything on the ground. She placed the bowls gently on an ebony tray, where they glowed against the dull cement floor like four magnificent pieces of jewelry.

"Be careful when you handle them," the maid said to her. "They are very expensive. They change color in response to heat. Why don't you take the soup to the main living room and serve the mistresses? I will bring the rest of the breakfast as soon as it is ready. After they dine, we will provide food for the staff."

"Where is the main living room?" Ven asked.

"It is the first and largest room in the house, facing the entrance that we passed earlier this morning," Song said. "But you are not yet allowed to use the front door. Your astrological sign is in opposition to that of Third Mistress, and Master Nguyen fears you might cause her great harm if you don't take precautions. Follow this path to the back door."

Song placed the lids over the exposed soup bowls and pointed to a narrow lane of bricks that led to the rear of the great house. Like magic, the bowl covers also took on the glistening hue of emeralds, as though light shone through them from inside.

Stepping from the kitchen, Ven was dismayed to see that the path forked into three separate routes. All led into the house, but through different doors. After a moment's hesitation, she drew a deep breath and chose the path that led to the entrance nearest her. Finding the door unlocked, she turned the knob with her free hand and pulled it open. The rusty hinges groaned.

She found herself in a dark and damp room filled with half-naked men sprawled on tatami mats. At least thirty, maybe forty of them were crowded into the confined space. They roused lazily as the bright, crisp air from outside poured in. Some muttered curses under their breath. Others burst out laughing when they saw the frightened look on Ven's face. She took several steps back, her hands gripping her tray. She turned around and hurried back to the second path.

But fate seemed to toy with her that morning. As she approached the house for the second time, the corroded metal door before her sprang open, and a man stormed out, colliding with her. Though she was normally not a graceful woman, she spun around, using her back to absorb the impact of the blow while she balanced the precious load. She recognized the angry face of Master Long, just inches from her own. He had the smoothest skin she had ever seen on a man.

"Watch where you are going," he snapped. Adjusting his robe, he sauntered past her and disappeared behind a clump of taro plants.

With her heart throbbing, Ven pushed the third door open with her elbow. The first face she saw in the room was her husband's. He grinned at her, showing the same toothless smile she had seen the night before when he had removed her wedding veil.

***

Ven lowered her glance and kept her eyes glued to the floor, which was overlaid with beautiful blue-and-white tiles. Its surface was so highly polished that she could see her reflection as clearly as if she had been gazing into the river. The room occupied a large portion of the main house, an expanse of roughly thirty by seventy feet. The sturdy walls were made of cement mixed with peppercorns. As the temperature outside dropped, the heat from the peppercorns would help keep the room's temperature at a comfortable level. Ven knew that this system of construction was a luxury that only the rich could afford.

Her husband stood at the foot of a spiral staircase, once again dressed in his groom's outfit. His head was shaved except for three little spots: one above his forehead and two at the sides, above his ears. For the first time, Ven noticed that the haircut made him look like one of the fairies' servants who carried the peach of immortality at the gate of Heaven, a scene often depicted inside Confucian temples.

Behind the young Master Nguyen was a massive black-lacquered divan decorated with a mother-of-pearl mosaic illustrating the life story of Kuan Yin, the goddess of mercy. Its craftsmanship was exquisite, and Ven could not help admiring its beauty. She paused, temporarily confused.

"Come in and close the door behind you," a harsh voice said.

She lifted her head and saw that the voice belonged to a woman in her sixties, the oldest person in the room besides the matchmaker. The dowager lay on the couch, reclining. Her face was cocked upward to study Ven, and she wore an expression of undisguised disapproval, as though she were regarding a piece of spoiled meat. One of her arms stretched over the back of the divan, and in her hand she loosely held a long, ivory opium pipe. Her other hand held the mouthpiece of the pipe a few inches away from her mouth. She wore a black robe, which hung on her flat chest like a scarecrow's rags. Its severe color accentuated the pallor of her skin, and her purple lips, discolored from opium, pressed together like oily earthworms. She wore no jewelry except for a bright gold collar, which encircled her neck like a brace.

"Move closer. Meet your second and third mothers," she said, pointing to the other two women.

The matchmaker seized the opportunity to make herself useful. She reeled toward Ven, her back curved torturously to the ground.

"Come over here, girl. Pay your respects to your mothers-in-law. Bow and offer them the soup."

Ven moved toward the divan, keeping her eyes on the immaculate floor. She could see the women's reflections in the tiles as they studied her. The matchmaker tapped on her legs and whispered to her, "Kneel down."

Like a puppet, Ven fell to her knees. She raised the ebony tray to her brow, so that all she could see was the side panel of the couch. "First Mother," she said to the goddess of mercy's inlay, "please have some sparrow's nest soup."

First Mistress ignored her. Instead, she waved the pipe to Second Mistress, who sat across from her on a burgundy velvet pillow. The gesture promptly animated the woman. She reached into her blouse for a silver pillbox the size of a betel nut. From the corner of her eye, Ven watched her spoon out a brownish, rubbery substance, using a gold pin. She roasted this resin over the flame of an oil lantern for a few seconds, checked its consistency with her thumb and forefinger, then rolled it into a small round capsule and placed it in the older woman's pipe.

A few feet away, a younger woman slouched in an oversized armchair, holding a lute against her chest. This, Ven deduced, must be the beloved Third Mistress. Her tiny bare feet were stretched out on top of an ottoman. Ven saw that her feet had been bound in the Chinese way when she was a child, so that they were now no larger than those of her seven-year-old son. But she was not an entirely traditional woman — her teeth, instead of being stained with the lacquered juice as was customary, were pearly white.

A shirtless young man in his mid-twenties knelt beside Third Mistress's stool. He massaged her delicate feet with coconut oil. Each movement of his hands made his muscles ripple under his tanned skin, like the stout cords of a fisherman's ropes.

Just as Song had said, Third Mistress was an exceptionally beautiful young woman. She did not seem to be a day older than twenty-three. Her luxurious jet-black hair was parted perfectly in the middle and twisted into a tight chignon. A few strands fell down the sides of her face, caressing her flawless skin like streaks of dark ink on white canvas. She leaned her cheek against the fretted neck of the lute while her fingers plucked at the strings and made a lazy, melancholy tune. A red crepe-de-Chine breast band across her bosom accentuated the elegance of her long neck.

Second Mistress rose to fetch an ornamental screen embroidered with a pheasant and placed it in front of the older woman. The device protected First Mistress's pipe from the draft so its flame could stay lit. And, of course, she liked to keep her activities from prying eyes. Next, Second Mistress removed a transparent shade from an oil lantern. Through the partition, Ven could hear the loud sucking noise the old woman made with her pipe and the gurgling sound of the liquid being churned in the bowl.

Suddenly everything stopped, including the music that wept from beneath Third Mistress's slender fingers. First Mistress dropped her pipe and fell back. Her eyes closed. Her lips tightened. Her chest seemed to stop moving. For several seconds, no one made a sound.

Then the music resumed. Second Mistress turned to Ven and said, "It is time to offer First Mother her soup. It will help to keep her opium down."

First Mistress sat up and opened her eyes, still holding her breath. She grabbed a bowl of soup from Ven's hands and took a sip. With a scowl, she put the bowl back on the tray and spat the soup into a copper urn on the floor.

"It's cold," she snarled.

Ven looked at the soup bowls. Their emerald glow had vanished, leaving the outer shells pale. Beside her, the matchmaker uttered a cry of dismay.

"What kind of miserable cook are you?" the older woman went on. "When did you prepare this soup, last night? You wasted a perfectly good dose of opium that could have helped relieve my arthritis — not to mention my valuable sparrow's nest. Didn't your mother teach you anything?"

Ven tried to speak, but only incoherent sounds came from her throat. She stuttered, "I am so — so very sorry, First Mother."

"Sorry?" The older woman scowled. "Is that all you have to say?"

"Control your anger, Lady Nan," came a man's voice. "It is her first day in this house. She is allowed a few mistakes." From the top of the spiral staircase, Master Nguyen descended, holding a fan in his hand. He moved down the steps with the grace and ease of a lion emerging from its lair. His relaxed movements softened the tension in the room. All of his wives sat up straight in their seats, eager anticipation on their faces.

"This miserable girl dared to disrespect me on the very first day of her wifely duties," First Mistress told her husband. "If I don't correct her now, she will never give me the respect I deserve."

"Of course she will," Master Nguyen replied. "After all, you are her first mother. Remember when you were in her shoes, Lady Nan? Have some pity on the poor girl." He walked over to Ven and picked up a soup bowl. After sniffing its aroma, he took a small sip. Ven kept her eyes on the ground, taking in the complicated craftsmanship of his shoes. Master Nguyen replaced the cup on the tray, then patted her head with the handle of his fan.

"Good flavor," he told her. "Next time, tell Song to carry a clay stove with her and enough hot coals to heat it up. You don't serve soup or tea to us unless we are ready to receive them. Do you understand?"

"Yes, Father."

"Good," he said, turning to Third Mistress.

"Have a good morning, sir," Ven said. "May the gods in Heaven bless you with a thousand years of happiness."

But Master Nguyen didn't hear her. His attention was riveted on his youngest wife. Scowling at the young masseur on the floor, Master Nguyen grabbed him by the shoulder and pushed him from his kneeling position to sprawl on his side. "Get out," he told the man. "Your job is finished in here. Go back to the garden and tend to your duties."

The young man withdrew without a word.

Master Nguyen knelt beside the footstool facing Third Mistress. Taking a satin handkerchief from his sleeve, he wiped her feet clean of the coconut oil, then laid them back on the ottoman. Looking at her tenderly, he said, "There, all done. Tell Song to rebind your feet before they begin to hurt you."

Third Mistress smiled, showing her teeth. She cooed, "Thank you, dear husband."

Ven abhorred the look of those awful white teeth, which reminded her of perfectly aligned kernels on a corncob. Clearly they had never been exposed to the bitterness of black lacquered dye. Yet secretly she admired her young mother-in-law's courage in being a modern woman, despite her bound feet. Ven would never have dreamed of being so bold.

Third Mistress shifted her gaze to Ven. "You can get up now, daughter-in-law. If the master likes your soup, your job here is done. Take my son back to your wedding chamber and watch over him."

"Not yet," First Mistress interrupted. "Since there is nothing more for you to do here, you should work in the rice field. There is plenty to be done there. Then come back at noon to cook lunch. As you may have found out from that gossip Song, we are short of servants in this house. You will have to do your part."

"I am not a servant," Ven said. Her throat was dry.

"True, you are not a servant," First Mistress snapped. "You are much lower than that. You are a daughter-in-law. It is known under Heaven's laws that you owe us your servitude. Do you think I came easily to the position I hold today? Do you have any idea how hard I had to work and how many years I spent under my mother-in-law's rule so I could earn my place in this household? You are the first wife. Someday you will have the same privileges I have. But until then, you are a slave here. One more word from you and I will send you back to your parents' home. And I will personally cut off the ears of a barbecued pig head and send it back with you, so I can tell the whole world what a disgrace you were."

Ven swallowed with difficulty. To be sent back home was unthinkable, especially with the earless head of a pig. That was the common punishment for a licentious woman who failed to save her virginity for her wedding night. She could not bear to live with the shame, even though it was a lie. After all, her husband would not reach puberty for at least another six years. Bowing low, Ven left the living room through the back door.

On the brick path, she met Song, who was carrying a large tray covered by a copper lid. A few bamboo wrappers peeked from under its rim. Hearing the last words of First Mistress's scolding and seeing the nervous look on Ven's face, the servant girl paused. But the door opened, and the little boy, seeing Song, cried out, "Breakfast, break-fast," jumping up and down in excitement.

First Mistress called to Ven as the women laughed together. "Don't forget your husband. Come back after your work is done in the kitchen. For now, leave him to eat with us. Later, you can take him to the rice field."

chapter three

The Messenger

MAY 5, 1916

*I*n his later years, Dan Nguyen would recall little about his wedding at the age of seven to Ven, his first wife. He would always remember, though, the long hours that he spent riding on her back while she worked in the fields. At that time in Thua Thien Province, growing rice was strictly a human enterprise, requiring long hours of backbreaking labor. Unlike the other farmers in the Cam Le Village, Ven always worked alone.

Each night, at about the same time the chickens nestled down in their cages, she took her young husband to bed with her. In the dim lantern light, he watched her undress until only a single layer of cloth covered her golden skin. Dan developed a habit of falling asleep against the soft cushion of her breasts. Redolent of fresh mud mixed with mint oil, the scent soothed his active mind and sent him to a world of dreams.

Each morning, he woke to find himself curled up inside a basket, woven from sheaves of wild bamboo, rocking to her rhythmic motion. He never recalled being lifted from his bed. He only woke when the sunlight was strong enough to hurt his eyes, despite the straw hat that Ven placed over his head. When she sensed him stirring, she would pause from her chores to attend him.

On the rock-strewn ground under the shade of a star-fruit tree, she fed him breakfast. Dan loved those tiny banana pies in sticky rice, which she steamed in coconut milk. She knew how to make the rich vapor seep inside the bamboo wrappers, just enough to turn the heart of the pie tender. After breakfast, he would return to the basket for another ride on her back. Sometimes he chose to sit under the tree and play with his toys — a group of hand puppets she had made for him from old clothes. The figurines' eyes, noses, and ears, even their hair, were embroidered over the faded fabric. With his eyes closed, he could feel the threads that formed their little faces, rough against the tips of his fingers. As she worked, Ven would watch him and wave from time to time. Her eyes were slender like the leaves of willow. Each time she looked at him, Dan knew he was safe.

In mid-March, his father and first two mothers had gone out to sea. For six weeks now the house had been hollow without their lively company. As far back as Dan could remember, this was the longest period of time his parents had ever been away. Even his third mother, Lady Yen, had begun to worry. After dinner each night, instead of watching him play puppets with Ven, she sat on the veranda in her favorite armchair. As she waited for his father, her fingers strayed over the strings of her lute, creating music sad enough to make the Heavens cry.

His father owned a large ship, the *Lady Yen*, which he used for his fishing expeditions. Dan had never seen the ship, but he knew that she was docked far away, on the other side of the mountain. His father had told him stories about the lush green jungles that bordered deep saltwater lagoons and the thousand-mile coastline where his ship roamed free.

Dan wondered if one day he, too, would be a sailor. He wished to see with his own eyes the incredible sea, which according to his father was a hundred times larger than the Perfume River. He also liked the idea of traveling to distant places. But he did not want the influence and responsibility that the *Lady Yen* gave his father over the other men in the village. The very fact that the crew preferred to remain for a few days in their captain's house after a long trip at sea, instead of reuniting immediately with their wives and children, attested to the power of his father's command.

One morning in early May, after she fed him breakfast, Ven returned to work in the rice paddy, leaving Dan on the ground with his toys. The hours dragged by. From where he stood, Dan could see the back of his house across a lean path and numerous terraced fields. A smell of rice alcohol soiled the sunny morning. Dan recognized with a chill the sight of the time-teller, Big Con, lurching toward him. He knew the scarred face, the staggering walk, and the sound of wine guzzling down his throat. Now and then, the man stopped, mumbling something, probably a curse, under his breath. From his spot in the shade, Dan watched Ven impatiently, waiting for her eyes to meet his. He wanted her to take him away.

Like other children of this village, Dan was familiar with Big Con. The time-teller had become a monster that mothers used to scare their children at bedtime. No one knew where he came from or who his parents were. Dan was convinced that one late evening, the gate of Hell was left unattended and several creatures had slipped into Earth to haunt the children. Among them was the time-teller. On his hands and knees, Dan crept away until he was concealed behind the trunk of the star-fruit tree, away from the man's view.

Thirty paces away, Ven was engrossed in her work. Her knees were deep in the mud, and her back bent parallel to the earth. Out of the corner of her eye, she also noticed the drunk. But she thought he was too far from them to cause any harm. If anything happened, she could get to the boy before the man did. Judging from the way he was trampling around in an ivory bamboo thicket, she believed that he was just searching for a shaded place to nap.

Ven had little fear of the time-teller. To her, Big Con was merely an enigma. The story she had heard about him began when he was an infant. A fishmonger found him at the riverbank at the break of dawn one day. He was naked and gray like the color of dead grass, and every orifice of his head was covered in leeches. She wrapped him in two panels of banana leaves and later that day sold him to a blind fortune-teller who had no husband or children. The price she asked from the old woman was twenty copper pennies. The psychic paid the price and took the infant under her roof as if he were her own son, naming him Con.

The child's new name generated little ambition in him, if any, as it literally meant *a boy*. The fortune-teller gave him the name for a reason. Besides the happiness of having a son, the woman was consumed with fear, mostly because of her unexpected fortune. The earth was filled with malignant spirits who were jealous of the prosperity of the living. By calling her son Con, she was hoping the simple name would help the boy escape the envy of the underworld.

When Con was old enough, the soothsayer sent him to school to learn the ABCs — a new writing method that had taken root with the French presence in Vietnam, replacing the old vernacular language with its demotic characters. Little Con was a gentle soul, so fragile that during the Harvest Moon Festival it was difficult for him to play the popular game known as "catch the chicken." As hard as he tried, he could never lasso a fowl. In all of his childhood years, never once did he raise his voice, nor did he cause any trouble to anyone in the town.

When he was eighteen, Con went to work for Magistrate Toan, then the town's mayor, as a tutor to the young children of his third and fourth mistresses in their private mansion. Fourth Mistress was a young, rosy-cheeked woman who enjoyed a midday rest on a hammock strung between two rambutan trees. She liked Con to stand at the foot of her swinging bed and read her long chapters from the famous novel *Kim Van Kieu* by the poet Nguyen Du. This was an adventure story of a young girl who turned to prostitution in order to save her family from poverty, leaving behind the love of her life. The tale had a happy ending, as the lovers were reunited after many sorrows. Each time Con came to the final verses, Fourth Mistress would press her hands above her generous breasts to express the buoyancy of her feelings. Sometimes, she even pulled her pants up past her knees and had him massage her legs.

One afternoon, Magistrate Toan brought home a dozen policemen. In front of several shocked witnesses, Con was handcuffed and sent to jail. What happened in that moment, and why, was known only to the Heavens above and the parties involved. No one dared to question the magistrate's decision. Con had no relatives, except for his adoptive mother, and so his arrest was not a matter of concern to many.

The poor fortune-teller, however, was grief-stricken over the unfortunate incident. She remained in her little cottage on top of the hill, overlooking a tiny garden, which she had planned to sell one day in order to get Con a wife. Forgotten by the rest of the world, she waited for her son to come back. Shortly after Con's imprisonment, a farmer found the body of Magistrate Toan's fourth wife, badly beaten and strangled, buried underneath a haystack. Her hands were clasped over her breasts. Her face wore a shocked expression.

In front of the community hall, Magistrate Toan announced to the villagers that Big Con had murdered his wife. Of course, everyone realized that was a lie. She was still alive the day Con was arrested, and the whole town knew it. Besides, who would believe a polite and fragile boy like Con could commit such a hideous crime? Still, no one dared to say anything against the powerful Magistrate Toan. To cross him was certain suicide. With no one to speak in his defense, Con was tried and found guilty of murdering Magistrate Toan's wife. He was sent to death row a few days later.

Soon afterward, Con's mother died in utter poverty. As for Magistrate Toan, due to his advanced age, he finally retired. His son, Master Long, took his place as the town's mayor.

At the prison in Da Nang, Con found a desperate way to avoid the firing squad. He signed a contract with the French government to serve in one of its dangerous rubber plantations without salary. To most people, the ranch was a death camp because of its horrible living conditions, incurable diseases, and inhumanely hard labor. Yet to Con, it was his only chance for survival. He disappeared for almost nine years.

To this day, Big Con still chanted a popular song about life on a rubber plantation. Even now, a short distance away, Ven could hear his mournful voice.

> *There is no way out of the rubber camps*
> *Men enter those gates in their physical prime*
> *Only to leave when they are inches away from Death's door*

Ignoring him, she wiped the perspiration off her forehead and returned to the field. To keep her mind busy, she kept repeating a poem she had learned as a child, a traditional farmer's mantra for a successful rice season.

> *January is the time to celebrate the New Year*

She sang the first verse while separating a bundle of shoots, blocking the time-teller's voice out of her head. To her, January was a reminder of the dark wedding chamber where she had sat frozen, waiting for her husband. Her memory held barely a trace of festivity, except for the faded sound of firecrackers and the cheerful slurs of intoxicated guests outside her bedroom window.

> *February is the time to plant beans, potatoes, and tomatoes*
> *And then wait for Heaven's tears*
> *Turn to March, these plants will be reaped*
> *Let's summon the help and dry the beans in heaps*

As she worked alone in the rice field, Ven's voice rose over the tiny sprouts she had just planted. She remembered one day in March as if it were yesterday. Her hands had acquired new blisters from ten long days of peeling peas off their vines. Many of them bore traces of her blood. After all her hard work, her mother-in-law First Mistress had decided that the peas were only worthy of consumption by the chickens. With each handful that Ven fed the fowls every morning, she shed bitter tears, but she knew that to complain would be useless.

April is time to rent a pair of oxen

Her mind chanted the familiar song before the words could escape her throat.

Then it is time to rotate the soil, get ready for May's rice season

She had walked many miles under the hot sun each day since April, turning over the earth with a plow to prepare a seedbed. Under her direction, the water buffalo trudged ahead of her. Encircling their shoulders like a shackle, the wooden implement cut, lifted, and made furrows in the soil. The land, flooded by a copious channel of river water, took on the consistency of dense clay. Like the animals, Ven felt the handle of the farming tool wrapped around the small of her back, pulling her downward until the mud rose up to her knees. She had to use every muscle in her body to keep the exhausted animals in a straight line, even when the stubborn earth refused to yield.

Early in the morning, don't forget to soak the rice until the skins turn yellow

She could hear the time-teller's uneven voice as he mimicked her singing.

When the germination has occurred, scatter these sprouts in the muddy meadow
In a few weeks, the buds will become young shoots. Pull them up from their roots
Then hire the help to plant them in the rice field. Only then can you go home and rest your weary heels

Ven laughed. The optimistic ending of the poem always infuriated her. She moved from row to row, pushing each new plant firmly into the wet earth. Her lips tightened, and the pain in her back intensified. *"There will be no rest for a girl named Ven,"* she sang out. *"Only someday when she is as useless as a crippled old hen."* The time-teller guffawed.

Ven straightened at the distant sound of rapidly advancing hoofbeats reverberating in the otherwise silent countryside. Through a cloud of dust at the end of the main road, she saw a man clinging to the back of a galloping horse. The rider's hands shook the reins, trying to make the animal go faster.

The white uniform he wore was familiar, even though the dust of the road had turned it dull brown. He was one of Master Nguyen's sailors. On his face, Ven detected the wild look she often saw on the condemned servants her father-in-law disciplined on the veranda, slashing their backs with a long whip made from the tail of a ray fish. The horse flared its nostrils. The drumming of its hooves threw a rain of dirt on the time-teller, who slouched in the shade of the bamboo bush. He jumped up and roared in anger, waving his fists.

Ven threw down her bundle of rice sprouts and ran after the horse, waving her torn hat in a vain attempt to get the rider's attention. In seconds, the sailor disappeared around the turn of the road.

Ven rushed to Dan's side. Without a word, she grabbed him by the waist. Her sturdy legs flew across the fragile earth levees that separated the rice paddies as she instinctively chose the shortest way home.

Ven entered the house through the back door, pulling the boy along. The living room was vacant. Third Mistress was out in the front yard, where the gardener was teaching her the finer points of trimming rosebushes. The sadness that had haunted her in the past few days had lifted. Ven could hear her tinkling laughter echoing against the walls of the empty den.

In the middle of the garden, Ven and Dan found her leaning against the gardener's arms. His hands lay atop her delicate fingers, helping her to hold a large pair of scissors. On the ground around them was a carpet of red rose petals. They continued to prune flowers off the vines, creating a cascade of scarlet.

The mud-spattered sailor careened through the front gate. His horse strained against the harness, prancing a few more steps before the rider brought it under control in front of Third Mistress and her companion. The sailor leaped from his saddle. One of his feet got caught in the stirrup, and he fell before them.

"Danger, great danger is falling upon us, Third Lady," he wailed to her feet, beating his fists on the ground. "Please forgive me, for I am bringing you bad news of the master."

Ven watched her mother-in-law's face turn white. Third Mistress dropped the pruning shears and grasped the gardener's hands.

The sailor continued, "Master Nguyen and his two wives were arrested last night, along with the rest of his crew. The bearer of the order of arrest was a French magistrate, who led a company of soldiers from the palace. Master did not want to comply, so a scuffle broke out before they were all placed under arrest. During the struggle, I escaped." He doubled over, gasping for breath.

Third Mistress fell back into the gardener's chest. In a shaky whisper she said to the him, "Take me inside. My head hurts under this strong heat."

The young man caught her in his embrace, lifted her up, and carried her into the living room. Because of her bound feet, she could not have made the short journey on her own, even if she had not been in shock. The sailor staggered a few steps behind them. As they walked by, Dan took hold of his mother's hand. The gardener didn't seem to see Ven and Dan standing at the doorsill. He brushed past them and deposited his mistress on the divan.

With gentle strokes, the gardener touched Lady Yen's cheeks, massaging her skin until her color was restored. With her large, somber eyes, she searched the room for the sailor.

"On what grounds did they arrest my husband?" she asked.

"Piracy, madam. Our Royal Highness, the king himself, was abducted last night from his bedchamber. The leaders of the kidnappers are Thai Phien, Le Ngung, Tran Cao Van, Phan Thanh Thai, and Vo Van Tru. Many of these men are fishermen. Furthermore, both Masters Phan Thanh Thai and Tran Cao Van are our master's longtime friends and confidants. There were rumors that they were planning a revolution against the French. If our master is convicted of any of these alleged crimes, either as a sea bandit or a rebel, he will be put to death." The sailor waited for those words to sink in. Then he continued, "I thought you would have heard this news about the king already. The French have posted news bulletins all over the country since last night."

"The king is missing, and the Royal Court thinks my husband is involved?" Third Mistress raised her voice. "This is the most ridiculous news I've ever heard. Everyone in the Cam Le Village knows that my husband is neither a politician nor a thief. All he was and always will be is a family man and a proud fisherman. Nobody in this town will let this unjust incident harm one of its most beloved citizens."

The gardener interrupted in a tense baritone. "We have to find out what exactly the French said in their communiqué about Master Nguyen."

All eyes shifted to Ven, who stood watching the scene in silence. Third Mistress propped herself up on her elbows. A glimmer of hope brightened her eyes.

"Please, Ven," she said, "you must go right away and find out more news. I can't think of anyone who can handle this job better. No one saw you when you were brought here under your wedding veil, and you are so common-looking that no one would suspect your relationship with the Nguyen family. Song, on the other hand, is too clumsy. And I can't let these men go. I need them here to protect me."

"I can't do it!" Ven exclaimed. "I don't know how to read or write. What good am I when it comes to reading a news bulletin?"

"You, indeed, are the right candidate," pressed the lady. "You don't have to be literate to get the news. Just ask someone to tell you what the note says. May I remind you that you are Master Nguyen's and my daughter-in-law? Your unwillingness to help me with one simple request disappoints me and will be reflected upon you for many years to come. However, if you honor my wish, I will be certain that once the crisis is over, Master Nguyen will reward your loyalty and courage handsomely."

Ven knew that she had no choice. Looking at her mother-in-law, she asked, "Where do you want me to find this information?"

"The news is always delivered either to the time-teller's cabin or to the community hall," the gardener replied, regarding his nails. His features held a certain refinement, reflected in his red lips and dark eyes. At first glance, he could have passed as a sibling of Third Mistress. "Everyone knows that this is the way news has been carried through hundreds of years. Must you ask such childish questions at this time of crisis?"

Lady Yen raised her forefinger in front of the gardener to silence him. Her long lashes fluttered as she said to Ven, "Go to the time-teller's cabin. Avoid the community hall, since it is probably full of curious spectators. Take Dan with you. I dare not be trapped here with that demanding child."

Seizing her husband's arm, Ven left the house through the front door. Dan did not resist, looking at her with fear in his eyes.

They had reached the front door when Song called out to them from the kitchen. "Wait for me," she said, "I am going with you."

chapter four

The Time-Teller

I do not want you to be alone with that miserable time-teller," Song said to Ven as they left the mansion. "You have heard the stories about him. I think I should go with you to his hut."

"If you want to," Ven replied.

Song pointed the way toward a path in the bamboo thicket. "You remember when you first came here, I warned you not to trust him to report the time accurately?" she reminded Ven. "That's not his worst trait, by far. He is one of the most dangerous men in town, especially when he is drunk."

"Why don't the elders strip him of his duty?" Ven asked.

"They would rather put up with his misbehavior than face the madman's wrath," Song replied.

About six months earlier, Big Con had walked into the Cam Le Village a completely different person after having been gone for nine years. At first, people didn't know who he was. His face was a mask of thick scars, running in all directions like a map of the

Imperial Palace. His head was shaven clean, like a monk's. He was a small, wiry man, but he exuded the ferocity of a cornered mongoose.

He chose a wineshop in the market, sat down, and started drinking sticky-rice wine and eating pork. In the course of two hours, he drank three liters of wine and downed three servings of grilled meat. Then, staggering, he stood up, spitting saliva through his purple lips as he slurred, "Give me an IOU. I'll pay you later."

The shop owner was a short, broad woman with a flat nose and black nostrils that flared in apprehension. She shook as though she were catching a cold. "Please, sir," she said, "I don't have enough capital to extend such large credit. Please pay your balance before you leave."

He raised his eyebrows like a war god, used the back of his hand to flip the wooden table upside down, and kicked the stool in her direction. "How dare you not trust me?" he growled. "I am Big Con."

He waited for his words to sink in. The other customers in the shop hid their faces in their food. He stood still for a moment, then continued. "I was born and bred here on this spot. That bastard Toan owes me some cash. I am going to look for him and retrieve what is rightfully mine. Then I will be back to pay you, you stupid mare."

The woman dried her eyes with the dirty hem of her shirt and said, "I don't dare to distrust you. It is just that I am too poor to sustain a debt as large as this one, Sir Con. My children will surely be hungry tonight."

He reached behind the counter for two more bottles of wine. Before shuffling out of the shop, he added, "Make another noise, and I will burn this dog shed down to the red mud on the ground. Then you will know what it is to be in debt. If you don't believe me, cluck for the police, old hen. See for yourself which one of us is a wolf, and which one only scratches in the dirt."

The woman shut her mouth with both of her hands, struggling to turn the sobbing in her throat into something that sounded like an attack of hiccups. He gave her a final glare and walked out. Two curious children followed him, but their mother ran out from her hiding place, snatched them up, and held them to her chest. He looked at no one and headed toward the wide road that led to Magistrate Toan's mansion. It was high noon. A few scattered clusters of cloud skidded across the sky that November day. His face was as red as the sun. The alcohol seeped through his body, turning his head like a pinwheel. He felt gigantic, invincible, and full of anger.

The horrid temperature made him mad. Perspiration pricked the skin on his back like a thousand hungry red ants. He gulped through the two bottles of wine in an attempt to fend off the heat. Instead, it seemed to expand inside his head. He yanked open his shirt to bare a chest that, like his face, was crisscrossed by scars. Swaying, he sang the only song he knew.

> *There is no way out of the rubber camps*
> *Men enter those gates in their physical prime*
> *Only to leave when they are inches away from Death's door*

Big Con had never had the pleasure of passing through the door of Death, he sometimes thought. Heaven as he knew it had rejected him a long time ago. And Hell, he believed, had moved inside his head, so there would be no need for him to claim the devil's throne. His thought of the devil reminded him of Magistrate Toan, and he cursed out loud.

It was then that the people of Cam Le Village first learned the extensive vulgarity of his wrath. He was worse than a fishmonger who had not made a sale all day. He damned Magistrate Toan's ancestors all the way to the powerful man's front steps. Everyone was sure that the magistrate would come out of his library and put a bullet in Con's chest without hesitation. Big Con, after all, was a condemned man with a prison record.

However, the moment that Con burst through the gate onto his enemy's property, what he instead faced was a vicious dog, the size of a grown deer and just as brown. It lunged at him from behind a lilac shrub. With white fangs dripping with foamy spit, the beast seized his forearm and knocked him off balance with its weight. Con fell off Magistrate Toan's front porch into a thornbush. The ferocious animal continued to snarl and pull at him. Big Con cursed louder. With his free hand, he smashed an empty wine bottle against the hard pavement. The shards gleamed under the harsh sun.

But Con did not use the weapon against his relentless attacker.

Instead, kicking and screaming, he scraped it across his own face, making several deep cuts. Like a man possessed, his eyes rolled to the back of his head and his mouth gaped. Blood spurted from the wounds, mixing with the sand around him.

To Con, mutilating his face was his strategy. His injuries would make his enemy appear guilty before the police. No judge would believe anyone could be crazy enough to inflict so much damage on himself. Contrary to popular belief, Big Con had never fought a battle in his life. When faced with a confrontation, he simply disfigured himself. The scars he bore were his trophies, telling the turbulent tale of his life.

Seeing the intruder's frantic movements, the dog paused. It seemed to forget even to growl. Then, as if Big Con's behavior were too outrageous even for an animal, the creature retreated under a shade tree and proceeded to lick the blood off its paws. Con continued to cut his face and chest with the sharp glass, screaming. Not a soul on the street witnessed the gory scene; even the sun discreetly hid behind a tuft of white cloud.

A loud explosion shattered the air, drowning out Big Con's frenzied cries. On the front step of his house, Magistrate Toan appeared, holding a gun. The tip of his pistol, pointed toward the sky, emitted a lingering trace of smoke. The dog yelped as it leaped behind a lilac bush.

"Which one of the devils are you?" Toan asked in his most intimidating voice. "Why are you disturbing my home?"

Big Con remained on the ground, covering his face in his hands. He was no longer screaming or cursing. The only sound that came out of his throat now was a soft and pitiful mewling. "Does the name Big Con sound familiar to you?" he moaned to the older man. "You killed me once in the past, Bastard Toan. Why don't you try it one more time, see if you can finish the job?"

Magistrate Toan cocked the muzzle of his gun toward Big Con's chest. His eyes narrowed into two thin slits. "Get off my land," he warned the drunk.

Big Con pulled open his shirt. The sun shed its golden rays over the exposed flesh of his chest. He said to Toan, "If I die, I will become the most awful demon and forever haunt your family."

The old man hesitated. One couldn't become a magistrate by being weak-minded.

He placed the handle of his gun against his lip and eased into an armchair. Under the shade of his tin roof, his face appeared as a blur among the shadows. Baring his sharp teeth against the steel pistol, he gave himself time to think. Things had changed since the days when he ruled this village. Now, even a soft-spoken coward like Con, the tutor, had become a monster, a potential killer.

Magistrate Toan formed his lips into a pleasing smile — with a little clever thinking, he had found a solution for his problem.

He would not take this lowly dog's life. Instead, he would make a killer out of him. With the right amount of persuasion, Big Con could help him take care of certain enemies, the ones that had power and positions in society. And if Con got killed, Magistrate Toan would be rid of the pest without dirtying his fingers. Either way, he would come out ahead. He was extremely satisfied with the splendor of his wit.

He said to the drunken man, "Oh, come now. I didn't recognize you. Why would I want to murder you, Teacher Con? You and I are bound by a dear and brotherly friendship, and I was stricken with grief over your unfortunate tribulation. When did you arrive in town? I am disappointed that you did not notify me sooner. I would have told the cook to prepare a feast for us. Fowls are extremely succulent at this time of year."

"You are a snake," Big Con snapped. "I am well aware of the sort of devil I have to deal with."

"Please, don't use that language with an old friend." Toan's charm was relentless. "Come inside. Sit next to me! Tell me what you want. Give your orders, and I will execute them."

Big Con sat up. The alcohol had evaporated from his brain, and he felt a dull throbbing from his wounds. The pain made him weak at the knees. He yearned for more wine, the only thing that could make him strong and invincible again. "I came here to claim what is rightfully mine," he said to the magistrate. "I want compensation for my incarceration."

"How much do you want?" Magistrate Toan asked.

Big Con tried to think of the largest sum that he could. "Five silver dollars," he said.

Magistrate Toan rested his gun on the floor next to his feet. He took his handkerchief, which he used to wrap his cash, from his pants pocket. Then, he held out five silver coins. They gleamed in his hand, beckoning. Big Con did not trust the old coyote enough to touch his money.

"It is all right," the old man urged. "Take them. Like you said, they are your compensation."

Big Con reached out his dirty hand, but the old man's reflex was faster. He folded his bony fingers to conceal the money and asked in a half-joking, bitter manner, "Are you certain that five dollars would be sufficient for your needs, Teacher Con? I suspect that if I give it to you, you will be back here tomorrow asking for more. I will not be the sort of bank that will grant you unlimited credit. Perhaps we will understand each other better if I ask you to come up with a bigger sum."

Big Con swallowed hard before he answered. "Five silver coins are plenty, sir."

Toan shook his head. "Let's fix a sum of fifty dollars to accommodate your drinking habit for the next thirty days. What would you do for that amount, Teacher Con?"

"Fifty?" gasped out Con. "Certainly I would do whatever you please for that much money."

The magistrate released his hand, once again displaying the sparkling coins. Con touched them carefully. This time, the old man gave him the money and said, "There will be fifty silver coins for you in my house, in exchange for a small favor you can do for me. Do you remember Officer Dao, the man who arrested you nine years ago?"

Big Con nodded as his brain conjured up the image of the policeman.

Toan continued. "For some time now, this bastard has wanted to get rid of me. If I am dead, then no one will take care of you in this town. Do you understand me?"

"Say no more," Big Con cried. "Consider that man a problem no longer, Sir Toan. I will take care of him."

"Excellent. Make sure that he is dead," said the old man.

The magistrate opened the gates and saw his guest out. As the drunken young man staggered back out on the street, Toan returned to his armchair. A smile darkened his gaunt face.

✦

To get to the time-teller's cabin, Song led Ven and Dan for an hour along a path through a tangled thicket of bamboo. The rough and pointy leaves scratched at their faces like sharp fingernails, leaving red lines on their skin. Looking at Dan's sweaty face, Ven wished for a touch of wind to ward off the intense heat. At last they arrived in a rough clearing at the foot of the mountains.

Big Con's hut was located on a small hill, surrounded by an immense forest. Song signaled for Ven to follow her. They went around the cottage to enter through the rear, stepping over a narrow pasture of green grass.

As they emerged at the side of the humble dwelling, Ven took Dan by the hand. In front of them, the hut stood on four twisted, termite-eaten posts. Through a rectangular hole of a window, where a tattered drape fluttered, Ven saw that the house was dark and moldy. Cobwebs spread their grubby filaments over the entrance, and the sunlight danced across the fragile strings.

"Look over there," Song said.

Following her glance, Ven saw the time-teller sprawled on the ground in front of his home. His mouth was wide open, showing a large coated tongue. He was snoring loudly. An empty wine bottle lay a few inches from his fingers. Ven's eyes stopped at his crotch, where the creased fabric was darkened with his waste.

Ven turned to Song. She felt the urge to flee, but one of her sandals got caught in the exposed root of a tree. She tripped, blurting out a startled sound. The time-teller opened his eyes and looked straight at her. His irises were the same color as his tongue, bleached and cloudy.

He hoisted himself up, grabbing the bottle by its neck and holding it in his hand like a weapon. Rage seeped into his eyes. The women pulled closer to each other. Dan, caught in their embrace, reached up to look over their arms.

The time-teller cleared his throat. In a rough voice, he asked, "What do you want? Why are you coming here to disturb me?"

A cloud of flies circled around his crotch. Their wings made a loud buzzing in the hot air. Big Con attempted to squash the bugs with his empty bottle. After a few tries, he lost his temper and smashed the bottle into a tree. Fragments of broken glass exploded onto the ground around his bare feet.

Ven stepped forward. "I came looking for the news," she said. Her sharp voice grated on his nerves, but her open-palmed gesture told him that she was harmless.

He looked up into her face. The murkiness left his eyes, but he still wore a mask of somnolence. "It's you!" he said. "What do you want?"

Ven repeated, "I came here to get the news."

"What kind of news?"

"About Master Tat Nguyen and his mistresses," Song said.

Big Con brushed his hand in midair. "Get your gossip at the community hall like everybody else."

Ven took another step forward. She was close enough to see the scars on his face. She pressed on. "I was told to come here. Please tell me if anything has been posted since yesterday."

Ven stood her ground. Their eyes locked for several seconds, then he shrugged and pushed his chest forward. With a manner as majestic as that of a king, he stretched his hand toward an oak tree at the side of his cabin. Several posters were pinned against its trunk. A few of them featured sketches of Master Tat and Lady Nan. Under the pictures, words written in black ink marched in neat rows. "Those are your news bulletins, madam," he said. "They came this morning."

"Can you tell me what they say, especially these?" Ven pointed at the papers that bore the portraits of her parents-in-law.

He shook his head. "I haven't read or written in several years. I don't remember much anymore. If you can't read, then get off my property."

Ven reached for the posters. Her fingers picked at the nails that fixed them against the tree.

"What are you doing?" the time-teller yelled. His thunderous voice startled Dan into tears. Song held him in her arms.

"Since you are not going to tell me what is in the notices, I am taking them with me," Ven said.

"Don't you dare leave with that announcement!" Big Con strode toward her with a warning look. Ven turned to him. The pine tree behind her had two branches, like arms extending right and left, seeming to block her path. She leaned back against its trunk as fear rose to her chest.

"Please, don't hurt me," she whispered to him. "I just want to get the information on these posters. What can I do to make you help me?"

He halted in his track, thinking for a moment before he said to her, "I miss the company of the Wine Fairy. For ten copper pennies, I'll read you the notice."

Ven reached inside the cord of her belt, where she kept her money. Her hand found the warm metallic coins, slippery in her own sweat. The money was strung into a loop, all pennies. Under her fingers, they made a clinking sound as they moved against one another. Big Con's eyes lit up, and with his clenched fists, he seemed to be fighting the urge to snatch the cash.

Ven counted her money slowly and carefully several times. Then she looked up. "I only have eight pennies." She opened her hand to show him her cache.

Big Con swallowed. Golden beams of sunlight danced on his shaven head as he seized the money. "Move away," he said. "How can I read when you are blocking my view?" He pushed her aside.

Big Con came closer to the announcements, his nose only inches from the tree. He squinted and scratched his hairless skull, stammering over each syllable like a young pupil reciting a difficult poem for the first time in front of a strict teacher.

"Cap-tured Re-bels," he began. "From-the-Court-of-Hue-came-this-an-nounce-ment-"

As he read on, the time-teller seemed to adjust to the strange characters on the paper. He delivered the message faster and with more confidence. "This day, the second of April of the Dragon Year (lunar calendar), known in the Western calendar as the third of May, 1916, it was revealed that a group of rebels had persuaded our young emperor, King Duy Tan, to escape the Purple Forbidden City. At first, these radicals pretended to fish at Hau Ho, forging palace passes to visit the emperor. Then they docked their boat in Thuong Bac to receive His Royal Highness. As of today, the Imperial Court has not been able to ascertain the emperor's whereabouts. The leaders of the rebel group, Thai Phien, Le Ngung, Tran Cao Van, Phan Thanh Thai, and Vo Van Tru had plotted against the French protectorate over Vietnam. They should not have involved our young king. His Majesty has not yet seen his sixteenth birthday, far from the maturity needed to make decisions to move mountains and conquer seas. Other rebels in the same group have been arrested, including Tat Nguyen, the captain of a Cam Le fishing boat, and his two mistresses, Nan Nguyen and Ly Nguyen. They will be given the death penalty. The executions will be carried out in their hometown two weeks from this day. This action is intended to show other rebels that the Court at Hue is intolerant of insurgents of any kind —"

Ven turned grayer than the bark of the tree against which she leaned to keep herself from falling. "Impossible! Utterly impossible!"

Big Con continued to read. "Upon searching the *Lady Yen,* thirty large gunpowder packages were found in the lower compartment —" He scrutinized Ven's face. "What does this mean?" he demanded. The drunkenness had completely vanished from his eyes.

"I think I have gone mad," Ven muttered. Then, pushing herself away from the tree, she grabbed Dan in her arms and ran down the hill. Song chased after her.

The time-teller sniffed his string of coins and watched his visitors disappear into the thicket of bamboo leaves. He sucked his teeth noisily and mumbled, "Where is that cursed wineshop? I need a refill."

chapter five

Inferno

It was dark when the two women and their young charge turned into the lane that served as a shortcut to the main gate of Master Nguyen's house. As the last streak of daylight disappeared, the moon rose on the opposite side of the sky, as if trying to outshine the sun. Despite their combined glow, the evening was gloomy. Clouds hovered overhead. Between the chrysanthemums and orchids along the side of the road, the twittering of crickets sounded.

As they approached the house, Ven saw a carriage, drawn by a pair of auburn horses, parked outside the main gate. She recognized the beautiful animals as Master Nguyen's pride and joy, to be used only for special occasions. Ven imagined her parents-in-law sitting on their expensive divan in their living room, and a sense of relief washed through her. She watched as one of the horses neighed, while the other pounded its hooves on the gravel.

The granite gates rolled on their hinges. Standing in the opening was Third Mistress. In her arms she clutched a small box. Her lute hung on a strap on her back, vibrating with each step she took. A coachman jumped from his seat to assist her. Ven saw that it was the young gardener. The handsome couple stepped through the gates, which closed on their wheels, making little sound.

Noticing Ven, the gardener looked terrified. He pushed the Third Mistress inside the carriage and hopped into the driver's seat, yanking the pole that guided the animals to urge them into motion. Lady Yen's embarrassed face peeked out the window of the carriage as it began to move.

"Stop!" Ven called to them. "Where are you going?"

Her voice disappeared down the empty street without an echo. The carriage picked up speed, and Ven saw that the driver was having trouble managing the spirited animals. They pulled at the pole, straining each time he cracked his whip.

Ven understood the horses. She had tended them in the stable for the last few months, brushing and feeding them. That wasn't the way to handle them, she thought. She pushed Dan into Song's bosom. "Hold him," she said to the maid.

Before Song could react, Ven charged after the fleeing coach. Her stride was strong, and soon she was abreast of the horses. The gardener slapped harder at the lead, pushing them to a more furious speed. Still, Ven held her pace.

"Go away!" he screamed at her. "Stop chasing us!"

Anger fed her determination. She rushed past the two horses, reached out, and seized the closer animal's ears, allowing it to drag her along.

The gardener turned the whip on his pursuer, hoping she would give up the chase. The first lash unraveled the knot of her hair. His next blow struck her head, then another landed on her back.

Ven felt the rough leather's sting ripping her skin every time it touched her. Blood ran down her face, blurring her vision, filling her mouth with the metallic taste she knew so well. Gritting her teeth, she tightened her grip on the horse's ears. The animal snorted with pain, and its forelegs buckled. Its sudden halt jerked the second horse back. The pole that connected the two animals snapped in half as the carriage swerved to a stop.

With nothing to break her momentum, Ven shot forward like a cannonball. She rolled over twice before landing facedown in the road, limp.

Once the adrenaline subsided, pain and dizziness overwhelmed her. Blood dripped into her eyes, and the clouds of dirt raised by the carriage obscured her vision. From somewhere behind her, Ven could hear Lady Yen wailing.

She got to her feet and limped toward the noise. Her skin was scratched and torn, but as far as she could tell, no bones were broken. Through her tangled hair, she saw the moon peeking between the clouds, whitening the rock-strewn road. About ten feet away, the gardener was removing the broken implement from between the horses. Ven strode to the carriage and raised her voice over the sharp weeping of Third Mistress.

"Why are you running away with that man?" she asked her mother-in-law. "They are going to behead half of your family in two weeks. What am I going to do with your son?"

"What else am I to do?" Third Mistress pleaded through the carriage window. Her hands grasped the bars so tightly that her knuckles were white. "I heard about the news soon after you left. Surely the police will kill me, too, if I remain in that house. They will find me guilty by association. You are not a stupid person; you know I am too young to die a virtuous death like a proper wife. It wasn't in my contract with the Nguyen family. My son is now your husband. My duty to tend him ceased the day he married you. Ven, the boy is your responsibility, not mine. Let us go in peace, I beg you."

From the front of the carriage, the gardener's head poked into the passenger compartment. "Time to leave," he said.

Lady Yen pulled a silk handkerchief from her sleeve and pressed it to her eyes. A beautiful fragrance emanated from its fragile tissue, making Ven swoon. She found it difficult to argue with her mother-in-law. Words seemed to fail her every time the lovely young woman looked at her with her mournful eyes. And her language! Ah, Lady Yen was an eloquent speaker. Words streamed from her mouth as smoothly as oil poured into a lantern.

"Take this jade and my lute." Lady Yen took off her gold necklace and handed it to Ven, along with the delicate instrument, through the carriage door. Curiously, Ven inspected the gold chain. It was finely made but secondary in beauty to the round piece of jade, the size of a Chinese penny, that hung from it. The stone's surface glowed in the moonlight. In its center was a fine mesh of gold lattice woven together to form a Chinese character.

Third Mistress continued. "I had these two precious objects as a young girl in China, long before I entered the cursed house of Nguyen. They have never left my side until tonight. The letter in the middle of the jade is my name in Chinese, and the lute — I think you know its story. Playing it was how I made my living in the years I worked in the opera troupe. Now I have other plans. Give these things to my son when he grows up, so that a part of me can stay with him. Take good care of him and help yourself to anything in the house that you want in order to start your new life."

Before Ven could reply, the horse-drawn carriage again rolled down the pebbled road. Lady Yen sank back into her seat and drew the blind over the window. Ven fell to her knees and wept loudly and openly for the first time in her life. Tears had the same salty, bitter taste as her blood.

Wrapped in Song's embrace, Dan watched Ven's confrontation with his mother and the gardener with a sense of desolation. Although he didn't understand everything that was said, he could feel the storm of emotions that poured from them — a thunder of cries, a hail of sadness, a rain of anger and confusion. Not until after the carriage had disappeared around the bend of the road did Dan realize it was over.

The maid helped Ven to her feet. They held on to each other and walked back to the mansion. Behind the gates, Dan's peaceful home had been transformed into a vacant tomb. The night was aging. With the strong wind that came from the river, the clouds parted. Once again, the moon and a canopy of bright stars illuminated the gray sky. Dan imagined that all the lanterns in his house had ascended to the Heavens to engage in a wild dance, leaving his dwelling in darkness.

He followed the adults to his bedroom, where Song rekindled an oil lamp. Though its flame drove the dimness from the room, it did not save Dan from the terror he was feeling. His fear intensified as he watched the women's gigantic shadows skip ominously on the walls. Although they were just a few steps away, Dan felt alone.

Leaning against the windowsill, Ven undressed. Under the glittering light, her naked back was covered with welts. Dan examined the angry marks with fascination. Some were swollen, trickling blood. Her hair was also crusted with dried blood. Outside, the wind picked up. A chilly breeze rushed into the room through a gap in the window. Ven shivered but stood her ground, too exhausted to move.

Song floated into the room like a ghost. The surface of the full water basin in her hands swayed in rhythm with her movement. Using the fresh water, the maid helped Ven to clean her wounds. She held on to the frame of the window, letting her head droop against her arm. Her face blanched from the pain. She let out incoherent sounds, which were obscured by a much louder noise from outside — the sound of an automobile engine.

The neighborhood dogs awoke and added their voices. Soon, the road in front of Dan's house was alive with the sound of dogs barking, children wailing, and the confusion of the roused neighbors.

Ven reached for her shirt. "Shut off the light!" she ordered Song. The room plunged into darkness.

Dan searched for Ven blindly, and she sensed his need. Like an eagle tending its young, she flew to his side. Her arms enfolded him and her voice, with its usual gentleness, whispered in his ear the magical phrases that always calmed him.

"What time is it, Song?" Ven asked. They had not heard the time-teller's gong all night. Without it, time seemed to stretch out to eternity.

"It is the hour of the rat, madam," Song replied.

Dan tried to recall the lessons Ven had taught him about how to tell time. According to the Chinese astrological cycle of time, twelve animals represented equal intervals in the day. In the Western system used by the French, each animal sign corresponded to two hours. The hour of the rat extended from 11:00 P.M. to 1:00 A.M. The next period, from 1:00 to 3:00 A.M., would be the hour of the ox.

As if to confirm his thoughts, Ven said to the girl, "It's midnight. Who would come at this hour, other than thieves or policemen? No matter what kind of people are out there, I don't think we should let them know that we are here."

In the dark, Song nodded.

Dan felt himself being lifted up from the bed, carried across the room, and laid down inside a small space. The scent of wet bamboo filled his nostrils. Ven had placed him in the basket that she used to carry him on her back while working in the rice fields. Now the container became his sanctuary.

She set his mother's lute in the carrier beside him. He reached for her hands on the handles of the basket, wanting to show her that he was very scared. But she seemed lost in worry.

Outside the window, under the whitish moon, a sedan drove up to the main gate. Running in a double file behind the vehicle was a troop of soldiers, clad in brown uniforms. The dark-blue socks covering their ankles showed that they belonged to the palace army. The sound of their marching boots reverberated on the gravel road, pounding in Dan's ears. Each soldier held in his hand a burning torch made from a strip of dried rubber that had been dipped in gasoline and wrapped around the end of a bamboo pole.

Following Ven's instruction, Dan drew farther inside the basket. As the automobile came to a halt, so did the tight phalanx of soldiers. In order to go from the gate to the main house, they would have to pass by Dan's bedroom, which was situated on the right side of the path, hidden behind a large garden.

Song was the first one to sneak out through the window. Hiding herself behind some cherry trees, she reached back to take the basket from Ven's hands. Dan closed his eyes and felt himself being swung through space like a jackfruit. The experience sent a wave of excitement through him, in spite of his fear.

As the wind rasped in his ears, the lute next to him vibrated. It was as if the wind had become fingers walking atop the strings. The song ended when the maid caught him in her arms.

Ven climbed out last, making a thud as she fell from the windowsill onto the wet soil. With Dan curled in a fetal position, the maid fastened the basket around Ven's back. Ven crawled on the grass to get under the raised wooden walkway that cut across the garden. Song followed her a few steps behind.

Once they found an ideal place to hide, she unhooked the basket from her shoulders and swung it in front of her. She wanted Dan to watch what was happening with an unobstructed view. From their position under the esplanade, with the thick floorboards above their heads and the wind to muffle any sounds their movements might make, the women and Dan could spy on the visitors without much fear of discovery.

$$\asymp$$

*F*ollowing gruff orders from inside the vehicle, the first two soldiers fell out of rank and ran to the front of the car. They propped their torches on the ground on either side of the house's main entrance. Placing their hands against the black granite, they pushed open the gates and stepped aside for the car to enter. The dark and luxurious sedan, reflecting the fires in the soldiers' hands, took on the color of a cockroach's wings. Its thick glass windows hid the passengers.

The majestic car lumbered along the white-brick path and stopped in front of the veranda. Like the tail of a massive scorpion, the military men kept up with it. Their feet clobbered the bricks, sending a chill down Dan's spine.

The back door of the car swung open, and two men stepped out. Dan felt Ven's hand wrap around his face. He wanted to pull away, but she was too strong. Her work-roughened fingers left just enough room around his nose for him to breathe. From somewhere above his head, he could hear her whisper with disbelief. "Oh, dear God, it's Master Long," she said.

"And his father, Magistrate Toan," Song added.

A third man emerged from the car. He wore a strange black suit, and his face bristled with light-colored fur that sprouted like the brushing end of a new broom. His eyes reflected the light like a housecat's, as he scanned the surroundings with an imperial mien. The two Vietnamese men stood beside him. Their bodies appeared diminutive as they bowed, bobbing their heads like two excited pigeons during the mating season.

The foreigner looked at Master Long and spoke a string of odd words. His thick fingers sliced the air in counterpoint to his bizarre speech. Magistrate Toan leaned closer to his son and cast a brief but expressive glance at the foreigner. "What did the French captain say?" he asked.

"The mandarin wanted to confirm that we have taken him to the correct address of the rebels," Master Long answered. His short, pomaded hair copied the Frenchman's style, in contrast to his father's traditional headdress.

Magistrate Toan urged his son, "Tell him yes, quickly."

Master Long said a few words to the French official. As they conversed, Magistrate Toan stood next to his son, waiting impatiently to receive the information from the foreign dignitary. "What did he say just now?" he asked, seizing his son's arm when the two men grew silent once more.

"He wants to search the entire place for clues of the rebels," Master Long translated. "Also, he ordered the arrest of everyone inside, regardless of age."

Under the shadow of the hiding place, Ven exhaled. "Bastards," she said under her breath. "It is unfortunate that our master placed his trust in these poisonous people. They are dangerous not only to our family, but to the very air the Cam Le Village breathes."

Song placed a finger against her lips to plead for Ven's silence.

On the veranda, Master Long, followed by his men, traversed the long walk to the living room. Once they disappeared behind the door, Dan listened to the sounds of furniture being thrown on the floor or smashed against a wall. Through the opaque windows, he caught sight of a torch leaping from room to room. Shadows of men danced against the white parchment paper of the windows. Their images reminded him of the stories his father often told about monsters who were half men, half goat, and who ascended from Hell to steal the souls of the living. Dan covered his ears with his hands. Still, he could not block out the sounds of destruction.

Outside, in front of the ornamental vase on the wooden stand, Magistrate Toan and the French mandarin awaited the soldiers' return with visible impatience. The magistrate, with terror in his eyes, studied the foreigner, hoping for some positive words, dreading to see a frown. More than half an hour went by, an eternity to Dan, before Master Long and his men emerged from different doors of the house and reassembled in the courtyard.

Master Long stepped out of the living room, staggering under the load over his shoulder. A few strands of pearls peeked out from his front pockets. His face wore a grin. Like him, the soldiers clutched large bundles on their backs. With each step they took, the clanking of metallic objects stirred the night like the rattle of ghostly chains. Others came from behind the house, leading Dan's entire collection of barnyard animals, including cows, horses, pigs, and cages of poultry, as well as a pair of oxen Song had rented the month before from a farmer in the neighboring village. Under the men's prodding, the animals moved in rows, following the fires held high in the soldiers' hands.

The French official and Master Long exchanged some words. But the foreigner did not seem satisfied with Master Long's response. He turned away and folded his arms in front of his chest. Master Long tried to speak, but the mandarin became livid. In front of the shocked soldiers, he blurted out some loud comments, then strode to the sedan and kicked its front tire.

Looking at his father, Master Long explained, "The mandarin wanted to know if I found any evidence against the fisherman. When I told him that I had found nothing, he wanted to examine these bags. Once I informed him that they contained the fortunes I had confiscated from the rebels' home, he lost his temper. He even called us a bunch of greedy monkeys."

"I see," the old man whispered, trying to maintain an air of poise.

"Do not worry, Father," Master Long said. "He will soon cool from his temper. Then, I shall provide him with the evidence he needs in exchange for these profits in our hands. Be merry, because tonight we have stumbled upon a great fortune."

From where Dan sat, he could not see Magistrate Toan's face, but he clearly heard the sound of his laughter. He wondered if this could be just a nightmare. The things he had witnessed seemed outrageous. Yet Ven's hand against his mouth assured him that he was not dreaming.

Dan's legs grew numb from staying in the same position for too long. He stirred, but Ven held him tighter. He tried to peel her fingers off and at the same time kicked the bamboo basket with his feet. Ven would not yield. Though her silent strength dominated him, the boy would not be still. The bottom of the basket scratched against the sand beneath it.

"Who's there?" Magistrate Toan called out to the dark garden from his vantage point on the veranda. Dan saw the old man's face, looking straight at him.

The boy froze. Magistrate Toan's sharp eyes seemed to hypnotize him, making him weak with fear. Several torches pointed toward the wooden walk. Unfortunately for the refugees, the combined lights were strong enough to reach their hiding place. However, as they remained unmoving, the soldiers were unable to make out their cowering figures under the floorboards.

"Who's there?" Magistrate Toan repeated. When dealing with the villagers, he always used his most intimidating voice, and its tone played a crucial role in implementing his power.

The Frenchman pulled out a pistol from inside his jacket. Without a word, he cocked the gun and aimed at the garden. Dan was hypnotized by the dark, round opening of the gun. He felt helpless, like a chicken waiting for an ax to fall on its neck.

Song touched Ven's hand. Her voice was barely audible above the rustling wind. "Listen to me, madam. Move away quickly from this place after I surrender. Take care of the young master. If you want him to stay alive, don't let them capture him."

Without waiting for Ven's reply, Song ran out from her hiding place. She raised her hands over her head and cried, "Please don't shoot me. I am just a lowly servant. Have pity on me."

Master Long whispered something in the foreigner's ear, and the man placed his gun in its case, which hung around his waist under his jacket. At the same time, Magistrate Toan waved his fingers in Song's direction, and two soldiers ran to seize her. Together they dragged her across the yard to face the old man. She pulled against their grasp, but they twisted her arms behind her shoulders, forcing her legs to bend. Beneath the swirl of hair, her face was as white as her shirt. Her head fell to her shoulder, and she swooned.

"I heard talking," Magistrate Toan shouted at Song, waking the girl up. "Who else was out there with you?"

"I was alone," Song whispered. "What you heard might have been my prayer to Heaven, sir."

Ven crept from under the wooden path, pulling Dan and the basket deeper into the darkness of the shrubbery. She muttered in his ear, "Did you see what trouble you have caused Song? Please stay still from now on, I beg you, Master." But her voice contained more sorrow than reprimand.

Her pleas were unnecessary. Dan would not dare to move even a muscle after what had happened. Nevertheless, he could not tear his eyes from the spectacle that was occurring thirty paces away.

Despite his age, Magistrate Toan jumped closer to Song with the ease of a panther. He snatched a burning torch from a soldier. With his other hand, he grabbed a handful of her hair, pulling her head backward, so that he could look down at her. The torch came down near her face as their eyes locked. The magistrate's nose was only inches from hers.

"Speak to me, slave," he shouted. "Who else is hiding out there? Say it before I scar your face with this torch."

"Nobody is here but me, sir," she said with difficulty.

He brandished the fire closer, until her hair was the same shade as the roaring torch. From a distance, it looked as if her hair had caught fire. Song closed her eyes.

"Where are they then? Where is Lady Yen?"

"My Third Mistress left with her son in a carriage late this afternoon. I know not where she is heading. A true servant shall not be inquisitive about her mistress's plans, but simply obey her order. I stayed behind because I have no other place to go, and it was her wish for me to remain here."

"Why?" he asked, as he handed the torch to one of his men.

"To guard their home until she or the master comes back. Alone in the house, I became frightened, especially when an army of strangers came in at midnight. I did not know what else to do but hide."

The magistrate couldn't seem to take his eyes from Song's face. She took a step backward, but the two soldiers tightened their hold on her arms, forcing her to be still. The flickering tongues of the fire made her rosy skin flush and her eyes glisten. With his right hand he toyed with the gold band on the third finger of his left hand, thrusting his finger in and out of the ring with increasing speed.

His voice lost its severity. "You are indeed a very attractive servant. Your master is a blind man to ignore such a beautiful flower right under his roof."

Song said coldly, "I am a married woman. My husband may have passed on, but I am devoting the rest of my life to him. Please have respect for the dead, sir."

"Hmm," the old man said with a frown. "Now that you mention the word *married*, where is that daughter-in-law of the Nguyen family?"

"She also ran off. I think she is returning to her family."

"That miserable wench," Magistrate Toan said. Then, after a brief pause, he turned to a soldier and ordered, "Send out a search warrant for all of them in the morning. They couldn't have gone very far, especially that peasant bride. It will, however, be a difficult assignment to hunt for her, since no one in this town seems to have ever seen her. I understand that the fisherman's family hid her in shame even on the night of her wedding feast. Her features were said to be too coarse for her to pass for a lady. I think we will have more luck finding her at her maiden home than waiting for her to resurface in this town."

Master Long took the old man by the elbow. "Father," he said. "I think it is time for us to leave."

The old magistrate nodded. "Make sure every animal is out," he said. "Then burn the place down. The owner of this house once held a noble status among the fishermen in the village. Reducing his property to ashes will teach the rest of his men a lesson and keep scavengers away." Turning to Song, he said, "As for you, little girl, you are under arrest and will be prosecuted later. I will personally act as judge to determine your fate."

He ordered to Song's two captors, "Take her back to my mansion."

Magistrate Toan led the march toward the Nguyen family's main house, holding his torch up high like a flaming sword. No longer a feeble old man, he strode forward, a fierce and bony soldier, ready to fight. At the front door, he paused to give the soldiers time to get outside the gates of the compound. Master Long stood in the garden, watching his father twirl his weapon in the dark night. A proud smile blossomed on his face.

The first thing Magistrate Toan burned was the wooden stand that supported the eucalyptus in the shape of a phoenix. Its ancient wood caught fire readily. Soon, the weak blaze reached the sculpted tree, and sparkles of embers crackled and flew like tiny stars. Next, the old man set fire to the panels of doors as he ran inside the house. Through the windows, Dan watched as his father's library went up in flames. The magistrate dashed from room to room, applying the spark to anything flammable in sight. The flames, small at first, shone in the darkness like so many lanterns. Slowly they coalesced to form bigger fires, licking at the walls like a thousand red snakes. The strong wind helped fuel the flames. Before long, the sulfurous hue of the inferno climbed to the magnificent roof, and the sky lit up in brilliant orange.

The smoke darkened the air as the breeze dispersed it. Frightened sparrows flew from under the carved roof-panels, where their nests were glued like cement to the tiles. Their shrill cries were lost in the thunderous roar.

Part of the roof fell to the ground. A cloud of dust rose above the fire, spreading the ashes of the hundred-year-old mansion. Magistrate Toan reappeared at the door like a demon, with the raging fire behind him. His arms were spread outward. His face was covered in sweat. Dan heard the laughter crackling from the depths of the old man's lungs. His mind had been overrun with terror at the first sight of the magistrate and his soldiers, then secretly thrilled by the splendor of the fire. Now he was consumed by the knowledge that he had lost his home forever.

Again, Ven cupped his mouth with her hand. Her tears fell onto his face, blending with his own. Before his vision was blurred completely, Dan saw Master Long. He, too, was watching the fire. His glasses reflected tiny specks of bonfire.

As the men were leaving Dan's house, Magistrate Toan threw his torch inside the bedroom that Dan shared with Ven. It landed on their wedding bed and burst into a chrysanthemum of flame.

chapter six

The Reunion

he fire burned all night, bringing down enormous portions of the house. On one side, the entire brick wall collapsed. The tile roof fell into the rooms below. The exquisite furniture, impeccable artwork, and haunting memories of Dan's once-happy family were all consumed in flames or buried under debris.

No one in the Cam Le Village dared to come within a hundred yards of the smoldering ashes for fear of the old magistrate. The sumptuous mansion had always brought pleasure to their eyes and pride to their hearts; now they watched through the cracks of their doors as the centerpiece of their town was converted into a useless ruin.

Steps away from the wooden path, Dan emerged from his basket. A few red cherry blossoms, caught by the wind, swayed in midair before landing on his head and shoulders, then falling to the ground. Their scarlet petals looked like drops of blood against the lifeless grass. With a leaden heart, he padded down the walkway, searching for Ven.

A loud crash drew his attention to the remains of his bedroom. A heavy block of concrete lay on the scorched ground, and above it, through a cloud of dust, he saw a gaping opening in the wall. From this cleft, Ven emerged, brushing dirt from her palms. He barely recognized her through the soot smeared on her face and the exposed portions of her arms. On her head she wore a conical straw hat fastened with a wide band of fabric to keep the wind from sweeping it away. In the usual fashion, the black cloth band would have been secured under her chin. Instead, Ven had wrapped it over her mouth and nose.

Dan looked into his wife's slanted eyes. Though they were nearly hidden underneath the brim of her oversized headgear, he felt a wave of relief. He spread his arms and waited for her to come to him.

"You are awake, Master Dan," she said as she picked him up.

With her fingers, she applied dirt all over his skin and clothes. Dan wiggled, trying to push her away and wiping his face with the back of his hands. His struggles only made the oily soot spread, until he resembled a sad jester in an impoverished opera troupe.

"Stop!" he screamed.

"Please, young Master," she urged him. "We must keep our identities a secret. You can see for yourself from what happened last night, the magistrate and his son are very dangerous men. We cannot have them recognize us in public."

"Can we leave here?" he asked.

She shook her head.

"Why not?" he insisted.

Patiently she explained, "We must beg for food and gather news of your parents at the community hall. And we must remain in town. I cannot take you back to my grandparents' home. Magistrate Toan said that he would look for us there."

"Where will we sleep?" Dan asked. He had always been afraid of the dark, and the thought of spending another night in the garden was daunting.

"Don't worry, Master. I'll find a warm and safe place for you to rest, away from the guards and soldiers." The determination in her voice kept him from asking more questions.

*T*wo weeks passed in a deceptive calm. No one in the Cam Le Village paid much attention to the two new beggars haunting the entrance of the community hall — a burly woman dressed in filthy rags, carrying a little boy inside a torn bamboo basket on her back. Everyone assumed the child was her son. Although most villagers disliked the sight of strangers asking for food instead of working, paupers were common, and it was unremarkable when one disappeared and another showed up. The earth had always provided an abundance of food and fuel. Through the act of giving alms to the less fortunate, the well-to-do would gain recognition for their good deeds and win merit in Heaven.

The townspeople were preoccupied with their own sorrows, as they yearned for news of their missing sons, husbands, and fathers. In nearly every family, a loved one had been arrested at the seaport. The whole village's destiny was entwined with that of its bold fishing captain, the ill-fated Master Nguyen.

The boy spent most of his time playing with his soiled puppets while his "mother" begged for food or money. His mournful expression, too sad and mature for a child his age, seemed to darken each time a soldier crossed his path. His guardian showed no emotion as she inquired about the posted news from the literate passersby. She listened to the tidings with outward composure. Yet an astute observer might have noticed that under the large straw hat her eyes betrayed a spark of emotion that seemed like pain.

*L*ate one morning, the crowd of distraught wives and mothers in front of the community hall was startled by the sound of motor vehicles rapidly approaching. With the permission of the guards, the women hastened into the street. Beneath a cloud of russet dirt from the distant road, a dark sedan rushed toward the villagers. At the turn of the street, it stopped and glared at the pedestrians with its headlights.

Behind the car rumbled a much larger conveyance. No one in the town had ever seen this type of transportation before. Like the car, the new machine was drawn forward by neither man nor beast. Its enormous body seemed as gawky as a giant water buffalo, and just like the animal, it snorted forth smoke and water. Under the blazing sun, the people of the Cam Le Village at last saw their lost relatives riding atop the wagon.

With expressions of agony and acceptance, their imprisoned loved ones looked back at them. Seated on a wooden plank in the truck's open back, the captives had been riding from Hue City since the previous evening. Soldiers of the Royal Court, carrying impressive firearms, accompanied them.

The sedan surged forward, swallowing the road with furious speed. Its sudden movement dispersed the villagers in every direction. Amid the confusion, the truck followed the sleek automobile through the crowd.

The women cried out when they saw the convicts up close. Signs of physical abuse were visible on every one of them. Recent wounds lay atop old ones in various shades of blue and red, turning their faces into living masks of torture. Their hands, too, bore testimony to their suffering. When the prisoners were arrested, the guards had pierced their palms with an iron poker and inserted heavy rings through them. A chain through the shackles connected the men like a string of human beads. With brutal efficiency, the device served to keep them from escaping, as well as to help transport them from one place to the next.

Despite their anguish, the villagers understood the severity of the alleged crime. Throughout Vietnam's history, the atrocities committed by pirates had infuriated the authorities. Sea bandits had looted coastal cities, getting away with murder and mayhem, for years. On those rare occasions when some of them fell into the government's hands, they were shown no mercy. Upon seeing their menfolk, the women ran alongside the truck without fear for their own safety, until the vehicle was brought to a sudden halt.

Master Nguyen and his two wives sat among the captives. Unlike the others, their eyes were blindfolded with black rags. Their expensive clothes were torn, covered in blood and the filth of the road. Master Nguyen's headdress, the elegant silk panel that had always been folded in neat layers on the crown of his head, was torn and slanted toward his ear. Yet he still remained stoic, as was fitting for a man of his stature.

First Mistress, on the other hand, resembled a broken puppet. She was shaking uncontrollably. Her face was the sickly beige of an opium addict's during a fit of withdrawal. She turned toward the noisy crowd, calling out for sympathy. Her supplication was cut short when a soldier smashed the butt of his rifle into her face. The blow broke her nose and knocked her to the wooden floor. Jets of blood sprayed from the wound. Her companion, the subservient Second Mistress, reached around blindly in search of her. The soldier jerked the chain connected to the younger woman's shackle with his foot, restricting Second Mistress to her seat.

When the clock inside the community hall struck twelve times, the villagers' true torment began. Magistrate Toan, who had been concealed behind the dark window of the sedan, stepped out to announce that the hour for the capital punishment had arrived and that this would be the villagers' last opportunity to bid farewell to those they loved. He ordered a number of his men to hold back the crowd while others unhooked the back door of the truck. The prisoners inched single-file toward the opening, descended a few steps, then jumped the remaining distance to the ground.

Master Nguyen and his two mistresses were the last to make their way toward the opening. Sightlessly they fumbled for a wall to guide their steps but found none. It must have been a frightening experience for them, feeling the sunlight that penetrated their coarse blindfolds, yet being unable to see.

A couple of soldiers on the truck shoved Master Nguyen from behind. He fell forward and crashed into First Mistress. She, in turn, staggered ahead. Like a toppling line of dominoes, the prisoners collided against one another, while the iron shackles pulled at their hands. Dan's parents were dragged across the truck bed by their bloody palms and flung onto the earth like three rice sacks. The laughter of the soldiers carried above the distressed cries of the onlookers.

Among the hysterical women, a beggar, whose face was half-covered under a large conical straw hat, watched the scene with visible sadness. After the prisoners were assembled in front of the community hall, she withdrew into a shady grove that faced the marketplace. Behind an oak tree, the little boy was waiting for her. Traces of tears stained his muddy cheeks. He raised his arms toward her.

"Save my daddy, please," he said.

The beggar took his head between her hands, drew him toward her, and kissed his forehead several times. Tears also welled up in her eyes. "I can't, young Master," she said. "I can only try to save you."

She lifted him up and laid him inside her basket. With a sweeping movement, she swung it over her shoulders and started off.

"Where are we going, Ven?" the boy asked in a faltering voice.

"We are going home, young Master. They are going to kill your father at the doorstep of his mansion. Custom requires that a pirate must be executed in front of his own house. Because his crew spent so much time there, they will meet their fate in the same place. It is your duty to watch this ritual with a calm and strong mind and then judge for yourself: Does this bloodshed require revenge? Let this experience guide you into adulthood. Someday, I hope you will raise your head and say in the enemy's face, 'I am the son of a man you killed because of your own greed. And now it is my turn to claim your life.' And then you will draw back in order to watch life ebb from his eyes. When that time comes, I want to be right next to you."

Snug in his basket atop his wife's shoulders, Dan cried until exhaustion claimed him. Even while he slept, the image of his father and two stepmothers in their helpless state tormented his thoughts. Ven made no effort to assuage her young husband's grief. When at last he stopped sobbing and fell asleep, she was thankful for the quiet.

After a few more turns on the dusty red road, they approached the tall brick wall of their former home. At the entrance, behind a few large fir trees, a couple of soldiers slumped against the hard concrete, fast asleep. Military hats, made of straw and decorated with tufts of horsehair, covered their faces.

Ven used a post placed at an angle against the wall to hoist herself up a few inches. Looking into the garden, she saw no one. The desolate ground baked under the hot sun, lonelier than a cemetery. Ashes swirled in the wind like flakes of wild pollen.

She lifted Dan out of the basket and tossed him over her shoulder. The boy woke groggily. She hurled the empty bamboo basket to the other side of the wall. He stretched his thin limbs around her. His breath, like the muggy air, was hot against her neck. Then, with the boy's legs wrapped around her waist and his arms holding her neck like those of a little monkey clinging to its mother, Ven's limbs were free to help her to spring over the wall, using the post for support. After perching briefly on top of the barrier, they landed on a soft bed of grass. Ven used her back to absorb the impact of the fall.

Once they got to their feet, Dan thought he heard a car engine over the gusts of wind that sighed above their heads. The wicked noise that had rung in his ears for the last two weeks grew louder. Was fear making him imagine the sound? The alarmed expression on his wife's face told him she heard it, too. She reached for the bamboo basket, urging him to climb inside.

From his basket, he saw the dazzling light reflected from the shining top of the car over the far end of the tall wall. Behind it waddled the truck, bearing its cargo of human misery. Moments later, the pounding footsteps of the soldiers reverberated in the humid air. Above the clatter, Dan heard the cries of the victims' relatives, who panted after the two vehicles, reaching up in a vain effort to touch their loved ones' hands.

His wife remained calm in the midst of the chaos. She stood at the edge of the yard, examining their surroundings. The garden was made up of a number of rectangular plots of well-kept grasses, separated by wooden paths. Parts of it were far enough from the main house to have been spared from the fire. At the corners near the wall were clusters of mango, guava, and jackfruit trees with thick foliage, which merged to form a canopy over the compound's ornate entrance. One of the tallest mango trees had several branches reaching out over the main pathway. Without hesitation, Ven climbed the tree, holding on to its branches as she moved upward.

Dan wrapped his hands around his wife's neck and crouched lower in the basket. Although her burden was awkward, she moved with skill and precision. Soon they were thirty feet above the ground, looking down at the road through a thin curtain of leaves.

Balancing on a horizontal branch, Ven shifted the basket in front of her. Dan remained motionless, but his mind raced with curiosity. All around him, green mangoes in various stages of growth dangled on their thin stalks.

The fruit reminded him of the little prizes his father had hung on the branches of the cherry tree at the beginning of every New Year's celebration. For as long as he could remember, that tradition was his father's way of rewarding the servants for their hard work. He scratched his nose and blinked away a few tears. His wife made no gesture to comfort him.

"You have cried enough, young Master. Now please be still," she said to him.

He twisted to face her with a pleading look. "I don't want to be here. Please, Ven, please. You cannot make me. You have no right, for you are not my mother."

She set the basket on a wide horizontal branch that forked outward like the two grasping jaws of a pair of pincers, less than two feet away from the tree trunk. In her eyes he saw an unfamiliar expression that terrified him. "Be grateful that I am not your mother," she said. "She has abandoned you. She chose to value herself and a lowly gardener over you, her own son. As for me, the gods have cursed me since the day my grandparents sent me to the house of Nguyen. And now you are becoming a heavy load for me to handle, but I am bound to you under Heaven's law. I assure you, young Master, I have had many moments when I was tempted to leave you. But I knew that if I did, my conscience would forever haunt me. I made a vow to take care of you. I hope that you will always treat me with the respect due to me as your lawfully wedded first wife.

"You don't want to witness the gruesome details of the execution? I am afraid that I cannot spare you this dreadful sight. In order for you to harbor the revenge in your head and the bitterness in your heart, you must witness the death of your father at the hands of his enemies. Only then will your grief be so profound that it will force you to seek payback. Now, be silent."

Dan covered his eyes with the palms of his hands. Ven urged him to look down, and he obeyed. The crowd's tumult roused the two sluggish guards, pushing them to their feet. They stood at attention, holding their firearms against their trousers. The dark sedan arrived at the entrance, followed by the truck and a team of guards.

*A*s the convoy came closer, Dan could see the faces of the condemned, and he heard them praying aloud. He recognized his first mother even though the soldier's blow had turned her nose into a swollen purple mass, like the skin of an overripe eggplant. Splashes of ruddy blood covered the front of her black dress. She was sixteen years older than her husband, but this was the first time Dan saw her show her age.

The boy's eyes shifted to his father. Tat Nguyen held his blindfolded head erect and seemed undisturbed by his physical discomfort. After the guards repeated the procedure of shoving the prisoners from the truck to the ground, Master Nguyen marched through the squad of uniformed men, following the tug of the shackle. The punctured hole in his palm had replaced his sight and was now showing him the way.

The people of Cam Le Village were restrained behind a barricade. Dan could hear their frustrated cries rise like a human storm, as their anguish deepened. Family members called the prisoners' names with love, hope, and tenderness. Adding to the din, they hurled curses at the magistrate and his son and called for vengeance and justice.

Inside the mansion grounds, a group of soldiers toiled under the supervision of Magistrate Toan to prepare a killing site. From the truck, they unloaded stout bamboo poles, three or more feet in length and solid enough to serve as house beams. With heavy mallets, they drove each post into the ground alongside the brick wall, between the walkway and the garden. Soon a symmetrical pattern emerged, with the poles six feet apart on either side of the main path.

Next came the digging. A few feet in front of each stake, the soldiers excavated an open pit in the rocky ground. Dan counted a total of thirty-three pits. From his hiding place, the execution area seemed to drape along the mango branch, separated by thirty feet of empty space and a thin veil of foliage.

"Bring in the prisoners," said the magistrate.

The convicts filed through the main entrance, followed by the soldiers. Magistrate Toan waited for them at one corner of the garden, near the first pole. One by one, he unlocked the shackles to release each man. The captive then was led to his designated plot, where a guard stood at attention.

No one said a word or tried to escape. The physical and mental tortures inflicted on the fishermen during the past two weeks had left them in a state of exhaustion that was compounded by their long period of hunger and thirst. Each man was forced to bend down in front of his killer, who then tied his hands to the bamboo stalk. The prisoners knelt on the loose stones, looking at the open graves behind their executioners. The holes stared back, hollow and vacant, like the eyes of Death.

Master Long guarded the first three posts on the right side of the main walkway. His prisoners, Master Nguyen and his two wives, knelt before him with their hands tied behind their backs. The afternoon sun beat down on them. Master Long tilted his head to the side, trying to keep the bright glare off of his glasses. He wiped perspiration from his forehead with a handkerchief and shifted his expensive leather shoes on the torrid sand.

Turning to a soldier near him, he said in a tight voice, "Sai, go and fetch me some refreshment."

The young soldier ran to the road. Moments later he returned, holding a goblet of fresh coconut juice. Master Long snatched the beverage, and a splash of it sprayed the condemned man. Master Nguyen's tongue darted out, and he closed his eyes to savor the drink's freshness. Next to him, Master Long made loud gulping noises as he emptied his glass. Once finished, he sighed and tossed the glass back to the soldier. The man caught it clumsily using both of his hands. A foolish grin broke wide on his face.

On the mango branch, Dan felt faintly warmed by the weak rays of sunlight that penetrated the leaves. In the silence around him, he heard a thumping sound, like a drum against his rib cage. His parents on the ground below seemed miles away. He observed each gesture they made. He was the audience, viewing a play directed by destiny from thirty feet above the stage. Like any spectator, he could not interfere with the performance. All he could do was watch.

Magistrate Toan reached inside his *ao dai* tunic for a pocket watch and glanced at its face. He walked across the white gravel road and stood before Master Nguyen, who lifted his head.

"Do you have a last request?" Magistrate Toan asked.

"If that question is addressed to me, then the answer is yes," Master Nguyen replied.

"What is your request, sir?"

"I would like to have my blindfold removed. And I urge you to give my two mistresses the same consideration. If you won't grant them this small favor, then I shall keep mine on."

Magistrate Toan tapped his foot on the ground, thinking for several seconds. In his most domineering tone, he ordered one of the guards, "Take the coverings off their eyes." The soldier responded instantly.

Master Nguyen blinked, adjusting to the brightness around him. He looked about the garden, searching for his two wives and the rest of his crew, then turned to face the ruins of his home. What he saw exceeded the capacity of his imagination. He gasped, using all his willpower to keep still. But, in spite of his efforts, his emotions exploded out of him like the howling of a wounded wolf. Next to him, the two women wept.

The outburst startled Magistrate Toan into taking several steps backward. With a whoop of surprise, he fell into the open grave behind him. Master Nguyen yanked at the bamboo stake that secured his hands and sprang against the hard ground. The guards subdued him with a shower of punches, not stopping until he lost all power to resist.

Dan watched his father's head tilt and hang motionless. He wondered if the beating had killed him. A tremor passed over Master Nguyen's body, and his eyes opened.

The condemned sea captain waited for Toan, assisted by his son, to climb out of the grave before he exclaimed, "What has happened to the remainder of my family? Where are my son and his mother? Who is responsible for the destruction of my property?"

"Everyone in your family escaped the fire," said Magistrate Toan. "But they cannot hide for long, because I am sending out search warrants for their arrest. And it is I who was responsible for destroying your charming home."

Master Nguyen burst out laughing — a terrible sound that expressed more pain than his earlier outburst. "All survive," he muttered, as if the sound of his voice would somehow confirm the validity of the news. Looking up at Toan, he asked, "Why did you do it? What have I or any member of my family ever done to offend you?"

"Treason," the old magistrate said. "You have committed a great crime against the country. You have been found guilty of having conspired to aid the young emperor's escape, as part of a greater plan to overthrow the French government. I am just an ignorant old man. I am following orders from the Court at Hue. The Office of the Royal Prosecutor has required me to exercise its power and mete out justice in this area."

"I am innocent of those accusations," replied the captain. "If you are interested in the facts, just ask your son. Master Long knows as much about my business and political affairs as I, since he is handling some of my estates. He can vouch for my neutrality when it comes to politics. I am and have always been a businessman, and my position as a captain of a small fishing boat is not nearly eminent enough for me to be involved in any political activity. Only thirty sailors serve under me; and they, too, are innocent of all crimes. It must be a conspiracy —"

Magistrate Toan interrupted. "What you ask is impossible. My son knows nothing about you or your affairs, Sir Nguyen."

"Tell me then," said the captain. "Since it is the stem of my misfortunes, what has happened to King Duy Tan?"

"His Majesty was arrested three days after his infamous escape, at a town called An Cuu. The prime minister, Sir Ho Dac Trung, was in charge of carrying out a judgment against the king and his supporters. This is the result of his trial." He reached inside his long sleeve to pull out a golden scroll — the imperial order he had received from the Court at Hue. With a flourish, he unrolled the paper and read its contents.

This letter is addressed to all the mandarins in the Court at Hue. The royal prosecutor has concluded: "At first, these men pretended to fish at Lake Tinh Tam, forging the emperor's handwriting to create false permits. Then they aided the emperor's escape on a boat at Thuong Bac Port. They fed the young king inferior quality rice at Ha Trung and chicken rice soup at Ngu Binh Mountain. His Imperial Highness has suffered through a series of storms, winds, and dust throughout his journey. All of these crimes were part of a scheme designed by these accused."

Magistrate Toan rolled the paper back to its original shape and continued. "Unlike all of you, His Highness has escaped the death sentence, but he abdicated immediately and is now in exile, somewhere in Africa, on an island called Réunion. The court has appointed a new king, who reigns in Vietnam at this moment — King Khai Dinh. His Majesty is from a long line of royal blood, as you may know, and has always been destined to be a true king, even in his cradle. The king's father was the late King Dong Khanh."

Magistrate Toan glanced at his pocket watch again and said, "The moment has arrived. It has been ordered that the prisoners must cease to live by the hour of the goat. This is now the hour of the goat." He raised his hands to summon the soldiers.

"Wait," said the captain. "I have one more request."

The old magistrate shook his head. "I can only grant you one favor, which was removing your blindfolds."

"You must listen to me," Master Nguyen insisted. "I'll trade my fortune for one final wish."

The old man snorted with laughter. "This is a very ridiculous offer, since I already possess everything you once owned."

"No doubt," said the prisoner. "However, my real treasure lies hidden away, and I am the only one who can show you the map that leads to it. You must trust me, for I am a pirate. And you know, pirates often bury their wealth. A vast treasure could belong to you, Sir Toan, if you grant me a final wish before I depart this world."

"How can I believe this so-called treasure really exists?" asked the magistrate, who was losing patience.

"My request is very simple. My son's life and the lives of my sailors, all are insignificant to you; however, I am responsible for their safety. Release them, or put them in prison if you must, but please spare them from the death sentence. They are no threat to you, nor are they criminals under any court of law."

"How much money are we talking about, Captain?" inquired the magistrate.

Master Nguyen's eyes were half-shut. "More than you can imagine, Magistrate Toan. It sleeps in the bosom of the earth, waiting to be uncovered."

Magistrate Toan looked to his son. Master Long, in turn, merely shrugged. The old man turned to the prisoner. "I have no reason to trust you."

"And neither have I any cause to accept your word," replied the captain. "I can only hope that you will spare the lives of the people I just mentioned once I leave this world. After all, one must grant a dying wish, regardless of the conditions."

"All right," conceded the old man. "I will honor this agreement."

"In that case, send your men outside. I must disclose this information in confidence."

Once again, Magistrate Toan turned to his son. "Get your men to untie the prisoners and take them outside the gates," he said. "Make sure that no one else is in this garden, except for the captain, his mistresses, and me."

Master Long made an effort to hide his disappointment. "Must I, too, go outside, Father?"

"Indeed, you must stand guard over the prisoners."

Master Long instructed the soldiers to carry out his father's command. The fishermen were released from their posts. The shackles were once again passed through their swollen palms, and the chain was threaded through to connect them. The granite gate was re-opened. As they passed by their captain, the sailors bade him farewell, saluting him with titles of respect. They then returned to the road.

Magistrate Toan turned to Master Nguyen, who wore a look of pride.

"Tell me the location of the map," the magistrate demanded. "As you can see, I intend to keep my promise to you."

"Thank you," Tat Nguyen replied. "Half of the map was tattooed on my back. You can check it if you wish."

Magistrate Toan studied his opponent. Slowly he strolled a half-circle around the bound prisoner, so that he could look at him from behind. With the swiftness of a hawk, he tore open Master Nguyen's tunic. In the bright sunlight the map appeared before the old man, covering a large portion of the captain's upper body with a detailed landscape and an inscription in the old vernacular. The magistrate leaned closer and read out loud: "The priests make charms out of nature by aligning the constellations, the sun, and the moon." He scratched his chin and asked, "What does that mean?"

Master Nguyen replied, "It is a favorite verse of mine, written by Taoist monks in China during the early seventh century. It means just what it says, nothing more. The map will lead you to the treasure."

In the mango tree, Ven repeated the verse softly as if it were a mantra.

Toan narrowed his eyes. "For the lives of your son and your crew, tell me where the treasure is. I have no patience for riddles."

The captain smiled. "If I could remember where I hid my riches, I would not have bothered to record their location in a tattoo. Besides, searching for it will be an exciting adventure for an old fox like you. Have I gained your trust now, Magistrate Toan?"

"Where is the other half of the map?"

"Before I answer that question, allow me one more inquiry, just to help clear my mind."

"By the Heavens, what is it?" cried the old man in exasperation.

"Why are you destroying my peaceful home? Could it simply be vengeance? I do not remember ever offending you."

"No, you haven't," replied the magistrate. "There is no reason, except for —"

"Except for?"

"There cannot be two suns in the sky nor two kings in one country. You and I cannot exist together in this town. I must destroy you before your strength and power outshine mine. This opportunity could not have come at a better time."

"Your words ring of truth," said Master Nguyen. "Thank you for your honesty."

"Now, tell me where the other half of the map is."

The captain said, "It is tattooed on my son's back. Once you find him, you can copy the map if you wish, but you must spare his life as we have agreed."

Upon hearing these words, Dan jumped with fright inside his basket. Behind him, Ven made a surprised sound from the back of her throat. She should well be familiar with his body by now. Nevertheless, Dan felt his wife's hands creeping up along his torso. She lifted the thin fabric of his shirt. Soft wind walked its fingers along the small of his back, where the skin was as white as ivory. Dan could not remember getting any tattoo, nor could he comprehend why his father had lied to the old magistrate. His wife, however, understood. She squeezed his little body in her strapping hands.

"Prepare for the deaths of the condemned Tat Nguyen and his family," Magistrate Toan announced.

Sai, the same soldier who had handed the beverage to Master Long, now returned to the garden. In his hands he held a small tray containing a dry lump of red ink and a large Chinese brush made from sable fur. Some of the ink had been ground and mixed with water inside a clay bowl to form a viscous paste. Standing before the magistrate, he raised the tray to his brows.

The old man picked up the brush and dipped it in the thick ink. When he drew it closer to Master Nguyen's face, the tip of the instrument dribbled red liquid onto the white sand. Carrying out the executioner's ritual, Magistrate Toan drew a line around the prisoner's neck, marking the place where the cut would be made. From the gates, the sound of a tambour lifted, hollow and rushing like the galloping of wild horses. The magistrate made the same marks on the necks of First and Second Mistress. They wailed as they felt the brush on their skin.

Another soldier appeared. With his palms open, he handed Magistrate Toan a scimitar. The sharp edge of its curved blade reflected the sunlight, gleaming like a crescent mirror.

Ven knew what was going to happen next. She wrapped her hand around Dan's mouth, silencing him before he had a chance to scream. Thirty feet below them, Magistrate Toan picked up his weapon with two hands. Dan shrank back and closed his eyes tightly, trying to escape the dreadful scene. When he reopened them, his father's head was flying in the air like a shuttlecock. It landed with a soft thud on the ground underneath his basket.

Dan's gaze was riveted on the decapitated head, which lay facing the sky. His father's eyes, still wet with his spirit, seemed to look straight at him, recognizing who he was. A faint smile passed over his bloody face. And then, as though the fire inside him was extinguished, his features grew dull.

Warm fluid spontaneously squirted down Dan's legs. He had lost control of his bladder. Ven loomed above him with her arms tight around him. Magistrate Toan was erect and triumphant. He inhaled deeply as though he were absorbing the spirit of his enemy, then turned to face the two bound women with his weapon.

Beneath the mango tree, the swatch of green grass slowly took on a bright shade of crimson.

chapter seven

Two Silver Dollars

At the first sight of blood spurting from Master Nguyen's neck, Ven collapsed against the tree, half-fainting. The stricken look Dan gave her reminded her of her duty. She would not allow the scene beneath the mango's branches to steal her will to fight. Anger seized her throat, and she fought the urge to scream, shake her fists at the Heavens above, or confront the enemies below. For the sake of her young husband, she concentrated on formulating a plan to save both of their lives.

From the ground rose the acrid smell of spilled blood, like the stench of a slaughterhouse. Magistrate Toan puffed out his chest. In his hand he still held the sharp scimitar. Kneeling, he wiped the blood off its blade by stabbing it repeatedly into the soil. A soldier approached the bamboo posts, where the corpses dangled like marionettes whose strings had been cut. Before each grave site, he placed a small wooden board inscribed with the death sentence.

Ven glanced at her husband. Never before had she seen a child weep in such total silence. Above them, the indifferent sun scorched the earth with rays strong enough to wilt the mango's leaves. Another soldier moved down the walkway, carrying three round plates the size of Ven's hat and made of woven rye straw. He grimaced when he came to the severed heads of Master Nguyen and his two wives. Using his thumb and forefinger, he lifted them by the hair and placed one on each tray. As Ven looked down into the dull, bloodstained face of Master Nguyen, she felt a wave of nausea and she, too, broke into silent tears.

Magistrate Toan moved among the bodies, using his sword to cut the ropes that tied them to the poles. Deliberately, the old man spat on the gore-encrusted torsos, aiming at the raw flesh of the necks, where the ruptured arteries could be seen. The soldiers pushed the corpses belly-down into the open graves. No sticks of incense eased the passage of their spirits. Their expensive clothes were torn, and their claylike bodies showed through the tatters. Under the old man's direction, a guard flayed the skin that bore the tattooed map from Master Nguyen's back. Only then did the magistrate allow his men to complete the burial.

Once the last shovel of dirt fell upon the graves, the troops left the garden, taking the victims' heads with them. Ven followed Magistrate Toan with her eyes and saw him climb into the dark sedan, where Master Long waited. Almost as an afterthought, Magistrate Toan opened his window and ordered his men to place his enemies' heads at the entrance of the house. Soon the three trays hung from the branch of a fir tree under the hot sun, a cautionary example for the villagers.

Ven watched the car roll down the pebbled road, trailed by the team of soldiers on foot and by the truck bearing the remaining prisoners. She lost sight of them, and once again the garden was immersed in loneliness.

*T*hat night they hid in a clearing behind the single remaining wall of the kitchen. Ven lay on her back, studying the dark sky. The waning moon did not rise until the time-teller's third round. Dan cuddled against the fold of her arm, sleeping. Ven watched him, and the signs of his ordeal broke her heart. After their weeks as beggars, his once-round body was now angular and bony, as small as a bird's.

Ven held his hand in her rough fingers, pressing it against her nose. In the impenetrable stillness she inhaled his faint, childlike warmth.

Her head throbbed as though a handful of rocks were forming under the flat surface of her brow. They rolled restlessly from one side to the other each time she tilted her head. Ven gritted her teeth and pounded her temples with her fists, moaning. She had been out in the sun for too long in the past few days, she thought. Overcome with exhaustion, she drifted into a restless sleep.

When Ven woke up, the sun was rising in a cloudless sky. Dan sat with his back to her in the shade of the brick wall. He had found a bunch of taro in the ashes of the kitchen garden, and he was picking out the tiniest bulbs from the tangle of roots, popping them unpeeled into his mouth, and crunching them. In a pile near his feet were the larger corms, which contained a bit more nutrition.

Ven remained on the ground, unable to move. A fever spread through her body like fire. She was desperate for a drink, but her withered tongue was unable to form the words to ask for one. She concentrated on her husband's back, making a slight rustling noise with her hands in the parched grass to get his attention. At last she managed a single hoarse word.

"Please!"

Dan turned around.

"Water," she whispered.

Dan regarded her as though she were a stranger. Then he got up and disappeared from her view. Returning with a clay bowl of water, he stooped and held the cloudy liquid to her lips. She drank a little, clutching her head to prevent her brain from bursting.

"Come, Ven," the boy said. A look of worry showed through the dirt that covered his face. "Have some taro roots with me. I don't know how to cook them, but I have saved the biggest pieces for you."

The water replenished her strength, yet the awful pain persisted. Until now, she had never thought about herself. She bit her lower lip and said nothing while her mind churned. She had no money. The last copper pennies were gone long ago. But her poverty was not the issue, for she did not even feel strong enough to walk to the town and fetch a doctor.

Ven got to her feet with effort. The hammering in her head grew worse. Leaning on her husband, she took baby steps toward the garden. She remembered the purple *Ricinus* leaves that used to grow along the back fence. Every farmer knew this wild herb got rid of a headache faster than any bottled medicine. Gratefully, she found the plant had survived the conflagration. She laid its fronds against her forehead and held them in place with a turban of black cloth. Exhausted, she returned to the kitchen and collapsed into the shadow of the wall, where she sat as immobile as an earthen jar.

Under her direction, Dan smashed a knuckle of gingerroot into the juice of a lemon that he had found on the burned ground nearby. Ven straightened to unhook her clothes. With his palm the boy smeared the ginger-lemon paste over her body. Its heat suffused her skin in waves. As she drifted in thought, her husband's prayer echoed in her ears. "Dear gods, please save my Ven."

She woke sometime in the afternoon, feverish, bathed in perspiration. The headache, far from dissipating in her sleep as she had hoped, had gotten worse. Her breath rasped, and her limbs shook with a palsy.

Dan sat some twenty paces away and watched Ven. Her quivering body and the unusual heat that emanated from her filled him with dread. When she looked at him, her narrow eyes held none of the tenderness he yearned for.

"I cannot take care of you any longer, young Master," she said.

"No, do not say that," Dan cried. He sprang to her side and touched her face with affection. "Eat some food," he said. "You will feel better soon."

She shook her head. When she spoke, her voice was like the wind. "I have thought of nothing but you in my sleep, and now I have come to a conclusion. This is not a simple decision for me to make, nor will it be easy for you to accept. Trust me, poor child, I know your anguish. Fate has inflicted a great misfortune upon you, and your life has not been of sufficient length to bear yet another. Oh, Dan, if only I could, I would not hesitate to cut the flesh from my body to feed you.

"My strength is fleeting. I am seized with a terrible illness, and I cannot be sure how much worse it may grow. It is called malaria, and I have had it before. Perhaps this time it will overcome me. But before Death turns me cold, I must find a way for you to survive." She paused, catching her breath.

"Stop! I am scared," he screamed.

"You must listen to me, young Master," she said. "I need you to understand. I belong to you, and I shall remain with you so long as life runs through my veins. Only Death could part us, and now I can feel it in my bones. Before I die, I want to find you a home that can give you food and shelter. I must not wait too long. We cannot escape this place, so we must find a way to ensure your safety among your enemies, even as they are searching for you. And where could I hide you? Where is the very place in this village that no one will look for you? I have found the answer. Indeed, my sole consolation is the fact that, at the height of my malady, I have come upon a plan to save you."

Dan did not fully understand what she said, but he sensed her seriousness. "Do not send me away," he begged her. "Come and sit with me. We will have lunch together, Ven."

She stood up and searched for her straw hat, which lay nearby with the rest of her clothes. The boy watched her with fear in his eyes. He gathered the taro roots in his hands. "Please, Ven. Eat something. You'll get your strength back. Then we will leave here together."

Ven sat up and faced the burned wall. Her shoulders shook. In a flat voice she said, "I can't, young Master. You eat the food. I would not rob you of your last meal in this house."

The boy froze in consternation. "What do you mean, Ven? Where will I eat? Who will I live with?"

Ven buried her face in her hands. "Tonight you will eat at the house of Toan, on the floor with the rest of the servants."

Dan stepped back, transfixed with horror. The taro roots fell from his hands. "No, no," he wailed. "I cannot go to the house of Toan."

"We have no choice. To save you, I must sell you to Magistrate Toan's family. If I die, you must pursue revenge for your parents and me. If I survive, I will be right here watching over you."

Dan ran out of the kitchen. Ven somehow found the strength to catch up and seize his arm. The boy struggled to get free. Despite his screaming, she did not release his wrist. He fell to the ground. "I hate you," he moaned, beating her feet with his fists.

Ven lifted him across her shoulders. His weight temporarily threw her off balance. She rested against the wall, waiting for a wave of dizziness to pass. "I am sorry," she muttered. "Let us go while I still have some strength. Since I can no longer offer you any assistance, I must break off my relationship with you."

With the boy sobbing against her neck, Ven gathered his clothes and tied them in a bundle. She put her straw hat on her head to shield her burning eyes from the torrid sun. As she eased through the back fence, she moved so slowly that she thought she would never reach the road that led to town.

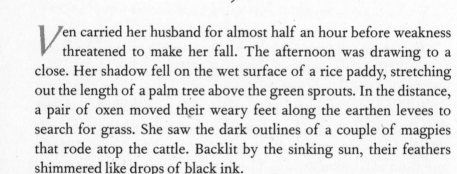

Ven carried her husband for almost half an hour before weakness threatened to make her fall. The afternoon was drawing to a close. Her shadow fell on the wet surface of a rice paddy, stretching out the length of a palm tree above the green sprouts. In the distance, a pair of oxen moved their weary feet along the earthen levees to search for grass. She saw the dark outlines of a couple of magpies that rode atop the cattle. Backlit by the sinking sun, their feathers shimmered like drops of black ink.

Ven stopped and swung the boy down from her shoulders. Holding him by his upper arm, she led him across the fields. Beneath their feet, the drying mud was bumpy with the imprints of hasty footsteps.

"Do you really plan to sell me?" Dan whined. Tears melted the dirt on his face into black streaks. "Have pity on me, Ven. I don't want to die like my father. I want to live."

She walked faster.

"Please, Ven," he said. "I do not want to be without you. I already miss you so much. Please let me stay with you, just one more night together, I beg you."

The entrance to the village came into view from behind a row of areca palms. On the right was the house of Toan. Several haystacks, like bald hills, sat outside its front gate next to a group of jackfruit trees. As a farmer, Ven realized that in order to gather that much rice straw, Magistrate Toan must control hundreds of acres.

She felt as though she were about to enter a tiger's lair. How would she face the enemy? What would happen if Magistrate Toan or his son recognized them as the missing fugitives? Only fate could decide what would happen next. She felt light-headed. Hunger and illness once again overcame her.

She stood at the gate, holding her husband's hand. Red tiles covered the top of the entrance, which was supported by a pair of black wooden posts. Two enormous iron doors, also painted black and ornamented with white porcelain carp — a sign of prosperity — closed on each other and were secured with an iron hook. Thick walls of sun-dried bricks bordered the compound's three acres. Beyond the gates, a long courtyard led to a two-story house. Its front porch overhung a doorway decorated with images of dragons and phoenixes, painted blue and red against the golden panels of the doors.

Ven turned away. It was impossible. Her husband was right: she needed to eat and rest. Somewhere in her head, a much louder voice urged her to carry out her plan. Sweat broke out on her back as though she had been pulling the plow across the field all morning. She lifted the front panel of her shirt and wiped her forehead. Slowly, she turned to face the large gates.

She saw no one inside. In the front yard, a handful of pigeons pecked lazily at a bowl of rice crumbs. Next to them, a row of leafy-stemmed orchids with large, droopy flowers bathed under the harsh sun.

"It must be done," she muttered to herself and inserted her fingers through the peephole to unhook the gates. Turning to her husband, she said, "You wait here. From now on, if anyone asks, I am your mother, and your name is Mouse."

"My name is not Mouse," the boy argued. He was looking inquiringly at Ven. "It's Dan. My daddy said in the old language it means tiger, not mouse."

"You were born in the hour of the rat, were you not? The magistrate's men are searching for a boy named Dan Nguyen. As long as you remember that your name is Mouse, you will be safe. Understood?"

"Yes, Ven."

Ven strode through the gate, looking neither right nor left. Her husband leaned against the wooden post and watched her.

From the kitchen, a brown dog dashed through the courtyard toward her. It jumped forward, aiming its sharp fangs at her throat. Ven let out a shriek. She fell on the ground, waving her hat to protect her face. Her voice echoed in the empty garden, while the dog's barking roared like a thunderstorm. "Help me, please, somebody!"

No one answered. The dog lunged to bite at her feet. Ven used the hat as a weapon to fend it off. The animal snapped its jaws and tore the straw brim into shreds. "Help me, anybody!" she implored.

A woman dressed in a black silk outfit rushed out from the back of the kitchen. Her hand held a large bamboo stick. In the corner of her mouth hung a toothpick. Despite the horror of her predicament, Ven watched the young woman with astonishment. Even though she carried more weight on her stout frame, her face bore the features of the maid Ven knew. Song cracked her cudgel on the back of the beast. Shouting, she chased it across the courtyard until it disappeared under a lilac bush.

Once the animal was out of sight, Song returned to the intruder. Seeing Ven's sickly pallor, she dropped the staff from her hand. Her toothpick also fell at her feet. "Are you ill, Mistress?" she asked Ven.

Ven pushed herself up from the ground. Blood welled from the wounds in her right hand where the dog's teeth had punctured her skin. She tore a piece of cloth from the front panel of her shirt, then wrapped it around her palm.

Song stared at her. "Why have you come here? Are you mad? Didn't you hear that Magistrate Toan has just executed thirty fishermen? Leave now, before he returns and kills you, too."

Ven took the maid's hand to steady herself. "That monster!" she exclaimed. "Heaven will damn him for betraying a dead man's last wish. But the devil has never seen Dan or me. No one in this house has. Please, Song, you must help us. Don't tell anyone the young master's identity."

"Do you think I am your enemy?" cried Song. "I am and always will be a faithful servant to the Nguyen family. Why are you here in this house of calamity? And how can I help?"

A sad smile brushed Ven's face. "As you can see, I am not well," she said. "I can no longer care for my husband. Bringing the young master to this house is the only way to save his life, since no one would think of looking for him here."

Song clasped her hand to her mouth to hide her shock. Ven wondered what had possessed her to be so frank. It was a great risk for her to trust the maid, but she had no other choice. She said, "Song, for the short time that I have known you, you have shown nothing but great kindness. Please help me protect the last bearer of the Nguyen bloodline. I will owe you my deepest gratitude." She fell on her knees before the maid.

From inside the living room, a woman's voice stirred in the hot air, as scornful and haughty as the afternoon sun. "Who is out there, Fifth Mistress? If it is a beggar, do not waste your time. If you want to give anyone our leftover rice, feed it to the pigs instead. We do not need those beggars to glorify our family name. Do you hear me?"

Ven caught the frightened look on the girl's face. "Fifth Mistress?" Ven asked. "Which of the men granted you that title, the father or the son?"

"My life now belongs to Magistrate Toan," the girl replied. "If you want to leave the young master here, you must make an arrangement with his first wife, the old mistress. Come with me." She turned from Ven to lead the way.

❧

Across the long courtyard they went, until Song left Ven to wait on the front porch while she disappeared behind a panel of doors. In a large room that resembled the backstage of an opera house, the peasant woman stood alone, peeking through the entrance.

"What took you so long out there?" Ven heard the same sour voice shrill beyond an ivory partition that shielded the room behind it. Its surface was decorated with a mosaic sculpture of a nude model made from little pieces of blue jade. The girl in the picture reclined on a beach and seemed to smile and wink at Ven.

On the right and left sides of the screen, a pair of ancient verses were engraved into the wooden beams of the house and glossed with a layer of golden paint. Its original color had since faded, and the ink had become rusty. Above the inscriptions hung an advertisement for baby formula cut out of a French magazine. The fat, happy faces of the babies in the photographs were as foreign to Ven as the tin cans that bore them.

In the far corner of the room, Ven saw an ornate mahogany cabinet. Behind its glass door was a china bowl filled with chicken eggs that were waiting to be eaten. The dish sat atop a white marble tray.

Ven shifted her view to the rosebushes nearby. Their white flowers, blooming broadly under the encouraging sun, were within her reach. Despite her dismal situation, she studied the petals and could not help admiring their fragile beauty. How simple and untroubled they were, in contrast to the rest of the house. She looked at her hands. Under the blood-soaked bandage, the wound seemed to have stopped bleeding.

Song pushed the partition aside. Ven remained on the front porch, looking through the door. She would not dare cross the threshold. In the center of the room, she saw an elderly woman, dressed in lustrous black satin. The old lady reclined on a bench, holding a cup of tea. Ven recognized the emerald glow of Master Nguyen's soup bowl in her bony fingers. She concealed her anger by keeping her eyes low. A child about six years old played at the old lady's footstool. She held in her hands a bottle of colored liquid and a small metal loop. In the soft light of the room, the little girl made soap bubbles by twirling her loop through the air.

Magistrate Toan's first mistress scrutinized Ven through sunken gray eyes. Thick saliva, a mixture of betel juice and limestone powder, filled the tiny cracks on the old lady's lips. From afar, the sharp look in her eyes, the wrinkles on her thin face, and her shockingly red mouth reminded Ven of a monkey in an expensive costume. Ven fell to her knees and knocked her head against the stone ground.

"Who are you?" the old lady asked. Her voice echoed through the cavernous room.

"I am a beggar, Great Lady," Ven replied.

"Our door does not open to beggars. Leave this place at once."

Ven looked at the old mistress. "I am not here to beg for food," she said. "I have a small affair to discuss with you."

"What sort of affair?"

Standing in a corner, Song said, "She wants to sell her seven-year-old son to the house of Toan."

"Why does she not speak for herself?" the old woman asked. "Where is the boy? I do not see anyone but that beggar woman."

Ven crawled on her knees across the marble floor to get closer to the old lady. Her mouth was dry from the fever. "The boy is waiting by the gate," she said.

"Seven years old," the old lady said, sipping her tea noisily. "He is too young to be a servant in this house. What can a starving child do that could be worth the rice that we feed him?"

"I can teach him the duties and responsibilities of a skilled servant, Old Mistress," Song replied.

The old lady gave Song an angry glare. "You are now a mistress," she said to the girl. "In front of the servants, you should behave like a lady. You do not teach somebody to be a slave. It must be innate, like an ox born to plow the fields, or a dog to guard houses."

Ven implored, "Have a heart, Great Lady. Think of it as a good deed for your life in Heaven. Only a small payment will save a hungry child and his mother."

Master Long came into the room, carrying a book. He removed a Western-style felt hat and fanned himself; then he touched the little girl's black hair and asked, "Why is a beggar in our living room, First Mother?"

The old lady answered, "She is selling her son. A small household affair, which need not trouble you." Turning to Ven, she ordered, "Bring the boy in. I want to see if he is fit to serve my first grandchild. A seven-year-old slave is worth three silver dollars."

Ven thought of Dan waiting outside. Her protective instinct rose, and she considered leaving at once. Seeing her uncertainty, the old lady said irritably, "Well, go, will you!"

Ven did not forget to bow to the old mistress before leaving the front porch. On her way out, she picked up the stick and her torn hat. This time, she was ready to fight the dog if necessary. It hid somewhere behind the tall brush and growled at her.

At the wooden gates, Dan sat and waited for her. He jumped up as soon as he recognized her faded brown shirt. Ven waved for him. Seeing the blood on her hand, the boy gasped in fear. His face bore a sadness so expressive it seemed part of his personality.

"Come with me," she said to him. "The old mistress wishes to see you. Please behave yourself, and don't forget anything that I have taught you."

She turned to the house, looking back now and then to make sure he was behind her. The boy plodded along. His eyes were glued to the thick shrubbery, from which the dog's snarling could be heard. Soon they were at the front door of the main living room.

Master Long sat on a chair on the front porch, watching Ven and her husband through the thin lenses of his spectacles. Without a word, he grabbed a handful of rose petals to wipe the dirt off his leather shoes. Then he scattered the bruised flowers on the floor and resumed reading his book.

Ven pushed the boy onto his knees, facing the old mistress. On the bench, the old lady lay with her eyes closed and her mouth open, making little snorting sounds in her throat. Song stooped and whispered something in her ear, which roused the woman from her nap.

"My grandchild, where is she?" she asked, searching the room with her ancient eyes. Once she spotted the little girl, still playing with her bubble toy nearby, the old lady smiled, and she recovered her poise. "Where is that beggar and her son?" she asked.

"This is my son, Old Mistress," Ven replied. Her hand rested on the boy's shoulder, keeping him on his knees.

"What is your name?" asked the old lady, looking at Dan.

The boy searched Ven's face before he answered, "M-mouse."

"How old are you?"

"Seven."

Anger appeared on the old woman's face. She kicked the footstool. "Ill-bred scoundrel!" she screamed. "Always address me as Old Mistress, do you understand?"

Dan shrank back, more in surprise than fear. "Yes, Old Mistress," he said.

"Your mother also told me that you are seven years old," the old woman went on. "From the look of those tiny hands and feet, I think you both lied to me. It is inherent in a beggar's blood to lie. You just cannot pull those tricks on me and expect to get more cash. I can see that this boy is six years old — much too young to work in this house! However, I have pity for your wretched condition, and my grandchild needs a servant. I will buy this slave despite his age. But because of his inferior quality, I will only pay two silver dollars."

"Have mercy on us, Great Lady," Ven cried. "My son is seven years old. He was born in February, the year of the rooster. We would not dare to lie to you."

"Shut your mouth," the old lady snapped. "I have decided. If you do not like the price, you can take him with you and face the famine together."

Sitting up in his chair, Master Long snapped his fingers to get Dan's attention. "Come over here, Mouse," he ordered.

Dan seized his wife's hand and stood his ground. Ven pushed him away from her. In a solemn voice she said, "Come now, the master calls for you. You should run to him." Step by step, Dan moved toward the man as a convict draws near his guillotine. The images of his father's death still burned in Dan's memory.

Master Long reached out to grab the boy's thin arm and pull him closer. Terror deepened on Dan's face. Lifting up the child's shirt, Long examined his torso, carefully checking his front and back. Finding nothing out of the ordinary, he said, "Go back and bid farewell to your mother."

Ven knew that Master Long and his father would continue searching for a boy with a tattoo. Thankful for her father-in-law's wit in his final moments, she muttered a prayer for him under her breath.

Old Mistress whispered to her grandchild, "Little May, that boy is my gift to you. He is now your new servant. Do you like what grandmother gives you?"

The little girl laughed, clapping her hands together and spilling the soap liquid on the floor. She glided and pirouetted across the room until she came face-to-face with her new present. Shyly, she reached out and wiped a tear off his face. Dan stepped back.

"Don't cry," the girl whispered. The plastic loop in her hand traced along the side of his cheek, forming a small bubble that smelled like flowers. He forgot himself and grinned at her.

The old lady turned to Song. "Fifth Mistress," she said. "Go fetch Tutor Lo for me. I need him to draw up a contract for this drifter to sign. One must be careful of a derelict's capricious mind."

When Ven left the great house of Toan, two silver dollars clinked inside her pocket, next to the contract. She remembered the cold touch of the black ink on her mangled hand when she laid her fingerprints across the document. She recalled the boy's hysteria as he clenched her torn shirt, and the strong hands of the servants who had pulled him away from her. She could not stop crying.

That night, and during many nights that followed, Ven battled her illness in the burned ruins of the old kitchen. Hidden in the murky stillness of the abandoned house, she slipped in and out of consciousness, having a recurrent nightmare in which she was tied to a bamboo post in front of a shallow grave. Several times she woke to her own screams. The crescent moon above her became the gleaming scimitar. Her body pressed deeper into the ground in those confusing moments, and the delirium intensified. She shrieked and wept until she lost consciousness.

After several weeks, she felt her strength begin to return. Ven went to the community hall to beg for food more substantial than the morsels she found by scavenging through the garden. There, she learned from the gossips of the Cam Le Village that the house of Nguyen was haunted. Tales were rampant of the ghosts that dwelled in the ashes of the mansion. Many a villager had heard the unearthly screams at night. Now, hardly a soul dared to pass by the ruins of the once stately house.

In Ven's mind, it was a place she could never leave. Each day after begging for alms in the village, she returned to the place of woe and watched the moon stroll across the night sky.

Slowly, the dusty road in front of the mansion fell into disuse. Weeds grew up to cover the shattered entrance with their greenery. Even the few remaining walls continued to disintegrate with the torrential rains. Fallen mango fruits covered the bare earth, rotting under the sun.

However, at night, when the silver moon spilled its eerie light over the treetops and a faint mist rose from the quiescent land, the cries of the ghosts would echo clearly, lingering in the gentle wind like a never-ending song.

Part Two

NINE YEARS LATER

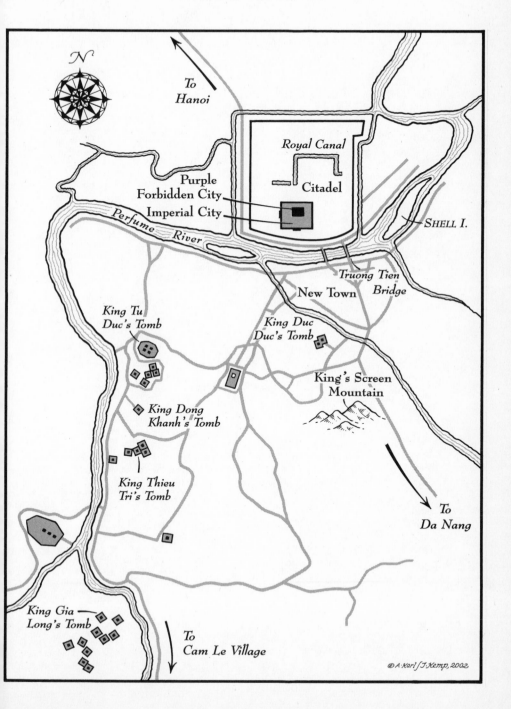

To
Hanoi

Royal Canal

Purple
Forbidden City
Imperial City

Citadel

SHELL I.

Perfume River

Truong Tien
Bridge

New Town

King Tu
Duc's Tomb

King Duc
Duc's Tomb

King's Screen
Mountain

King Dong
Khanh's Tomb

King Thieu
Tri's Tomb

To
Da Nang

King Gia
Long's Tomb

To
Cam Le Village

© A. Karl / J. Kemp, 2002.

chapter eight

A Marriage of Propriety

THE CITADEL OF HUE, SEPTEMBER 1925

*I*n the early autumn of 1925, a mandarin and his son from the Imperial City of Hue were invited to open the Harvest Moon Festival that would take place a few weeks later in the village of Cam Le, four miles south of the citadel. Acting in the name of the emperor, Minister Chin Tang and the young Master Bui Tang agreed to officiate at the three-day celebration along the banks of the Perfume River. Together they would lead the townspeople in giving thanks to the gods of the soil and the harvest — the sovereign lords of the terrestrial world.

In the letter Minister Chin wrote to the mayor of Cam Le to confirm his attendance, he also implied that his son, who had just passed his seventeenth birthday, was a proper candidate for marriage to Master Long's only daughter, Lady Tai May. The Toan family eagerly accepted this suggestion but expressed its wish for the two young people to get acquainted during the festival before any further arrangement for their union would be made.

The young lord, Bui, had passed his childhood with his father behind the high stone walls of the citadel. For as long as he could remember, his mother had lived separately in the apartments of the emperor's first wife in the heart of the Purple Forbidden City, where she served as a lady-in-waiting for the Queen Mother, the majestic Lady Thuc. The quarters where his mother stayed were probably the most secluded in the citadel — except, of course, for the king's private bedchamber, into which no outsider would be admitted on any account. Bui formed vivid impressions of the nobles' luxurious and decadent lifestyle through the descriptions his mother offered each time she visited her family, which could be as often as twice a week for a few hours during dinnertime.

Around the Imperial City, located inside the citadel, were the complexes of six ministries — the Exchequer; the Justice Sector; the Chancellery; the Ministry of Forests, Navy, and Shipbuilding; the Ministry of Religion and Ceremonies; and the Ministry of War. In this elite society Bui's father, Minister Chin Tang, held a distinguished position in the branch of religion. As a third-rank mandarin, he had endowed their family name with a degree of nobility. But Bui quickly learned that the title itself generated little income or respect in the king's court. To other mandarins, his father was merely a scholar, teacher, and secretary for the royal family. Chin Tang possessed no arable lands or properties that could produce any earnings. In fact, according to his mother, if she had not taken the employment in the queen's palace, they would have gone through Bui's entire inheritance much faster and would have left him penniless when they died.

Bui grew up inside a small, protected enclave known as the "ministers' section." Located behind the eastern gate, it was a series of guarded rooms that the king had reserved for mandarins of his father's stature. Except for a handful of holidays and special events, when he was allowed to venture outside his home, he spent his days inside his bedroom reading ancient scriptures with a private tutor or playing with the neighboring children. Now Bui was ready for his first trip beyond the walls of the citadel.

The prospect of escaping the confines of his childhood home sparked in him a thrilling flight of the imagination. His spirit longed for the freedom that lay beyond his orderly, formalized existence. Besides the chance to enjoy some rural entertainment, the excursion represented Bui's journey to marriage. He might leave this place a boy, but in the eyes of the world, he would come back a man.

The wait was excruciating. The female servants his father sent to help him prepare for the journey seemed to irritate him deliberately. These were the older, more experienced maids, who had served his family for several decades. By now they should have been able to read his thoughts and understand his moods. Yet, to his surprise, they acted like a herd of oxen, slow to move and just as dumb. The sight of them crashing into one another, stumbling over their large feet, and dropping his expensive Western clothing on the floor infuriated him. Venting his frustration, Bui cracked his riding crop on their backs and sent them screaming into the garden. Still, this sudden outburst did not satisfy him. He wished he were strong and skillful enough to break their tough hides and leave scars, so he could teach them a lesson they wouldn't forget.

On the day of his departure, an hour before sunrise, a cannon announced the opening of the gates to the fortress. Shortly afterward, the bell from the faraway Pagoda of the Celestial Lady, west of the citadel, tolled its persistent knell. Its chime vibrated in deep and long strokes to the ruddy dawn. The crowing cockerels of nearby villages responded with their usual zeal.

The monks had always been the first ones to rise inside the citadel. Bui usually lay comfortably in bed, watching his window through half-shut eyes to catch glimpses of the monks' dark shadows as they moved toward the eastern gate, begging Heaven to preserve the king's well-being. Another hour would go by before he heard the door of his father's room creak on its wooden hinges. Then came the young maids, holding red lanterns in their hands and making a faint rustle in the hallway with their cotton shoes. He waited until the servants' soft hands nervously touched his shoulders through his thin blanket before he stirred.

That morning, in the comfortable darkness of his bedroom, Bui woke to the distinctive perfume of sandalwood oil that the servants sprayed on the altar of the earth gods in the garden. It was the first time that he did not wait for the maids to wake him. Wrapped in his blue satin bedspread, he sprang up and left the warmth of his bouncy Hong Kong mattress. The new bed had been sent to him as a preemptive wedding gift from the Toan family. Bui adored his new present. Lacquered and brass-trimmed, it served dual purposes: a place to sleep and a fashionable trunk in which he could hide his valuables. Its ebony wood, renowned for its magical properties, was said to ward off evil forces.

At the center of the room, a blue-and-white urn containing a flaming wick afloat in sesame oil had managed to burn for several years to nourish Bui's weak spirit. His father had explained to him on several occasions that since Bui was a gift sent from the underworld in response to his parents' prayers, they must constantly make offerings to ensure that the gods would protect him. Bui never opposed any of these superstitions since they served well to endorse any unruly actions he might commit and to shield him from all the trouble he made.

He stood facing the copper jar on the floor, unfastened his coverlet to leave enough room so that he could urinate, and swayed his hips from side to side to direct the flow into the vessel, unsuccessfully. Later, the maids would clean up the puddle he left on the floor. Pushing aside the screen of his bedroom, he stepped out into the chill.

The earth was still fogged over from the night's soggy breath. As he watched, shivering, a cool autumn wind rolled across the vast enclosed field and scattered the mist into a walled garden full of flowers, cherry trees, frangipani, and flame trees. All of the plants and walkways in his garden circled around a small pond — a typical design for the dwellings in this section of the citadel. Between the properties, several simple paths merged and formed a larger road, leading to other areas of the fortress. Running alongside this road was the wall of the Imperial City. Its majestic height and thickness protected the king's estate from all those living around him, making his home a city within a city.

From behind the Great Eastern Gate, the sun emerged, dimming the lingering stars in the bronze sky. Bui sat on a quilt placed on the ground, touching a silver chain around his ankle and staring at the four brightly lit lanterns hung from the garden walls. In front of him, a single file of porcelain vases with sprouting orchids of different shapes and colors sat against the backdrop of a miniature landscape — all built from a single piece of stone. When he was younger, the intricate forms of these rocks above the pond had suggested mountains, animals, and human forms, a magical world full of mysteries.

His father had pointed out a small path in the rocks along the water's edge that led into a dark cave, carved between the granite shoulders of the minuscule mountain. It was, he said, the road to Nirvana as described in the Buddha's scriptures. For a long time, Bui held on to that belief. Sometimes, in the middle of night, he would jump from his bed and run outside to examine the tiny pathway, checking for any subtle changes. The moonlight trickled wanly over a couple of statues that were losing themselves in a game of chess. Each time Bui studied them, they seemed to stop and look wonderingly at him. In the pond, the goldfish, nibbling at the moon beneath an island of water lilies, slowly transformed into illusory dragons and white carps. Now, the tiny clay figures of peasants, temples, and fairies no longer held the enchantment he had felt as a child. Filtered through his adult eyes, the scenery seemed foolish and crude. He got up from his seat, wondering if he should find his father and remind him of the journey they would make today, but decided to wait until breakfast to raise the subject.

In a small room behind his bedchamber, the maids had half-filled a large basin with heated water for his bath. Its steam rose against the darkness, and a mixture of lemongrass and jasmine scents filled his nose. He closed the silk screen and dropped the bedspread on the floor before he slid into the sweltering tub. Today he must cleanse his whole body. Sometime during this expedition, he fully expected to consummate his union with his soon-to-be wife.

As a young man of privilege, Bui was intimately familiar with the soft female flesh of the pubescent maids who worked for his family. He never needed a bath to impress these lowly servants, with their skin toasted brown from the harsh sun like the color of mud. When and if he achieved the conquest of his betrothed, it would be different. This would be the first time Bui experienced the pleasures of a painted face and a delicate body. Like opium smoke, the same earlier excitement rushed through his veins.

After the bath, he hurried into his dressing room. From an armoire full of clothes, he selected a crisp white shirt and a pair of brown French-style trousers. Even though the French had influenced Vietnamese culture since 1862, most families inside the citadel still wore the traditional costumes. Yet, all sense of style seemed to have changed ever since the thirteen-year-old Prince Bao Dai returned to the palace from several years of study in Paris.

The Imperial City had not recovered from the shock of seeing its future king with his new slick hairstyle and the strange Western suits on his back. Soon, several young lords, including Bui, underwent a similar fashion transformation. The reason for the prince's hasty return to the Purple Forbidden City was that his father, King Khai Dinh, was gravely ill. Under pressure from the chief ambassador of France in Hue, the Vietnamese councilmen — nobles belonging to the royal family — had chosen His Majesty's only heir to succeed the throne.

Bui had been among the crowd of mandarins on the day, just a few months earlier, when the prince's formal investiture had taken place in the throne room. That was the only time he had seen the young prince in a Vietnamese ceremonial costume. Just like his idol, Bui was drawn to the French culture like a nail tugged into a magnetic field. He never desired to be clad in another *ao dai* garment again, if he could help it.

In front of a large mirror, Bui examined himself in his brown pants, white shirt, and black velvet shoes. Would the reflection in the mirror impress the country girl who would be his wife? His black hair, shining with pomade, was slicked back along the sides of his head and combed to a point above the nape of his neck like a duck's backside. He studied the unblemished cotton fabric of his shirt and fingered the big belt buckle that rested against his belly. A thick twenty-four-karat gold chain — one of his few remaining possessions that had not yet been sold to support the family in proper style — ran from his waist to his pants pocket. He fixed on his image with an intensity that could almost cut through the mirror's surface.

Then he smiled. Any country girl, no matter how rich her family may be, would be fortunate to have him for a husband.

Through the crack of his bedroom door, he heard his father's voice. The maids were coming to fetch him for breakfast. He smoothed the front of his shirt, checked the crease along his pant legs once more, and went outside.

>≻—

On the sidewalk in front of his apartment, Bui spotted a group of male servants carrying hammocks and five-colored parasols, preparing to take him and his father to the riverbank. He went into the dining room, where his parents were waiting. His mother, tall and nervous, sat on the edge of her chair at the head of the table. She greeted him with a grin of gleaming black teeth. The Queen Mother had excused her from her duty this morning, and here she was, on the verge of tears the moment she saw his face. A bowl of glutinous rice in black chicken broth sat untouched a few inches from her bent elbows. That was not unusual, as she never ate at home. It was more economical for her to dine with the other ladies-in-waiting at the palace. Bui would eat her food after he finished his.

At the other end of the table with his face down, the back of his bald head parallel to his plate, was Bui's father. He looked up to acknowledge his son with a faint nod, blinked at the early sun, and returned to his breakfast. Friends of his parents often told Bui that he was the very image of his father, as if it were a compliment. Whenever he heard this, Bui would rise to his feet and leave the room, slamming the door behind him.

As he joined his parents at the table, his mother turned and waved her fingers. The movement of her arms jingled a collection of gold bracelets against one another like the sound of a chime. She said to him, "I was set at liberty by the Queen Mother to formally bid you good-bye before your departure. If it were up to me, I would go where you go. But I cannot, not only because I am a woman, but also because I am bound with higher responsibility than a mother's duty. You will forgive my absence, won't you?"

He sat on a chair next to her, quivering with the anticipation of his journey. His father paused from time to time to look up at him. The way the minister's sparse features disappeared into the folds of his bulbous face reminded Bui of a distant full moon. He wondered how his father could carry a face so big without spraining his neck, especially given the vigorous way he nodded his head in response to his wife's conversation. Bui turned his attention to the plate of food that had begun losing its steam.

His mother talked on as if he were not there. "Just imagine, soon your son will be able to take off the silver chain around his ankle. Did the monk not tell us that his bond to the gods would be severed when he found a wife?" She turned to him and said, "Now, before you grow into a respectable young man, hurry with your breakfast. I cannot stay here all day."

Bui touched his chain with the tip of his shoe almost absentmindedly. The silver bracelet felt cold against his skin. His mother's words, laden with superstition, echoed in his head. He had to acknowledge their wisdom. For more than seventeen years, the chain had served its purpose, not as a piece of jewelry but as a paranormal connection that linked his spirit to this world. Soon it would be time for him to shed this bond. He felt reckless at the prospect of becoming an adult, like a prisoner on the verge of freedom. Unable to finish his meal, he got up from his seat and followed his parents outside.

The servants stood at attention while Bui hopped into the hammock they held suspended between their shoulders. His Western clothes contrasted with the dull uniforms they wore. Above him, the wooden beam that supported the swinging cot bowed with his weight.

Without looking back, Bui could feel his mother hovering in the doorway of their compound. He tried to avoid the embarrassing moment when he had to bid farewell to her. She might have understood his restlessness, but her tears reminded him that he was still a little boy. He did not want to linger a moment longer than he had to. He had waited long enough for this day. As he and his father neared the river, he saw a small brown vessel docked at the shore. On the boat's side, his family's name was written in black letters. Bui jumped off the hammock, abandoned his father, and ran ahead.

Moments later, they weighed anchor and were swept into the main current, heading west. Bui leaned over the rail, studying the boat's sharp prow as it cut through the water. The sailors aligned themselves in two rows and paddled. Around him the dreary northern winds swept their impatient tentacles across the river, changing the tiny, white-crested waves to icy gray. He was too excited to notice the cool air. Like a sparrow skimming over the river, he watched the landscape running to meet him, then falling behind, as the vessel carried him toward his future. Less than an hour passed before a crewman pointed out the Cam Le Village. It looked like a small chip of bark floating in the distance.

Along the bank of the Perfume River stood a crowd of curious spectators. Bui had no trouble distinguishing the mayor's family. They were the only ones dressed in fine clothes, and they were waving at him and his father.

Bui watched the crowd give way before an old man who took each step carefully behind a walking stick. With clawlike fingers, he clutched at the scrawny twig as though it were a vital limb. His body was nothing but a skeleton, hidden under several layers of expensive silk tunics that were held in place by a golden belt. His thin neck stretched forward like a bird's, and his shoulders arched in a permanent shrug that seemed to reach up to his dangling earlobes. Tufts of white hair, resembling straws that had been bleached by the sun, straggled across his naked head and disappeared beneath the back collar of his tunic.

Next to the old man walked a young girl. Her delicate face was shaded by an elegant yellow organdy hat, woven from sheer cotton, that circled her head with a stiff brim. The sides of her hair were pulled up and hidden under the bonnet, while the rest of it cascaded down her back in the latest style. Bui noticed her lips, deep and rosy like a lotus bud, pressing together as she helped the old man down the narrow, soggy path. The chilly breeze murmured above the water, and the girl's white tunic fluttered against her thin waist.

As his boat approached the pier, Bui overheard the old man's complaint. "Wait for Grandfather's old feet to move, little May. I am using all of my strength, but this road is too long."

She held her arm around him, guiding his steps through the waiting crowd.

With the help of a sailor, Bui jumped off the boat. He looked up. The first thing his eyes registered was the girl's beauty. Instantly, everything else around him seemed to recede into the distance. He was scarcely aware of a servant's voice announcing his father's name. He moved across the wet sand toward her, unable to keep himself from staring. Hungrily, he licked his dried lips and swallowed. The girl looked right through him with her large, hypnotic eyes as though he were not even there.

He turned around. He saw nothing out of the ordinary behind him — nothing except a humble servant approximately his age. The boy was shouting Bui's name, announcing his arrival to the Toan family on the dock. One glance at him, and a thought flashed through the young lord's mind.

He wanted that slave's face as his own! With its elegant brow, strong cheekbones, and generous mouth, and framed by a thick mane of hair that was tied at the back like the long tail of a horse, it possessed the interesting traits that his own face lacked. Even decked out in the extravagance of his clothing and jewelry, Bui was aware of the dullness of his features. He felt like a peacock whose lively feathers had been singed.

Then he heard a gentle voice, coming from the girl's mouth, as clear as the bell from the pagoda. "Thank you, Mouse," she said. And a smile blossomed on her face.

chapter nine

The Phoenix Dance

P lease, gentlemen, follow me," said the slave to Bui and his father. "The carriage is this way."

Bui drew a handkerchief from his pocket and dabbed his forehead. A short distance ahead, the magistrate and his granddaughter walked down the path that led into the village. The young lord followed them, allowing himself to be guided by the servant, as he kept his eyes on the girl. In his heart, pride blended with a twinge of insecurity. He had no doubt that she was the fairest noblewoman he had ever encountered, or that she would soon belong to him. Yet her looks intimidated him.

Her father, in contrast, was a portly man in his early forties, with eyes so timid they hid behind his glasses. Next to him, clinging like a strand of wild ivy, was a shadow of a woman. Her face was as blank as a sheet of paper and well hidden behind the thick locks of her black hair. There were remnants of beauty about her narrow face and in her large, frightened eyes; yet overall, she reminded Bui of a once handsome painting that had faded with time. He wondered if she was the girl's mother. No one had included her in the introductions.

A blue-white metallic carriage with four wheels waited for them at a bend of the road. The slave hopped into the driver's seat. The coach, at first, looked to Bui like a fusion of two rickshas, doorless, with two benchlike seats and a collapsible hood. It was pulled by a sturdy white horse that stood, blinking calmly, between two metal shafts.

From inside, Magistrate Toan motioned for Bui and his father to step up into the vehicle's charming interior, which was richly upholstered with purple velvet. There were embroidered cushions for the passengers' backs and a bearskin rug on the scrubbed floorboard. Bui stumbled on the step and would have sprawled on his face had the magistrate not caught his arm in his bony fingers. His cheeks burned as he muttered an apology. He sat erect and tense across from the girl, hoping that his silent uneasiness would be mistaken for calm. She looked back at him, one of her elbows leaning on the arm of the seat. She had the same look of intelligence that he saw in the magistrate, but her expression was much kinder.

His father exclaimed, "This car is like the king's chariot, which is only used for His Majesty's pleasure to drive around the imperial garden and to entertain important guests."

"You and the young lord are my important guests," replied the old man. Turning to Bui, he asked, "How did the young master enjoy my present? That bed had been in my family for a very long time. It is a small token to express our sincere hopes for this friendship and respect for your impeccable tastes."

His father answered for him. "All of the mandarins' quarter buzzed with the praises of the Toans' generous gift. My son is a very fortunate lad to have received such attention from your family, which, of course, he clearly doesn't deserve."

The old man waved his hand. A cloud of sadness passed over his eyes, and he said ruefully, "That was my very first wedding bed. I have no use of it now, since my wife has passed away. My second and third mistresses preferred the impoverished, chaste, and simple lives of the religious world and have entered a nunnery. I am now relying on the companionship of my fifth mistress. I wish you many decades of happiness, like I had in my earlier years."

"What about your fourth mistress?" Bui asked. The magistrate ignored his question. He smiled and looked outside. Feeling impatient, Bui beheld the smallest marketplace he had ever seen. It sat in the center of a square behind the town's main entrance, having fewer than twenty vendors and a handful of shoppers.

The carriage rode along the bricked wall, and the road soon narrowed into a simple path. The earth beneath them was hollowed into tiny canals, covered with planks in a man-made system that supplied water from the river to the fields. Bui had never seen this before. He marveled at the thought of riding atop a thin layer of wood, and he winced each time the carriage swayed on its wheels. He did not want to be thrown from the vehicle and dirty his expensive clothes.

The horse came to a stop under a large red-tiled awning. Beyond it was a mansion, protected by thick walls and iron-barred gates. The old magistrate said with glee, "We are here, at last. Welcome, Minister Chin Tang and Master Bui Tang. Please pardon our humble home. We are indeed delighted at the honor of your visit."

As the carriage passed through the black iron gates, Bui counted at least fifteen young maids in pink cotton uniforms running back and forth under the supervision of a plump woman dressed in a black silk outfit. Some were sweeping the courtyard, using brooms made of the leaves of the areca palm tree. Others hung strings of incense on long bamboo posts.

They drove into a long courtyard, and Bui found himself surrounded by a cluster of buildings. These wealthy country mansions, he observed, shared a lot of design traits with the Chinese houses that he had seen in New Town, across the river from the citadel. All of the elements of nature, including the directions of the winds, the flow of the river, the contour of the land, mountains, trees, and bushes, were taken into consideration before the house was built. Here the entire property was laid out on a square piece of land, built to accentuate the benevolent forces of the earth.

There were three separate quarters. The main one was a two-story building that stretched horizontally and faced the gates. On either end was a long, narrow wing. Looking from above, the compound took the form of the letter *H*. The kitchen was at the northeast corner, next to the back entrance. From its finely carved roof to its thick bluestone foundation, the entire structure was covered in gold plaques, a sign of the owners' gratitude to the gods. In the middle of the front yard, the carriage came to a halt.

Bui reached for the links of silver around his ankle, which had been catching the hem of his trousers since the beginning of the journey. "Can I take off this trinket now, Father?" he asked.

"By all means," replied the minister. "You are now an adult; you can do anything you want. What are you planning to do with it?"

"I'll give it to the less fortunate," he said and unfastened the chain. Easing down from the vehicle, Bui smoothed his neatly combed hair and scanned the scenery around him with a satisfied look. As he passed Mouse, who was unloading their suitcases from the back of the carriage, Bui threw his outgrown good-luck charm at the quiet slave and said, "Here is your tip, my good man."

Magistrate Toan's fifth mistress ran out to meet her husband and the guests. She was the same woman in the black silk outfit Bui had seen at the gates. To him, she appeared a bit overweight, yet still striking.

"Song, my fifth mistress, is waiting to receive you, gentlemen," said the old man. Then to his wife, he said, "You will show the mandarin and the young lord their guest quarters so that they can rest up from their journey." And he excused himself.

Minister Chin Tang bowed and replied, "I follow you, Lady Song."

The servant picked up two of the guests' valises in each hand. Song took the largest one from him. "Let me help you, Mouse," she said as she led the way down a long sidewalk.

The guest chambers consisted of a series of rooms linked to one another by means of indoor galleries. They were built as an extension to the stately main house, and the first of its two antechambers rivaled the Imperial Palace in its splendor. Their furnishings were works of art from a bygone age, and a new coat of white paint surrounded the windows, which looked into the court. A faint smell of mustiness reinforced Bui's speculation that this area had not been used in a long while. With each compartment they passed, the fifth mistress opened the windows, letting the fresh air enter the stale interior.

Through the circular-shaped entrance, Bui could observe the rest of the estate. On the other side of the main structure, another side-house belonged to Master Long, his wife, and their daughter. Immediately behind the main complex, alongside the high wall in the rear, were the kitchen and the servants' apartments. Bui had been told that his future in-laws were wealthy, and now he was taken aback by the opulence of their property. He saw more of the long cones of incense, hanging from the ceiling and spiraling down almost to the ground. As the son of the minister of religion, he understood that the fragrant resins had been burning since the full moon of the month before. As long as they went on smoking, their owners would be protected from ill fortune.

Along the inside of the curved brick wall, lanterns shaped like fish, butterflies, and buffalo were mounted at intervals, in preparation for the first night of the festival. Next to them were trays of moon cakes made of lotus flowers and egg yolks. The fifth mistress explained to Bui's father that it would be imprudent for a noble house such as Master Long's to ignore the power of the underworld, especially when their honored guest was the minister of religion and ceremonies. Therefore, the mayor had hired a geomancer to identify the precise locations for these sacred offerings, in hope of attracting benevolent spirits when the harvest moon reached its apogee the following night. Once inside the building, the ghosts would watch over and protect the living.

They came to the end of the hall, and Lady Song paused in front of a plain blue door. "This is your room, young Master," she said, setting down his suitcase. "Make yourself comfortable and rest. A servant will come and notify you when it is lunchtime."

She bowed to him and quickly disappeared with the slave behind a bamboo partition that seemed to lead to a small backyard across from the kitchen area. Bui yawned, exhausted from the few hours of traveling. He kicked the door open and entered the vast whiteness inside.

*T*hat night, the eighth moon showed her glittering face in the star-stained sky earlier than usual. However, her radiant beauty was diffused by the torrent of light coming from the streets of the Cam Le Village. It was a night of lanterns, varying in size and shape, reflecting one another like thousands of glowworms. At seven o'clock, the servants from the house of Toan opened the heavy gate to allow two dozen monks to pass through. In their hands, they carried more lanterns.

In the middle of the courtyard stood a circular altar made of freshly cut wood and bamboo stalks, stacked like the steps of a pyramid. Candles, incense, sandalwood bark, and moon cakes occupied its surfaces. Once the holy men were inside, two servants handed out drums, gongs, and castanets. After choosing an instrument, each monk took his place around the altar, forming a circle. Fiery lights exaggerated their impassive faces. To many, they were no longer flesh and blood, but had become living statues of stone.

Minister Chin stood high on a pedestal, apart from the rest of the worshipers, facing the altar and the main entrance. He pressed his palms together in front of his chest. Long stems of incense sprouted out of the tips of his fingers, puffing scented smoke. The minister closed his eyes and led the monks in the opening phase of the ceremony — the chanting of holy verses. In this night, he must mend any broken seams of this village by leading the obligatory chanting for at least several hours, so that the land could recover its supernatural powers and yield more crops during the next season. Only with his sincerity would he ensure the harmony of the townspeople and the prosperity of his host.

The Toan family closed ranks behind their distinguished guest. The old man, too feeble to stand, hunched in an armchair. Everyone else stood under the lanterns, holding bundles of incense. Their robes made soft rustling sounds in the cool evening. Without looking back, Minister Chin could feel their curiosity burning the nape of his neck. His many years of standing in the throne room among his colleagues had inured him to such looks.

The minister relished the opportunity to display his prowess in the harvest ceremony. Despite the crudeness of this town, he was satisfied with the trappings of wealth in this farmer's house. As for his son, he did not need a professional matchmaker to paint a picture of how lovesick the poor lad had become under the spell of that slender girl. To him, they seemed like a perfect match, and this trip could very well be the beginning of a marriage of propriety. More than ever, he knew he must exercise his vast stature before his future in-laws.

The chanting ended, and a servant struck a deep gong. The minister expanded his chest and shouted into the sudden silence, "I, Minister Chin Tang, have come to this town in the name of our emperor." It was time for the festival to begin.

*B*ui lowered his head and chewed his nails, struggling to control his impatience during the mantra. It seemed unbearable to him that he could do nothing but watch the girl from a distance. The night was rapidly advancing, and he had yet to be alone with her. Each time the wind blew, he waited for it to lift her hair away from her neck, where the collar of her tunic caressed her white skin. He wanted to seize her, and to peel her robes away bit by bit, so that he could see more of her flesh. Instead, he stood among the flickering lanterns and watched her recite Buddhist scripture, until his father intoned the conclusion of the chanting ceremony.

When it was over, a young maid came out to inform the mayor that tea was ready. Master Long opened the living room's panel of doors. To the guests' awe, the enormous space, supported by elegant carved mahogany beams and decorated with exquisite furniture, opened like an ancient temple before them. Except for the old man, who excused himself to the bedroom in the back, everyone passed silently into the large room, following their host.

Once they had all taken their seats around a table with a red marble top, Master Long turned to the minister. "Would you like to enjoy some opium with me after the children leave for the carnival at the river?" he asked.

Before the minister had a chance to reply, his son interrupted. "A carnival?" he cried. "I am fond of all carnivals." The fact that he had never experienced a carnival did not dim his enthusiasm. "It would be my pleasure to escort the young lady," he continued, "but I do not know what to expect of this particular street party. Tell me, what is its nature?"

Master Long looked at his guest of honor and said, "Let the minister explain the purpose of this feast, since he is more qualified to do so than anyone else in this room."

Minister Chin signaled for a maid to replenish his cup of jasmine tea. He glanced outside into the courtyard. The monks had all gone, but behind the tall wall, the excited noise of revelry was building. In a calm voice, he said to his son, "You should not have asked me to explain this spectacle. I am a firm believer in the theory of introspectionism, the latest European doctrine, by which all life experiences should be observed through one's own eyes, rather than through others' influencing thought and feeling. You, my son, must tackle the unknown with open arms. Trust me, you will find it entertaining."

Bui leaned forward with his hands pressing against the marble surface. "Come now, Father. Certainly you would not expose me to the risk of failure in front of the young lady because of my lack of knowledge. I am thrilled at the prospect of this mysterious festival, but I cannot say that I would enjoy making a foolish mistake."

Minister Chin Tang smiled. "I suppose you are entitled to a brief education. The Harvest Moon Festival is a time for young people to practice their belief in romantic love. I am glad that you will have a chance to witness the festival, since we do not have this sort of entertainment in the Purple Forbidden City. But I want you to understand the rules of the game before you join in." He sipped at his cup of tea and then laughed self-consciously. "So much for the theory of introspectionism." He continued.

"Each year on this very night, when the moon is one day shy of becoming fully round, everyone who is young and single is free to join the carnival in search of true love. Dress yourself in a costume and choose a mask to hide your identity. Once you are disguised, you may enter the phoenix dance. Then, you will be treated just the same as everyone else at the fete, despite your rank or your wealth. Without the help of a matchmaker, or any prearrangement from me, you can exercise your wits to woo the girl of your dreams. The trick is to learn her character well, so that you can find her in the crowd. Do not worry if you are not successful. You will find this girl, or rather, her parents will find us tomorrow. Then you will know what to do. When you are tired of this childish game and wish for my help, you can return here and look for me." He turned to the mayor. "Am I being too presumptuous in my description of the festival, Master Long?"

His host gave him a gratified smile. "No, sir, not at all. I think you have predicted its exact outcome. Any parents in this village would be honored to have the young master for a son-in-law. I only need to add one minor detail in order to prepare the young master fully for the evening's gaiety. In this town, the phoenix dance takes place on the river, not on dry land."

"What is a phoenix dance?" Bui asked.

The mayor replied, "The legend says that a phoenix captures the heart of its true mate by expressing its passion in dance. Nothing can be more effective at impressing a fair maiden than a love song composed only for her, or a poem about her beauty. Given that you are a young man of great virtue and courage, I have no doubt that tonight the moon god will reward you by sending the most beautiful girl in the dance straight into your arms, young Master."

The screen that blocked the living room entrance was drawn aside, and a servant appeared. Bui recognized the handsome slave named Mouse. "Please, everything is ready," the slave said. "The horses are harnessed to the carriage. Would Master Bui and Lady May like to join the festival now?"

Bui got up from his seat and walked toward the slave. He had to look up to face Mouse, and the difference in their statures offended him. "Are you the coachman for the evening?" he asked.

"Yes, Master," replied the young man. Unlike most servants, he did not avoid Bui's eyes. He seemed relaxed yet courteous. His serenity triggered an aversion in Bui, and he folded his hands into fists.

Without turning around to face the mayor, Bui raised his voice in a tone of disgust. "Must we be exposed to the potential dangers of being placed in the hands of this inexperienced slave? Is he the only coachman in this house?"

Tai May, who had been silent in her seat until now, spoke up. Her voice was filled with sudden excitement. "I beseech you, young Master. Mouse is my slave. Besides that, he is my friend, confidant, and a precious gift from my late grandmother to me nine years ago. By taking us to the carnival, he is only fulfilling his duty to me. You can rest assured that your safety is in the hands of the best driver in this town."

Those passionate words from her pretty lips turned Bui's ears red with shame.

Mouse bowed his head before his young mistress as though he was thanking her. "It would be my honor to drive you to the feast, Master Bui," he said.

Before Bui could find a proper reply, Mouse bowed again and disappeared behind a screen. The rest of the Toan family got up from their seats. Magistrate Toan's fifth mistress addressed Master Long. "I would like to accompany your daughter to the festival," she said. "I think it is wise for the young lady to go with a chaperon. I promise I will not interfere with their games."

Master Long nodded with a smile. "Indeed, a good idea. I entrust my daughter's happiness to your hands, Lady Song."

On the way out, Master Long pulled Bui aside. Under the shade of a large hibiscus shrubbery near the entrance gate, the mayor whispered into the young lord's ear. "Listen to me. Do you desire my daughter?"

Bui bobbed his head in the dark. He wanted to tell this man how much he coveted the beautiful girl, but words failed him. Master Long examined his features. In the gloomy shadows, the older man could just see Bui's small eyes. He saw no trace of good looks of any kind on his common, arrogant face. It would be just as well. The boy would appreciate his daughter's beauty all the more. The trace of a smile turned up the corners of his mouth. "Will you promise to obey my instructions implicitly?" he asked.

Once again, Bui nodded.

"Then listen carefully." Master Long seized Bui's forearm to emphasize his seriousness. "My daughter's boat is painted white. There will be two lanterns shaped like butterflies hanging from its bow. It is important that you recognize her before eleven o'clock. That will give both of you a chance to get acquainted, since the festivities end at midnight." He looked up and signaled for a large figure standing nearby to approach them. "Take this man with you, young Master. Surely you have heard of Monsieur Jean Luu, the famous opera singer."

Bui beheld a barrel-chested man with an androgynous face concealed under a thick layer of white powder. Being from the citadel, Bui had heard of the singer and was impressed to find him at this rustic celebration. "Indeed," he said.

The mayor continued. "Tonight, at my request, he will sing all of my daughter's favorite songs. With this songbird, I am sure that you will triumph." He led Bui and the singer toward the entrance.

The same silver carriage that had brought Bui and his father from the river was now waiting for him under the bright moonlight. Lady Song and Tai May sat close together on the bench behind the driver's seat. There was no breeze, and the temperature had begun to rise. The slave was lowering the hood to both sides of the wagon. Bui walked closer, but Mouse was so engrossed in his work that he did not hear the young aristocrat's footsteps. With an exasperated gesture, Bui grabbed the servant's long hair and dragged him a few paces away.

"Never bar my path, you fool." He kicked the slave. Then, he mounted the step and slid inside, choosing the seat opposite the beautiful girl. For a second, their knees touched, but the contact was soon over. She avoided him in the same way that fire shrank from a waterspout. In the awkward silence, he feasted his eyes on her face. Her expression was blank.

Next to him, the pale and oily opera singer wiggled his oversized rear into the seat and started to hum. He rummaged his fingers, with their long scarlet nails, through a small moneybag that was hooked around his shoulder. Bui watched in amazement as the tenor took out a piece of red color-coated paper and a hand mirror, and blotted his lips with its dye. Once his lips matched the shade of his nails, the man heaved a deep sigh of pleasure. When he turned and met Bui's astounded glare, the singer smiled broadly and offered his cosmetic tools.

"Would you like to try some color on your lips, Master Bui?" he asked.

He shook his head and moved away as far as the narrow bench allowed.

Mouse urged the horses into motion. The carriage left the house of Toan and joined the celebration that was already making the streets ring. All those who were young and single, or older and married and still attracted to the gaiety of the carnival, mingled through the village with candles or lanterns in their hands. Their shrill laughter and conversation filled the night. Together, the pedestrians formed a mile-long path of flickering lanterns, descending toward the river like an incandescent snake. Above them, the moon was a circular window open to a heavenly world, where golden lights shone through.

The carriage took Bui and his companions through the Cam Le Village and approached the Perfume River by a road crammed with people on foot. Mouse had chosen his route so that his passengers could admire the moon-soaked scenery along the way. Sitting across from May, Bui cast a few stolen glances at her. But her face was averted as she concentrated on the view at her side. No words were exchanged among the company, and the only sound was the tenor's tedious humming. To his right, he saw a long and bumpy path cut through a thicket of endless cornfields.

As the carriage turned onto a crowded street filled with lights, Bui noticed a large vacant property situated a distance from the road. Trees and shrubs obscured the crumbling brick walls, which were covered in vines. As the moon struggled through a sea of foliage, its filtered light revealed the ruins inside. The sharp edges of burned bricks jabbed upward into the sky, so faint that they appeared at first like phantoms. Eeriness rose from the deserted grounds, and Bui was aware of a chill wind — or was it his own imagination?

"What is that place?" he asked.

The girl paid no attention to Bui's query. The older woman replied, "That is the haunted estate of the Cam Le Village. It once belonged to the Nguyen family. Its owners have been gone a long time."

"Haunted?" Bui asked with excitement. "Is it really filled with restless ghosts? Has anyone seen them? What do they look like?"

His questions were interrupted as the carriage took a sudden turn, tossing him against the wall of its cabin. Bui cursed the coachman. When he fell back into his seat, the cheerful tumult outside his window recaptured his attention.

Soon the coach reached the end of the street, where it split into two smaller paths that led to the river at different sites. Each opening was lit by a pair of torches, one burning on either side.

A man advanced from behind a tree and drew the horse to a halt. "Excuse me," he called up to Mouse. "You must leave your vehicle here if you want to enter the carnival."

"How do we get there?" Mouse asked.

"The men follow the right path, and the women the left one."

Mouse jumped from his driver's seat. He opened the door and told his passengers what he had just learned. Bui leaned back in his seat and looked at his wife-to-be. His legs were stretched out in front of him, blocking her exit. Surely she must acknowledge him before they disembarked.

The girl sat on a white quilt. Her face was smooth and delicate. Bui detected fine specks of ground pearl on her powdered skin. Yet, underneath the vulnerable demeanor, her dark eyes betrayed a sense of will that made him look away. She lifted her hand and offered it to him. The tips of her fingers barely touched the palm of his hand. He shuddered at the slight contact.

"You have my best and sincere wish for a successful evening, young Master," Tai May said in a calm voice.

He seized her hand in both of his. The heat from her skin shot through him like lightning. He opened his mouth, not knowing what he was going to say. "I promise I will find you on that river tonight" were the words that came out.

*B*ui took the right path with his opera singer. He was still drunk from the girl's touch and the bewitching look in her eyes. Around him, a new source of noise rose over the shouts of the crowd — the cries of the mask-sellers. Each vendor carried hundreds of different costumes, made from either colored paper or coarse cotton. The revelers hastened to purchase a mask and its complementary outfit.

For himself he chose a dark-blue peacock mask and an elaborate costume depicting the bird's vivid feathers and for the opera singer he purchased a brown monkey suit. The effeminate man murmured a sound of disparagement, but took his gear from Bui's hand. He searched the crowd for the coachman, but Mouse had disappeared. The slave had shed his peasant skin to become part of the crowd, just another among the many mask-wearers.

On the bank of the river, a boat-renter approached Bui. His face was covered in pockmarks. Some of the scars were so deep that they resembled little black holes in his skin. The man bowed to him and said, "Would you like to rent a boat, my lord?"

Bui scrutinized the boatman's face, laughed, and poked his finger against the man's nose. "More than anyone else in this place, you should wear a mask, my good man. You are frightening the customers. Give me your most expensive boat."

The boatman bowed lower. "Right this way, my lord," he said. "Do you want a steersman as well, sir?"

"Yes," Bui said enthusiastically. "I want everything. Tonight must be perfect. This money should be enough to cover it." He thrust a handful of coins into the boatman's hand.

*T*he river air was chilly but abuzz with excitement as Bui's boat entered the tumultuous scene. The dull thumping of the drums along the riverbank accompanied the higher pitch of female voices, echoing through the vast space above them. As in the mating ritual of birds, the male singers answered coyly, adding new verses to the familiar songs that the women sang. Then, communicating through the music, they searched for one another. Hundreds of tiny boats floated like fallen leaves, pushing against one another as they maneuvered for favorable positions. The brilliant light of lanterns, sparkling as though they were the rarest, most expensive jewels on Earth, reflected on the water surface.

With marvelous skill, the helmsman Bui had hired was able to escape the men's area and advance toward the women's boats. The young lord stood up, despite the cool wind cutting through his paper costume. He could hear the stirring of the oars and the clashing of the boat's keel against water. A short distance ahead, he spotted Lady Tai May's white canoe floating like a swan among a flock of black ducks. At its tip, just as Master Long had predicted, hung a pair of lanterns shaped like butterflies. He recognized her almost instinctively. She was dressed in all white, and her outline was defined against the dark river and sky. He noticed her mask, which resembled a butterfly's wings. Next to her was the fifth mistress of Magistrate Toan, who wore no costume. The stout woman was rowing, and her gentle rhythm kept their wooden vessel a few paces ahead of the other boats.

Bui struck his boatman on the shoulder. "There," he said, pointing. "Get me to that white boat." And to the opera singer, he ordered, "Sing, sing this instant. Let your voice be heard."

The brown monkey opened his mouth, and music streamed from his lungs. His voice, rich with melody, instantly prompted a couple of women's sampans to draw near. The admirers' shrieks and clapping filled Bui's heart with pride. He recognized the priceless value of his songbird.

"Sing louder," he urged the tenor, banging on his back as if beating a drum, and the man complied. His voice swept higher, and for a moment, the girl on the white boat seemed to notice him. She cocked her head and listened.

Bui soon found his vessel surrounded by the singer's amorous aficionados. Many of these ladies had recognized the opera singer's famous voice, and their passionate cries reverberated in the dark night. Some even threw Bui bouquets of flowers, realizing he must be a man of wealth to have hired such an important tenor. As the women's boats approached, they reached over and tried to snatch the peacock mask, wanting to see his face. He fell back into his seat, covering his head. The boat rocked with a violent force. Even the skillful helmsman was having a difficult time steering his vessel.

"Stop singing, you fool," Bui yelled. To his newly acquired fans, he snarled, "Get away from me, you filthy farmers."

But now he had offended the peasants. Their happy cries turned aggressive. With a yank, one of them pulled his mask away. In minutes, his peacock feathers flew about his boat like the remnants of a torn flower.

Fortunately for Bui, the attack stopped abruptly. Someone or something on the river had captured the women's attention and drew them away from his boat. In the riotous atmosphere, he heard the spellbinding sound of a lute. The melody drifted through the air, soothing the angst of the game. The chaotic river was restored to its calm.

With his hands over his face, Bui was able to see between his fingers. He watched a boat gliding atop the water. Its owner wore a black hooded cloak that made him resemble Death. The light was so faint that no one could see the details of the man's features or how his fingers were dancing on the strings of the instrument. Bui saw the white boat advance. The slender girl who was supposed to be his wife got up from her seat. He watched Death take her into his arms.

Outraged, Bui turned to his steersman. Under the moonlight, he caught the man's dull smile. To vent his anger, he struck the grinning face with his fist. There was a note of hysteria in his voice as he cried out. "Take me to that boat. Now! Now! I want to see his face."

The helmsman's smile turned into a fearful frown, and he cried out in pain. Yet he remained unmoving in his seat.

"Are you deaf?" Bui said. "I command you to take me to that boat."

The peasant shook his head and replied in a flat voice, "I can't, my lord. It is too late. She is already inside his boat."

All around him, the carnival continued. However, to Bui, it was over. He had lost the phoenix dance.

Mouse's throat went dry. He looked at the girl in his arms. She was the only daughter of a village mayor, and he was her slave. On this river they were probably the most unlikely match conceivable. But she had chosen him! By walking into his boat, not only did she defy her family and risk losing everything, including her own reputation, but she had also spurned the visiting mandarin and his son. Mouse's spirit lifted. Tonight, thanks to the festival and the cloak of darkness, his status did not matter. Her strength ignited in him the courage to love like everyone else.

Her butterfly mask pressed against his chest, its wings undulating like the river. He leaned closer and inhaled the gardenia scent of her hair. She had not changed her fragrance for as long as he had known her. Somewhere beyond a group of floating boats he saw the young lord, white-faced with rage. He knew they would suffer for this later, but he did not care. The world around him melted away.

She lifted the disguise and peeled it away from her face. Mouse watched, riveted by every gesture. She gathered her hair — dark and rippling down to the small of her back — and pulled it over one shoulder so it lay above her breast. The moon outlined her features. He saw her eyes, slanted because of her high cheekbones and shaped like the spreading wings of a distant swallow. They widened when she looked at him. She was smiling. He stopped breathing, unable to tear his eyes away.

For a long time, they stood in the middle of the sampan, holding each other without uttering a word. The boat rocked, drifting farther away from the festive area of the river. All that Mouse could think of was how happy he felt. Now his love for her was no longer a secret. He reached his arms farther around her waist. He could feel her hand slip through the opening in his cloak and rub his back. She raised her head, and the tips of their noses touched, briefly. He heard his voice whisper, "Mistress."

She winced and pulled away. The boat swayed. Without his sturdy stand to keep her balance, Tai May staggered and grabbed the air. He caught her hands, helping her to sit on a wooden bench. Then he fell to his knees in front of her. She sighed, her hand touching his face. "Do not address me with that awful title, not tonight, not ever," she said.

He nodded, fascinated by her mouth. He had heard the young cowherds talk about the French kisses, in which a man explored his woman's mouth with his tongue. The strangeness of the act had seemed so erotic that it made him squirm with anticipation. Vietnamese never kissed; to express affection they took long, deep sniffs at each other's skin. But in the dim glow of the lantern her lips were full and wet, so inviting that he ached to taste them. He sat at her feet, dazed and full of desire.

She glanced down at the lute on the floorboard and asked, "Who taught you to play that sad song?"

He explored the instrument with his fingers, and a melancholy sound rose from under his hand. "It is my mother's favorite ballad," he replied.

"Your mother," she echoed. "She is the one who lives in the haunted mansion."

Mouse felt the blood drain from his head. He was horrified by the knowledge behind her remark. The secret he thought that he had buried so deep was now exposed. "What do you know about Ven?" he said.

Her mischievousness turned to confusion. But Mouse was too upset to notice. She clutched her hands in her lap and said, "I am sorry if I am intruding on your privacy. Please forgive my curiosity. My only desire was to learn about you." After a moment, she added, "We have always been friends, have we not?"

Mouse frowned. "Did you tell anyone in your family about her?"

She shook her head.

He took her hands and looked into her eyes. "If you ever do, Tai May, you will place Ven and me in a grave danger. There are men in this village who want to hurt us." Out of a corner of his eye, he saw a sampan approaching. He fell silent and turned away, letting go of her hands. His face was hidden behind the hood of his cape.

Two people in blue pirate costumes rowed by. The woman lifted up her mask and waved happily at Tai May while her companion threw a pigskin filled with wine to Mouse. "Take this, young lovers," he called. "Have a drink to show respect to the old gods of the moon. May they bless your great future together with a wedding." He laughed and sculled off. Their voices dimmed as their vessel hastened down the river.

Mouse watched the couple pass through the crowd of boats, until he and Tai May were alone once again. He brushed the hood away from his head and shifted his position so that he could look at her. He cleared his throat, and said, "I was abandoned nine years ago. Ven, the woman you saw in that haunted house, is not my mother."

"Then who is she?"

The innocent look remained on her face. He could not bring himself to lie to her, but he hated to sadden her. "She is my wife," he said.

Tai May flinched as though he had just slapped her face. Mouse could not bear to see the hurt in her eyes. He realized that this was what the musicians meant when they sang about a broken heart. No wonder the love songs always made people weep.

"Do you love her?" He heard her gentle voice.

"Yes, I do," he admitted. "But not the same way that I love you."

When he got the courage to look up again, Tai May was holding the jug of wine in her hands. She shook it and said, "Tonight, we must drink every drop of this wine to forget about your dreadful predicament. Instead, you can recite a story for me."

"The way I always do at your bedtime?" he asked.

"No." A sparkle of fun seemed to return to her. "This time you must play the lute while you relate the tale, like a true storyteller at the market."

He heard her laughter, light and tinkling, as she put her foot forward to touch his. Was she trying to hide her disappointment about his past? The river was silent except for the soft splash of waves against the boat and the rise and fall of distant jollity. He chewed his knuckles. "Would you still have come to me if you knew I had a wife?"

She whispered, "I love you dearly, Mouse," and slid closer to him. "I find you faithful, honest, and deserving. With the witness of Heaven above and the underworld below, I solemnly pledge my truest words. I will never regret what I have done tonight, nor would I hesitate to do it again."

He closed his eyes, inhaled deeply, and planted his lips on hers. At first the contact was so soft that he wondered if he had just kissed the empty air in between them. Then he felt her mouth open slightly, and her breath caressed his face. The tip of her tongue passed along the border of his lower lip. He raised his eyelid and peeped out in sheer incredulity. Through his lashes, he saw her looking at him.

He encircled her in his arms and laid her down on the bottom of the boat. The hood fell over his head and shielded them from the rest of the world. He tasted her mouth and was aware of her trembling in his embrace. Instinct urged him to thrust himself against her body, to stroke her soft breasts, to make himself one with her. With a gasp, he broke away.

"I must stop," he panted, "before I can no longer trust myself."

"No," she moaned.

The moon was hidden above masses of dark clouds. Most of the lanterns were extinguished as the villagers were leaving the carnival. The only light that was left was a lantern hanging at the bow of Mouse's boat. "I should take you home," he said.

"Not yet," she said. "Stay with me. I don't want to be alone."

Around them the wind picked up its pace. He turned and faced her. She was still shivering in her cotton dress. He took off his linen costume.

"You never told me, who are these men that want to hurt you?" she asked as he pulled the cloak over her shoulders.

"The most important one is Magistrate Toan, your grandfather," he replied.

chapter ten

The Break

The next morning dawned cold and cloudy. During the night, the winds had shaken most of the gold plaques from the outer walls of the house, and they lay scattered on the ground. At the house of Toan, just as the restless sun mounted the horizon, the thick carved door of the guest house that faced the courtyard was flung open. Moments later, two shadows stormed through it. They were Minister Chin and his son. In his haste, the minister did not fasten his gray satin tunic. His loose garments flapped in the wind, much to the surprise of the two female servants who were sweeping the patio. Neither of them said a word to the guests. They merely stood aside to let them pass.

"What a misfortune," Minister Chin said to his son, as he ascended the steps that led to the owner's living room. "But before I confront that girl's father, I must understand something. Have you told me the entire story of last night's events?"

"To my best recollection, sir," was the young man's reply.

Bui had never been refused by anyone until his experience at the phoenix dance. Now, several hours later, rage still coursed through his heart. He would never forget the image of the girl leaving her boat and stepping into the arms of a stranger. She had made him feel less adequate than a peasant. But now it was his turn to shame her in front of her elders. His father, one of the king's ministers, would make certain that the Toan family name was of no account in the Court at Hue unless they agreed to disown the girl. Bui gnawed at his nails. From time to time he paused long enough to wipe the tips of his fingers along the pristine fabric of his shirt. Soon, dark trails of blood streaked the glossy cotton.

His father reached for a way to open the panel of doors but found them bolted. He stopped and turned to the young servant nearest him, a short, thin girl who was clutching a broom in her hands. "Let me in!" he demanded.

The maid was so nervous that the left side of her face was twitching. "Is there anything wrong, sir? Did we sweep too noisily and disturb your rest? If we did, I beg you and the young lord to accept a thousand apologies."

"Shut your mouth," he barked. "This matter doesn't concern you. It is the face of your master that I am looking for. Wake him up and tell him —"

From behind the thin wall of doors, the sound of furniture being moved interrupted Minister Chin. Wooden clogs clobbered against the tiled floor, and the entrance to the main living room burst open. Magistrate Toan's buxom fifth mistress stood at the door, holding a candle in her hand. Her hair was tousled, and she squinted at the stark sunlight. Seeing the minister's face, she took a step back and pressed her hand against her chest. "Can I help you?" she asked in a weak voice.

Minister Chin swept past her and entered the dark living room. "I must speak to the girl's father before we leave here this morning."

The young mistress extended her hand toward a richly upholstered reclining couch with silver inlays around its edges. The polished metal reflected her candle, winking at Minister Chin. "Will you please take the best seat in the house?" she said to the minister. "I will summon my son-in-law this instant. While you wait, the servant will bring hot tea to warm you. I beg you to have patience and try to forget any unpleasantness that is troubling you."

Minister Chin remained standing as he recognized the voice of the mayor, coming from behind the ivory partition. Silently, the minister turned his eyes to Master Long's silhouette, outlined against the mosaic sculpture of a female nude carved into the screen. The mayor's voice seemed to emerge from the figure's blue-jade mouth. "Unpleasantness? Certainly in my house my guests should not be feeling any sort of discomfort."

Master Long pushed the screen aside and walked in. Following him was the slow, silent woman who had never been properly introduced to the guests. From her expensive garments and the jewelry sparkling in her hair, and the mere fact that she always stayed within three paces behind the mayor, Minister Chin assumed that she was his wife. The woman stepped behind a painted post and merged with the thick gloom. Her husband came forward and bowed before the minister.

"A servant informed me of your desire to speak to me," he began. "Sir Chin, it is my duty as your host to ensure that all of your wishes be met. So, here I am, at your disposal. I have but two questions: Has any member of my family offended you or the young master? And does it have any relation to the phoenix dance last night? Please speak freely, since your presence in my humble home is a matter of great honor to us. I urge you to reconsider your decision to leave on such angry terms."

The minister gathered his loose tunic and fastened it against his body with a mechanical twist of his fingers. "So, you are aware of the humiliation my son had to endure at the carnival?" he asked bitterly. "I wonder if it was a premeditated action, a deliberate means of rejecting him, an indication that in your eyes he is not suitable to seek your daughter's hand in marriage."

"Dear Heaven!" Master Long exclaimed. "What has made you think this? I give you my word that I do not know what happened between the young master and my daughter. My words were mere speculation. Now that I am aware of the problem, let me summon my daughter. She must apologize and beg your forgiveness for her ill manner. Minister Chin, I also want to emphasize that I desire nothing more than to bring about a marriage between the two young adults. After today's festival, I will find a proper matchmaker, and you will see how simple it is, this affair." He laughed, a cackling sound, and wiped his forehead with his sleeve.

"I am afraid that it is too late," Minister Chin said, taking a seat on the divan. "We both know how your daughter feels about my son. Maybe she was born to mate with another peasant, like the man she met on the river last night."

"What man?" the mayor asked. A splash of surprise washed over his face. He turned to Bui. "Did she not invite you to join her in the phoenix dance? Who else on that river could have a better voice than my tenor, or bear a more popular name?"

Bui was slumped in a chair. On this comment, he sat up and responded, "There was someone in a death cape, playing a butterfly lute. I consider him no one, but your daughter apparently thought he was a prince. She even abandoned her boat to be with him. I left the river alone and walked straight to your mansion, almost getting lost on the way."

Master Long struggled into a chair nearby. "Who was that man? Did you get a good look at his face?"

"No, sir. It was cloaked behind his dark garment. I tried to come closer to their boat, but it seemed that I was bound by the rules of the game."

"I must speak to my daughter," the mayor said, as if he were talking to himself. Looking up at his honored guest, who was still perched on the ornate couch on its raised platform, Master Long had lost his earlier buoyancy. His voice came in a whisper. "It is not too late to fix this matter. Please leave everything in my hands. We might have had an awkward beginning, but the festival is not yet over. Please stay!"

The faint echo of his voice bounced off the high ceiling, as if to mimic his supplication. The minister shifted his attention to the front of his gray tunic. Master Long glared at Fifth Mistress. "Lady Song," he scolded, "I trusted you with my daughter last night. How could you allow that incident to happen in such an irresponsible manner? Have you now at least the decency to reveal to us the mysterious man's identity, or must I begin the investigation?"

Magistrate Toan's fifth wife answered, "I came to the feast as a chaperon to the young lady. As I said to you last night, I was merely there to ensure her safety. I did not interfere with the games."

"Do not speak to me in that tone, madam," he screamed at her. "Remember your position in this house and answer my questions: Who was she with? And where did he come from?"

A look of disgust flashed across the young lord's face as though he had just spotted a dead rat on the floor. Master Long turned to follow Bui's eyes.

Standing at the threshold of his living room was his slave, Mouse. The servant stood erect, tall and triumphant, holding his daughter's hand as if she were now his woman. Her large dark eyes fluttered, but they were filled with a deep happiness. A black cloak swallowed her.

"Please, Father," she said to him in a calm manner. Clearly she did not understand the damage she had done. "Do not blame Fifth Mistress for my doings. It is not her fault. If there is anything you wish to know, you can ask me or Mouse." She looked up at the servant.

Master Long jumped forward. His hand seized her cloak, and he yanked it off her. "I will not speak to you until you take this filthy rag off," he shouted. "Get out of here this instant. And do not leave your room until I have decided on an appropriate punishment. Go! Or I will be compelled to strike you in front of my guests." With a shove, he sent his daughter sprawling backward on the tiled floor. Mouse leapt to her side.

Behind a painted column, Master Long's wife uttered a frightful sound. Her voice punctured his anger and depleted it at once. "Do not fret, madam," he said to her. "I am sorry for what you have just witnessed. But I implore you to take your daughter out of my sight. Let me resume my conversation with my guests."

He shifted his attention to Mouse. The blue veins around his temples were bulging under his skin. "Do not touch my daughter with your dirty hands," he said. "How dare you treat your own master this way? Where is your sense of duty or your conscience? I took you in during a great famine and gave you food, a home, and an education. I had great ambitions for your future because I recognized your gifts. Until now, no man has found himself in such a favored position in this house. But you are robbing me of my only daughter. Dear gods, I have been harboring a hive of killer bees in my sleeves for nine years." His forehead was slick with sweat. Finally, he pointed toward the entrance. "Leave my presence! Confine yourself in the kitchen. And pray for Heaven's mercy while you are waiting for me there."

※

*B*ui lifted up a corner of the parchment from a window and peeked outside. Sunlight had broken through the clouded sky, and the sparkling droplets of dew atop the rose leaves had nearly evaporated. Somewhere in the distance, the gong of the time-teller's last round announced the morning. Bui wanted to spy on the girl, but she had disappeared into her own room. He could see her silhouette pacing behind the opaque screen of her window. Frustrated, he diverted his attention to the adults inside the Toans' living room.

From the reclining couch, his father rose. "Sir Long," he said, pronouncing the mayor's name with an indolent yawn, "do not bother to discipline your daughter for her ill manners and her loose conduct. It is too late for a girl her age to learn. I have made up my mind to withdraw my son's offer of marriage. We will be leaving as soon as possible."

"You cannot leave, Sir Chin," said the mayor. "I promise you her behavior will change. Please pay no heed to her. She only speaks like any fifteen-year-old who has all the spoiled willfulness that a mother's excessive affection can bestow. Beneath that rebellious veneer, she is an excellent child."

The minister walked his fingers along the rough stubble of his chin. Toward the back, a burgundy tapestry that veiled the entrance of an anteroom was moved aside, and Magistrate Toan's face materialized. No one knew how long the old man had remained behind that partition, observing the tense scene. With dragging steps, he shuffled into the room. As usual, his harsh voice preceded him. "You must not beg the guests to stay, my son. No one in the Toan family should ever have to beg from strangers. We may not have an impressive title in the king's court or reside in the citadel, but we are a class of businessmen. We have our own lands and an entire village of laborers. Our fortune has no fame or nobility, especially the kind that has the reputation without any of the benefits. It is Minister Chin's obligation to be here in the name of the emperor. And our feast is not over until tomorrow night. Sir Chin, you would not let a private matter interfere with your duty as master of ceremonies, would you? As for the wedding, it shall be carried on as agreed." He sat on an ebony chair decorated with carved dragons.

"I may not have any choice about leaving this town," the minister said, "but what makes you so certain that we desire to be associated with your family, especially after the dishonorable secret that your granddaughter has just revealed?"

"The girl's dowry," Magistrate Toan said with a chuckle. "That should be enough for you to change your mind. Not to mention her enormous inheritance of lands that is worth one hundred twenty-five thousand silver pieces, which she will receive upon my death. All of this wealth will belong to the house of Tang in return for your cooperation. A very lavish offer for such an untalented lad, don't you agree?"

Bui stepped forward, puffing with indignation. "Do not insult me!" he exclaimed in a high-pitched voice. But his outburst was cut short by a signal of his father's hand. Minister Chin paced the length of the living room, lost in thought, and then resumed his seat.

"I take pride in being an honest man," the minister said. "It is difficult for me to decline such a generous offer. But untalented as my son may be, he still deserves better than wearing a slave's secondhand shoes."

He rose and saluted the old man and his son. Bui followed him.

"Two hundred thousand silver coins as her inheritance, plus her dowry," the old man called after them. Then he added, "That is my final offer. But you need not give me the answer right away. Tonight, my servants will prepare a pipe of highest-quality opium for your pleasure. Do not refuse, since I have already made all the arrangements. Only let me warn you that my persistence is legendary."

Minister Chin opened the door and let himself out. Bui ran after him. The courtyard opened before them, spotless under the bright sun. The sky was blue, dotted with white, billowy clouds. Fresh roses scented the air, reminding Bui of the aromatic steam that rose atop his mother's morning cup of tea.

"With that dowry," he said to his father when they left their host's front porch, "we can become landowners, and we can buy a great house similar to this one. Is there anyone else in the mandarins' quarter who could do these things?"

His father seized his shoulder and shook him. "Have you no religion, no morals, that you harbor these thoughts in your head? What is wrong with the life you have inside the citadel, enjoying a high status among the elite of society?"

"We are not rich, Father," Bui said. "With your meager income, you have three mouths to feed in our family, plus the servants. How long can we go on living as we do? Why must we refuse the old man's offer so hastily? This marriage is a means for us to add more strength to our name, and a chance for me to get revenge on that arrogant girl. I beg your forgiveness for speaking so frankly. I never dare to correct you, my elder, but I wish you would reconsider the Toans' proposition. It gives us much to gain and nothing to lose."

Minister Chin sighed and led his son in the direction of the guest quarters. "Bui, you are a good lad, but you are much too young to understand that money is not the source of happiness. Our pride and heritage are the ultimate treasures, which no amount of money in the world can buy. By accepting their offer as they try to pass us a rotten piece of fruit, we will sacrifice our family traditions and values. Is that what you really want?"

His father's voice receded into the background. Across the long path leading to the kitchen, and through a thicket of durian trees, whose foul-smelling fruits with prickly rinds reminded him of the sweat of a peasant's body, he caught a sight of his nemesis, the slave. He watched the youth tiptoe through a small back gate, carrying a black knapsack across his shoulder. There was no one else in the courtyard, except for his father, who was searching Bui's face for an answer. Only Bui observed the slave. Should he follow the peasant in case he was attempting to escape? He imagined the terrible punishments the youth would face if he were captured, and, of course, Tai May's reaction to her lover's woe. He wanted to see her suffer a sudden, horrible, and devastating shock. He thought furiously, scratching his head as though the sun had made his scalp itch with its robust rays. Next to him, his father waited. He struggled with the impulse to alert the Toan family of the furtive escape that he alone was witnessing.

He looked at Tai May's window. Her shadow was still flickering against the semitransparent screen. He watched her bend over and comb her hair — her long, lustrous river of hair. Then he watched the slave's back, floating down a small road. He measured the growing distance between them with his eyes. Bui opened his mouth, drew in a deep breath, but let it out soundlessly. Dimly, he was aware of his father's high, cracked voice, saying something about his ancestors.

Bui started to run. "I will think about your words later," he yelled to his surprised father. Brushing aside the durian branches, he bolted through the back gate and hurried down the narrow and dusty road, keeping an inconspicuous distance from the slave.

*M*ouse wound his way through the cornfields that lined the narrow path. Bui realized that the slave was heading toward the main street. It was the same road they had taken to the carnival the night before. Behind the marketplace rose the twin pillars of the town entrance, two massive gray columns that stood under the orange sun like a pair of powerful guards. Their tips, decorated with carved stones that resembled lotus blossoms, were nearly hidden by the foliage of ancient oak trees. Beyond the portals, the golden earth, like the vast sky above it, spread out to infinity. Bui understood that once the slave stepped outside the village, he would become a free man.

However, to his surprise, instead of heading toward the bazaar, Mouse turned toward the east, picking his way through a cornfield. Soon, Bui could only distinguish Mouse's dark hair and the top of his knapsack over the immeasurable sea of auburn tassels. Without hesitation he, too, melted into the field's embrace.

They walked a few paces apart for almost a half hour under the hot sun. Bui was tired and thirsty. The muddy ground, oozing water from under its surface like perspiration, seized his feet. Somewhere inside the endless cornfield, he lost his leather shoes. Ahead of him, the slave did not show any sign of slowing down. A few more turns, and the field ended.

As the sky opened up, Bui found himself facing a ruin. Mouse, with an air of confidence, entered the wasteland through a crumbling portal. Recognizing the sharp edges of the brick walls and the wildly grown, unkempt shrubs and weeds, Bui realized the slave had led him to the back entrance of the infamous haunted house. A sighing wind above him, like the groans of troubled ghosts, beckoned Bui to come forward and explore the mystery inside. He followed the path into the compound and hid in a wild chrysanthemum bush.

He watched the slave approach a woman in her mid-thirties. Bui had never seen anyone like her. It was as if all the spirits of this wrecked place had taken on female form. Dressed like a beggar with clothes that were tattered and muddy, she was as brown as the ground she stood on. Her tangled black hair hung down her back. She opened her arms, and Mouse fell into them.

The slave's voice sounded like a child's. "Ven," he said, "I have come to seek your advice, for I have gotten myself into a great deal of trouble at the house of Toan."

chapter eleven

The Rose

Dan Nguyen remained still in his wife's strong embrace. Her scent, the familiar mixture of freshly turned soil, mint leaves, and garlic, reminded him of the days he had spent as a child riding on her back. For nine years, she had been the keeper of his soul on this damaged ground. Countless times he had come to her, broken and frightened. Each time he saw the warmth in her eyes, his spirit was renewed. He reached for her hand, his favorite part of her body. Smooth on top, callused on the bottom, it reminded him of a dog's paw.

For several minutes he heard no sound but his wife's soothing voice. Then he was aware of the humid air rushing through the trees, and his farmer's instinct sensed rain. He looked up. Through a curtain of willow fronds, swaying in the breeze, he saw patches of piercing blue sky, free of clouds. Could he be wrong about the rain?

Ven's voice, melodious as singing, brought him back to his surroundings. "I knew it was trouble when I saw that girl in your boat last night."

Dan drew back and looked at her. "You saw us together?" he asked.

She nodded. "I saw you, and so did the rest of the town. You inter-fered in the mating dance between Magistrate Toan's granddaughter and that young lord in the peacock costume. Didn't I advise you to keep away from that family's troubles altogether? If only you could hear the rumors that are flying through the town. But it is too late now. We are in trouble because of your impulsive conduct."

"I had just as much right to take part in that festival as anyone else," Dan said. "Last night was the first time I could see Tai May, not in the manner of a servant waiting for his mistress's command, but as a man admiring the beauty in his woman."

She slapped him, then felt instantly sorry. "You cannot look upon the enemy's offspring with adoring eyes. Have you forgotten our quest for vengeance, the sole reason for us to remain in this village?" She searched his features. "Must I remind you that up on that mango branch, you witnessed your parents' brutal slaying? And their killer, old Magistrate Toan, is still alive, wrapped in silk embroidered robes. He wears clothes with stitched knots so finely made that they can only be prepared by the hands of children, who will eventually go blind. Every year he purchases a new imported black silk hat, topped with an ivory finial and decorated with the rarest feathers. And yes-terday in the community hall, he invited more than two hundred guests for the harvest moon celebration, so they could enjoy bird's nest soup and opium. How can this go on? How will you face your parents in the afterlife?"

"It's too late," he said. "The enemies know I love her. It was you who sold me to the house of Toan, and fate brought Tai May and me together. No one can prevent what a heart desires. I can never be what you want me to be." She took a step back and closed her eyes. Her face was taut.

A thumping noise pounded in his ears. It seemed to come from all around them. He recognized the relentless echo of a loud drum, three intervals of nine continuous beats. It was the village's urgent warn-ing that some catastrophe had occurred. In her eyes he saw that she, too, knew the meaning of that pulsating sound.

He turned to the north. Past the endless golden pastures of Cam Le, he could make out the tiny pillars of the town's entrance and, beyond them, a succession of beautiful rolling hills. As the huge gates were closing toward each other, the view before him slowly vanished. He knew that his fate had been sealed behind the locked doors. Above, the swollen sun was trying to burst through the leaves. Dan watched the beams of light shooting through the shaded canopy to create a dappled pattern on the ground, like the metal bars of a jail cell. Ven put her arms around his shoulders.

He pushed away from her and looked for an escape. The town's north gates would be protected by the watchful guards. To the south, the river stretched its silver body along the edge of the village and then divided into canals and streams to crisscross the green landscape until it reached the end of the earth.

Over the clamor of drums, he heard Ven's surprised scream. He turned to look at her. A lock of hair stood up above her head like the crest of an angry rooster. To the side of the back fence, he saw a broad section of shrubbery shake violently. There, to his shock, Dan spotted the round red face of the young lord, Bui Tang, son of the proud minister from Hue. Bui, realizing he had been caught spying, dashed from his hiding place and charged toward the exit. Dan dove after him like a falcon pursuing a rabbit. Ven followed, her ragged clothes streaming behind her.

Dan grasped a handful of Bui's carefully styled hair and pulled. The teenager gasped as his head was wrenched back. But the rest of his body continued to thrust forward and curled into an arc under the bright sun, like a taut bow aimed at the sky. Then, as his feet came out from under him, he fell to the ground with a thud. Dan's momentum pushed him over the fallen boy. The impact of his dusty foot made an imprint on Bui's tailored shirt. Out of Bui's mouth came a gurgling sound, and he curled to his side, clutching his stomach. Ven approached and studied the teenager on the hard soil. "Pick him up," she said to Dan.

Bui moaned. With his eyes half shut, he seemed to ignore the two shadows above him.

Suddenly the quivering mound beneath Dan's palm sprang up and erupted into a cloud of dust. Dan felt sand, like streaks of fire, shoot into his eyes. He collapsed to his knees and groped at his face in agony. Before his vision dimmed into darkness, Dan caught a flash of white shirt floating against the blue sky. Behind it fluttered a black tuft of his wife's long hair. Her hand came down, and he heard a scream. There were more rustling sounds. Her hand came down again. He heard a pounding like a wooden pestle striking the hollow well of a mortar. Another scream. Then silence.

Dan tilted his head toward the warm sun and listened. Tears streamed down his face, and the redness before him grew thicker. He felt as though he were peering into a pool of blood.

"Ven," he called. His hands felt the empty air. The aroma of garlic and fresh mint returned, signaling her comforting presence.

"I am here, Dan. Are you all right?"

"I can't see. What has just happened? Did you kill him?"

"No."

"Did he get away?"

"No, I just knocked him unconscious," she said.

"Dear Heaven!" he cried, temporarily forgetting the ache in his eyes. "What are we going to do?"

Ven did not answer him. Her soothing fragrance withdrew from his nose.

"Ven," he shouted. "Where are you? Do not leave me alone." There was no response, except for the distant drum.

He grabbed the front of his shirt and wiped his eyes. A flood of tears washed the sand from them in abrasive rivulets. Gradually, the blur in front of him settled into thousands of tiny specks of light. Inside this circle of illumination, he saw Ven's face.

She stood before him, clutching a kitchen knife in her hands. A few feet away from her, Dan saw Bui lying on his stomach. His knees were bent. His hands and feet were suspended over his buttocks, tied together with a stout rope. The young lord rested one side of his face against the sand, puffing through a corner of his wide mouth. His eyes, dark and fluid like a duck's, were blinking without recognition. A deep red handprint spread across his cheek.

"Come, come, calm yourself," Ven said. "I just went inside and looked for a cord to tie up our spy before he fully regains consciousness. Do you need any help?"

Dan drew in a deep breath. With his restored vision came a wave of relief, but he was now an outcast. In one day, whatever life he had hoped to build with Tai May was dashed. When they had left the river, he was sure that they would be together and he would kiss her until the end of time. The hypnotic drumbeats seemed to be growing louder or coming closer. He could no longer distinguish their sound from the throbbing of his heart.

Ven put down the knife and disappeared again behind the kitchen wall. She came back, holding a large straw hat in one hand and a wet cloth in the other. "Here," she said. "Clean your face. It will make you feel better."

Dan pressed the damp cloth over his forehead. "What are we going to do?" he asked.

Ven tied the hat strings under her chin. "I must go to town and learn some news before we decide on a plan." Sensing his hesitation, she added, "If I am certain that they are hunting for us, we will leave this place together after nightfall. For the time being, it will be much simpler for us to hide from the guards. Tonight, if the villagers are allowed to celebrate the harvest moon, we will have more luck getting away."

Dan pointed to the young lord, who lolled on the ground like a bound pig. "When are we going to release him?"

"He will not be released."

Bui let out a scream. "Let me go."

Ignoring him, Ven picked up the knife. He struggled against his bonds. Looking at Dan, he called, "Who are you people? What is this vendetta between you and the Toan family? If they are your enemies, I see no reason for you to harm me or hold me hostage. By imprisoning the son of the king's official representative, you are committing an offense against the Imperial Court. Release me this instant, if you ever expect to beg for my mercy in the future."

"We cannot let you go, young Master," Dan muttered. "You spied on us, and in doing so, you forfeited your freedom."

Bui fixed his eyes on the knife in Ven's hand. The muscles in his neck tightened, and he yelled with all his might, "Help me, somebody! Help!"

"Shut your mouth," Ven shrieked. She flew to the hostage's side and pressed her knife against his neck. "Do you wish to die? Just say one more word, and I will grant you the favor."

"Calm down," Dan said to the prisoner. "We will not harm you."

Bui shut his eyes. The burly woman's shadow blocked the sun from his face. He did not dare to look at her, towering above him like a giant, ready to extinguish his life the same way she would squash a bug. He began to cry, softly and bitterly.

"Are you hurt?" Dan asked the teenager once his sobbing had subsided.

Bui responded only with a lot of sniffing. He glanced at the beggar woman.

Dan said, "Speak if you want, but remember to keep your voice low."

The prisoner spoke as though he did not want to. "What do you have in store for me? You cannot leave me here alone in this haunted house overnight, not while there is a full moon. As you must know, ghosts thrive on the yin effect that the moon creates. I would die from terror."

"If there are ghosts in here," the woman interrupted Bui, "they would not bother to haunt you. Instead, they would come after those who are unjust under the eyes of Heaven. Why would you fear the dead unless the true origin of your demon is your own conscience? Is that not what you are truly ashamed of — the reflection of your hateful heart?"

"I am not afraid of any inner demons!" he exclaimed. "It is the legends of the disturbed ghosts, this wretched place, and your hostile companionship that I fear."

"This place is our home," Dan said. "You have chosen to enter our property as an unwelcome guest and challenge our hospitality. Aren't you ashamed of your behavior?"

"Forgive him," Ven said. "Under the elegant exterior, the young lord is well aware of his shortcomings. You, my husband, although a slave, are richer than he is in several ways. He wishes to see you trampled and dishonored, so that he can reclaim the confidence and masculinity that you took away, not to mention the beautiful girl and her fortune."

Bui whispered in horror, "Who are you, woman? How can a lowly beggar know what my thoughts are? And why do you speak like an educated person? Are you the phantom of this haunted ruin?"

"No," she said. "Although some town folks might think that I am an apparition who has not yet matured into a ghost, I am actually the wife of that slave, who is the only surviving offspring of the Nguyen family. I must go now. If you place any value on your life, stay still and do not try to escape." Turning to Dan, she whispered, "I will try to get back as soon as possible, young Master. Keep a close watch on the prisoner. Do not let him out of your sight. If he screams again, stuff rags in his mouth."

"Be careful, Ven," he said.

She bent toward the ground in the courteous way of a wife bowing to her husband. Still hunched over, she concealed the knife under the front panel of her tunic. "I will try to come back before night falls. If you are hungry, look behind the wall. Your supper is being kept warm on the brick kiln."

She vanished behind the back door, choosing the road that led toward the community hall.

After Ven had gone, Dan repositioned his prisoner so that he was sitting with his back against the trunk of a weeping willow tree with his hands tied behind it. Dan sat down a few feet away and reached for his knapsack. From it he withdrew a birch-bark sewing kit, whose surface bore symmetrical carved designs and repeated patterns of bamboo and plum trees, symbolizing an everlasting friendship. Dan chose a couple of bamboo loops from the box and used them to stretch a piece of cotton cloth.

He held a thin needle close to his face and passed a silk thread through its eye. With a deft twist of his shoulder, he raised the needle high in his right hand and pointed the tip downward, while his left hand held the frame steady. Then, like a machine that had been oiled and put into motion, his fingers and arms moved through the rapid series of automatic gestures that drew his mind into the tedious, comforting ritual of needlework.

Hours passed. As he plied the long strands, the image of a red, raised petal took shape on the taut surface of the fabric. Ignoring the prisoner, Dan worked faster. His eyes tracked the gleaming needle with the keenness of a hunting animal.

The rain he had predicted earlier was coming. As the weather changed, the distant sky collapsed like a deflated balloon. Flashes of lightning slashed across the Heavens. The willow trees above him writhed in the wind, and now and then a loud thunderclap boomed. The earth plummeted into darkness, until his embroidering became an impossible task.

Dan rose, placing his handiwork carefully inside his bag. Striding to the back gate, he scanned the cornfields for his wife. There was no one in sight. The main road that threaded the Cam Le Village's wide rural plain was now black with dust from the storm. Above it, the fog spilled its damp wisps over the rippling hills and terraces. He stood still, listening. The only sound now was the air moving; the drum had ceased its pounding.

Behind him, the prisoner shifted his thin legs against the uneven grass. Dan heard the scratching sound of Bui's back brushing against the willow tree's sturdy trunk and the popping of his knuckles as his hands wiggled to break away from the constricting rope. He turned around, and the prisoner flinched. The bruise on his right cheek was swollen and shiny, like the skin of a ripe persimmon.

"I changed your position and tied you against that tree so that you could be more comfortable," Dan said. "Do not force me to restrain you the way Ven did."

"I am sorry," Bui whispered. His voice was lost in the bellow of nature.

"What did you say?" As Dan came closer to the bound teenager, the wind whipped at his hair.

"I am sorry," the prisoner screamed. "My hands are falling asleep. I am cold and hungry. And above all, I am scared. The storm is coming. If I get wet, I will surely become sick. Just let me be. Do not torment me anymore with your threats."

His mention of hunger nudged a painful twist in Dan's stomach. Raising a finger to the captive, he said, "Some supper will help you forget your discomfort. What I find will be yours to share. But while I am behind the kitchen wall, you must not try to escape. I will not hesitate to take your life to protect my liberty. Now stop your whining. It is an effeminate trait."

Bui cast his eyes on the sewing box and said, "What could be more effeminate than your embroidery? A man should never touch women's tools, let alone create pretty flowered ornaments like a subservient housewife. Is that how you are trained as a slave in the house of Toan, to do needlework?"

Dan thrust his fist in Bui's face. "Be careful of your comments. We are not here to exchange opinions, or to make a false friendship. You are my prisoner. That position gives you no ground to mock me. Now keep quiet, or I won't feed you."

He stomped behind the broken wall. The smell of coconut milk made his stomach grumble in anticipation. Ven's supper consisted of an earthen pot full of banana pies wrapped in bamboo leaves — his favorite meal. Through the crack of the kiln, he saw that the fire had died away. All that was left inside was a seam of gray ashes, still shaped like little lumps of charcoal. He took the lid off. Grabbing the container's cold handles with both hands, he carried it outside.

Spotting Dan returning with the food, the prisoner's eyes narrowed. He licked his lips, and his Adam's apple thrust up and down. Soon the scents of sticky rice and bananas filled the open air, blending with the rising mist. Dan placed the clay pot on the ground a few steps away from his captive. Bui leaned forward and peeked at the contents. He grimaced.

"Is this the sort of food that beggar prepared?" he asked. "It looks dirty. Don't you have any other dishes that are garnished with meat?"

Dan unwrapped a pie and held it in front of the prisoner. The outer layer of the sticky rice was glazed in a bronze coating of cooked banana juice. A few milky drops of coconut condensation were dripping down its side like tiny pearls. The vapor of its sweetness filled Bui's nostrils, and he swallowed noisily. Dan pushed his hand closer. The young lord leaned forward and devoured a piece of pie. His face relaxed in satisfaction.

Dan turned away, searching the distant fields again for his wife. A few chilly drops of rain fell on his face. He stood still in the earth's vastness and desolation. He did not feel the coldness of his exposed skin in the seething wind, nor did he notice the slicing rain. Behind him, the faint cries of the young lord grew quieter. Dan was aware only of the doomed land under his feet, and the sense of death that was rising from its muddy ground. He thought about how foolish he was, to have imagined that he might be left in peace to love the grand-daughter of the enemy. Ven was right! His impulsive conduct had cost him and Ven what little was left of their freedom. Now the old vengeful magistrate was loading his rifle and recruiting an army of men, so that he could hunt them down like two escaped convicts.

The more he thought of Tai May, the more his heart ached. For nine years she had been so much a part of his life. He was conditioned to protect her. How could he fathom a world without her smile, her voice, or her presence? Above all, he could not forget the long kiss they had shared. He wished he could simply go back to being her slave, loving her in silence. At the same time, he wanted to run away, to hide from all of his troubles. Until Ven returned, he had no place to go. He and the boy were both prisoners in the haunted mansion.

"What are you waiting for?" Behind him, the hostage cried out. "Give me some more of that peasant food."

chapter twelve

The Toad and the Goldfish

Ven felt the midday sun beating down on her head as she left the ruined mansion. She clutched at the knife under her shirt as she plodded along the outer ridge of the road. The sunken fields on both sides of her path gleamed with puddles of water that lapped up and spat out her shadow intermittently.

At the bend in the road, she paused and looked back. On the verdant mound of the kitchen floor, her husband stood with his dark hair tossed by the wind. One of his hands fumbled inside his knapsack. She knew every item in it, treasured tools of needlework she had watched him carry on his back for years. They had once belonged to her; now they were his.

He had loved the hand puppets she had made for him out of old clothes when he was a child. Yet she was certain that his inspiration did not stem from her or the simple toys she made with a few colored threads. His desire came from that slender girl from the house of Toan.

One spring day two years earlier, he had come to her for advice. His eyes had glinted with a strange fever; his cheeks were rosy, and from the excitement in his voice, she could tell that the boy was sick with an illness more powerful than she could cure. He could not stop smiling. His teeth glittered like ivory, reflecting the bright sun. Her heart ached with spite.

"Ah! Ah! Did you know I took the young mistress, Lady Tai May, to the Trui market yesterday?" he had said to her in his cracking, adolescent voice. He shifted his weight from side to side in agitation. "You cannot guess what we saw at the market, can you?"

"No, sir, I really cannot."

"Roses," he blurted. "Beautiful red roses, just like the ones we used to have in our garden before the fire. I bought one bloom for my mistress with my wages, but the heat made it wilt." He paused and drew near her, then asked in a whisper, "Ven, will you teach me how to embroider? I want to make a flower for my mistress that will remain fresh for eternity." That was when she knew he had forgotten his blood feud with the Toan family.

The same afternoon, she gave her husband the sewing kit. It was a birch box that she had spent more than two years carving with lively images of plum and bamboo trees, using the only tool she had — the antler of a roe deer. A few days later, she had bought him the first fabric. And then she taught him how to embroider, hiding her jealousy inside the silken threads they had chosen together. Like tea leaves steeping in hot water, Ven's emotions swelled in the brew of her censorious silence.

Now, even with the town in mayhem and his life in danger, he still wanted to embroider. It was almost more than she could bear. He was right to have blamed her for sending him into the enemy's house. In her perfect plot for revenge, she had not envisaged the power of that girl, or the way her husband blushed each time her name was mentioned.

An old song, like a faded memory of her childhood, rose to the tip of her tongue:

> *The female toad gave birth in a goldfish's pond.*
> *The young tadpoles looked just like goldfish's fry,*
> *So the goldfish adopted them and brought them up.*

"What happened to our children?" the toad cried to his wife.
In the middle of the night, he came to the pond and asked for
*   his sons back.*
But the goldfish humiliated him, saying that they
Could not be his offspring, for toads were land animals.
A tree frog listened to the quarrel nearby and said to the toad,
"Why argue? Every species reproduces its own kind. . . .
"Calm yourself, and do not continue with this dispute,
*   Let the goldfish bestow care on your children;*
One day, when their tails fall off, they will return to you.
*   And that is the natural way."*

Hot air leaped across the fiery ocean of cornfields, scorching her face. Thinking of the toads, she wished for her husband to return to her, not only for the cautious weekly visits when he could escape his duties at the Toan mansion, but also as her sole contact with anything resembling a family.

She picked up her pace, as if to leave her troubled thoughts behind. The song continued to stream from her mouth, softly as first. And then like the humming wind, it soared through the air:

Those goldfish were truly thieves.
Greed like a blob of pond scum had blinded them,
Without giving them time to think.
The tadpoles became toads and went home to their parents.
And while the goldfish cried over his losses,
The family of toads was reunited and lived happily together.

She was floating with her song beside a bright checkerboard of golden fields when tramping feet thundered behind her. She stood rigid, yet fully aware of her surroundings.

"Where is this dumb beggar going in the middle of a curfew?" asked a mocking male voice.

With a slow gesture, she hooked the handle of her knife inside her waistband and turned around, her hands knitted together against her stomach. Dark veins bulged along her forearms, highlighting her muscles. Her eyes took in the muddy tips of the men's shoes and then the dark-blue socks around their ankles. She counted four pairs of soldiers' clogs scuffing the dirt in front of her in their usual intimidating way. One of the men, the captain of the guards, slammed his fist at her shoulder, forcing her to take a step back.

"We asked you a question. Must we stand here all day while you stare at the road?"

"No, sir . . ."

"No, sir, what? You are under arrest for breaking the curfew. Did you not hear the warning drum?"

"Yes, sir. I heard it loud and clear. Can you tell me what has happened?"

"We are looking for an escaped slave from the house of Toan, who may also be a kidnapper. No one is allowed to roam the streets until we find him."

"Why do you trouble me? I am not a slave," she whispered. From under her lowered lids, she was watching their every move. She saw the leader's shoes shuffle closer until the front of his brown shirt pressed against her nose. His skin oozed the unmistakable odor of opium, sweet and acrid.

One of the soldiers seized the meaty part of her arm in his gnarled fingers. "Listen to us, she-monkey," he said in a thick voice. "You do not talk to Mr. Sai, the town's police chief, in that tone of voice."

The rest of the men closed in around her like a pack of staghounds. Their nostrils puffed air in excited bursts, as though they were waiting for a signal from the master of the hunt.

Ven looked up at the leader's face for the first time. He had prickly black hair, and dark-brown specks of tar dotted his large yellowish teeth. His eyes were half shut; his face was puckered into an idiotic, hallucinatory grin. Using both hands, he scratched his head repeatedly — a gesture that reinforced her impression that he was sleepwalking.

No one moved while the captain's attention wandered across the fields and finally back to Ven. His eyes lost their glazed look as he ordered, "Who has the rope? Tie her up."

Ven brushed away the hand on her arm and plunged forward.

Before she could get far, the captain of guards was blocking her path. More hands, like the hooks of a fishnet, seized her. She struggled to break free.

Sai raised his sparse eyebrows to form two exaggerated half circles. With his fists he delivered a series of punches to her chest. The skillful blows of the experienced guard were unlike any she had encountered in common fights. She had no breath to scream; her lungs could produce only a chain of muffled hiccups. With his eyes still half shut, her captor clutched the scruff of her neck, pulling her upward, while the other men twisted her arms against the small of her back. Holding her in that position, they wrapped a rope around her wrists and fastened a knot. The captain released his fingers. Ven fell to the ground, immobilized.

The soldiers yanked her to her feet. She stood before Sai again, red-faced, with a trail of saliva trickling down her chin.

"Why are you running away?" he asked.

"I don't have to answer any questions," she said. "You have no right to arrest me."

"Do you defy us?" There was something eerie in the way he referred to himself in the plural.

Ven tried her best to project an air of meekness. "No, sir," she mumbled.

"We think you did," he barked.

The blows rained down again, harder this time, pummeling her chest with a dull agony. The men released her arms, and she fell flat on her face. Flashes of lightning exploded in her eyes. On her tongue, she was aware of the metallic, earthy soil, which reminded her of the taste of blood. She choked, unable to speak.

"Stubborn brute, why are you silent all of a sudden? Let us hear your sharp tongue once more," the captain said.

She closed her eyes. Her mind opened into a world that was filled with nothing but gray sky. The captain's voice rasped above her, like the relentless wind: "Another drifter on the way to town. Sooner or later, we'll find that runaway slave . . ."

Someone grabbed a handful of her hair. Ven struggled to her feet as she felt herself being dragged down the road.

Outside the community hall, an ancient banyan tree threw its shadow across the ground. The rich colors of harvest goods brightened the marketplace, an impressive testament to a successful farming season. Soybeans lay in mounds on the rectangular veranda, waiting to be divided among the landowners. Near the front entrance of the hall, ears of corn were strung high from one tree to another, drying in the sun. Beneath them, the massive courtyard was full of vehicles of all kinds — carts, wagons, horse-drawn carriages, and a dark sedan caked in brown mud.

In back of the redbrick hall, a dismal scene was on display. A desultory herd of oxen and cows chomped the few strands of limp grass that clung to the hard-baked soil under the dying sun, while their owners — hapless peasants arrested for curfew violations — sprawled silently inside. Above them, beyond the tall foliage, strong winds pulled forward masses of dark clouds. A storm was moving in.

In the great hall, the harvest moon banquet was winding to an end. Upon a dais that was furnished with a thick, soft carpet — the highest and most honored seat in the house — Master Long, his elderly father, and the guest of honor, Minister Chin Tang, sat cross-legged, sharing a pipe of opium and a burning oil lamp. Long's mouth drooped to the side, and from his throat escaped a damp snore, like the gurgling of a kettle.

To his right sprawled the old magistrate, draped in a formal outfit — a dark-blue silk tunic and a headdress of similar color. He was clutching a half-eaten cow's shank in his misshapen fingers. His lavender lips stretched almost to his earlobes as he tried to gnaw the meat off its bone.

The minister of religion was clothed in the fine satin of the Imperial City's official uniform, with its outer tunic of glossy purple-blue. A gloomy look shaded his face. Before him was a lacquered bowl heaped with grilled chicken, beef stew in curry sauce, and fried shrimp wrapped in rice papers, all of which appeared to be untasted.

Underneath the platform crouched a pack of dogs. Watching the bone in the magistrate's fingers, the animals panted and salivated, occasionally biting one another's ankles in frustration.

A few feet away from the dogs, a cluster of less important residents — the Cam Le Village authorities and senior citizens — sat around a tatami mat covered with dirty dishes, fish bones, and empty lobster shells. A black pipe, shiny from the addicts' greasy handprints, was being passed from one person to another. The droning sound of air churning atop the lantern was as steady as the buzzing of flies over the leftovers. Some of the men were waiting for their turn to partake of the pipe, while others leaned back and held the opium smoke in their lungs with mouthfuls of hot tea, served to them by orderlies.

Ven huddled in the far corner of the hall, lost among a crowd of a dozen bound prisoners. The smell of the stale food, mixed with the peasants' strong odor, numbed her mind. Her arms remained roped behind her back. The knot was so tight that she could no longer feel her fingers, except to sense that they had swollen like ten gigantic bamboo sprouts. Now and then a gust of wind rushed through the great door, and she shuddered.

Not far from her was a pack of scavengers — homeless, addicts, and orderlies — the dregs of Cam Le society who came to the banquet for leftover food and opium. Among them was the time-teller. He sat on the ground with his legs wide apart. Working with silent intensity, he scraped the burnt residue from the opening of a pipe with a crooked spoon. His face was flushed from the smoke he had inhaled; even his scars, normally grayish and distended, were now pink and oily with sweat.

Ven shifted her buttocks, searching for a more comfortable position. Her mind was awake, but her limbs felt as if they were trapped under heavy blocks of concrete. She straightened her cramped legs, and as she did so she knocked over a stack of dirty dishes someone had laid close by. Their loud crashing noise carried above the shrill clamor of the hall.

The sound woke Master Long. His eyes, clouded and bloodshot, turned in her direction. Soon the sharpness returned to them, accompanied by a sudden anger. He pounded his fist on the copper food tray, sending a vigorous vibration through the surrounding table-ware. The room became silent.

"Who — ?" His scream echoed through the hall, sounding like a long lowing of a cow. He staggered to stand up, but as one of his toes caught the hem of his tunic, he fell back.

The silence continued until Master Long's voice again rose. "Who broke the dishes?" He searched the hall until his eyes rested on the time-teller. "Big Con, my favorite lackey," he said. "You are sitting near the peasants. Surely you must know who that clumsy brute is. Lean over and give him a slap in the face for me."

The time-teller looked up. He licked a corner of his mouth, and Ven shuddered at the sight of his black, furry tongue. Everything about the man frightened her. He threw her a look that reminded her of the emptiness of a well. She sat frozen, watching him until he lowered his eyes and resumed his scraping.

Master Long's voice barked again, more impatiently this time. "Raise yourself, time-teller, and hit that miserable fool who broke the town's dishes. Teach him a lesson, Big Con. You must show us your strength, which we have already paid for with the free supper and rice wine."

The time-teller pushed himself to his feet. As he relaxed his fingers, the spoon slipped from his hand, making a hollow clatter when it hit the stone floor. Ven watched him move closer until his body filled her vision. She lifted her head, closed her eyes, and waited.

Then she heard his voice again for the first time after many years, as though he were speaking directly to her. "I will not hit her." His speech rasped, as if rusty from disuse.

"Why not, you weak-minded coward?"

She heard the movement of his body, and then the vast shadow receded. "I am not drunk enough to strike a bound woman," he said.

The guests exploded into savage laughter, mocking the time-teller's weakness with their guffaws.

"Shut your mouths, now. All of you, be silent!" shouted a reedy voice from the center of the dais.

Ven opened her eyes. Minister Chin Tang, with his chest pushed forward and hands folded into fists, stood on top of the platform. His small eyes bore a resemblance to those of the young lord her husband was holding prisoner at the ruined mansion. However, on this man's face, those eyes gleamed with authority.

"Say not a word about being prudent," said the minister in his purest accent. "Why should all of you bother with a lowly beggar when you are supposed to be searching for my son? I have exhausted my patience sitting here all morning and part of the afternoon, waiting for news about his return, while all you could do was eat, drink, smoke, ridicule, and judge things that do not concern you. If the mayor of this town is not disturbed by my son's absence, then let me summon my three sailors, who are waiting by the dock, and conduct my own search. I will not sit here, safe from harm, while my son's life may be in danger. Gentlemen, I bid you farewell. Enjoy your feast and do not expect any kindness in my annual report to the king's councilmen about your town."

The old magistrate leaned on his son's shoulder, struggling to stand up. Not until his eyes were at the same level with those of the irate minister did he speak. "Sir Chin," he said, "I assure you, your son is not forsaken. Right this instant a search is being conducted. My men are combing this village section by section, gathering every clue that might lead to his whereabouts. So far, no one has claimed to have seen or talked to him. Unless the young master left Cam Le this morning, sooner or later we will indeed find him. For the time being, I beg for more of your patience. What good would it do if you stir up a crisis among these ignorant villagers? Allow us, your true allies, to express our faithful friendship and service for a few more hours."

"You will never find him," Ven shouted. "I am the only soul in this place that knows where the young lord is."

The silence in the hall was deafening. Outside, the autumn earth seemed to smoke. Rain was coming. She shrank back to the floor, shutting her eyes. The old magistrate sat up. When she looked up again, her eyes locked glances with him.

"Who are you?" the minister asked, jumping down to the ground.

Ven's mind was flooded with panic. *What are you doing, Ven? You have taken one step too far on this road; there is no turning back now, except to face the consequences.* This might be the only way she could save Dan.

"Where is my son? Do you want to tell me where he is or should I beat the information out of you?" the minister cried as he rushed toward her, his robes rustling through the long room.

Ven felt him seize her shoulders. "No, no torture," she gasped. "It would not do you any good. I will not tell you under any circumstances, unless you give me your sacred promise that you will listen to my story and protect my family from all harm and grievance. Only you, as the king's minister, could provide a just ending to the harrowing tale that I am about to reveal to you. Your son is safe. It is us, the lowly slaves and beggars, who are in great danger."

Hearing her words, Magistrate Toan resumed his former position, half-sitting, half-lying on the carpet. But now his every muscle was taut, alert. Next to him, his son roused from his drowsy state.

"I swear to you my promise, deeply and sincerely," the minister said. "Tell me where to find my son, and I will recompense you to the best of my efforts. You speak as though you are a victim of great injustice, and from what I have seen in this town, I have reason to trust you. Just begin by telling me who you are. How can a lowly beggar speak so eloquently, even more so than many educated men in this place?"

The sincerity in his demeanor persuaded her to trust him. "I was the daughter of a poet," she said. "My father passed away when I was a young girl. Even though I did not have an opportunity to learn the proper vernacular language, I grew up among poets and writers and acquired a different type of education — the ability to express myself through speech. I confess, poverty was the main reason for my grandparents to send me to this town nine years ago, a slave-bride to the rich house of Master Nguyen. There in his cursed mansion, I witnessed a massacre." She jumped up from her sitting position, feeling warm tears on her cheeks. Looking at the old magistrate, she screamed to him, "Toan, do you know who I am? Can you guess it now, or do you want me to tell you my name?"

The old magistrate's hands were clutching at his tunic. He was as menacing as ever, and his looks were as scathing now as they had been nine years ago. He assumed a knowing smile and interrupted her with a shout.

"Sir Chin, I know exactly where your son is. Let us take you there this instant. Do not listen to that woman. She is a criminal who has, unfortunately, escaped the court's justice for several years. Guards, seize her at once."

The minister raised his hand. "Do not move. You can see for yourself that she is already immobile. I will not let you shut her up." He turned and said to her, more kindly this time, "Take me there now. We will use a carriage, and you can tell me every page of your life on the way. I promise that as long as you present me with the truth, I will keep you safe from your enemies."

She felt his hand reach into the cradle of her bound arm, and then her whole body was being lifted. The crowd parted, and she saw Master Long hurrying toward them. His jet-black hair fell over his glasses. His face wore the expression of one who has just encountered a ghost.

"All of you, go home," he said, addressing the hall. "Curfew is in effect from this moment on." To the minister, he said, "I am coming with you. My father will join us later, after he finishes taking care of certain business."

"That will not be necessary, Sir Long," Minister Chin said. "Follow us if you must, but I need to have some time alone with the prisoner. I am borrowing one of your carriages."

Master Long bowed and murmured, "As you wish, sir."

Ven stopped listening to his voice, stopped looking at his pale swollen face. Walking slowly, she let herself be guided out of the great hall and into the courtyard. The rain was here at last. Its singing echoed in the air and piped in the bushes, like sparrows chirping. The warm caress of the raindrops seemed to wash her anxiety away. The minister was next to her. She had nothing to be afraid of, now that she was under his protection.

Ven held her head high as the minister led her to a black-lacquered carriage and helped her into its richly cushioned interior. Its springs sagged as a coachman sprang to the driver's seat. Beneath her, she could feel its wheels begin to roll.

"Where is my son?" the minister asked her.

In a firm voice, she directed the coachman to take the main road and head east toward the haunted mansion.

chapter thirteen

The Heart of a Butterfly

For Dan Nguyen, the sight of the dark sedan coming down the long, straight road late that afternoon reignited all the disturbing sensations he remembered so well from his childhood: hiding in the mango tree, feeling the wind brush his body, and watching his father's head fly through space. On the highest mound of dirt, he stood alone, holding his knapsack as the rain soaked through his thin clothes like a waterfall. The roar of the car's engine — deep, sustained, and unyielding — vibrated in his ears over the hiss of the downpour. The vehicle's squat metallic form crawled along the muddy route like a giant dung beetle.

The prisoner behind him screamed. He, too, had seen the intruders.

Dan's blood drained from his face. His enemies were here at last, looking for him and the young lord. He rushed back to the weeping willow tree, where his prisoner was bound, writhing as if he were on fire. Dan took off his shirt and swung his knapsack over his bare shoulders. Once his hands were free, he gagged the prisoner, using his torn shirt.

"Now will you be quiet?" he cried.

Muffled sound continued to pulse from the other boy's throat. But Dan could see a flash of triumph on the young lord's flushed face implying that he was no longer afraid.

Dan sprang to the other side of the willow to untie the rope that was restraining his prisoner's hands. The sound of the car engine hemmed him in. He looked up. Before he could tug apart the stubborn knot, the car drove up to the mansion's main entrance. He and the young lord were standing on the ruin that had once been his family home. Four hundred feet ahead, across the empty veranda and the unkempt garden, the black granite gate was overgrown with thick, thorny underbrush. He watched the entrance glow in an eerie rectangular light, like the doorway to Hell, as it reflected the car's headlights and the fading sun. The unflinching glare made him feel small. He must find a place to hide. Without Ven and her limitless wisdom, he would not want to confront the enemy.

Finally pulling the knot free, Dan grabbed his prisoner's head in both his arms and crept along the ground, pulling the boy with him until they were behind a collapsed wall of the kitchen. To his surprise, the sedan remained in front of the gate, with its headlights trained on the main walkway.

He took cover near the earthen stove, which stood on three small piles of broken bricks about a foot high. Ven had used the wall to protect the stove from the wind when she cooked. Now it served as the only shield to hide Dan and the prisoner. Sprawled there in the mud on top of Bui, he listened. Above the purr of the vehicle's motor, he could hear another, more distinct sound: the fast galloping of horses that seemed to come from behind him. Dan turned around and saw two carriages racing down the rutted road that led to the back of his home. He recognized the coaches of the house of Toan.

Dan shrank into the earth in a paralysis of terror. He was surrounded, his escape blocked at both the front and back. Fear seemed to add new strength to his body. He rode on top of the other boy, using his body weight to press the young lord's scrawny trunk into the mud. He raised his eyes above the clay stove and spied the carriages, which were pulling up behind the taro bushes that marked the remains of the garden.

He looked at the first chariot and saw a figure outlined against the mysterious red satin screen that illuminated the vehicle's entrance. To his surprise, his wife's body came into view, hunched against the rain. He saw her stringy hair and tattered clothes. Her hands were tied behind her back, making her walk somewhat unsteady, like the shuffling gait of a drunk.

Following her was the young lord's father, Minister Chin Tang. His head was held high in spite of the downpour, and his dour visage, rising and falling behind the fence line, grew darker as they drew closer to the door. Twenty paces behind them was the second carriage. Master Long, glistening in a black trench coat, stepped out. He waddled through the puddles like a brood-hen. Four guards in uniform and the Toan family's coachman accompanied him, armed with metal clubs of various lengths and shapes, walking up the road toward the back entrance. The gravel from the street crunched under their booted feet.

Dan felt the young lord squirm beneath him. The bruise on the outer rim of his captive's eye was the color of a grape. Against the wet soil, his shaggy black hair was caked with the silt and ashes that had spilled from the stove. His jaws were opening and closing, chewing at the rag. Droplets sprayed each time he breathed, like a fish gasping for water.

The first person who walked through the gates of his mansion was Ven. She cocked her head to scan the ruin, searching for him, wet tufts of her hair wafting in the wind. He could see her eyes catch the light.

"Dan, where are you?" she called out. The garden returned her words in a disdainful pitch, like the echo of a temple bell. "Do not hide yourself and the young lord any longer. Come out and greet Minister Chin."

A gust of wind teased the trees, and their thick leaves cackled at her suggestion. Dan remained silent in the vanishing twilight.

"Please, Dan, hear my plea. I have related our story to the minister, all of it, including the dark deeds committed by our enemies. He promised he would not harm you. Come out from your hiding place and answer any questions he might have for you, not as a prisoner to a judge, but as a man to his compassionate friend."

He heard the minister's voice, full of authority, as he asked Ven, "Is this the exact spot where the crime was committed?"

"There was no crime, dear sir," came the voice of Master Long. "Nine years ago, the Cam Le Village indeed harbored a great secret. However, the stories that this peasant is relating to you are nothing but a bald-faced attempt to elicit your sympathy to an atrocious villain. The owner of this mansion was once a famous pirate, who was sentenced to death by the Court at Hue. He did not deserve your pity, not even the smallest drop. My father was merely an executioner, fulfilling his devoted duty to the Purple Forbidden City. He should not be blamed for his obedience to his country."

"Spare me your self-righteous speech," Ven spat. "Really, was it part of your devoted duty to burn down the condemned man's house, steal his fortune, and send troops to hunt for his surviving offspring? Did the death sentence include his entire family? Or did you take pleasure in beholding such punishment carried out at your command?"

"Where is my son?" He heard the minister's voice, now plaintive. "Bui, can you hear me?"

Upon hearing his name, the young master shook under Dan's weight. He watched the prisoner's face widen into a smile, as if he knew his captivity was all but ended. Deliberately, Bui winked his bruised eye at Dan.

Dan's eyes darted in every direction. The flashing sky, twisted tree trunks, green shrubbery, and the people in front of him, all melted into a blur as though they were figures in a watercolor and the rain was washing them away. In a daze, he dismounted the prisoner. His shoulder bumped against the brick wall, shooting a current of pain through him. The fear was gone, leaving him as hollow as the sky.

He sprang to his feet, pulling Bui up with him. His fingers closed around the young lord's throat. How easy it would be to end this life with just a simple twist of his hands. He retreated toward his once-stately house until his bare feet touched the rough concrete of the veranda. From there, he could observe both entrances. Bui shuffled along with him.

From behind the wall of leaves, the automobile's engine rose to a whine, followed by a loud crash. In the ruby light before him, he saw an explosion of squiggling vines, like the bursting of a water serpent's nest. The sealed gate split open, and the garden was bathed in brilliant brightness. He watched the ancient door lift off its hinges and dangle to the side as the sedan bounded forward. It crossed the white pathway and roared in his direction.

Dan wrapped his arm around the young lord's neck, elbow pointing outward. The boy fell back against Dan's bare chest, blinking away the rain in his eyes. From nearby, Ven ran toward him, her body swaying from side to side to maintain her balance. Behind her the men were closing in. Although their faces were in shadow, Dan could make out the metal rods gleaming in their hands.

"Stop!" he screamed, pushing his free arm forward, palm facing at the car. His head turned from side to side, observing the enemies in both directions. "Do not make another move, or I will break his neck." Bui moved feebly in his arm, fixing his eyes on his father.

"Who are you?" Minister Chin Tang asked.

Blinded by the headlamps, Dan closed his eyes. His wife replied for him. "That young man is my husband, son of Captain Tat Nguyen."

"Impossible," exclaimed Master Long.

"Let my son go," the minister said.

"No, I will not," Dan said. "Stay where you are. I do not trust your intentions, nor yours either," he said, pointing his finger at Ven. "Why are you bringing these intruders here to my parents' resting place? Did that devil Toan promise to spare your life in exchange for mine? Tell me now, announce my death sentence before they do."

Ven backed away. "You are mistaken, young Master. I am not betraying you. One thing I have resolved, and that is to stop at nothing to restore your liberty. The fact is that I have persuaded the minister to lend his empathy to our misfortune, and he is willing to search for an opportunity to free us from all charges. Please release the young lord at once, before you upset the court official further and turn him against us."

Dan glared at her, wide-eyed. "How could you do this without consulting me, Ven? It is a dangerous scheme. I am convinced that my plan to escape is far better than yours. At least that way, I will not be forced to hurt young Master Bui."

"You will never escape this place," the minister replied. "Not if you hurt my son. Do not blame your wife for bringing us here. I have shut down the festival, and the guards are searching the village. Sooner or later, with or without her help, they would be on their way to this mansion. Now, for the last time, let go of my son. Afterward, I will listen to your complaint because, truthfully, you have aroused my curiosity."

Above the churning of the trees and the quiet rumble of the car engine, Dan heard the galloping of yet another team of horses. The squeak and clatter of fast-turning wooden wheels accompanied their frantic gait. Night was falling in earnest now, and the sky was changing to the color of dust. He turned his eyes to the distant road, but darkness was quickly transforming it into a deep tunnel of shade within the sea of silhouetted corn tassels. A ball of fire was shaking and floating toward his house, as if searching for him.

The others followed his gaze and were quickly as transfixed as he was. Once the light came close enough, it resolved into a big torch that was propped next to the driver's seat above two sweat-lathered stallions.

Master Long stomped on the ground and cursed. Turning to his coachman, a short, bony, middle-aged man who had served his family for more than two decades, the mayor ordered, "Go and find out who just arrived. If you see my daughter, do not let her in — especially if she expresses her wishes to see Mouse."

The coachman bowed and withdrew.

On the white-brick pathway, the bumping and crackling sound coming from the sedan pulled Dan back to his surroundings. He tightened his hold on the prisoner. The car's front door swung open, and he saw the captain of the guards step from the driver's seat. Without a word, he unlocked the back door and looked inside.

A wrinkled and misshapen hand thrust from the murky compartment like the jagged hood of an excited cobra. It clasped the captain's hand and would not let go. Dan watched the old magistrate crawl out and shuffle forward with halting steps. One of his hands was concealed under the long skirt of his tunic. His milky eyes seemed to search the sky before they lit on Dan. Straightening, he pushed the captain away to proceed unassisted up the path. Tonight, Dan noticed, the old man was walking without his cane.

Before the veranda, the garden leveled out, creating a raised platform of grass. The old man stopped there with his back hunched and
his feet apart, like a toddler learning to stand for the first time. The
captain was behind him, holding a folded chair in one hand. With
the other he held a broad bamboo umbrella above his employer's
head. He shoved the chair into the soft earth and waited. The
umbrella, woven from tufted rush, deflected the raindrops with a
light tinkling sound. Toan lowered himself onto the seat. His eyes
never left Dan's face.

"Where is your mother?" he asked Dan, leaning forward. His
right hand was still clutching at his abdomen inside his long tunic.

Dan said nothing.

"You are here," Toan said. "That unsightly bride of yours is here.
Where is your mother?"

Minister Chin Tang took a step forward, facing the magistrate.
"Why must you insist on learning his mother's whereabouts, Sir
Toan?" he asked.

Magistrate Toan ignored him.

"The reason is quite simple," Dan interrupted. He looked calmly
at the minister, but his voice quivered with emotion. "He has been
looking for a map of buried treasure. You may not believe me, but
this man is a thief and a murderer."

The night crackled with a thousand hissing noises like the moans
of addicts whose opium was wearing off. Some of these sounds came
from the magistrate's throat. He threw another warning look at Dan.

"Oh!" the minister exclaimed. "This story is getting more interesting. If there really has been a crime, I will investigate it. Tell me more
about the treasure."

The old man laughed. "There is no treasure. Do not push me too
far, contemptible slave. You will regret it."

Dan took a deep breath and spoke quickly. "One half of the map
that led to the pirate's treasure was tattooed on my father's back."
As the memory of his parents' massacre seared his mind, he was unable to stop the words that flooded from his mouth. "It was this man
who flayed it off my father's body after he killed him. By gathering the rest of my family together, the magistrate wishes to find the
other half of the map." Turning to Toan, he cried, "What are you

going to do? Kill me? It is too late for you to intimidate me. I no longer fear you."

In a rage, the old man strove to stand up, but his strength failed him. He folded himself into the seat. For several seconds he crouched in his chair with his hands inside his tunic.

"How do you know so well what happened that day?" the magistrate finally asked.

Dan pointed toward the dark foliage that lined the edge of the yard. His prisoner seized the opportunity to wrench himself away and hurl himself toward his father. Dan paid him no attention. "I was on that mango branch," he said. "I saw what you did to my parents and their corpses."

A thin smile creased Magistrate Toan's gaunt face. He slapped his thigh, making a clapping sound, and then shook his head in disbelief. "What a miserable twist of fate," he said. "However, I would venture a guess that you are in possession of the map's second half." He paused, pointing at Dan's bare torso. "I see that you don't have it tattooed on your body, contrary to the story I was foolishly led to believe all these years. But tell me, where do you hide it, or should I consult that beggar wife of yours?"

"You would only be wasting your time, sir. The Nguyen family never shares its secrets with an outsider, including the in-laws," he said. For the first time, he realized his prisoner was no longer by his side. He spotted the short, dirty young lord cowering behind his father, chewing a fingernail. The rope that had bound him lay at his feet.

Dan held his face in his hands, realizing his mistake.

"I hope you are right," said Toan. "But somehow my instinct tells me different. Do not worry. I have plans for both of you, fates that are more gruesome than death. You might, perhaps, find yourself surrendering any information I have requested more willingly than you anticipate. Ah —"

"Enough, Sir Toan," Minister Chin snapped. "I did not expect you to be such a malevolent old demon. Just to think that this morning I still considered accepting your family's proposal of marriage. What a mistake that would have been! You can rest assured that I will take pride in pursuing this investigation until it reaches the Imperial

Court's attention. You will be reproached fairly for the sorrows you have inflicted upon these unfortunate souls. Stop now, or you will lose yourself forever."

Magistrate Toan gave a gloating laugh. As he raised his hand from under his tunic, a sharp report sounded somewhere between his fingers, followed by a trail of sparkles like the brilliant tail of a shooting star. Dan jolted to his feet. Somewhere in the dark near the back entrance, he heard a woman's voice, rising above the horses' frightened neighing.

The old man paused, tilted his head, and listened to the men yelling. Under the harsh glare of the dark sedan's headlights, the rusty pistol in his hand breathed thin traces of white smoke. Minister Chin did not move or speak, looking stonily at the magistrate. Then, like a tree falling, he toppled to the ground. His face sank into the wet grass, and his hands stretched out, embracing the earth. A few steps behind him stood his son, babbling in his shock. Streaks of precipitation ran down the teenager's face, blending with his tears.

"Now you shall disclose nothing," said Toan. "Foolish man, you should have remained quiet. You gave me no choice but to kill you. I do not need any more witnesses, except for a handful of my devoted servants. Who else wishes to stand in these lowly peasants' defense?" His eyes scanned the crowd.

Dan watched Bui collapse to his knees. His head rolled from left to right as if he were trying to wake from a bad dream. He touched the wine-colored bullet hole on his father's back and examined the blood that tainted his fingertips. He looked up with an expression of disbelief.

Across the veranda, looking back at him was the dark vacant eye of the gun muzzle. Bui gave a loud wail and clapped his hands together in front of his chest. His eyes rolled back in their sockets as he tried to avoid gazing at the gun. "No, please do not shoot." His teeth chattered with each word. "I cannot die. There is so much that I have not yet done. Please, sir! Have mercy on me and put that weapon away before —"

Another explosion, and the shooting star once again soared its magnificent streak across the yard. This time, the noise seemed to carry higher into the sky, and the dark branches above Dan came alive with the flapping of birds' wings. The young lord fell back against the soft bed of grass. From the tiny black dot that the bullet had torn into his forehead, blood trickled out, almost as dark as his hair. He lay on the cold ground, eyes wide open, forever trapped in an expression of disbelief. Faintly, his lower lip was still moving, but his words had died away.

"Elder Toan, you have not lost your excellent aim," remarked the captain of the guards.

The magistrate replied with a chortle.

Female voices again sounded from the back entrance. A torch glowed through the pitch-black space, disappearing now and again among the thick, droopy willow branches. Then came the hasty footsteps splashing across the rain-soaked ground, and the guards roused from their stupor. They turned to face the intruders, and the iron bars gleamed in their fists. Dan saw his wife step toward him. Her robust frame blocked him from the sinister old man. Yet his fiendish laughter was something she could never save him from.

"Quick, while they are not looking," she urged him. "Run and save yourself. That old devil will not kill you, not while he is still searching for the map. Leave this place while you can."

He shook his head. "I will not leave you behind, Ven."

As he worked to unfasten the tight knot on her wrists, a guard approached from behind him. The man lifted his metal club, preparing to swing at Dan. He heard his wife's loud screech. She lunged forward, and her shoulder shoved him from the soldier's path. She lowered her head and charged into the guard's chest. The collision knocked the man backward; his weapon slipped from his fingers. She fell on top of him. The knife that she had been concealing leapt out from inside her waistband. It lay a few steps away from her, its keen edge gleaming against the dark soil.

"Run, I tell you," she said. "I am only a peasant. Dead or alive, it is the earth that I belong to. You must not worry about me."

He took off at a run, his knapsack bobbling on his shoulders. Something flashed ahead. It was the same torch Dan had seen earlier. Now it tossed its bright head several times and charged toward him. The outlines of two women, clutching each other's arms, emerged at the single remaining step of his house. Dan recognized the familiar figures of Tai May and her mother. Seeing him, Lady Long screamed, her voice piercing the night like a police whistle. Behind them was the coachman. Long scratch marks, as if made by an animal's claws, cut along his right cheek.

"Ah, Mouse, thank Heaven, you are alive." Tai May fell into his embrace, panting and smiling. The torch wobbled in her hand. "I heard gunshots. The thought that something might have happened to you nearly made me die of fright."

Over his shoulder, she saw the approaching guards, and her smile faded. Their shiny weapons reflected the fire in her hand. She whirled her flame at them as though warding off a pack of wolves. "Get away," she shouted. "Leave him alone! I'll scorch your faces if you come nearer."

The men paused in their tracks. Lady Long picked up rocks and threw them at the confused soldiers.

"I must go," Dan said. "Farewell, Tai May."

"No," she said, seizing his hand. "Take me with you. My carriage is waiting by the entrance. I will not stand by and watch them kill you, Mouse."

"I cannot," he said, pulling away like a wild calf. "Stay away from me. You are the enemy's daughter. I must live to get revenge for my family." He saw her wince, so he stopped. His hands slipped off hers, and he experienced a painful sense of loss. *I will never kiss her again,* he thought. Then he started to run.

"No," she said, running to keep up with him. "I cannot give you up. Take my hand and let us go together, if you want to get out of this town alive." Dan slowed his pace. He was trying to be cruel to her, but his attempt failed miserably, for her compassion had melted the anger in his heart. He grabbed her hand and together they flew into the shadows of the old kitchen.

Shifting on his chair, the old magistrate called out to his guards, "Pay no mind to that foolish girl. Kill her if you will, but do not take that rascal's life. Not yet. I want him alive enough to speak."

Master Long shouted to the men with all of his might, "Stop your chasing this instant." He pointed his forefinger at his father. "If my daughter is harmed, I will personally strangle you with my bare hands. You may have banished my ill-fated wife into a world of insanity, stripped her of any last shred of confidence, but you will not destroy my daughter. No more! Look around you. The dead are everywhere. Because of you and your miserable thirst for fortune, I became a criminal. But it must end here."

The stunned magistrate shrank away from his son's outburst. Whirling, Master Long walked toward the sedan. The old man muttered, as though talking to himself, "She is just a girl! There will be plenty more children who could make a man happy. Why must you allow one child to ruin our plan?"

Before getting into the driver's seat, the mayor turned to his father. "Do not worry," he said. "I will bring that slave back. And as for my daughter, I shall take upon myself the responsibility of educating her from now on. She is mine, and you cannot take her away from me."

He hurled himself into the leather seat and slammed the door. As the car rumbled down the sandy hill, he felt each bump of the uneven ground under his feet. Through a break in the tree line the pasture opened up. He saw his daughter and the slave, their bodies close together, running. In her hand, the torch sputtered like a sick heart, dying yet refusing to relinquish its life.

>⊱—

Down the familiar path Dan ran, his arm around Tai May's waist, pulling her along. The rain had stopped, but the willow branches, sodden with water, whipped at their faces. He stumbled at times, aware of the steep shelf of rock cutting into his bare feet. Although she was small and delicate, she was able to keep up with him. About fifty yards ahead under a couple of torches, he sighted the back gate. Behind it stood a couple of men. They were smoking hand-rolled cigarettes and whispering together, guarding the three horse-drawn carriages thirty paces away.

Dan halted and fell into a crouch, pulling Tai May down next to him. The rough grass poked at his legs like crawling insects. "Not another step," he whispered, "or they will see us."

Behind them, the black car climbed the same path Dan and Tai May were on. Its grumble stirred the guards, and they turned to look in its direction.

"What should we do?" asked the girl. Somewhere in their flight, she had dropped her torch, and now they were in darkness.

Dan rose and searched the fence line, barely visible ahead. His eyes found a small breach in the hedge, where some stray animal had dug through. "Let's go," he hissed, and sprang up. Without looking back, he could hear her delicate panting a few steps behind. Straight into the steaming night, he guided her toward the opening in the fence. She crawled through first as he stretched the escape route wider with his body, forming a canopy over the ground. The hedge creaked above him, threatening to snap in half.

Once she was safely on the other side, he wiggled through the mud, slick as an eel. The last carriage was parked a short distance away. On the narrow lane, the silhouettes of the guards danced in front of the sedan's window. Their hands gestured in midair as they appeared to converse with the driver, whose car was too large to pass through the gate.

He grasped her arm and threaded the way down the sparsely covered slope that led to the road. Her white dress flapped like a frantic bird's wings, prompting the men to spin around. The dark sedan roared, retreated, and leaped forward. Its grille tore through the gate, ripping at the loose vines. The car burst into the lane with strands of greenery wrapped over the hood like a wreath. The two guards fell off the path into a shallow ditch nearby, as flakes of wood rained on them.

Dan hopped into the coachman's seat and stretched his hand down toward Lady May. Sweating, he waited as she struggled to mimic his jump. After a few unsuccessful tries, one of her feet found a post, which she used to propel herself higher. Dan caught her in his arms, feeling his knees buckle the instant her body was crushed against his. Gently, he deposited her on the bench, finding it difficult to peel himself away from her touch. The automobile turned its headlights in their direction. Its engine puffed at a standstill, and the driver honked his horn.

As Tai May settled into her seat, Dan seized the reins and urged the animals into motion. The horses strained against their harness under his expert guidance. The carriage rushed forward, then spun around. The U-turn nearly sent both of them flying off the ledge. The driver of the dark sedan poked his head out and yelled something. Dan looked back and recognized Master Long's face, but the coach was already too far away to hear him.

The clouds parted, and a sliver of the full moon drifted into view. Bars of silvery light slid across the bobbing heads of the horses. He could only distinguish a short section of the road ahead. Dan held the animals to a steady speed, relying on his familiarity with the surrounding cornfields. The sound of Master Long's car engine reverberated a short distance behind, and occasionally its headlights, like a pair of wayward suns, lit the side of his carriage.

"Where are we going, Mouse?"

He heard her timid voice, like the silver bells that hung from the stallions' necks. He turned to her and shouted over the bellow of the wind, "My name is not Mouse. It is Dan Nguyen."

Cornfields, more cornfields, and a banyan tree around the corner of an intersection moving backward at a furious speed — his mind played these images he knew so well. And then he heard her voice again, saying, "I know what your name is. Song told me."

The carriage was climbing the hill. A hundred yards ahead, he spied the town entrance. The two ancient wooden gates, bolted and studded with iron, were closed. Next to these opulently decorated portals was a small vent that was cut into the brick wall as a way for animals to enter or leave the village. The market, normally bustling with rich villagers in satin clothes and vendors hawking their wares, was now flooded with guards. Dan counted at least ten men, mounted on horseback, their backs erect. He gave the lead a quick yank, and his vehicle came to a stop. Behind him, the sedan stretched across the road, blocking his path.

He felt the warmth of Tai May as she snuggled near him, taking the reins. She looked at him, and he saw his own reflection in her eyes. Dan put his arms around her and hugged her, breathing her sweet smell, feeling her tears fall onto his shoulder. He tilted his head and kissed her cheeks. Her face was hot against his skin. She brushed her lips along the side of his neck. He gasped with surprise and excitement.

And then she said what he dreaded. "I cannot leave with you. If I do, my grandfather will never stop chasing us. We are young, inexperienced, and we have nothing."

He grabbed her shoulders. "We have each other. Is it not enough?"

"No, it is not," she said. "I will always be a reminder of what happened to your family, and how you want to destroy mine. Sooner or later your love for me will turn into hate, because I will be preventing you from carrying out your duty."

Dan pulled away from her. More than ever he was forced to face the painful truth of their doomed love. She touched his face with an unbearable tenderness. "I will help you escape," she said at last. "I have a plan."

Even during this last hour she was still thinking of his safety. He was struck by the thought that he might abandon his search for vengeance altogether, as long as he had her by his side. But in his mind the thought of Ven rose. Envisioning her fate in the hands of the magistrate, he stifled a sob. Tai May was right about his obligation: Blood can only be washed away by blood. For Ven, and for his family, he had no right to be happy. With a heavy heart he muttered, "It's the only way." Each word sounded like the mournful note of a dirge.

"When you leave this town," she said, "go to Hue City. It is a large place, and you can blend in with the crowd. No one can find you there."

"Without you, I can never be happy," he said.

With her mouth close to his ear she said through tears, "Climb inside the carriage and conceal yourself, and do not make any move until you hear my voice." She pressed a finger against his lips, preventing him from arguing. He did as he was told.

Not until he was inside the vehicle's compartment did she flick the leather rope, allowing the stallions to trot another twenty yards forward. With a nervous gesture, she stopped, tilted her head, and looked at the uniformed men.

Master Long waited inside his car. Now that the carriage had halted, he could look out the window and keep an eye on his daughter and the runaway slave. His legs astride, his arms raised, the mayor stretched in satisfaction. Any minute now, they would surrender. In truth, he could not imagine any possible escape for them, except perhaps another pointless chase if they cut across the field. Through the windshield he saw the outline of the carriage, immobile. Time trickled by. Fifteen minutes stretched into an eternity. He did not expect this stillness; it felt wrong. He wondered whether he should make the first move. The soldiers waited for his order.

"Not yet," he mumbled. "Not just yet . . ."

The wheels of the carriage rolled again on the pebbled road. The policemen started, and their horses pranced nervously. The soldiers' hands went to the left sides of their waistbands, grabbing the handles of the metal clubs. Resuming their flight, the runaways made a brusque turn and plunged into the cornfield. At the same moment, the guards kicked their boots into their mounts, causing them to bolt forward. Just as Master Long had envisioned, the chase entered a new phase of excitement. However, this time it involved an entire team of policemen.

Master Long slammed his fist against the steering wheel and cursed. It was late, and he yearned to capture the runaway so this night would soon be over. With a reluctant effort, he put the car into gear and stepped on the gas pedal, joining the pursuit after the last horseman.

In the cornfield, the fugitive carriage came to another unexpected halt. He heard his daughter's scream above the neighing of the frightened horses. Under the yellow darkness of the moon, he saw the back of her vehicle sink into the ground, as though the soft earth were swallowing its wheels. The horses' front legs, attached to the yoke, swam helplessly among the wilted corn plants. His anger turned to fear as he thought of his daughter's safety. He kicked open the door and sprang outside.

Brushing the men aside, he drew near the sinking carriage. Its door was ajar, but the inner compartment was empty. He found his daughter alone in the driver's seat; her hand clutched a small piece of cloth. Between her fingers, he could see an embroidered red rose, exquisite in its craftsmanship.

"Forgive me, Father," Tai May said. "Mouse isn't here anymore. I have set him free."

chapter fourteen

The Scarecrow

R un, young Master. You must not worry about me." Ven's words to her husband took the last of her breath, and she let her head drop back to the ground. She had fought the same battle for so long that she was exhausted. Painfully, she raised herself and saw Dan fleeing with the girl from the house of Toan. She had succeeded in giving him a chance to get away. Above, birds were shrieking inside the thick curtain of leaves.

The guard rose to his feet — a tall man in a disheveled brown uniform, his long hair and thick beard whipping about him in the windy night. Red-faced with anger, he swung his leg. Ven felt the toe of his boot crash into her torso, somewhere between her fifth and last ribs. For a moment, her vision blurred, but she did not wince. She fell back, gasping, with her face again smeared into the soil.

The guard placed his foot on her head, saying, "Magistrate Toan, give me permission to crush this she-devil's skull, sir."

The old man clasped his hands together, dropping the gun on his lap. "No, do not do so," he said. "Do not throw garbage out just because you have to clean up the house. You might find an opportunity to reuse it later." He paused, and then continued, "I remember the woman who uttered those very words to me, my mother."

Behind him, the captain of the guards exclaimed, "Truer words could not be said at a better time! The ancient one must have been a remarkable lady, possessed a great deal of wit and cleverness. You have inherited many of her superior traits."

"Indeed I have," the old man agreed. He fingered the gun on his knees, touching its copper barrel languorously. His rheumy eyes were clouded in gloomy reminiscence.

Then the murkiness vanished from his eyes. He dangled the gun before his face, leaning back against his chair. With a look of intense concentration, he fastened his eyes on Ven. "Bring that beast closer to me. It is time for me to reuse my trash. You all witnessed that beggar, in her insanity, kill the king's minister and his son." He signaled to the same guard, whose foot was still planted across her head, and continued, "And fetch her knife, too."

In the aftermath of the rain, the air was heavy with moist foreboding. The other three soldiers moved slowly across the veranda and whispered to one another. They paused while the longhaired guard bent down and grabbed a handful of Ven's mane. "Get up!" he shouted, and gave her head a mighty yank.

Ven cleared her throat and expelled a large spume of mud toward the old man. "Murderer!" she shouted. "You may be playing with justice, but your end is drawing near. I knew your plan, and I can read your evil thoughts. Do not expect my husband and me to take the blame for your murderous acts. I would die before I would admit to your accusation. As long as there is a single breath left in me, I will expose you."

The guard's fist slammed her left cheekbone and sent her swerving a half circle in space. She collapsed on her side, coughing a black tooth onto the ground. The old man bared a smile, stained brown from opium sediment and the viscous juice of betel nuts.

"Bravo," he cheered. "You speak eloquently, like a scholar. But now, prisoner, I must inform you that I will not satisfy your wish to be terminated from this earth. You will live, and your case will be tried in court, so that the massacre you committed can be punished, in the name of justice and for the respect due to the departed. Only then shall the judge determine your fate. I imagine your sentence would very likely be death by hanging."

Two guards drew closer. She felt her body being lifted up from the wide plot of ground. "I would rather die than be pushed around by you animals," she cried to the guards. In their hands, she was dragged across the yard until her face was inches away from the pointed tips of the magistrate's shoes. She stopped struggling. She wanted to stain his expensive sandals with her bloody spit, but the pain in her mouth made it impossible for her to pucker. She raised her head, wanting him to see the defiance in her. The old man took her kitchen knife from the longhaired guard. In his softest voice and most polite manner, he ordered his men, "Hold her still and pry her mouth open."

She was the only one who did not understand what he was planning. His men seemed to recognize his intention. She was pulled to her knees. One of the soldiers seized her bound wrists and held them as another grabbed the crown of her head. Captain Sai extended his left palm across the bridge of her nose and clutched her cheekbones. His other hand parted her lips, hooked his fingers over her lower teeth, and forced her jaw downward. She found herself locked in position with her mouth gaping open, waiting. The hinges of her jaw screamed in agony.

The magistrate rose and bolted forward. She could smell the musty odor of his clothes. His sparse eyebrows, with hairs as long and translucent as a cat's whiskers, shrouded his eyes. He inhaled, and Ven felt there was no air left between them. The knife gleamed in his hand.

Ven tried to back away, but her captors kept her planted on the ground. Her lips were stretched wide and her chin was wet with saliva. Wide-eyed, she watched the old man and realized for the first time what was about to happen. She screamed, only to find that her voice screeched to its highest note and dissolved. The recognition of her helplessness drove her to the brink of insanity. She listened to her mind shrieking, *Oh, Heaven, please let it happen quickly.*

The old man seized her tongue with his thumb and forefinger, which were wrapped inside a white handkerchief. She struggled to break away, whipping her head from side to side, but the soldiers tightened their hold. She looked in fright at her tongue, wedged inside the cotton fabric. The pain of her flesh jammed in the old man's fingers caused her eyes to swell with tears. She watched him give it a few quick pulls before he tightened his fingers and flexed his arm. With each tug, Ven felt her innards being hauled up through her throat. The blade flashed through the air above her.

"You will not die," he said to her. "But you shall hold your silence forever."

He sliced the blade into her. At first, she did not feel the pain; her mouth was already on fire. Blood splattered into her oral cavity like a flood pouring through a collapsing dam after a heavy rain. She gasped for air when the liquid rose up to her nose. She could hear the soldiers yelling in disgust as she fell to the ground, her open mouth making a strange, hurtful howl. Her feet dug the soil in uncontrollable spasms.

The magistrate stood before her, shrunken and wrinkled like a three-day-old carcass, with the blood-splattered handkerchief in his hand. She saw a gray morsel of flesh lying on the snowy fabric. His voice seemed to come from far away as he gave an order to the captain.

"Arrest this prisoner in the name of the law. Hang her against a post for the rest of this night so that she will not escape. I want you to inform the minister's sailors about his tragic end at your first meeting with them tomorrow morning."

"What should I tell them?" came the voice of Captain Sai.

"Tell them that you are deeply bewildered at what happened here tonight, that the minister and his son were gunned down by a lunatic who has been a runaway fugitive for the past nine years. And tell them that to carry out this arrest, I will personally escort the convict to the Purple Forbidden City. However, there is a slight probability that this female criminal may not survive the journey, since as you all may see, her mental illness causes her to commit excessive self-destructive behavior."

His voice faded. Somewhere above her, the harvest moon showed its sallow face beyond the thickets of leaves. Ven lay still and drifted into a world of silent agony, as the darkness slowly claimed her.

*I*t was past midnight when the time-teller made his first round along the main roads of the Cam Le Village. As usual, he was intoxicated. And as usual, the world seemed to dwindle down to one last staggering man and his creeping shadow. The quiet town seemed as isolated as a cemetery.

Big Con shook his head and cursed. His voice traveled through the hollow darkness, as if he were screaming into a bottomless well. No one responded to his vulgarity. Not a soul in the depth of night cared about his drunkenness, or the fact that he had missed his duty to announce the last two passages of time.

He lurched along, wobbling from one pothole to the next, not realizing where he was heading. The generous moon, hovering above the cornfields like the biggest lantern he had ever seen, held him spellbound with its ashen glow. Or perhaps the enormous opening that he was looking at was simply the sky's pulsating anus, spitting at him a rain of slippery, fatty, yellow excretion in its indifferent, wordless manner. He let his mind float, drawn toward the mesmerizing orb, while he held the wine bottle in his stiff fingers. The ground beneath him was littered with tiny frangipani flowers.

The stillness of his surroundings reminded Big Con of his time-telling obligation, and he reached into his pocket. Instead of the metal gong and its padded hammer, he found a handful of tobacco, mixed with the fuzz of his garments. He sniffed at the foreign object in his palm until his nose detected the distinctive, pungent smell of tar. The puckered scars on his face relaxed in a grin of satisfaction. He stuffed the wad under his upper lip, where the skin had sunken a little because of his missing incisor. Sometimes the taste and sensation of nicotine wedged inside the gap of his gum could summon up enough vigor to ignite in him the urge to fight.

Ahead, the house of Toan was still illuminated with glinting lanterns, a sight that stirred his curiosity. Weaving down the uneven road, he abandoned the hypnotic moon and focused instead on the enchanted dwelling before him. The intermittent shine filtering through the cracks of the mansion's gates sparkled on the raindrops that clung to the corn leaves.

Big Con thought he heard a human sound coming from somewhere behind the brick wall. However, it was not singing; nor was it talking. To him, the noise was more like the sigh of the wind rasping through trees and bushes on a drizzly day.

He stood at the gate a long time, looking at it, waiting for the ferocious dog to come charging from behind the lilac shrubbery to snarl its hot breath through the keyhole. Then he recalled that the damnable beast had been dead for several years now. His toes, curling from the memory of the sharp fangs and frothy spittle, kicked the wooden gate cautiously. It felt cold against his skin, but it swung back. The courtyard glistened from the afternoon's rain. There seemed to be no one inside. The sound he had just heard must have been the wind.

He wound his way through the partial opening. The light he saw came from the main living room. Against the bright parchment, Big Con perceived several shadows moving. He paused, tilted his head, and shut his eyes for a moment. The gob of tobacco in his mouth released a constant, bitter juice that teased his tongue.

He swallowed and drew a breath. The itch to fight burned in his mind, and he sauntered forward. Tonight, he would demand an assignment from that sinister magistrate. Maybe for a few silver pieces, he could harass some of Toan's current enemies.

To Big Con, picking a fight to get hard liquor was an old addiction, much like drinking and chewing tobacco. His hazy mind vaguely recalled a hot afternoon, a violent tussle with a mean dog, and then the promise of fifty silver coins, which had changed his position in this town from that of local pest to notorious killer-for-hire. That first verbal agreement was made here on the front porch of this mansion, when he had promised Toan he would eliminate a police officer.

He touched the depression on his upper lip, wincing at the unexpected surge of memory. It amazed him sometimes how his intoxicated brain could still retain such details after all these years. And yet he could not remember whether or not he had collected that money. The sudden recognition that he might have been swindled whirled up a wave of anger, like three evil spirits rushing through his body. *Ah, that slick old fossil!*

He paused on the hard pavement to throw his head back, unhinge his jaws, and tilt the bottle into his mouth. In his irritation, Con accidentally swallowed the tobacco leaves. "Not tonight!" he mumbled. "You are not going to cross me anymore. I have kept my end of the bargain. That Officer Dao was dead, was he not?"

No one argued with him, except for a slight moan that seemed to rise from inside his head. He closed his eyes and listened. The sound came again, relentless and agonizing. Fear tiptoed up his back, choking him. It was impossible. *Could the dead have come searching for revenge tonight?* He turned to flee the Toan property, slurring incoherent phrases as he ran. On his way out, before he could see the dark scarecrow hanging on a pole opposite the magistrate's house, he tripped and fell into its dangling body.

"I did not kill you, Officer Dao," he whined. "It was an accident."

The bottle slipped from his hand and rolled along the earthy embankment until it disappeared inside the field, leaving a trail of liquid. Big Con buried his face in his hands. The puffy scars were rough against his calloused fingers. His thoughts returned to that fateful day when he had gone looking for Dao, excited by the shiny silver pieces in the magistrate's hands. His mutilated face was still oozing blood when he reached his old enemy's home at the south end of town, behind the last rice field.

The officer he had encountered that late afternoon was no longer the fit, sinister policeman who had sentenced him to the endless torture of the prison plantation. The man he found was as taut and rotund as a watermelon.

Big Con had come up to the front door, looked inside with his red, drunken eyes, and bellowed out a curse upon Dao's three generations. His hand shook the neck of a broken bottle in the air. Its sharp edges were stained with his own blood.

He remembered watching the way the angry man stormed from his dining corner. In his hand he flaunted a well-polished ebony club.

Officer Dao knocked him down. Con emitted the deep bellow of a wounded cow, until the obese man kicked him in the face with the metal tips of his leather shoes. Con remembered spitting out his front tooth while grabbing one of the officer's legs.

Suddenly, a portion of the ruddy sky was blocked away from his vision, replaced by a mound of shuddering flesh. He pushed the mass off of himself and struggled to crawl away, but curiosity prompted him to look back. The policeman thrashed in the dirt next to his children's broken toys, clutching his chest. Blood drained from his face, turning it the color of young grass in early spring. The time-teller got to his feet and stood over the officer. It was his first and foremost unexpected triumph.

Since then he had become a new demon to the citizens of the Cam Le Village. Even though Dao had clearly died from a heart attack, Con's malignant aura became something people feared. As for him, the incident was buried deep inside his foggy mind, dulled by countless bottles of rice wine. However, from time to time, a villager would find him drunk and disheveled, sobbing and begging the gods for their forgiveness, just as he did now.

He touched the scarecrow's bare feet, banging his face against its toes. "Forgive me" was all he could say over and over again. As if in response, the dummy above him writhed feebly. In the calm of the night, he heard it moaning, and he realized with horror that the noise was not coming from inside his head. The bundle of rags resolved itself into a female shape. He could not tell if her hazy outline was a result of his tears, or if she was a vision. Gradually, he recognized her face. It was the beggar woman, dangling over him as if she had just descended from Heaven.

"— ep," she uttered in a voice like the keening of a desperate eagle looking for its young. Big Con noticed her black mouth, and his senses were overwhelmed with the tangy smell of blood. The beggar jerked against a wooden pole, tossing her head, and Con noticed the thick ropes that bound her. He fell backward, stunned. All at once, her body sagged forward, resuming the scarecrow position as if what the time-teller had just witnessed was nothing more than a hallucination.

He drew closer, touching her hair. The beggar responded with a slow upward twist of her head. He slid closer still; his fingers brushed past her hair and caressed her face. Like a cat rubbing against a piece of furniture, she pushed her head against his hand and tilted her face so that the moonlight could illuminate her open mouth. The darkness that was caked inside grew redder before him until it turned into a pool of blood. Some of it had coagulated and was affecting her breathing. He could hear the air rattle in her throat.

Without a word, he untied the ropes and received her in his arms. And when, after a long time, the whole world was melting away, and there was this sluggish, sullen woman against him, an excitement he had long forgotten slithered in, slowly at first. Then it burst through him, rousing every nerve in his body with a new rush of intoxication. With a hoarse cry, he pressed his burning face into her hair.

They walked across the fields, heading toward his hut. Her arm was wrapped over his shoulders while he clung to her waist, lifting her with every step. The alcohol seemed to have evaporated from his brain, and he no longer felt its influence on his limbs. He hesitated in confusion: what right had he to rescue a prisoner from the house of Toan? The question taunted him like a scornful parental voice, which he chose to ignore.

As they passed street after street, he held on to her body, feeling the soft and womanly curves, and his rough hand lingered. The bamboo forest circled them into its thickets. Big Con listened to the footsteps of the woman upon dried leaves, and he felt as though he had walked this road with her a thousand times before.

He took her to a small creek in the woods a short distance from his cabin. There, on a remote bank, they came to a thick bamboo floor he had built during the days when he was sober and needed to keep busy. Con laid the woman on her back. Her hair fell through the gaps of the platform, soaring along with the brook's current below. She looked at him with eyes filled with a silent despair that nearly brought him to tears. He understood that hopeless look, and there was nothing he could say to her.

Slowly, he unfastened her soiled blouse, unable to keep his fingers steady. After he peeled her tattered garments away, his hands glided across her skin, searching for the source of her bleeding. But her body showed no visible injury. Around them, the air was warm after the rain. The moon peeked through the broad branches and spied on the two of them. The beggar's anguished face was bathed in a light that turned her skin the color of ashes, yet she made no effort to push his hands away.

She lay before him, her head turned toward the water; his presence was beyond the range of her blinking vision. In this strange, awkward silence, she held her legs together, arms crossed shyly over her breasts. The time-teller took a deep breath, conscious only of the rise and fall of her chest. He was incapable of looking away. She, too, was trembling, as if anticipating a blow. She coughed, spitting some blood on the slick surface of the stand.

"Tell me, where are you hurt?" he asked her.

She turned to face him, but said nothing. Her mouth was open, like a hollow in a tree. A slight rattle seeped from it.

"You must show me your wound, so that I can help you. I see blood in your mouth, but I do not know where it comes from. Is it internal?"

She shook her head. Nothing in her eyes gave him a clue about her condition. Then she raised her hand and reached for his face. Big Con leaned closer. He felt her fingers touch the outer borders of his lips before they slipped inside. He was mystified by her fumbling gesture, until she caught hold of his tongue and yanked at it.

He peeled her hand away from his face. "Is it about your tongue?"

She nodded and opened her mouth wider.

"You cannot speak? Your tongue, and the blood —"

As if someone had just scalded him with a bucket of boiling water, he understood. "That old magistrate did this to you, did he not?" he shouted, and the sound of his own voice startled him.

Again, she nodded.

He took her hand and pressed it between his. She lay back with her eyes closed, peaceful. For a long time, they remained in each other's presence, listening to the night song of the brook, and the fresh vapor of springwater clung to their bodies.

"You stay," he said to her after a while. "You are safe now. Do not worry about that man any longer. I will be back with some herbs, and I will wash you. These scars have taught me many lessons about how to handle flesh wounds," he said, touching the crisscrossed marks on his face.

When he returned to the creek, he found her clothes lying crumpled in a corner of the bamboo stand. A few paces away in the silver stream, her bronze body steeped in the moonlight. She had taken a bath while waiting for him. Hearing his footsteps, she looked up and covered her body with her arms. As he stood by the bank holding a handful of sweet melilot buds, he saw her rise out of the stream, shimmering.

He turned into a statue, unable to believe the beauty in what he was seeing. Even her face seemed to have shed its usual plainness and glow with the sparkling, mystical world. He wondered if she liked him, and the thought sent a wave of panic through him. He watched her get dressed with the wonderment of a once-blind person seeing the sunset for the first time.

When she was done, he said to her, "I have found some herbs for you."

Warily, she took the yellow blossoms. There was little trace of blood left on her, only trails of fresh water trickling down her clean hair.

"You must chew them until they mix with your saliva —" He paused in the middle of his sentence, realizing the improbability of his suggestion. "Let me help you," he mumbled, stuffing his mouth with the herbs and avoiding her eyes.

Once the bitter medicine was crushed thoroughly, and his saliva became strong with its essence, he raised his eyes and looked wonderingly at her. The woman leaned forward with her mouth partly open. She found his hands and seized them. Big Con shut his narrow eyes, drew in a deep breath, and pressed his lips against hers. He felt her cool body, quivering as she pulled him closer to her breasts. The strength of the peasant woman was like strong wine, rekindling the fire in him. He tried to breathe; the forest swayed and his vision blurred. Just like two drops of water, they fused and became one.

As for Ven, she had found a sense of richness deep in her soul that was never there before. When she walked with ease into his cabin, she knew that she was finally home.

Part Three

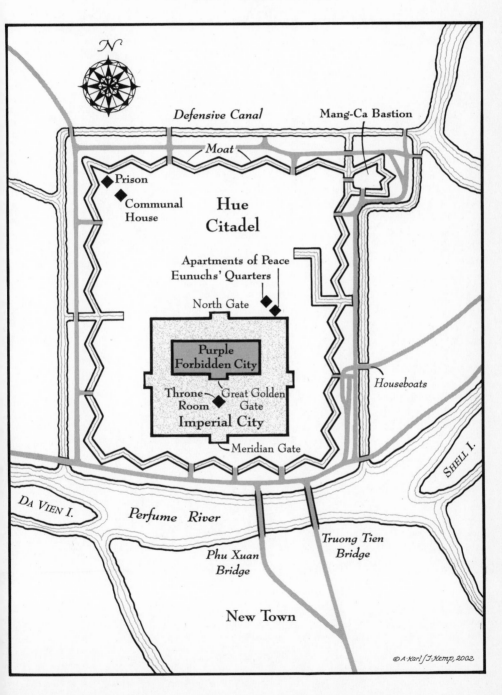

N

Defensive Canal

Mang-Ca Bastion

Moat

◆ Prison
◆ Communal
House

Hue
Citadel

Apartments of Peace
Eunuchs' Quarters

North Gate ◆◆

Purple
Forbidden City

Houseboats

Throne— ◆ Great Golden
Room   Gate

Imperial City

Meridian Gate

SHELL I.

DA VIEN I.

Perfume River

Phu Xuan
Bridge

Truong Tien
Bridge

New Town

© A. Karl / J. Kemp, 2002

chapter fifteen

The Apartments of Peace

L ady Chin was dying. In a tiny cell reserved exclusively for the terminally ill, the wife of the late Minister Chin Tang lay quietly among her pillows. As soon as her eyes opened to the blackness of the mosquito net above her bed, she wondered if this would be the night she would see her husband and son. If she remained perfectly still, she could savor the hope that they might come to her before morning. She did not bother to listen for their footsteps, for her mind was still sharp enough to understand that ghosts made no sound when they moved. Instead, she felt them reaching out as if they were fumbling for a tear in the fabric of her world, so that they could slip through.

For the past seven years since their deaths, she had spent most nights awake, drenched with a guilt that she alone could understand. But recently, in this confinement, she had begun to hear them. She knew she was near the end. So she clasped her hands above her heart, where her son, Bui, had laid his head and where she expected to receive him again. She knew that once the apparitions of her loved ones took shape in the darkness in front of her, it would be time to depart this place.

The night was fleeing. Through a round window on the wall to her right, the early sun sent its rosy rays over the stark branches of a dead oak tree. She could also glimpse a russet sky, like the healthy glow on a child's cheeks. With each day that passed, she felt herself lingering, like a guest that has outstayed her welcome. A rock the size of a grapefruit had grown in her womb, mounding under her abdomen like a fetus. She could hardly walk, for each step caused a searing pain that forced her to stoop and gasp.

Two weeks earlier, while attending her duties in the queen's bed-chamber among the other ladies-in-waiting, she had sprawled on the tiles, her face twisted in agony and her hands clutching her belly. A strange mist shrouded her eyes. The high ceiling above her had faded to a grayness like that of the silken counterpane that she had draped over her employer's lower body prior to the attack. Before she fainted, she remembered reaching toward the Queen Mother, Lady Thuc, who shrank away in her seat and cried out for the guards.

An imperial physician had rushed to her side. He discovered the tumor in her womb and advised that it had permanently enlarged the spleen, diseased the liver, and weakened the heart. There was no hope of recovery, since Death had also tinted the whites of her eyes a silvery shade of green. In the holy citadel, where she had lived most of her life, she had no immediate family. As for the distant rela-tives, none would agree to look after her. She was taken to the Apart-ments of Peace, one of the three royal buildings outside the walls of the Imperial Palace, where the women of the court spent their final days.

When she had first entered this rectangular room with its white-washed stucco walls, she was seized with a terror that had almost suf-focated her. The ceiling seemed so low that her initial impulse was to push it outward like a coffin's lid. She lay, alone and isolated, on the narrow cot, sometimes hearing the moans of unseen sufferers in adja-cent rooms. When the noise coalesced into a high-pitched siren inside her head, she screamed, begging the empty space for forgiveness. The thick walls responded only with the echoes of her lament.

Once her eyes became used to the lack of light, the starkness of her apartment seemed less intimidating. A bamboo bed was its only furniture. Exhausted from her outburst, she grew quiet, allowing herself to evaporate into the surroundings like a puddle in a desert. The gloominess began to suit her, as though it had always been a world she belonged to. She learned to acknowledge the existence of Death, its decaying miasma and its mystery.

Eventually she found a portal in her mind that she could cross whenever she liked. Through it she entered a white space where Death seemed peaceful and familiar; going there was like sailing down the Perfume River on a calm day. With each visit, she hoped to get closer to her ultimate destination. But each morning she would wake up on her bed, disoriented, relieved, and at the same time filled with disappointment.

Outside her window the cannon boomed, announcing the opening of the palace gates. Above its roar, she also heard drums and bells from the nearby pagoda. On the heels of the eager sunlight, an air of festivity crept into her vacant, orderly little bedchamber.

Lady Chin rolled to her side and looked at the wall. Beyond the usual sounds of the morning ritual procession, she was conscious of the steady, rhythmic pounding of hammers. Something was being built inside the Imperial Palace. Experience told her that the construction foretold some great event. She shut her eyes and forced herself to sleep.

Today, she was determined not to think of her husband and son. But still, in the cold stony room, with her back to the door and staring at the darkness, she could not help but wonder about them. To keep her mind clear, she longed for the company of the male servant who came once a day to bring her a meal. So far, he had been her only visitor. Custom dictated that once a lady entered the Apartments of Peace, she must go hungry as she waited for Death. This strict rule allowed no room for exception, and any servant found guilty of contravening it would be severely punished. How strange that anyone would challenge this tradition for her benefit.

The young man had first come to her during one of her fits of suffering. A large conical straw hat and wide chin strap covered most of his face, as though to keep his identity a secret. From the floor where she quivered on her hands and knees, groaning deep in her throat, he seemed to hover above her in a cloud of white light. She had looked into his large eyes and somehow found them reassuring, and his touch was gentle.

She did not fight when he bent down and lifted her in his arms. Then, floating in a gray void between being waking and sleeping, she was back in her bed. The servant's musky scent — the odor of young men — filled her nose. For a moment she was confused. Could that be her son returning from the grave to forgive her? As if to answer her, the man took off his hat.

A thin ray of light shining from under the door struck his face, but it provided her no clues. She could feel his hand withdraw from her neck as she relaxed onto her pillow. He fed her some warm broth, which filled her mouth with the bitter taste of herbal medicine. When he finished, Lady Chin remembered reaching out her arms, which protruded thin and angular from the long sleeves of her robe like two lotus buds. She wanted nothing more than to be held.

"Who are you?" she had asked him. "This is the house of peace. A surgeon sent me here, so that I can end my life with dignity. Why must you interfere? Were you sent by the Queen Mother?"

He shook his head.

"Then go, please," she told him. "I am in great pain. If the guards find you here, the two of us will be severely punished, and you may even face internment."

He reached for a warm cloth to wipe her mouth, but she pushed him away. She wondered if she had seen him in the palace kitchen, or in the old queen's parlor, or in the royal stables. She could hardly spit out her words. "If you are not acting on orders from Her Highness, then who gives you permission to be here? I have seen your face before, but I can't remember where."

Instead of answering, he vanished from her bedroom.

After that he came every day. Although they hardly spoke to each other, she was amazed at what joy she derived from seeing this quiet man, even for the short visit. More than the food he brought, she welcomed his presence, a warm contrast to the illusiveness of her other world.

><

S he woke to the sound of cautious footsteps on the stone pavement outside her room. The sickly dawn had matured into a robust afternoon.

She pushed to a sitting position and swept the mosquito net aside, then swung her feet to the floor. Even in the last days of her life, she must receive any visitors graciously, for she was a lady of superior station. The shy footfalls made her think of the servant. With her eyes closed, she could almost see him, treading nimbly along the old path that was covered with green moss. Then the door's hinges squeaked. When she opened her eyes, his tattered brown tunic was inside her apartment, together with a splash of sunlight. He cast a worried look at her; how honest his eyes were. She offered a weak smile.

The servant inched closer to her, his upper back bent to accommodate the low ceiling. He set a covered basket at her feet and stuttered a greeting.

"How y-you f-feeling, Aunty?" He seemed nervous.

She shook her head, reaching for a knot in her hair and trying to smooth it. The room took shape before her, cloudy at first, then with clearer details. She could see the weblike pattern of brown stains on the plaster, like clouds. The wall across her bedposts held an array of seven posters, depicting sketches of the criminal who was responsible for murdering her husband and son. She had asked the guards to post the bulletins there so she could look at them each day. The killer was a peasant woman. Her face was burned into Lady Chin's mind, especially the haunting eyes, which had now become an integral current of her river of memories. The fact that the murderer had never been caught was one of the few reasons she clung to life.

The servant knelt and placed his hands on her bony shoulders. A light breeze crept through the round window, ushering in a handful of wilted pear blossoms from the yard. She touched his face, feeling the strong cheekbones under his skin. The servant reacted with a jerk of his head, but he continued to hold her. Was it the poison from her pores that prompted him to flinch? Or was he hiding something from her?

"No need to be afraid of me, my dear son," she said.

He looked startled, and rather sad, as if she had said something outrageous. "I-I am not B-Bui, Aunty."

Her features contracted, and warm tears rolled down her cheeks. "I know you are not him," she said.

He turned his attention to the food. His skillful hands opened the bamboo kit and laid two bowls on the floor. She saw a couple of steamed chicken legs, thrusting from the white liquid. Part of her found the smell delicious, and this realization frightened her.

"No food, please," she wailed. "Why must you insist on feeding me? Don't you see that I am dying, and nothing on Earth can save me? All you are doing is strengthening me so that my suffering can last longer."

"Eat, please." He held the porcelain bowl in front of her, and she recognized the sweet odor of three-mooned rice — a special grain harvested after three lunar months and husked with the peasants' bare hands instead of machinery, so that each speck was as white as ivory and as soft as cotton. She turned her head away.

"Please have some food," he said again. She could hear the compassion in his voice.

"I am so scared, especially of your kindness," she said. "I don't know what you want from me. But during the past two weeks of your companionship, I have been filled with happiness. Why must you treat me with such tender care, which I clearly do not deserve? Young man, I beg you to let me go, because I cannot stand to be separated from my family any longer."

He nodded, placing the soup bowl in her hands. He gathered the rest of the food into the basket. With a light touch of his fingertips, he swept a strand of dark hair away from her cheek. He looked at her one last time, and then he was gone, slipping back to the world outside her tomb.

*L*ady Chin sat on the edge of the bed, the porcelain bowl in her lap forgotten. She gradually slouched back until the dish tilted and slid from her hands. She was not aware of the shattering noise it made against the cement floor, nor did she notice the soup that splattered on her legs. The pain returned to seize at her heart instead of her womb. Through the door overlooking the street she could see workers, their brown backs slick with perspiration, moving through the afternoon heat like cattle. With each step their flat soles slapped the burning soil, stirring up a cloud of dust that carried the vague aroma of roasted bamboo bark.

Her whole adult life had revolved around that smell. She thought of the forest behind the royal kitchen, the exclusive source of the special kind of bamboo used in carving chopsticks and toothpicks for the imperial family. She saw herself among the trees; the sun was high and the branches swayed. The delicate leaves cut her skin like sharp knives if she was not careful. She recalled the hours she had spent each day sitting by an earthen stove, inhaling the smell of burning bamboo, while the jumping sparks dotted the dark room like perfect stars.

Often the bamboo stem must be roasted prior to the making of utensils. Once touched by the flame, its texture became soft and malleable for a few minutes. During that time, it was easy to whittle with a knife. How many toothpicks had she carved in that kitchen? None of the other ladies-in-waiting had the delicacy and confidence for the job, and since each meal in the Imperial Palace required elaborate preparation, they all took part in the various cooking activities — except for her.

Squatting in front of the flame and blushing from the heat, she drew her hands along the bamboo. The slender, tapered end of the toothpick was used to remove food particles lodged between the teeth. At the other end, she cleaved the wood into a thousand splinterlike fibers and pounded them with a light hammer until they became soft. The Queen Mothers liked to use this end as a toothbrush after each meal.

She tossed in her seat. Why did her mind bother with this tidbit of memory during the last moments of her life? Was it a mechanism to mask the pain? She turned her mind inward. The snapshots of her past reminded her how monotonous her life had been. Those precious hours she had wasted in the frivolity of making toothpicks — oh, if she could have them back again!

"Lady Chin!"

A head, bald as her kneecap, poked inside her chamber. She recognized the narrow face, the round eyes without lashes, and the golden earrings that had once been blessed by a Tibetan monk. The sight of the man's homely features brought a smile to her face. It was Ung, her oldest and dearest friend from the private building across the yard — an elderly eunuch, once the royal chamberlain. Now he had been cast into a home outside the walls of the palace for men of his kind.

In 1914, during the reign of King Duy Tan, the employment of eunuchs had been officially eliminated. The remaining castrati were sent to the queen, or to serve in the royal harem until they died. When the eminent Lady Thuc was confirmed as Queen Mother, Lady Chin's son, Bui, must have been about nine years old. The servant was probably in his early sixties when he assumed his new duty at Khon Thai Tower, the lowly job of tending the royal chamber pot for the Queen Mother.

Like most of the ladies-in-waiting, Lady Chin never knew what he looked like, for he had kept out of sight. No one knew much about him, his name, or the life he had led; and no one cared. Each day, he wandered through the promenades. With his shaven head bowed down and his hands clapped together in front of his chest, he resembled a studious monk.

Every time she caught a glimpse of him, he vanished into the gardens or behind a building. She wondered if the flash of brown from his tunic had been a mere trick of the eyes, or if she had just encountered a ghost. For many years, that lonely image had been the only evidence of his existence to the rest of the denizens of the Forbidden City.

One morning, she had gotten up earlier than usual. It was the day her husband and their son were leaving the citadel to lead a Harvest

Moon Festival in a village called Cam Le. This journey was to combine an official obligation with a personal mission: her husband had indicated that the trip could be an opportunity to explore Bui's possible marriage to the daughter of the town's mayor.

The anticipation of happy news lifted her spirits, and Lady Chin decided to enjoy a break from her ordained duty. After returning home to bid her family good fortune on their trip, she would have time to join the emperor's third and fourth ranks of concubines in Doan Trang Tower for a table of mah-jongg. It had seemed perfect — an afternoon of continuous gambling, without a care in the world, and soon, to be acclaimed as a mother-in-law.

When the cannon's first boom announced the opening of the fortress, she was winding her way down a shaded path that separated two gardens, muttering to herself and touching her hair to smooth any tangles. "Bui," she was rehearsing in a whisper, "because I am a woman and because of my higher duty, I cannot go with you on this trip. You will forgive my absence, won't you?" The wooden boardwalk beneath her feet had creaked approvingly.

Out of nowhere a brown shadow crashed into her. Before she could feel the wetness rushing down the front of her embroidered silk shirt, the rancid smell of urine exploded in her face. Lady Chin paused, covering her mouth in shock. The thought of her ruined garment brought anger flooding through her. She wondered how long it would take to run back upstairs and change. She had no time. In front of her, the old eunuch was on his knees. A copper urn lay on its side a few feet away.

"Old devil," she shrilled. "Look at what you have done!"

His wrinkled face was hairless, and his eyes were teary. He shook his head and groaned, "Heavens, Heavens."

Lady Chin pulled herself away. The putrid odor followed her. "How could you be so clumsy?" she asked. "Are you blind, old man?"

"I am very sorry, madam," he said, clutching his hands together. "I did not mean to soil your beautiful blouse. Please do not raise your voice. If the Queen Mother heard about this, she would send me back into the eunuch's quarters. This job is all I have left. Please do not take it away from me."

Lady Chin felt her anger dissipate into pity for the old man and panic over her wasted time. Stamping her feet on the wooden walkway, she strode away from him as fast as she could.

Three days afterward, she had been seated at the mah-jongg table when two soldiers came from the Ministry of Religion and Ceremonies. They were escorting a strange old man who introduced himself as Magistrate Toan, head of the Cam Le Village and the grandfather of the would-be bride.

She recalled his wizened frame, which seemed much too diminutive for the oversized headdress and loose-fitting attire he wore. His deep-set eyes under a thick layer of cataracts had projected an air of frailty. Whenever she thought of how much her life had changed since that fateful morning, she had to think of this man and the news he brought. To her, he was the devil's own messenger.

Years later, she could still taste the rancid horror in her mouth as she listened to the old man's grating voice telling her how her husband and son had been killed by a deranged peasant woman in the wretched village. Nothing could have prepared her for the shock. She realized that she was alone on this earth.

To this day, the magistrate had yet to answer her question, "Where is the criminal that shot my husband and son?" He had stood there, unaffected by her tears. When he grabbed her hand to express his sympathy, she had fainted. The iciness of his bony fingers was too much for her to handle. It was as if she were touching the hand of Death.

When she came to, guilt and loneliness pecked at her like the beaks of a thousand vultures. She was back in her room inside the Purple Forbidden City, while in the ministers' section, the bodies of her husband and son were being prepared for burial. It was late in the day, and the rain had just ended. She remembered seeing a rainbow arching into her window, like a viaduct from the world of the dead. Her family must be on its other side. She reached, sure she could touch the magical bridge with her hand.

The old eunuch huddled in a corner of her apartment. As if she had just awoken from a deep sleep and found that her snore was the reason for her wakening, she understood. He, too, must have seen the rainbow.

"Do not worry," she said to him. "The dead are not coming for you. It is I that they want."

She watched his mouth move, but the answer seemed to come from inside her. *No, madam . . . please step off the windowsill. . . .* She reached for a handle in the open shutter. Her bare feet were teetering at the ledge. Six stories below, crawling among the red roofs decorated with ceramic dragons and phoenixes, the concrete pathway curved like the silver body of a python.

"Please, madam," he said. "Do not jump."

"Why are you here?" she asked, wanting him to disappear yet accepting his presence because she was terrified of being alone.

"I came to return your blouse." He showed her the silk garment, washed and folded in his unsteady hands. "A thousand apologies to you. I got the stains out, and now it is just like new. Would you care to inspect it?"

"That will not be necessary. You may go now."

"I do not want to leave you," he said, taking her hand. His voice was calm and reasonable. "Come inside. Your world is here. You might find it cold and lonely, but you are not ready for departure yet."

"You sexless old fool," she screamed. "What do you know about the way I feel? I have just lost my husband and my son."

He reached past her to close the shutter, and she heard his thin voice. "All I know is when the time comes, you will see them again."

And with that simple philosophy, Ung had saved her life. The next day, he accompanied her to the funeral. Although she never saw her loved ones' bodies in death, the wounds the old magistrate had described remained in her mind as ugly images, magnified with each passing day.

※

Recognizing Ung, Lady Chin straightened up on her bed. She noticed the porcelain shards on the floor but made no effort to push them aside. Through the open door, the sandstone path was scattered with dried leaves, and the sky was a faded color of violet. The eunuch frowned as he stood at the top of the three steps. His fleshy nose was directed upward, and he sniffed as if testing the odor of her room.

She waved, and the old man clutched at his chest in dismay.

"Dear Heavens," he cried. "You have terrorized my spirit out of its cage."

"What is it, Mr. Ung?" Lady Chin asked, cracking a thin smile. "Have you seen a ghost?" Seeing the humorless expression on his face, she eased back in her seat. "Please, catch your soul and come in."

"I have just returned from the Han Estuary," he said. His hands moved through the air in a melodramatic gesture. "I went there to greet His Majesty upon his return. Two weeks of preparation for one of the most elaborate ceremonies since the Minister Albert Sarraut's departure a few years ago. Do you recall that party, with all the color-ful carts and the streets covered in red rose petals and silver glitter? This fete, by far, has been even more beautiful, a triumph — Oh." He stopped as his eyes adjusted to the dimness, and his mouth dropped. "Dear gods, I have not seen you for two short weeks, but, madam, how you have changed. How could this happen?"

"Why are you here, Sir Ung?" she asked. "Do you bring a mes-sage from Lady Thuc?"

He shook his head. "No, there is no message. I have just learned of your illness from a source in the queen's palace. I came immediately after talking with the royal physicians. They want me to report on your condition, since it has been more than ten days —" He fell silent, scratching his shaven head.

Her hands smoothed the bedcovers. "Well, you can give them the bad news," she said. "I am still alive. Come back in a few days, and you shall find my dead body, ready for burial."

There was a crunch from under his feet, and the ex-chamberlain jumped back. "Did I break something?" Seeing the fragments of porcelain shards on the floor, he bent to pick them up. "Has someone been bringing food to you, madam?"

She nodded. "A servant from the kitchen! I assume he was sent by the Queen Mother, but I am not sure."

"It does not matter," Mr. Ung said. "You have not lost your appetite, which means that the golden stream in Heaven is not ready to sweep you away. I must go and deliver the news to the infirmary. But I will come back soon, to take you out of this dreadful place. You got better just in time to join the celebration, because the emperor has arrived in Hue this morning. Oh, what a day it is! Seven long years we have had no king, while His Majesty was being educated in France. But now he is back, and so are you, my dear friend."

He flung the door open. Lady Chin rose to her feet. "No, you will do no such thing. I am not getting better."

He paused, and the enthusiasm drained from his face. She staggered toward him, feeling a cyclone of dizziness swirl inside her head.

The eunuch rushed to her side. She clutched the bedpost. "No," she breathed. "I-I am not leaving. These are the apartments of peaceful souls. People come here to die."

"But it has been ten days!"

"I am dying, sir, an extremely slow process. I know my body better than any physician. I do not want to trouble you or anyone else. Certainly, you would not want to bring the evil aura of death into the Forbidden City on this happy day, would you?"

The eunuch said nothing.

"Ah, the emperor has returned," she said, changing the subject. "That explains the thumping noises of construction I have heard all week. Tell me, has His Majesty's appearance changed much after all the years he lived in France?"

The eunuch took a seat beside her. "No one at the palace has had the blessing to catch a glimpse of the imperial countenance since he assumed the throne in 1925. His Majesty has grown quite large. In the royal tunic and golden headdress, he was towering and impressive like a dragon. We rode the twenty-mile train ride from Han Estuary to Hue in a heavy rain and then changed to a private automobile at the station."

"Were you chosen as part of the king's reception committee?" Lady Chin asked.

"By no means," he said. "I am just a curious old servant who was fortunate enough to blend in with no objection."

She smiled. "You are a cunning man. This gossip will ensure your popularity among the ladies of the court. But tell me first. What happened next?"

Ung beamed like a child. "From there, over the mountain to the citadel, ten miles of multicolored fanions fluttered in the wind to mark the route that our emperor would be traveling. People were everywhere. In spite of the downpour, the Vietnamese, mostly students and teachers, bowed to the ground anticipating the sight of our emperor, while the French huddled under their umbrellas and watched the spectacle. Nobody spoke or cheered like in the old days, only the sound of a cannon split the air. But the king decided to take a shortcut in his automobile, slipping away from the crowd the moment he disembarked the train.

"Outside the Imperial Palace, on the entrance square, parasols rose above a sea of heads, forming a new sky. A throne was waiting for the king on the wet ground. Soldiers presented arms while an orchestra played the French national anthem. His Royal Highness stepped out of his vehicle, turned to the foreign flag, and made the five ritual prostrations, much to the dismay of his people. Only then did he assume the sacred Throne of the Son of Heaven. Governor General Varennes made a formal speech in which he expressed France's wishes for a period of peace and happiness. The cannons fired again to conclude the ceremony. His Majesty came down from the throne and was taken in a palanquin inside the Forbidden City."

Lady Chin listened with shining eyes, then remarked, "By bowing to the French flag, the emperor expressed his allegiance to the foreigners, which would surely offend the Vietnamese patriots. You and I must be grateful that we have nothing to do with this moment in history. Thank the gods, Sir Ung, that your life is now an idle one. Just imagine how busy you would be if you were the chamberlain for the young king."

"It is a road my ancestors have chosen for me," he answered. "My duty is to serve in the palace to my last breath."

"Yes, but I doubt that His Majesty would appreciate the loyalty of an old eunuch after many years of living in France and learning the ways of a Frenchman."

She watched the muscles around his mouth sag as if he were deeply hurt by her words. "That is why I was sent to spend my twilight days alone in the eunuchs' quarters," he said. "If we examine our lives closely, we are not too different from each other, madam. But there is one thing that separates me from you. Even though I am waiting to meet Death, it cannot stop me from living."

She covered her mouth in her habitual way of suppressing her emotions.

"I miss our friendship, Lady Chin." The eunuch's voice was soaked in sadness. "If I should ever be in a similar predicament, I would expect your warm companionship until the end. Please let me be your escort for this evening's fete."

"I thank you for your kind speech," she whispered, covering her face. "It is too late for me to leave this place." She raised a finger as if to stop him from interrupting. "But it would be a great honor if you would tolerate my company tonight. I have been longing for a stroll and some fresh air. It is time for us to spy on our new king and gossip together."

"Well said!" Ung exclaimed. "It is a first step. What should I do? Where should I go?" He hugged himself with delight. "It does not matter. Wait for me, and I shall come back."

With a chuckle, he flung himself out the door. Soon his outline was scarcely distinguishable in the garden amid the evening fog. Lady Chin wiped her eyes with the front of her blouse and fell back against her pillows. In her heart, she already knew that the dead would not come to her tonight.

chapter sixteen

The Ballroom

S hortly before sunset, the eunuch returned. A few steps behind him marched four male servants from the royal stables. A wooden palanquin, shaped like an armchair and suspended from stout bamboo poles, creaked on the men's shoulders.

During the time the former chamberlain was gone, Lady Chin had managed to step outside her apartment to wait for him on the steps. Sometime in the afternoon, a heavy rain had come. The tamarind tree dripped water like a rusty cask, and the moist air was heavy and cool.

Ung had changed into a black satin robe embroidered in white with ancient characters, front and back. The stark colors of his tunic, its long graduated panels, and the way he swayed his hips when he moved made her smile.

Bubbling with excitement, he slid his hands under her arms and lifted her, at the same time shouting for the men to lower their conveyance. She strove to move forward, but her feet merely dragged against the ground. Once inside, Lady Chin lay back against the soft cushions of the chair, aware of her grubby appearance. In her two weeks inside the Apartments of Peace, she had molted like a snake.

The dead skin that clung onto her garments danced in the twilight like drowsy moths.

They started down the street and in no time were swept into a mass of spectators and palace officials. Ahead, a group of Buddhist monks dressed in saffron robes sounded intricate rhythms on gongs made of tortoiseshell. Their chanting rose above the boisterousness of the crowd. Tall men with curly hair and wild eyes chattered in French with their equally towering women, whose low-cut décolleté accentuated their generous cleavage. They responded with clattering laughter. Dogs howled, roosters crowed.

The deep pain was gone; now all she felt was a tingling sensation. It seemed to her that the tumor was tickling its fingers against the wall of her womb — an entity waiting to burst out. Merriment resounded in her ears, as if everyone were laughing with their mouths open. Nothing on Earth could dim the excitement of this evening's welcoming reception inside the king's chamber.

Through the throng, Lady Chin could see the rough stone wall of the Imperial Palace, also known as the Golden City. Her quarters in the Apartments of Peace stood on the northeast corner of the fortress, outside the confines of this hub of royal activity. On the opposite side was the Golden City's main entrance, the majestic Meridian Gate. To enter, they would follow a pathway teeming with carriages, pedestrians, and other palanquins along the city's border. That evening, to honor the emperor, the royal soldiers who guarded this enclave had been instructed to leave its doors open until midnight, as the festivities would continue until the morning.

"Come," the eunuch said to the lead porters of her conveyance. His hand rose high, showing the soldiers the two ivory emblems that bore the king's seal — the royal passes that would allow them to enter the inner sanctum.

Lady Chin looked up. The road before her widened into a limestone court. On both sides stretched rows of redbrick balustrades, decorated with carved fretwork and adorned with torches in the shape of lotus blossoms. In the background, the Meridian Gate's mass blended into the night.

Every time she entered the vaulted corridor beneath the gate, she felt the air become balmy and perfumed with sandalwood smoke.

The structure was built from large blocks of blue granite, reaching twenty feet in height. On either side spread out the two annexes.

Like an enormous turtle bearing a castle on its back, the Meridian Gate was topped by the Tower of Five Phoenixes. Its golden roofs, ornamented with carved dragons and pointed tips, crowned a circle of five buildings. All were connected by a labyrinth of open and closed galleries. The large front room, facing the courtyard, commanded a view of the surrounding mountains and villages. There, the emperor sat enthroned during important occasions.

Above the royal chamber was a large hall, covered with elegant copper plaques and reserved for the ladies of the palace. Lady Chin recalled a secret staircase in the back that led to it. From behind a finely carved grille, the ladies could watch without being watched.

She closed her eyes and allowed her senses to absorb the surrounding revelry. She thought of the tinkles of laughter that had echoed down the hallway, and the lingering taste of sweet rice wine. It had been a long time since she had been part of such festivities, but the impressions in her mind were still vivid.

She opened her eyes as the porters descended a long bridge. The faint lotus fragrance wafted through the air, and the view opened before her — the shimmering landscape of the Golden City, which in turn enclosed the Purple Forbidden City.

She gasped. In the deepening evening, the Imperial Palace was aglow with thousands of light bulbs, sparkling in hues from pastel pink to gold to purple. Here and there, she could distinguish glittering candlelight and illuminated lanterns, mere pinpricks of light in comparison to the splendor and power of electricity. This was the first time the palace had been lit by electrical current, installed in honor of the king's return.

Over a vast area outside the palace, landscapers had built a royal golf course. Green grass, trees, and shrubs were brought in, and artificial ponds and barren sand fields were now being added, the eunuch explained. Nearby, a stable housed the latest in modern automobiles. Her entire life, she thought, she had known this place as well as she knew her own countenance. Yet so much had changed in the past few weeks, she could hardly recognize the face she saw in the mirror, let alone the sights around her.

At the entrance to the Purple Forbidden City, the heart of the citadel, where the royal family lived, Lady Chin and her escorts were stopped by a troop of soldiers. The porters could proceed no farther. Here, outside of the Great Golden Gate, sat a red-lacquered and gilded altar bearing the traditional five offerings to the Buddha in water, incense, flowers, rice, and candles, along with His Majesty's ancestral tablets and other objects of worship. Lady Chin and Ung joined the guests performing the five ritual prostrations at the altar, while the non-Buddhist French and the younger Vietnamese mandarins left their cars in a field behind the Hall of Supreme Harmony and simply strode inside.

Lady Chin reflected that since the young king had gone to his boarding school in France, the Purple Forbidden City — perhaps the whole citadel — had begun to fall apart. Although many mandarins held on to the ancient traditions, the Court at Hue was overrun by Frenchmen. Most of the older officials had left their positions and joined revolutionary troops, such as the Indochinese Communist party led by the socialist Ho Chi Minh. Rebellions fomented in many regions in spite of the severe consequences — punishment by guillotine. The regions outside of Hue were beset with thieves, robbers, whores, and other malefactors. Every time a nobleman abandoned the safety of the citadel, he, like her husband and son, risked his life.

Lady Chin and Ung watched hordes of foreigners walk past the place of worship, ignorant of what it meant. She wondered how a young emperor who had spent his adolescence in a far-off land and was not attuned to the politics of the Royal Court could prepare to govern a crippled system such as this. She was far from educated, but it seemed to her that the way her glorious past had been interrupted by the murders of her husband and son was a microcosm of what was happening to her country.

Crossing into the inner palace, she had to cling to Mr. Ung for support, lest the arriving guests knock her down in their rush. The King's Chamber, the first building behind the Great Golden Gate, was a place that only a four-hundred-year tradition of architecture could have constructed. Multicolored lights led the guests across a rectangular esplanade and into a colossal hall.

On either side of the hall's entrance, glass partitions revealed a pair of bronze lions — the gatekeepers, side by side in their crouching stance. The intricate carving that made up their pensive features represented the passionate art of a bygone era.

The ballroom was slowly filling up. The traditionalists were clad in colorful silk ceremonial robes with headdresses, cummerbunds, and boots. The colors of their gowns denoted their station and rank in the court. Sky-blue royal robes embroidered with a large dragon were for the highest ranking, mandarins of the second tier wore orange jade, and the third rank sported green jade. Lower-ranking courtiers were not allowed to enter the main ballroom. They twirled and mingled in the front hall with men in suits and ties and women in long, slinky dresses. The royal family was also here, but presumably inside and on the top dais.

Lady Chin found herself awestruck by the display. The blazing lights reflected off the gold in the walls to spin kaleidoscopic images before her dazzled eyes, while the loud foreign music made her knees weak. Being a lady-in-waiting and accompanied by a eunuch, she knew that she could gain access to almost every room in the palace. The armed guards assumed that she was here on behalf of the Queen Mother. Her ivory pass and the blue of her uniform put her in a category far above the other courtiers and mandarins.

But that knowledge did not make her feel any better.

Lady Chin searched for an empty space to stand in the crowded hall. Without looking back, she was aware of Ung's presence, his warm body supporting her. She could barely hear his voice, even though he seemed to be shouting over the music.

"We must go toward the back and reserve a private room behind the bamboo partition, so that you can be comfortable watching the festivities away from the crowd. But I warn you, you will not leave until we catch at least a sight of His Majesty."

"Would you lead the way, then?" she asked, grabbing his arm.

*T*hey walked through a series of corridors that wrapped around the ballroom in the form of dragon's claws clutching a jade ball. She could see a portion of the sky above the walled garden; the yellow moon, sallow compared to the brilliant light on Earth, floated over a hedge of tall areca palm trees. The apartments neighboring the King's Chamber radiated the heat of the electric lights. Around her, the odors of perfumes and exotic cooking competed with the evil-smelling fumes of cigarette smoke, gasoline, and burnt gunpowder from the firecrackers.

Never had the Imperial Palace seemed so chaotic, so contemporary, and so congested. Even with gentle breezes drifting now and then from the Ngu Binh Mountain, her lungs were starved for air. A middle-aged Frenchwoman with marcelled hair and a powdered face drew in a mouthful of smoke from the tip of her long ivory cigarette holder. She looked incredulously at Lady Chin and the eunuch as they walked by. They ventured up to the second floor. A few hallways guarded by the palace soldiers led them into a private rectangular box, which was furnished with a row of armchairs.

Lady Chin strained to keep up with the old man. Her strength was ebbing, but she was not about to collapse inside this sanctuary. If she expired here, her death would be seen as a wicked omen for the royal family, whom she had served faithfully over a thirty-year span of her life. She would not want to cast such a shadow over them.

She sat. Her chest hurt. Her knees wobbled. A bitter, burning fluid rose to the back of her throat; still, she began to relax in this safe surrounding. From this booth she could spy on everyone in the ballroom without feeling like a small duck that was about to be crushed by the overzealous dancing feet of the guests.

"Well," the eunuch said to her once they settled on their seats, "what do you think of all this?"

She swallowed the acidic fluid. "It strikes me suddenly that I have become too old to appreciate the flood of Western culture. The world has changed so rapidly. There was a time I could smell the sweet smoke of incense and opium anywhere in the fortress, but that has long passed. I have only sympathy for the two Queen Mothers, who no doubt must have suffered a great deal with these changes, especially at their age."

"Shush! Shush!" said the old eunuch, pointing to the window. From a raised platform at the end of the hall, partially obscured behind a series of bamboo screens, the recognizable shape of her employer, Lady Thuc, came into view. The emperor's mother, Queen Huu Thi, and two other ladies were accompanying her in a game of mah-jongg. Their shimmering, wide-sleeved robes matched the gold in the furniture.

The emperor sat on a throne a few feet away from his mother. He had grown tremendously from the mental picture she had of him: a tiny boy in a dark school uniform and white knee-length socks. The new king Bao Dai was a handsome young man of nineteen, dressed in a gray Western suit. His hands, unlike those of his father, King Khai Dinh, were free of jewelry. His short crop of dark hair was combed back with pomade, and his full lips bloomed with the vigor of youth.

"How handsome His Majesty is," she said, studying him. "However, he is not what I envisioned as royalty."

"All I can say," the old man replied in a hushed voice, "is that the emperor is the new image this country so desperately needs. But look over there," he said, pointing at a stout stranger in a single-breasted blue jacket with a thin, carefully trimmed mustache that ridged his upper lip. Next to him was the same Frenchwoman she had seen earlier outside the ballroom, with the powdered face and soft, wavy hair. "That couple is Madam and Monsieur Charles, the ex-ambassador."

"His Majesty's adoptive parents," she added. She had heard their names mentioned repeatedly during her long years of serving the Queen Mother.

"Indeed. In Paris, they have an elegant building on Bourdonnais Street, where His Majesty has spent the past ten years learning political science —"

"At le Lycée Condorcet puis sciences politiques," she interrupted.

The old man raised an eyebrow. "How do you know its name, madam?"

"That was the very school my husband and I planned for Bui to enroll in, once he passed their admittance examination. We were planning a career for him in politics."

A wave of grief brought along the never-ending realization of her loss. What had she done in all the years they had been gone? How did she get here, unclean and disheveled like a discarded rag? She struggled for air, feeling as though she were drowning amidst the strange music. She was swept by nausea as she thought of her son.

This was the place where her destiny had taken its tragic turn. There, on the front steps of the palace, her husband had notified her of the proposed union between their Bui and the daughter of the mayor of Cam Le. And there, a few days later, Magistrate Toan, the angel of death, had come to deliver the news of her family's last days on Earth.

She thought of the young girl who might have been her daughter-in-law if only fate had not been so cruel. It gave her a bittersweet pleasure to contemplate what her son's future could have been. During the years when she was still in good health, Lady Chin had tried to attend as many opera concerts as she could to spy on one particular dancer. Her friend the eunuch had informed her that this was Magistrate Toan's only granddaughter, the girl her son might have married. In the wake of the scandal surrounding the death of her son, the girl's family sought to restore its honor by giving her to the palace. She was her son's widow before she was even betrothed to him. Because of the tragedy, no proper suitor would ever consider asking for her hand in marriage again.

To Lady Chin, the fact that Magistrate Toan had sent his only grandchild to the palace seemed strange. She sensed that more dark deeds were hidden behind the deaths of her husband and son. This girl might have held the key to her unanswered questions. She wanted to believe that Bui's last days had been joyous, but the expression of sadness on the dancer's face troubled her. She wondered if the loss of Bui's life had caused this young concubine to lose all happiness in herself and enter this chaste existence in order to venerate him.

Lady Chin became obsessed with the girl. One night after a performance, she approached the dancer, summoning all of her courage. When their eyes locked, she fought the urge to flee. After the grace of a lady returned to her, she pushed a proud chin forward and said, "I am Bui's mother. I want you to tell me everything you know about my son's last days." Her voice broke into a sob. "I want to know how he died."

The dancer cried out as if she had seen a ghost. "Leave me alone," she wailed. "I am not the reason for your losses. I have vowed never to speak of that incident for as long as I live. Please do not ask me to relive the horror of that night." She ran off into her dressing room. After that brief encounter, they never met again. Lady Chin could only watch her from a distance. The girl's singing had grown more distressed with time, like the cries of a wounded nightingale.

Beside her, the eunuch had resumed the conversation, but now his voice seemed a thousand miles away.

"I assure you, madam, for you, being a mother, would understand. These foreigners have many plans for our young king, including a secret engagement that is about to be announced this evening."

Her head, which rested against the railing of the mezzanine, felt like a sack of stones. The emperor got up from his throne and stood over his grandmother's shoulder, studying her mah-jongg tiles. "How on Earth did you learn this information, Mr. Ung?" Lady Chin asked.

"We eunuchs have ways to gather intelligence," he said, "but you and I are having a confidential conversation that should not be heard by anyone else. Also, the rapid development of journalism in Da Nang has opened my eyes to the world beyond our citadel. There are many facts about the emperor that we, the ultraconservatives inside this closed fortress, are not aware of. The French would like to see the royal family lie around and smoke opium while they run the country.

"This morning, while waiting for King Bao Dai at the Da Nang Harbor, I read an article in the *Nam Phong* newspaper. It reported that a romantic encounter between our lord and Mademoiselle Mariette Jeanne Lan Thi Nguyen flourished into a liaison while they were onboard the *D'Artagnan* for their return trip to Vietnam. They left the Marseille port and drifted across the Pacific Ocean, which took several months at sea. During this time, they met each other in an incident that was carefully orchestrated by His Majesty's guardians. She is a Catholic who has just finished her baccalaureate at a convent in Paris, la Couvent des Oiseaux, run by the nuns of Saint Augustine.

"Also, in the same article, it said that the French government has eagerly approved this relationship and viewed it as a positive step for the young emperor, a union that would help improve his image. But in my opinion, the conflict between the two cultures, Vietnam and France, may have unforeseen repercussions on politics."

"What do you mean?"

"Well, madam, the Vietnamese people were hoping that our new king would abolish the French influences from Vietnam. However, it does not seem likely. A young boy is sent off to France, raised by a

French ambassador to think and behave like a Frenchman. Do you think he would rebel against a culture that he was made a part of? His future wife, who is a Catholic, will also play a crucial role in his career. I doubt that her religion will allow him to have more than one wife. By contrast, his ancestors, by this age, would have had several concubines and established many families. Mademoiselle Nguyen's parents have been active in their religion. The fact that they were responsible for the construction of the first three cathedrals in the south of Vietnam has proven their wealth and power among the Christian community."

"What rank is her family in the court?" Lady Chin asked.

"I am afraid that they are not royalty, madam."

She sucked at her teeth. "That might pose an extreme barrier to the acceptance of the girl's relatives in the court, Mr. Ung. After all, it has been our tradition and prerequisite for the queen to derive from noble blood. No doubt this young woman belongs to a horrible class of businessmen. Oh, is it not bad enough that she is a commoner, does she have to worship the missionary god instead of the Buddha like the rest of us? I imagine that the councilmen and the Queen Mothers would refuse to grant their approval, and the king might have to look for his new queen somewhere else."

"Quite the opposite," the eunuch replied. "They have all approved of her. The mere fact that she is Vietnamese instead of some French girl is enough to make the royal family heave a sigh of relief. Just this afternoon, I learned that Lady Thuc has given her permission for the emperor to take a trip to Dalat, where he will have an intimate rendezvous with Mademoiselle Nguyen's family. I entreat you not to leave this social gathering yet, because tonight you are witnessing the making of history, Madam Chin."

"I still do not understand what the French want from us. Why can they not leave us to govern our country in peace?"

"Money, madam," the eunuch said. "Also, the missionaries see us as barbaric and heathen. They want to save our souls by persuading us to worship a popular Western god, and therefore civilize our people into the modern world. To them, we are just a colony, not an independent country that has any rights."

Lady Chin felt as if she had awakened from a long sleep. The eunuch's explanations had opened her mind to a world that was shut down when her family died. However, his voice was beginning to sound incoherent to her, as though he were speaking in another language.

Something else had caught her attention — a vision that emerged from a corner of the platform. For a second, her son seemed to appear in the crowd. Suddenly, she was very tired. She laid her head back against the railing and closed her eyes. Through her eyelids, she could still feel the intense heat from the lights overhead.

Below her, the emperor announced his early departure from the party, and some of the excitement seemed to leave with him. Something heavy crept up her chest. She must have drifted away, because when she opened her eyes, she was looking straight up at the ceiling. Against its white stucco dome-shaped lining, Ung's face was hovering like a moon. He wore the same helpless expression she had seen years ago, when he had found her teetering on the ledge of her apartment window.

He was shaking both of her shoulders. She responded by blinking her eyes while remaining perfectly still, no longer fearful, but in utter disbelief. Then she smiled, feeling herself float like a fully expanded balloon.

"Dear Heavens, madam, how are you feeling?" he asked. "What has happened?"

"Nothing," she replied. "Only, as you see, I just realized the true identity of the servant who comes by my room each day to feed me. In my delirium I did not recognize him at first."

"Who are you talking about?"

Her eyes were fixed on a young man who sat behind a bamboo screen. A thick canvas was stretched on a wooden frame before him, and on it, the emperor's portrait was taking form with uncanny likeness. Balls of colored thread lay scattered over the floor; some were sticking to his clothes.

"Are you referring to the queen's official embroiderer, Dan Nguyen?" he asked.

She nodded and closed her eyes once again. "Please take me back to my chamber and arrange for a meeting with that young man. I must speak to him."

chapter seventeen

The Portrait of the King

*T*he dancing guests cast flickering shadows on the inlaid dragons that capered across the marble floor. Above the mahogany parquet and solid hand-carved oak beams that formed the dais for the king's throne, the embroiderer sat, weaving a royal portrait. A fog of cigarette smoke surrounded his platform, caressing him with its cottony tendrils. As the fumes burned his eyes, the progress of his stitches slowed. Below him, the party was reaching its height of excitement.

Dan Nguyen hummed as he coaxed a strand of dark-brown silk into the coarse canvas, creating the lower rim of the emperor's left eye. Layer upon layer, he kept adding threads to the flat surface of the fabric, sculpting the curves of King Bao Dai's features in three-dimensional clarity. In his expert hands, the golden needle leapt like a flash of lightning, replicating the vision inside his head. Although he had created many likenesses in this fashion, the richness that materialized in his tapestries never ceased to amaze him. He examined each new image with childlike disbelief, as if somehow, like a spider, he had spun strands of life from his own veins and woven them into living art.

Above the deep cloud of pollution, the dome-shaped ceiling, composed of six enormous triangular ocean-blue crystals, spread fanwise to provide an overhead view of the sky. Twelve mahogany columns, embossed with gold dragons, supported this spectacular glass roof. From where he sat, Dan could see the rising moon, like a mellow chandelier; its light added to the brightness inside.

The full moon shining on the great house meant good fortune, and the throne was placed so that the emperor could have a commanding view of the universe and its heavenly bodies. Tonight the glorious sight went unappreciated, since the young king was weary from his long journey and, in spite of the ongoing party and lively company, had retired early to his bedchamber. The Throne of the Son of Heaven, lacquered in red and encrusted with gold, remained unoccupied.

Dan stopped embroidering, secured his needle in his black silk headdress, and looked at his pocket watch. He struggled to focus his attention on the portrait, but his mind wandered. The song he was singing contained the low rustling of the wind across a cornfield, a reminder of his life before the citadel.

He tried not to revisit the past often. Memories suffocated him, made him feel as if he had dived to the bottom of a river to explore a beautiful but haunted world to which he no longer belonged. At such times, his songs were gusts of wind that helped him restart his lungs. From the music came a thrill of anticipation. He could sense the approach of the one he longed to see — or was it the desperation of his fanciful mind?

According to the schedule of festivities, it was time for the imperial talent troupe to perform an act of the famous opera *The Jade Pin*. In his mind he could already hear the first stanza of the lyrics.

Where is his tormented lover?
With a baffled face and a turbulent heart,
Phan Sinh paced to and fro, in and out, in vacillation.
The gentle wind carried an aroma of incense,
And his sudden attack of anguish evaporated. He began to think of
    her again, unequivocally.
The sound of crickets chirping echoed in his ears,
Together with the cackles of roosters and hens, piercing his lonely
    heart.

*The beating of the gongs and the clashing of brass plates from the
time-teller signaled the last interval of night.
His book was set in front of him; he was unable to read. His lute
stayed hanging right beside him; he was in no mood to play . . .*

"Tai May, where are you?" he muttered. The sound of her name
poured down his body with the velocity of a waterfall. Dan was certain he had startled the entire ballroom with the intensity of emotion
in his voice. Judging from the blank expressions of the guards
nearby, no one had heard him. He retrieved the needle from his hair
covering and went back to the canvas.

So many years had passed, but Dan's memories of Tai May were
still painfully vivid. He had not forgotten anything about her face,
her body, and the willfulness of her personality. Time and again, he
had captured her features on canvas until he surrounded himself with
likenesses of her face. With his eyes closed, he could still feel her
warm breath gliding on his skin, taste her soft kiss, and smell the perfume of her powdered skin. She was constantly in his thoughts, from
the first sunlight that touched his eyes in the morning to the last
lantern he blew out at night. In his dreams he saw her, floating like a
princess among the dancing images in his mind.

He had taken her advice and come to Hue City, where he was just
another face in the crowd. At first he lived with some fishermen along
the edge of the river not far from the citadel. They were part of the
beggar community that included coolies, laborers, mussel-gatherers,
and sometime outlaws. The nearby market, famous for its size and
location, always needed laborers like Dan.

The beggars had welcomed him into their circle; they accepted
anyone who was homeless and starving. They were like the peasants
in his village, plain and guileless, but instead of scraping the soil for
food, they skimmed the river. Most of them had nothing beyond
what they earned in a day's labor and from begging, and from the
outset Dan had understood that he could never be one of them.

During the days when the work at the market was slow, Dan
had embroidered his tapestries. While the dusty wind sighed through
the tattered rooftops, he set up his equipment in a shed, bound
together by dirty rush sacks, to escape the harsh sunlight. And amid

its poverty he had created beautiful images that were suitable for a rich man's house. He sold most of his needlework to a shop at the market, keeping for himself only those portraits he had made of Tai May. He became known for his unique talent, and rich ladies hired him to embroider their portraits, often posing with their favorite Pekingese.

One day, a noblewoman, seeing the unusual style of needlework at the shop, had decided to question the merchant about the artist. With little difficulty she had found Dan in his home. It was an afternoon at the end of December. The northeasterly gale blew through the streets, warning of a storm. It was an idle day for the coolies because the harsh weather had forced the marketplace to close. Inside his hut, the wind had torn some of the split reeds off the mats that covered the roof. The tapestries he had made of Tai May flapped as he was trying to retrieve them from the walls and place them under the floorboards. When the noblewoman entered, he was so engrossed in protecting his work that he did not hear her. In fact, the lady had been there in the doorway for several minutes before he noticed her. She was examining the wall hangings with an expression of wonder. Not until the last tapestry was safely packed away did she speak.

"I admire your work. I did not expect you to be so young." Her voice was cool and steady in contrast to the rumbling of thunder outside.

"Thank you," he said, wondering how a woman of her importance had found her way to this poor section.

As if reading his mind, she said, "I saw your embroideries at the market. It took me a while to find out where you live, but I am a persistent person. And now I see the beautiful likeness that you did of the young dancer in the palace. She must have been a great inspiration for you to have so many of her images in your home. I must confess I am a little jealous, but she is a lovely model."

Even the booming thunder outside did not shake him as forcibly as her words. Dan's mind reeled. Could it really be Tai May that the woman was referring to? He had to find out. But he must be careful because he was a runaway slave. He took a deep breath and asked, "Do you know this dancer, great lady?"

"Of course. Every lady in the court talks about this girl. She is the disgraced granddaughter of a wealthy landowner from the town of Cam Le."

It had to be Tai May, and she was no longer with her family. He struggled to keep silent, lest his emotion betray his identity.

That same afternoon, the woman had commissioned him to create a portrait of her mandarin husband, accessorized in all his glory. In a matter of weeks he had created a life-size image of the old official, draped in his noble coat of arms with its ferocious blue dragon. The artwork caught Lady Thuc's attention. "I have seen your work, and I would like to meet you," she wrote in a letter to him. At that moment, Dan decided that he no longer wanted to be in hiding. Now he had a chance and a reason to enter the palace and look for his love. He could not worry anymore about his past or his safety when she was so close. The following day, he stepped into a red palanquin, shaded by a yellow parasol. Borne aloft by four liveried porters, he bade farewell to the workmen's grim neighborhood and entered his comfortable new quarters in the citadel. His new home was behind the legendary Lake of Serene Heart, one of the modest and secluded apartments reserved for artists of the royal family.

For the next five years, whenever he was summoned by the royal family, he entered into a small work area the shape of a bamboo birdcage without a roof. Its walls were a series of strings and beads, turned at an angle to allow him a view limited to his subject. It was located a short distance from the king's throne, so that Dan could embroider each requested portrait. The bored women of the court scrutinized his completed canvases, their yawns expressing their views of his fountain of ingenuity. The only relief he found from the monotony of his new occupation had been the performances of the opera troupe.

Dan liked the way their melodies translated his emotions into sound. The screens of glass beads surrounding him parted like the sheer curtains on a window. Sometimes he was given permission to part the curtain and get a full view of the room, but only for short intervals. Any time he watched too long, it would be the armed guards' duty to pull him away. They were there to protect the royals.

During one evening's entertainment, he had caught a glimpse of a slender body pirouetting among other dancers. She was facing toward him, but her eyes seemed to register only the dark beads that hung between them.

At first he thought he had nodded off and encountered her only in his dream. The plaintive melody shrieked as if someone were sharpening a knife against the outer wall of his skull. And somehow, incredibly, Tai May was dancing on the inside. Her skirts, like a white butterfly's wings, whirled under the green canopy of rosebushes outside his childhood home. After a time, he became aware that he was not dreaming. She was as real as the music streaming from the singer's mouth.

In a daze, Dan had gotten up from his seat. Barely aware of the warning looks of the guards, he parted the blinds and peeked through the opening. But the girl had moved away from the main stage, and he did not know where she had gone. Then, as the two guards seized him by the arms and pulled him away from the lookout point, he saw the white panels of her clothing some distance away, motionless. Had she recognized him, too? The curtain closed before he could see her face. After a moment, she turned and rejoined the rest of the dancers.

"I've found you, but it has never been in my power to give you happiness," he whispered to her form as it disappeared from his view. He pushed the guards away and sat back down on his chair. Never had it dawned on him what a great sacrifice she had made in order to save his life. To give him his freedom she had lost hers.

Through party after party he had sat and watched, needle in hand, observing the merrymaking of the royals. During ceremonies and rituals, he peered into the inner court, scrutinizing dozens of dancers, but he did not see her. It was as though she had vanished from the palace. And then, at last, came the evening when Lady Thuc had decided to employ the entire royal opera company to perform *The Jade Pin.*

That night, Dan had been assigned his own corner in a room filled

with mountains of food heaped on a low table, in the Japanese s
In front of him, the ladies reclined on their dainty seats, anticipa
the great event. The banquet consisted of roasted pheasants, de
rated in peacock feathers and surrounded by tiny black chickens
depict the gracious feminine character of the phoenix; a boar or
spit; several superb courses of fried carp; and enticing platters of oy
ters and clams. Between these major dishes were the smaller ones
rice, noodles, and other vegetarian delicacies, including sautéed snov
peas, mustard greens in three types of wine vinegar, and seaweed sal-
ads. Wine and spirits were served in carved silver cups next to large
gold-rimmed plates imported from Beijing, China.

Dan paid scant attention to the food that was served to him behind
his screens. He had never attended a formal feast; even divided from
the rest of the guests like an invisible man, he felt conspicuously out
of place.

In an unseen inner room, a lute flicked its first soft, lingering note.
Above the spectators' voices it sounded like the gurgle of a brook,
rising and swelling until it became a stream of melody. Through his
blinds, he saw Tai May. Her white flesh shimmered through the opening of a purple satin robe. As the tips of her satin shoes, ornamented
with glass beads, touched the tiled floor and the sweeping music
floated around her, she moved closer to the screen that obscured him.

She stopped, facing in his direction. The music halted and the
room fell silent. Too overwhelmed to breathe, he leaned closer to the
beaded blinds and parted them. This time there was no doubt in his
mind that she saw him. Her eyes were shining with teardrops. Her
face wore the same expression that he had seen the night she helped
him escape Magistrate Toan's murderous fury. That evening,
beneath the calmness of her face, she had plotted for his freedom. He
wondered what she was going to do now. He felt feverish.

She reached inside the crepe-de-Chine band that bound her bosom
and pulled out a piece of cloth. Dan gasped, recognizing the red
rose he had embroidered for her. The music lifted and she began to
sing. He retreated back into his seat. Her voice was choked with the
passion of the song's lyrics, which depicted the awakening of love
between two mortals. The words pierced his heart. Then she bowed

and pressed her face against the fabric, made an abrupt twirl, and returned to the audience. Dan sat frozen in his sanctuary, shaking and perspiring. She belonged to the king — just like his tapestries. But he knew she had sung and danced for him alone.

＊

While the world below him celebrated the young king's homecoming, Dan studied the door behind the dais, which led to the royal theater and the rooms reserved for the dancers. The moon was slanting through the glass ceiling. Looking out the window toward the pond, he could see reflections of silver on the rippling water, flickering among the shadows of the trees. A drowsy hibiscus drooped its branches over the misty bank. The scent of water lilies, subtle but distinct, wafted through the humid air that enveloped the jade building.

Dan stole another glance at his watch, and the humming died in his throat. The palace dancers were now well behind schedule. It struck him that the opera might not be performed this evening, and the idea was enough to make him ill. It had always been difficult for Dan, as a male official of the court, to obtain authorization to enter the inner palace during major events, even to do needlework.

Throughout the year, the Forbidden City celebrated a seemingly endless succession of festivals and ceremonies. Anniversaries of the births and deaths of emperors and queens, observations of the changing seasons, the year's end, the beginning of a new year, or respectful acknowledgments of lost souls and stray spirits — all demanded their appropriate rituals.

For each occasion the old queen would send out invitations to all the women of the palace, enclosing an agenda that generally included a lavish procession to offer tea, fruits, flowers, rice, and incense to the ancestors in the pagodas and temples in the morning, and bridge or mah-jongg games with entertainment from the opera troupe in the evening. During these rare opportunities, Dan knew he must exercise his charms and influence on the ladies-in-waiting, who prepared the guest list. The permits he acquired from them would provide him a few passing glances at his beloved Tai May.

For five long years, whenever he had gone to work, each evening he had tarried until the musicians and dancers began their rehearsal on a veranda along the great theater's wall. In his corner behind the thin barrier, he sat stiffly and searched until his eyes could discern his lover, waiting for her turn to sing. Each holiday, he went into the women's palace and watched her, like a lonely canary in a cage, singing and dancing for a mate that would never come. He knew that she was aware that he was right beside her, also caged but forced to hold his silence.

How he longed to leap forward into the court, shout her name, take her in his arms, and declare his love for her. But he knew what would happen if he did so. She was the king's property. If he dared to approach her, the guards would burst into the room and fire their rifles at them. To Dan, the idea of giving up his life for love often seemed preferable to the torment of his perpetual wait. But an inner voice would stop him from behaving impulsively. The voice belonged to his peasant wife.

Not knowing what had happened to Ven, Dan could only assume that she had sacrificed her life for his freedom. The last time he had seen her, she had been urging him to flee the ruins of the Nguyen mansion after they had witnessed the murders of the minister of religion and his son. Dan could only surmise that she must have been executed in some horrible way by the old magistrate.

If his wife were standing in front of him now, she would say, "You have cheated death more than once, young Master. Do not offend the gods by forsaking your life now. Remember all that you owe me, for I stayed behind to face a violent death in order to save you. During our marriage, you deprived me of liberty, love, and happiness. The least you must do now to repay your debt is to seek revenge. Release my woe!"

A few feet below him, the Queen Mother stretched her arms. Her shoulders shrugged as if she were cold, and the salmon headdress slipped down the front of her face, where it looked like a blindfold. She signaled to a team of ladies-in-waiting that stood nearby. Dan returned to his canvas; in a few minutes, he heard their wooden clogs clatter off.

He knew that revenge for his family was his obligation, but it had always struck him as unreasonable. How could he seek vengeance on the magistrate's family when his life was spared by his own enemy's granddaughter? If it were not for Tai May, he would not have survived to this day. He owed her a life. Tonight, in the brightness of his gazebo, the war of emotions seemed to strike him at a new level of intensity. The past that he believed he had escaped forever seemed to cling to him wherever he went.

A masculine voice rose over the room. The music that was playing from a gramophone scratched into silence, and everyone on the floor stopped still. Dan leaned forward, using one hand to part the beads so he could peek outside. A Vietnamese official in his mid-twenties was standing at the edge of the platform. The man's overweight body swelled uncomfortably inside a beige military uniform with a high-collared jacket that squeezed his neck, turning his face red. His stance — legs apart, chest high — allowed the rows of golden medals on his left breast to glow under the decorative Western light bulbs.

Dan noted that the transformation to European culture ended at the official's neck. The Vietnamese black silk headdress bound up his forehead in several layers like a bandage keeping the pressure from bursting out of his face.

"Ladies and gentlemen," he announced, "the royal opera company will not be performing tonight. They have been canceled due to the unanimous complaints of the audience, and, of course, the orders of His Majesty himself."

Spurts of laughter exploded in the crowd. The mandarin paused, tilted his head, and waited for the eruption to subside.

"Instead," he continued once the silence had returned to the stately hall, "for tonight's entertainment, we have decided to introduce a new talent from the motherland. Her expressive voice, superb diction, and fine sense of style have made of her an ideal interpreter of French songs. Mademoiselle Suzanne Therein will perform selections from Debussy's *Pelléas et Mélisande* (act one, scene two) in which she plays the role of sweet Genevieve. And now, for your listening pleasure, please welcome Miss Therein."

Dan winced and lifted a hand to his open mouth. He had been waiting the whole night for Tai May, only to be disappointed. He stood up. Balls of thread fell from his lap onto the tiled floor. Behind him, the guards bounded forward, apprehensive at his peculiar behavior.

"It is all right," he whispered. "Please, take me back to the Great Golden Gate. I have finished my embroidery for this evening."

chapter eighteen

Camille

*I*t was midnight when Dan passed through the Meridian Gate. Ahead he could see the outline of a roofed promenade along the bank of the river, marking the perimeter of the fortress. The moon was hanging directly on top of it. Dan was too restless to return to his apartment. Instead, he crossed over the Truong Tien Bridge and wandered into the streets of New Town, which had grown up around the outskirts of the citadel. He could already hear the sounds of night life on Morin Street.

Tonight, the whole country was celebrating the emperor's return. He had no intention of brooding alone, simmering in the sour broth of his sorrow.

Dan made a quick turn at a bend in the path, and the busiest street in Hue City opened before him, noisy and energetic. Half-naked children chased one another through the piles of garbage on the side of the road. Puddles of murky water in the gutters reflected the street lamps.

The city was infested with stray cats that squirmed cagily in dark corners or draped themselves along the houses' banisters as though to camouflage themselves. Their yowling echoed in the night. Everywhere he looked, commoners and noblemen pressed against one another, yelling and barking out the deep, hollow laughter that he had heard all day.

Above the clamor that surrounded him, Dan detected the subtler, more hypnotic sound of music being plucked from a lute. It seemed to be floating from the upper windows of a tea shop across the street. The melody was an old folk song he had often heard when he was a child. Now, it was being played in a slower and sadder style, lingering like a ghost from yesteryear. An unseen hand pushed him toward it.

To reach the entrance of the tea shop, he had to pass through a horde of drunken men who had had too much of a good time. The crowd condensed into a multilimbed mass that oscillated wildly, and Dan was caught in the middle, like a shrimp inside a spring roll. In striving to move forward, his feet slid on something slippery on the ground, and he could only pray that it was a banana peel. He fought his way to the sidewalk, and the heat from the nearby vendors hit him like an invisible wall of hot coals.

The tea shop stood five stories high. Dan entered a narrow door and saw that the first floor was a sort of living room, crowded with couches and lounge chairs. Most of the men sitting in them were hidden under large palm trees set in ornate ceramic tubs. He strained to hear the enticing sound from upstairs, but it was muffled by the much louder noise below.

Beautiful women in scanty dresses slithered in the dim light like the stray cats he had seen outside. Their faces were concealed in heavy makeup that made them appear as mysterious as the scents that emanated from their bodies. None of them paid any attention to him, a country fellow who was still wearing the traditional *ao dai* tunic and hiding his long hair in a formal silk headdress, so different from the fashionable linen suits and fedoras of the shop's regular clientele.

Somehow Dan found the courage to navigate through the crowd and wind his way to the wooden counter near the back of the hall. When a male bartender in black uniform looked his way, he asked for ten copper pennies' worth of tea.

Clutching the delicate cup, he sat in a lounge chair under the staircase so he could observe the lewd commerce taking place between the hostesses and the guests. His inner voice urged him to drink the tea quickly and go away, but curiosity kept him in his seat. He had entered because of the strumming lute; he must meet the person whose lullaby he had heard.

After fifteen minutes, Dan went back to the counter. The bartender lurched forward. He was an oak statue of a man, with a neck full of beard, sunken cheeks, and eyes so narrow that they swam on his face like two anchovies. His stringy hair was pasted over a large bald spot. He gave Dan a dark look. "What is it? Does your excellency see a girl you desire?"

"I h-heard someone p-play a lute from outside," Dan stuttered. "I would like to hire that person to play this particular song for me." He whistled a tune from *The Jade Pin*, which still haunted his mind.

The man chuckled. "Oh, mother of Heavens," he called out in false delight.

"What is it?" Dan asked. "Did I say something amusing?"

"Not at all." The grin remained plastered across his face. "It is just that you do not look like the type who would be a fan of our Camille. In fact, you are much too young. I am curious to know, has anyone recommended her to you?"

Dan shook his head. It seemed to him that things had become a lot more complicated than he had envisioned. He took a sip of tea.

"Listen." The bartender leaned forward. His breath was a sea of rotten fish, choking Dan to the verge of tears. "For the customer that has more than ten silver pieces in his girdle, there are joys to be had in feasting and taking pleasure in private with any woman in this place. The rooms upstairs are reserved for this purpose, and the higher the floor, the more expensive the girls that occupy its rooms. Look around you. There are so many beauties for you to choose. Why don't you look at someone else, some pretty little lips perhaps? Or do you prefer the wild and wicked type?"

Dan's resolve hardened. "I told you, I heard a tune as I was passing. Can your musician play any songs from *The Jade Pin*? If so, then it is imperative that I meet her."

The man paused, sucking his teeth. His eyes became two thin lines. Then, while Dan held his breath, he smacked his hand against the wooden countertop and said, "Have a seat. I will return shortly with Camille."

~><

D an again retreated under the staircase. From there, he could see the entire place with little effort. Clearly, it had undergone a major reconstruction. Remnants of an old design were still visible in the copper plaques that gilded the ceiling beams and the oval openings that led to the inner gambling rooms. Facing the entrance, instead of the typical partitions that were seen in rich houses, a crystal wall of falling water shielded the inside from the street's pollutions, at the same time enhancing the visitors' privacy. The mist that rose from the cascade smelled of burnt rubber, and its damp vapor coated the furniture like slippery oil.

He remained in the dark corner for some time drinking his tea. Through the cracks between the steps, he watched the customers' costly Western shoes climbing the narrow stairs next to the silk slippers of their women. Those who descended wore a uniform look of satisfaction, confirmed by their disheveled clothing and stupefied grins. Their smug faces were stamped with the heart-shaped imprints of lipstick kisses, making them look like pigs that had just passed the Board of Health's inspection and earned the red seal of approval.

Out of nowhere, a brush of warm air blew a harsh, flowery perfume into his nostrils. Dan turned and faced an attractive woman who was half-leaning, half-stretching along the upholstered back of his seat. Her hair was tied into a big knot above the nape of her neck. The violet light overhead formed shadows over her eyes and darkened the folds of her lips, giving her an owl-like appearance.

"Camille is here at your service," she said. "You are, I presume, visiting the Red Dream Hotel for the first time?"

He nodded and lowered his head. She laughed with a twinge of sadness. "I heard you are looking for some company," she said.

He inspected the tea leaves at the bottom of his cup and listened to the rattling of dice from the next room. The hostess slid down into the chair. The friction of her movement bunched her black dress together in the back, and for a moment, she looked almost nude. Dan could see the outline of her rib cage beneath the thin satin. Her eyes looked straight at him with a hunger that again reminded him of street cats. She swung her arm forward, catching his fingers in her nails. He found himself unable to look away from her sharp white teeth, bluish under the light as she pulled him closer to her.

"Do you understand the rules of this place, young farmer?" she asked. "If you request a girl, you are expected to pay for her time, unless you have no silver. In which case, you do not belong here and must leave at once."

"I c-came here with one wish," he stammered. Her perfume reminded him of the stagnant water in a vase of old roses.

"My dear boy, you have come to the right place," she said with an air of pride. "You can make any demands in this house. Nothing is so outrageous that it cannot be done. However, people pay here before they indulge in their desires. As soon as you make a suitable donation for my services, I will comply with your wishes."

He reached for the money sack that was hidden in the sash around his waist. Her greedy stare followed his every move. "Tell me then, how much?" he asked.

"It depends on how long you wish to keep me," she breathed. "For the first hour, I am worth a pair of silver coins. Eight more will provide you my devoted service for the entire night."

"What I need would take no more than ten minutes of your time."

She chuckled. "You are certainly inexperienced, young farmer. But do not fret! I assure you that I am a skilled teacher. What's more, we have several kinds of tiger-bone wines that will help to prolong your endurance. In the house of pleasure, there is no speaking of time, only satisfaction."

Dan picked out two pieces of silver and handed them to her. She pulled back, as if he had offered her a burning lump of coal. "Do not give that to me," she whispered. "Pay him."

He saw a shadow coming toward them from the other side of the hall. It staggered, and a clinking sound of metal echoed its footsteps, like an iron shackle being dragged across the floor. From the darkness above him, the face of the bartender appeared, with his thick black beard bristling. The giant stopped a few feet away from Dan and turned his eyes upon him. He thrust his hand forward, revealing a stack of keys wrapped around his wrist. Dan realized that the manaclelike sound he had heard was made by the keys clicking against one another. He placed the coins in the man's palm and watched them vanish.

"One hour," the bartender said.

"Where is my tip?" the woman cried.

Dan had never heard that word before. They were both feasting their eyes on him, clearly expecting him to understand what it meant. He searched for clues on the woman's face, and she fixed her eyes on his bag of coins.

"What is a tip?" he finally asked.

"My present," she said in exasperation. "And who has not heard of it? You must show your gratitude for my service."

"But you have not rendered me any service."

She laid a hand on his shoulder. "I will, soon after you settle all of the payment in advance."

"All right," he said, his patience wearing thin. "How much do I owe you for this great pleasure?"

"The smallest amount one would consider a tip is one half of the fee. But according to most of my customers, my talent is worth at least two extra pieces of silver."

Dan laid more coins in the bartender's hand and they disappeared like props in a magic trick.

"Thank you, sir," came the guttural voice above him. "You have been more than generous with the lady. But I beseech you not to forget about me. I, too, deserve a tip for two reasons: one, for bringing you this songbird. And two, it is I who will stand guard outside your door so that neither drunkards nor policemen will disturb you and Camille."

Dan gave his collar a frustrated yank. The entire evening had become one gigantic mistake. Silently, he cursed himself for walking into this tea shop, and he cursed these scoundrels for helping to make this attempt at frivolity utterly unbearable. And to think of all the nights this should happen! He looked up, hoping to catch any trace of penitence on their faces. Instead, he met two pairs of blinking eyes, gleaming with uncanny desire at the velvet pouch in his hands.

"Why are you making a fool of me?" he asked them in a low voice. "All I want is a song. Why must you tease me with this silly prank?"

"We have certain rules in this place," Camille said. "It signifies nothing whether you stay one minute or one hour — whether you have my company here at this table or in the privacy upstairs. The stated price always excludes the tips."

Dan raised his hand until the purse was inches away from the woman's face. He tapped his fingers, and the coins jingled. He watched her make a quiet swallow with the muscles of her throat. Next to her, the bartender scratched his beard.

"This is all the money I am willing to pay," he said, "including your service, your tips, his tips, and my protection from the law enforcers — ten coins. With this much silver, I could make you bark like a cur. And based on your disposition I am certain that you would, probably for a much smaller sum."

He threw a handful of coins in her lap. They bounced under the indigo light like the splashing of some liquid. She sat on the edge of her chair with her mouth open. "I will not make you do anything shameful," Dan continued. His voice was a lot calmer now, almost a whisper, but his enunciation made his words as clear as if he were shouting. "I won't even stay in your room for more than half an hour. That money is yours — all of it, if you agree to sing the song I requested and play your lute in accompaniment, the same way you have been playing upstairs. Will you do what I bid you, or should I leave this instant?"

She used both her hands to gather the coins and hand them back to him.

"Take your money, young farmer," she said. "I will sing you that song, and it will be both my present and apology to you."

"Wretched woman, have you lost your mind?" cried the bartender with fury. "Why are you, an aging prostitute, turning away a small fortune because of some misguided fan? Impossible — utterly impossible!"

"Will you be silent?" replied the woman. "This fellow has paid my fee and your tip in full. What more do you want, unless you intend to frighten away a perfectly generous customer and inflict such a bad recollection in his mind that he would never visit us again? Return to your station and serve people drinks. Leave me alone, so that I can do what you are hiring me to do: provide the entertainment. As for you, country fellow —" She grabbed Dan by the hand and pulled him toward the stairway. "You are coming up to my room."

"If you were a good whore," the man grumbled, "you would let me handle the negotiations with the customers."

When they reached a turn in the flight of stairs, she leaned against Dan's chest and whispered to him, "Once we are in my room, you must give me that sack of money. I, Camille, have made two vows in my life: never apologize and never volunteer my services for free. I simply do not want to share this fortune with the beast downstairs."

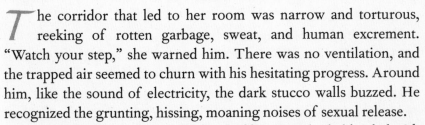

*T*he corridor that led to her room was narrow and torturous, reeking of rotten garbage, sweat, and human excrement. "Watch your step," she warned him. There was no ventilation, and the trapped air seemed to churn with his hesitating progress. Around him, like the sound of electricity, the dark stucco walls buzzed. He recognized the grunting, hissing, moaning noises of sexual release.

Camille marched a few steps ahead of him. Her body blended with the shadows in the hallway. All he could see was her thin white neck suspended in space. Dan wondered how many times a day someone in her position had to perform this ritual — walking on the sticky floor, listening to the droning in the wall, and all the while, pleasing men as part of her duties.

They reached the end of the hall. Her room was located on the far corner of the second floor, above the entrance to the tea shop. She motioned for him to wait as she turned the doorknob. The first thing his eyes registered was the moon, round and yellow, a melted ball of wax that splashed its light on him through the window.

"We are here, at last," she said. "A thousand apologies for that dreadful hallway. That cheap bastard Van Tong has tried to run this brothel without a maid service. Sooner or later, we will all succumb to more illness than the rats that live behind those walls."

"Who is Van Tong, the tea shop owner?"

She nodded. "Yes, that brute you met downstairs."

"Is that so?" he mused. "I was under the impression that he was one of the employees, a bartender or bodyguard."

Camille pushed the door shut, and the room brightened as the dark hall disappeared. Dan was aware of a faint fragrance of lilac. She tiptoed closer to him. Her feet — Dan noticed for the first time how small they were — tapped against the wood floor, beckoning for his attention. At the same time, her hands were on his shoulders, lingering for a moment before they slid down his arms, so slowly that he could feel himself respond with gooseflesh.

Looking up at him, her face was covered with so much powder that it seemed like a white mask. Crow's feet radiated from the corners of the eyes, which held no hint of emotion. Dan pulled away. Where did her spirit go? Where was the empathy that people like her were paid to provide? The mask embraced him with its hollow look, lacking all capacity to understand.

"The song," he reminded her.

"Is that all you really want?" she asked. "You are paying me a lot of money."

He nodded. Without Tai May, the coins had no value to him. *The Jade Pin* was his connection to her. The cycle of desire, reunion, and departure that he had experienced was a traditional aspect of life in the citadel. Forbidden love, hidden behind silken screens, had befallen the king's mandarins and concubines throughout history, and had been immortalized in literature and songs. Romantic frustration was part of the privileged life of the royal fortress. How could he, a lowly embroiderer, be bold enough to challenge the age-old customs? His only consolation was his song, which no one could steal from him.

The truly distasteful thing was getting the music of his heart out of this woman. Like the burnt wick of a candle, she stood inches away from the window. But he had come so far to get so close. His throat was constricted; he could hardly speak. "Just the song." He saw her lift the lid of a carved box on the mantel and pour his coins inside.

"The lute is in my bedroom. That way." She shut the container and aimed one of her fingers past his left shoulder. Dan turned. Through a semitransparent shade that separated the inner compartment from the room where they stood, he saw the outline of a bed covered with a red satin quilt. Behind it, his shadow was reflected in a wall of gleaming mirror.

A breath of wind crept through the window, and the thin curtain responded with a lazy twirl. The metallic glint of reflection faded to black for a fleeting second, and it seemed as if the mirror had just blinked at him, like the eye of some monstrous beast. However, when the same thing happened for the second time, he saw what was really happening: her movement back and forth from the window had intermittently blocked the moon and caused the illusion.

"With your permission," he said, his voice flat. "I would prefer to stay in this room while you play."

"Do as you please. I must change my dress into something more comfortable before I faint from this heat. I do not require you to do the same. I am certain that you are obliged by your own strict moral code to keep your garments on. However, if it is getting too hot in the room, you can open another window." She paused, then asked him, "Could I offer you some refreshment? All that I have is a glass of brandy."

"No, thank you," he said, having no idea what brandy might be. Probably some type of foreign tea, he guessed.

He saw her silhouette against the patches of light behind the sheer drape. Her naked arms were raised toward the ceiling, her body wiggling, her dress slipping past her breasts like a moth bursting out of its cocoon. Dan turned away, his cheeks burning.

He searched the room, keeping his eyes focused on its design and furnishings. Everything was set up in the Japanese style, with low tables and elongated cushions instead of chairs. A red scarf was thrown over a lamp to dim its light. There were pictures on the walls; strange sketches in black pencil. He saw portraits of a young boy in several of the drawings, along with the name "Camille" signed at the corners and personal remarks that made little sense to him. The rest of the portraits were a collage of unfamiliar men, some in uniform, others in suit and tie.

Dan realized that the paintings were just a part of Camille's larger collection — memorabilia of the lovers who must have passed through her life. On the mantel, next to the money box, lay an ascot left by some English gentleman. To its right were a captain's hat, a French clock, some smaller frames containing old coins, and other bric-a-brac. The objects were arranged like trophies, hiding untold stories below their sullied surfaces. He tried not to think about their meaning as he waited for her, avoiding contact with the mementos by keeping his hands folded together on the front panel of his garb.

Finally, the sound he had waited for coursed into the room. Her voice rose, high-pitched and grief-stricken.

> *With a baffled face and a turbulent heart,*
> *Phan Sinh paced to and fro, in and out, in vacillation.*

Her anguished voice, its intonation, its phrasing, accompanied by a familiar lute. He closed his eyes and saw a glimmer of the veranda of his home. Smelled the roses in the garden.

> *The gentle wind carried an aroma of incense,*
> *And his sudden attack of anguish evaporated. He began*
> *to think of her . . .*

His mind whirled. The song was so sad. He remembered waiting for his father to come home from a long journey. A lazy afternoon. The light, clinking sound of laughter. The singing struck every nerve of his body. Where had he heard those notes, those words, that sound before? It was as if someone had lifted a shroud off his eyes and darkness had turned to light. He . . . *remembered*. Of course, all those signs, the details that clattered inside his head . . . the tight knot of hair, those delicate feet, the drawings of the boy — images that led him back to the cradle of his youth. He saw, but he had also closed his eyes to things he did not want to see.

He made an abrupt turn to face her, leaning against the mantel for support. He did not realize he had knocked down some of her relics with the back of his hand, nor did he hear them hit the floor. The music stopped. She sat on the bed atop the red quilt, her fingers poised in midair. Fearfully, she lifted her eyes from the fretted neck of the lute and looked at him. She seemed to say something to him, but her voice was muffled, as though she were screaming through a wall. What was she saying? Van Tong? Why would she mention the tea shop owner at a time like this?

"What is your name?" he cried to her.

"Camille." She, too, raised her voice. "Don't you remember?"

"No, that is not true. Your other name!" He lunged toward her, heedless of the curtain between them. She looked purple to him through the veil. Her arms were wrapped around her chest, trying to cover her nakedness. He yanked the fabric away. "In my other life, my father called you Lady Yen," he said, and watched her face contort with anguish.

"Of my hundred names in this profession, no one has called me that in seventeen years," she wailed.

"Sixteen," he corrected her.

"Who are you?" she demanded.

He fumbled inside his collar until he found the piece of jade that had hung around his neck for as long as he could remember. The heat and oil from his body had polished it to a warm glow. It dangled at the end of a gold chain, sparkling in the light between his two fingers. "I am Dan Nguyen, your son," he told her.

She threw her head back and uttered a dreadful howl, with her hands extended toward him. Her body collapsed in his arms, slackening. In the reflection on the mirror, Dan caught a glimpse of something that almost made him swoon as well.

Spreading across her naked back, vivid in its details, was an elaborate tattoo. A coursing river and its bluish waves streamed down her spine, dotted occasionally in red marks. On both sides of this waterway, mountains, with their undulating crests, loomed in and out of seemingly moving clouds. In the center of this panoramic landscape, a monk bowed to a seated priest. And underneath them, in the old vernacular characters, was scrawled the second verse of the ancient poem: "Then they hold the constellations in their hands and peering at the sun, they find the road to Nirvana. Many invalids shall be cured at the door."

The last bit of the treasure map his enemies had sought so recklessly over the past sixteen years was now before him, as real as the woman who bore it.

chapter nineteen

The Red Dream Hotel

C lutching his mother in his arms, Dan Nguyen was transfixed by the reflection of her back in the mirror. There, in front of him, was the tattoo that completed the map he had beheld on his father's back at the time of his execution. Now he had the missing piece. He stored the images and the verse in a quiet part of his mind to be studied later.

Dan eased his mother down onto the springy mattress. As he wound the red quilt around her bare body, she seized the tip of his collar and held on, only letting go with reluctance when he peeled her fingers away. He noticed that her feet, though small, were no longer bound.

"My son," she moaned. "My own son! Wretched fate! I am being tormented by my past misdeeds." Her lips were shaking uncontrollably.

"You must not try to talk," he said. "Breathe deeply and slowly."

"Leave my room at once." She buried her head in a pillow. "I cannot bear to look upon you." Her voice trailed off into deep sobbing.

Raising his voice, he said, "I do not have any intention of reproaching you, madam. For sixteen years we have been strangers to each other. Let us not begin our first hour together with bitter words.

We have the rest of our lives to express our regrets. For the time being, I thank Heaven for our reunion, and that we did not perish under the enemy's hand like my father and his first two wives."

She looked up, her eyes brimming with tears. "Death," she whispered, "has many faces, and I know them all too well, for I, too, am dead inside. But tell me, how did my husband die?"

"The worst possible way, madam," said Dan. "I saw him in his last moments on Earth, on his knees and facing a grave. He died at the hand of Magistrate Toan, by means of decapitation. There was no mercy in the act. For almost ten years after his execution I lived as a slave in the enemy's house. I had to flee when my identity was exposed."

"Oh, no, no!" she gasped. "Please stop! This is much too much for my poor heart to bear. Just take your money and go away."

He shook his head. "Destiny has brought me to your door. I will not leave here until you answer my questions." He paused. Lady Yen was leaning back against the wall, her eyes as vacant as the mirror behind her. She stole a glance at a corner, where a thick rope hung within reach. He could read her impulse to pull this emergency cord and summon help.

"Very well, then," he sighed. "If you want me to disappear, you must tell me your story. Be sure to explain why you abandoned me, your own son. Was I too much of a burden for you to handle? Was my life not worth rescuing? I deserve to know the truth."

"No," she whispered, as she collapsed on her side. Her face was hidden behind her thick black hair. She put her hands against her ears as if to block out his voice. "Do not ask me these questions," she said. "I beg you. Spare me my last shred of dignity! The mother you are looking for is no longer here. She is dead. I, on the other hand, am just an empty shell, void of the past. For you, I have nothing and remember nothing. If you insist on humiliating me, I will have no choice but to alarm Van Tong, and he will get you out of my room."

"Please, be gracious and listen." He knelt at the side of her bed. "I will not allow you to forsake me twice in a lifetime."

Her tears felt warm on his hands. She reached for his silk headdress and unraveled it. His hair fell across his shoulders, dark and long. She brushed her fingers through it.

"I cannot say what you want me to say," she said. "The truth has been bottled up so deep, locked in me like I am now locked inside this bordello. Are you going to take your revenge out on me? Can you not see that I am suffering for the sins I have committed? What will satisfy you, besides my pitiable profession and my dreadful solitude? When will you believe that I am now settling my crimes with the gods?"

"But you must explain," said Dan. "Why are you selling your body? And why are you alone?"

"Because I am worthless as a human being. Because I have no skill or talent to be independent. And because I renounced my own son when he was most vulnerable."

"And why was I renounced? Why did you leave me behind to face a destiny that was worse than death?"

"Because," she screamed, "I wanted you to live!"

Her words seemed to exhaust her. Tears mixed with dark mascara ran down her cheeks in muddy tracks. "I wanted you to live," she repeated. "I knew my limitations. You would have already been dead if you were in my care. I gave you to that peasant because I trusted her instinct, her survival skills, and most of all, her single-minded devotion. I knew she would save you, as she would be able to blend in among the other farmers like a locust in the grass."

Dan stiffened. "You did not know that, madam. That peasant sacrificed her own safety on several occasions to save me. And in the end she died, so that I could live. Did your gardener give his life for you?" He fell silent, aware of the malice in his voice. To hide his embarrassment, Dan passed his hand across his brow and wiped away the perspiration.

"On the contrary," she said. "I entrusted my fortune to him and required nothing in return. He was a gambler. Most of the Nguyen family's legacies I took with me were spent to feed his addiction to laying bets. I found out, when it was much too late, that he owed several casinos in town an enormous sum, more than twenty thousand silver pieces."

She took a deep breath and continued, "To pay off this debt and save him from a dreadful end, I had no other choice but to sell myself to this brothel. What folly! He left me after I repaid his debt. My blind love for him carried me so far as to become a prostitute, only to be discarded. My gardener found shelter in another woman's arms, while I have spent the last fifteen years considering myself dead to the world. Now that you are here, my heart has awoken to beat again, only to suffer with the agony of the past. Oh, Heavens, help me!" She again gave way to sobbing.

"Stop your tears. Your troubles are coming to an end, madam," Dan said, standing up. "I will find a way to release you from this place. No other man shall walk into the tea shop and ill-treat you again. This is a promise I intend to keep."

"How?" she cried. "Unless you are a rich lord, I do not see how you will find twenty thousand silver coins, plus fifteen years of interest, to redeem my freedom."

"Oh, but there is a way," he said pensively. "The tattoo on your back, do you understand its meaning, madam?"

Her anguish faded. He could see then that she knew, as a sparkle of awareness crept into her eyes. He watched her fingers toying with the quilt's silken fringe. The clock ticked in the silence.

"How did you know about the tattoo?" she said finally. "You were only a small child when we parted."

"Madam, I knew about the buried treasure. The tattoo, the map . . . I knew its secret."

She gazed at the floor and did not answer. What was going through her mind? If only he could show her his true intention. If only Ven were here. "If you do not trust your own son, whom can you trust?" he asked.

He reached for her, and he could sense her again retreating. Her powdered face was inches away from him, impassive, stubborn.

"Do you want me to disappear?" he asked.

"I don't know," she said, hesitating. "Do you have a copy of my husband's tattoo?"

"No, and I don't remember its details, but I know who has the original."

"You must tell me then."

"Very well," he sighed, giving in. "My father's skin, which bore the first half of the map, is in Magistrate Toan's possession. I watched him as he removed it from my father's body."

"You must get it back," she said. "That man is our mortal enemy. Kill him before he escapes his Karma. And make certain that you see his blood spill. I trust you to carry out our revenge. Only you . . ." She shifted her eyes away from his face. Gathering her composure, she continued in a voice so soft he had to strain to hear her. "Only you, the last standing Nguyen, can restore our family's name and legacy."

"I am not, by any means, a killer," he whispered.

"How else can you reclaim your heritage?" she asked. "Can you ask the devil to return the map with peace and politeness? Or do you think that we can get justice by approaching the Royal Court to restore our name and property?"

"I will find a way to retrieve it, with no more bloodshed. Trust me when I tell you this: If violence were truly in my blood, I would have found a way to destroy him and his family long ago. I was a slave in his house for nine long years. That alone gave me countless opportunities. But there I was given shelter, food, and an education, and there I fell in love with an innocent girl."

"They destroyed us!" she said. "They killed your father. I am in a whorehouse, and you grew up as a slave. There was no mercy in the act — you said so in your own words. Blood can only be washed away with blood. Surely the gods in Heaven have kept you alive for that purpose. Don't you understand the principle of revenge?"

He did not; in fact, he could not begin to grasp the burden she had put on him. "I am not a killer," he said again. "If I murdered Magistrate Toan, I would risk my only chance of happiness with his granddaughter, whom I have loved more than anyone or anything else on this earth, including my own life. Avenge yourself then, madam, for I am helpless against the dictates of my heart. By asking me to commit a deadly act against her grandfather, you are asking me to cut away the only joy in my existence. I would rather let you kill me."

Lady Yen groaned and pulled at her hair. "How dreadful is Heaven's will! Is this a foolish game that was arranged by the vengeful gods? Dan, my poor son, how could you love the enemy's offspring? Now I know for certain that I will be trapped here in this bordello for eternity. Guilty as I was, I do not deserve such punishment. Look at me — my skin is drooping, my eyes grow gray, my beauty fades. I will die here, alone, suffering to my last hour." She sat up, pointing her finger at the door. "You must go, for I have no more to ask of you. As far as I am concerned, you ceased to exist on the day I left the mansion."

The clock struck, as if to signify that his hour in her room was coming to a close. In a solemn tone, he said, "I will find the money to buy back your freedom. And I will take revenge on the enemy as you ask of me. I tell you, he shall die! But together with his blood, mine will flow as well. Because in death I shall possess the freedom to be near my lover for eternity."

Without knowing how he walked out of her room, he found himself on the street. Away from her, the heaviness that had suffocated him lifted, and he could breathe again.

By the time Dan Nguyen left Morin Street, the night was almost over. The exhausted city was asleep, silent except for the lonely echoes of his footsteps. The yellow moon that had followed him throughout the evening was now a transparent ghost in the dark sky.

The main gates of the citadel were wide open. From the watchtower, a gleaming beacon whirled through the darkness every few seconds; it stopped momentarily to shine on him as he approached the gate. Beyond the light, the gloomy shadows of the guards, like clay figures sitting staidly under their small roof, nodded at Dan when he presented his ivory pass.

The royal city, just hours ago crowded with party-goers, was now deserted. Dan wound his way through the dark alleys. His hair whipped in the restless night air, and he felt naked without his silk headdress. In his hurry to flee the Red Dreams Hotel, he had forgotten it on the floor of his mother's bedroom. Would it end up among the souvenirs on her mantel?

What a fool he had been, thinking that he could escape his obligation. In all the years he had watched life as a spectator, he had been marking time, as surely as the ticking clock in his mother's room. Clearly he was, after all, just one more marionette in a puppet show orchestrated by some invisible force. A supreme being, perhaps? What about his free will, and how could he exercise it?

Again he thought of his mother's shrill voice: *Only blood can wash away blood, and you are the last standing man of the Nguyen family!* Through her words his ancestors' demands seared him like a flaming sword, and his entire life came to a new focus.

Dan understood that the answers he was seeking lay hidden within the walls of the Cam Le Village, and he knew he must go home.

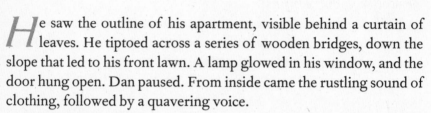

He saw the outline of his apartment, visible behind a curtain of leaves. He tiptoed across a series of wooden bridges, down the slope that led to his front lawn. A lamp glowed in his window, and the door hung open. Dan paused. From inside came the rustling sound of clothing, followed by a quavering voice.

"Master Dan Nguyen, is that you? At last you are home. I have been waiting all night."

Dan shaded his eyebrows to concentrate on the shadow. From the darkness emerged a wrinkled face, yellow under the lantern's glow. Dan recognized the king's former chamberlain, Ung, although he had never spoken to him before. Why was this man inside his living room? He stepped inside.

"I have important news to deliver to you," Ung said. His hunched form seemed incongruous among the shadows of bookshelves. There was no furniture in the room, except for a small chair at a corner. On the gray cement floor, a leopard-skin rug spread like a puddle of paint, catching the flickering light.

"You must go with me to see someone," Ung said.

"Who? And at this hour?"

"Yes, right this instant, sir. It was her dying wish to see you."

Dan gave a start of comprehension. "Lady Chin?"

"Yes, sir."

"She knows who I am?"

"Yes, sir. She knows that you have been bringing her the sustenance that has held her spirit to this earthly realm. She recognized you from last night's ball."

"She was there? How could she, being so ill?"

The eunuch pushed his chest forward and said, "I took her there. I convinced her that she should receive some fresh air. You must come with me, young Master. She gave me specific instructions to notify the Queen Mother, in case you refuse to comply. I hope that you do not force me to make that decision, Sir Dan."

Dan seized the old man's hands. "I cannot explain right now, but I am leaving the citadel, and I am asking for your cooperation. Lady Chin wishes to speak to me, for she has guessed something. Her intuition is accurate. I am about to reveal to her a secret that has been trapped in my bosom for all these years. She must not die without knowing the truth." Noticing the eunuch's baffled expression, he slowed his speech as if he were talking to a child. "Please, you appear to understand this matter. Before it is too late, I ask you to help save her soul. I need you to help me take her to the river for the last trip of her life. I cannot leave without her."

The eunuch took several steps backward. "I cannot do what you are asking me," he said. "She would not understand, nor would she survive such a vigorous journey."

"If you keep her in that dark room, you are only prolonging her agony."

"It is not a possibility, Master Dan," the old man said.

Dan pulled at his hair. What could he do to persuade this poor man to change his mind? "Wait here," he said. Leaving the old man standing in his living room, Dan ran into his sleeping quarters. He opened a simple mahogany chest and fumbled among his clothing until he found a silver chain. He took it back to the living room, only to find that his visitor had left.

Dan rushed outside. The eunuch was standing under a streetlight. His hands clutched the lantern.

"We will bring this to her together," Dan said, holding the bracelet in the lamplight for the eunuch to see. "Her son, Bui, once wore this chain around his ankle. Once she sees it, she will make her own decision about what to do."

The old man whispered, "Sir Dan, you overwhelm me with such secrecy. Who are you? And where are you planning to take her?"

"I am taking her to face Providence," replied Dan. "There, she will find peace through learning the truth — all of it, including my identity."

"Very well, then," said the eunuch. "Follow me. I will take you to her."

They set off in the direction of the Apartments of Peace. The tall frangipani trees that lined the path dropped thousands of white petals, dancing around the two men in the wind.

chapter twenty

The Bicycle

Long ago, when she had just gotten married, Lady Chin had received a generous wedding present from her husband: a bluish silver-white bicycle imported from a factory in Marseille. She never learned how to ride it alone, but she hoped to master it one day, so she kept it, still in its shipping crate, at the foot of her bed. Minister Chin Tang then belonged to the fourth rank of mandarins — the lowest tier in the court that would allow him to enter the terraces outside the throne room. One afternoon when he had completed his duties, he decided to take the vehicle and his wife out for a spin. For as long as she lived, Lady Chin would never forget that ride.

At first the excursion did not go well. The black saddle seat, where she perched in front of her husband, seemed ridiculously small for two adults to share. Her hands grasped the steering handle, next to a thin rod that held a rearview mirror. The long panels of her skirt were trapped between her thighs. And her feet . . . she remembered how difficult it was to rest them on the two tiny posts on the front wheel.

She was terrified. Her pose was difficult to maintain, and her sweaty palms kept sliding off the metal handgrips. But her husband was valiant. He seemed to foresee her every movement, cradling her in his arms to ensure her safety. While the vehicle rolled along the dirt road, she could feel him edging closer from behind. His warm breath burned the nape of her neck, and she could feel his heart thumping against her spine, as though a wild sparrow, trapped inside his breast cage, were flapping its wings.

They reached an empty field outside the citadel. The late-afternoon sun burned a red hole in the blue sky. Before them spread the hills, rolling and submissive, smooth as camel humps and covered with green grass. They were heading toward a mountain. Her husband's legs pedaled continuously as they climbed a soft path that seemed to lead them directly into the waiting sun. Then, before she could prepare herself, the ground dropped and she was looking down at a valley.

The wheels began to spin, slowly at first and then gaining speed. For a second she believed she was falling through a crack in the earth. It seemed so undignified to scream, but she did not care. Her shout escaped in large invisible bubbles, instantly stolen by the rushing wind. When her husband reached out and closed his hands over hers, massaging each white knuckle, she started to relax. Motionless, she savored his presence and the way the bicycle was purring against her thighs. Everything else evaporated, the sky, the earth, the green slopes that reached out to infinity. She was soaring like a kite.

His reflection in the mirror blushed. He clasped his hand around her waist and drew her closer to his lower body, his eyes closing. At the burning moment when the feverish sun came to meet the green earth, the bicycle came to a stop at the foot of the hill.

To this day, she was certain that Bui was conceived on that unforgettable afternoon, when she had learned how extraordinary it was to fly.

*N*ow, almost twenty-five years later, she could again feel the wind tugging at her hair as she floated along the river. The river! She had forgotten its name, the same way she did her own. Through the trees she could see the punctured sun, with its light leaking onto the nearby clouds.

Across from her, the embroiderer sat plying an oar. Even though her eyes were half-closed, she could see him moving steadily on the wooden bench. He was bare-chested. The muscles of his arms rippled like bronze waves saturated with sunlight, so healthy and beautiful that the sight of him reduced the ache in her eyes to a soothing pulsation. The splash of water under the boat grew louder until it covered her like a blanket.

Long ago on that bicycle, she remembered being absorbed by the tranquility of green hills and the specks of magpies that formed black freckles in the blue sky, and she recalled the feeling of ripeness in her body on that summer afternoon. There had been a place of sheer happiness in her then; no memory of fear even registered. If she could only go back there, into a world that held such vivid colors and details, if she could remember what it was like to love and live freely, she could find a way to enjoy this smooth tranquility now. Of one thing she was certain: She was once again flying.

Early that morning, when her dear Ung had brought the embroiderer to her room in the Apartments of Peace, she had been overwhelmed by the young man's earnest face and the fervor of his words. He promised her that if she came with him to the ill-fated village of Cam Le, he would show her the answers to the mystery of her loved ones' deaths and unveil the identity of their murderer. Sick though she was, how could she resist such an invitation? In an instant she had agreed to join him.

In the boat, he had strapped her in a palanquin; her ankles rested against its wooden legs, and silk handkerchiefs bound her wrists in place. "The wind is strong," he had explained to her. "Since there are only the two of us on this journey, it is urgent that you are secured to your seat while I row."

Over her head and attached to the sedan twirled a blue parasol — a round slice of Heaven, which had followed her since early dawn. Pink and purple satin pillows packed and supported her bony body, so that she could sit up and watch the scenery as the boat glided atop the water. In her hand she held her son's anklet, the talisman of her mission. The outrage of her family's massacre tore at her. She longed for the knowledge that would help her erase the hatred, and for that opportunity, she must keep herself alive.

She could see that the embroiderer was watching her between the strokes of his oar. Could he be the killer that she had been looking for all these years? The thought made her dizzy with suspicion. If he was, she would exact her revenge. Beneath her blank expression, her mind was ablaze. She knew she would not live long enough to witness his end, but she had set in motion a plan to make sure that he would pay. At the end of this journey, she would no longer have anything to fear or regret. A few more hurdles and she could die an emancipated soul.

The boat came to a small dock full of people. The embroiderer crouched in his seat, scanning his surroundings with the alertness of a disturbed cobra. For the first time, she could see the hatred on his face. Slowly he composed himself, dropping the paddle on the floorboard.

Turning to her, he said, "We are here at last, madam. Soon, you will meet your true enemy, who murdered your husband and son. I must warn you about his nature. Unlike anyone you have ever met, this man is extremely cruel and dangerous. If in fact death has not claimed him, then we may have just put ourselves into a tiger's lair. You are about to see the truth, in its ugliest form."

She said, "You do not need to tell me this. I am ready."

He cast a glance downward, avoiding her eyes. "I am a coward, madam. I am partially responsible for your son's death, and I know it is in your power to judge me. I realize by taking you here to meet the true killer, I will also be facing my own trial for the role I played in the crime."

"What role did you play in this tragedy?" she demanded.

"I was the one who should have been killed, not your son or husband. They should never have come to the Cam Le Village. But I must ask for your patience. I'll take you to the killer, and you will hear the truth from his mouth."

"How can you make a man confess his sins?"

"I cannot promise that he will speak," he said. "However, even the devil himself will not reject the final wish of a dying woman. I was hoping that you could plead for the truth from him."

She managed a tiny smile. "Will you be there, by my side, to protect me against the menace of this person?"

He nodded. The earnest look returned to his face.

"Sir! Over here!"

"No, let me!"

She became aware of the voices of the unemployed porters and beggars on the dock, looking to be hired by the rich merchants who brought their goods to the market in town. Their ragged clothes clung to their thin torsos, as if made out of river kelp, and smelled just as strong. Some of the men, the stronger ones, stepped into the water and with their skillful hands guided the boat to shore. She realized that the expensive garments on her body had attracted their attention, and now her vessel was surrounded with callused hands and sunburned faces. A few grimy fingers brushed at her skin, desperate to be chosen. The word *silver* was upon the tips of their tongues as they named their wages loudly.

Her companion leaped over the taffrail and landed on his feet among the strangers on the wharf. Wasting no time, the young man chose four men from the crowd. Ignoring the protests from the rest of the laborers, he stationed his employees at both sides of the boat and directed them as they hoisted her chair to their shoulders. Her parasol tilted, and sunlight poured down on her, bright and sudden like a slap.

Lady Chin saw the naked backs beneath her feet, marveling to think that after so many years, she was no longer inside the citadel. The embroiderer led her porters through a flotsam of rickshas, past wheelbarrows filled with fresh fruits and green vegetables. A few steps ahead, a pair of guards stood at the opening to the village's main road. Their faces, weathered from the harsh sun, looked dully at the newcomers.

"Identifications, please," one of them said. Dan produced the ivory passes from the royal palace, and the guards, though seeming unimpressed, stepped aside.

Cam Le was a village of white houses and thatched roofs, or houses that would have been white if the dust had not caked on their outer surfaces. Doors were open, and children ran naked in the streets. The women sat on the ground in groups of three and four, picking head lice from each other's hair and sewing rags together to make coverings for their bare bosoms. Cattle lived among the humans, eating the same grains from the fields as their owners, sleeping on the same tatami mats, until it came time for them to be slaughtered to complete the cycle of life. The sweet smell of roasted sesame filled the cool morning air.

There was so much simplicity in what she saw; it all seemed like a work of art — or Heaven, in its plainest form. She wondered if she had just died and crossed over into the peaceful world that she had spent her whole life looking for. Where had she gone wrong? She could have had this life. Happiness, anger, love, and jealousy — the basic human emotions were so simple in this idyllic context.

They emerged from a bamboo forest. Had she just dozed off without realizing it? She saw a grove of mango trees and heard sparrows singing in their branches. Fruits by the score dangled from thin stalks, their fat little bellies warmed by the sun. Never in her life had she seen so many mangoes in one tree. Their skins shone with a rich, glossy shade of green that made her mouth water.

The porters set her palanquin on a mound of wild grass. An abandoned field opened before her; the green was abundant and infinite, hurting her eyes with its shimmering brightness. In the middle of the meadow, she saw the remains of a crumbling, ivy-covered wall, lonely as a single mah-jongg tile. She looked up and saw the young man's face against the backdrop of a piercing blue sky.

"Where am I?" she asked.

"Madam, you are standing on the ground that was once my childhood home." He closed his eyes and drew in a deep breath. His arms extended outward, palms opened as if he were embracing the ghost of his past. "Over here was the living room with mosaic divans and bookshelves full of knowledge. The rich marble tiles were so well

polished that you could comb your hair looking at the reflection on the floor. Rare and antique paintings by well-known artists decorated the walls. I remember every detail, the fantastic colors, exquisite designs, and gentle aromas of my home." He turned and gestured, then continued.

"Look at that remaining wall! And those mango trees; they were among the few living things that survived a dreadful fire. Do they not seem to recite the horrors they have seen to anyone that would listen? Just hear their muffled voices." The wind wandered through a clutch of leaves, moaning an endless dirge of suffering. He continued in a toneless voice, "How can I find the courage to return to the very spot where my father and his wives were beheaded? They died at the hands of the same person who killed your husband and son. Look at this place! This is where your family was massacred."

Lady Chin rose from the chair with sudden strength. She recognized the sincerity in his voice, which seemed too youthful to be filled with so much misery. She wanted to speak, but the words died in her throat.

"Over there," he said, walking across a white-bricked path toward the front entrance. The gates had been broken from their hinges, leaving a large opening beneath a vinery awning. "This was my family's burial site!" he exclaimed. "I have not been able to pay respects to the dead in several years. With your permission, I would like to spend a few moments —"

His mouth dropped open as he noticed three lumps of dirt along the tree line. At first, she did not notice anything out of the ordinary. However, her second glance took in the explanation for his shocked expression: on top of the stone surfaces of the grave markers, fresh carnations lay in bunches, their petals still clinging to a few drops of morning dew. Somebody must have been in the cemetery prior to their arrival, paying homage to the deceased. Dan turned around, crossing the yard at a quick pace as if he were late for an important gathering. "Who has been here?" he shouted. "Can anyone hear me? Ven? Song? Are you listening to me? It is I, Dan Nguyen. Will you come out and see me again?"

His voice was lost into the limitless blue sky. No one replied, except for the birds flapping their wings. The porters looked at one

another. The embroiderer squatted and leaned against a stone pillar. He touched the flowers, as if to make certain they were real. Curiosity and sympathy flickered on the laborers' faces as they waited, huddled together like a pack of mules.

Lady Chin looked at the young man's face, taking in his dark eyes, full lips, and muscular frame. She saw the softness of his character, the strength of his body, and the vulnerability of his emotions. For the first time in their relationship, she truly realized that he was not her own son, no matter how much her mind had played tricks on her. Her son was timid, arrogant, and cruel. Her son bit his nails. Her son raped the servants whenever there was no one else around. Finally she understood her own reasons for embarking on this journey: she was not here because of the embroiderer's promise to reveal the truth about her loved ones' deaths. She had come for the trip that she should have made, along with them, seven years ago. She, too, should have perished in this remote village, along with her husband and son, together as a family in death as in life. Now it was time for her to complete her destiny. "Dan," she called. Her voice was no longer a whisper. "We must be going."

But it was too late. Her words were drowned by a buzzing sound, which grew louder. She recognized the noise made by a car engine. The dark rooftop of an automobile appeared at the end of the road.

"We cannot leave yet, madam," the embroiderer said, standing up. "We are about to have company."

chapter twenty-one

Wings of the Dragonfly

*T*he dark sedan, blue in the sunlight, crawled along the dusty road that led to the Nguyen mansion. Its metal roof showed through several tattered layers of paint like the sunburnt skin on the peasants' backs during the harvest season. Behind the car marched a double line of guards — men in white uniforms and straw hats carrying impressive firearms. Their cleated soles struck the packed earth, beating a shuffling rhythm that grew louder in the sultry morning. Before long, the vehicle and its legion drew to a stop on the other side of the entrance. Beyond the thick canopy of leaves, villagers watched with undisguised curiosity.

Lady Chin looked at the automobile's dark windshield, hypnotized by its size. The grumbling of the engine seemed to penetrate the earth like a malevolent entity. A whisper above her head, among the leaves, made her look up. Voices of the ghosts! She felt their presence as clearly as she felt the wind on her skin.

Dan grasped her hand. The warmth of his touch tethered her to the world of the living. She wanted to thank him but found no strength to make the sound. Instead, she returned her attention to the car.

The vehicle's door opened. White smoke curled from inside, caressing the grass like delicate fingers. The soldiers arranged themselves in a semicircle along the wall of the mansion, their hands cradling their guns like infants. More smoke emerged, making it difficult for her to see. The motor stopped its droning, and once again, silence ruled.

A black shoe jabbed the foggy space below the door, then crushed a tuft of grass. It paused on the green edge of the ground with its pointed, shiny tip aimed at her. Then slowly its twin appeared. Lady Chin sat still, mesmerized. Those were wicked feet — two black cats delivering the omen of evil. A faint odor of opium poppy wafted over the clean, sweet air. She was certain that the devil had come in his polished shoes to claim her soul.

Through her confusion she heard an unfamiliar voice, thick and drawling. "It is really you, Dan Nguyen. This morning one of the soldiers reported that you appeared at the dock, announcing your full name with the arrogance of a young lord. Naturally, I was incredulous. I had to see you myself in order to be convinced of such an outlandish tale."

Lady Chin looked up at the speaker. Prickly coal-black hair straggled over puffy, half-shut eyes. With each word he spoke, a trail of smoke trickled from a corner of his thin blue lips. His clothing was disheveled. The once-expensive silk garment was now crumpled and caked with dirt. One of his ears was flat, pasted to his head like soaked rice paper — the distinctive trait of an opium addict who has reclined too long on one side. She would have guessed that he was probably still in his mid-thirties, but years of indulgence had given his visage the leathery look of a much older man. She marveled that such an unkempt person would speak with such authority.

By her side the embroiderer stood with his eyebrows furrowed. "That voice," he muttered. "Where have I heard it?"

The other man leaned against the sedan's front fender. "You heard it for the first time in this garden, sixteen years ago, the day your traitorous father and his two wives were executed for their crimes. I heard your confession to Toan that you were hiding in that mango tree, and I, a lowly soldier then, was down here with the authorities, on the very spot where you are now standing. Refer back to your memory, young man."

"Of course!" the embroiderer said in disbelief. "You are Sai, the captain of the guards."

"Yes, indeed. You have a good memory. Only I am now Master Sai, the town mayor."

"What happened to Magistrate Toan?" Dan asked.

The mayor did not answer. Lady Chin watched them study each other like a pair of fighting cocks until the embroiderer broke the silence.

"You are not who I am looking for," he said, straightening. "Either you must leave my property at once, or state your motive. What are you doing here with a team of armed guards? Am I under arrest?"

"Come now, young Master Nguyen!" the mayor exclaimed. "Times have changed since you were last seen in these parts. The Toan family is no longer ruling the village. Since you know everything that happened here when you were a child, you know we share no bad blood between us. It was not I — it was he, Magistrate Toan — who was responsible for your sufferings. I was only a subordinate officer, a mere tool, like this firearm." He tapped the gun in the arms of a nearby soldier and laughed.

"Why are you here?" Sai's voice contained a trace of irony. "Since you are now liberated from the life of servitude, why return to the scene of your humiliation?"

"You have guessed it, sir. It is the magistrate that I am looking for, to even a score."

"Then you will need my help, young Master."

"Thank you," Dan said. "You are generous. But there will be no need to impose on you. I am capable of handling my own affairs."

Mayor Sai took a few steps forward until he towered above Lady Chin. His sparse mustache, enormous brown teeth, and red gums made her pull away involuntarily. The burning sun peeked out from behind his spiky head, and she had the impression that fire was bursting out of his mouth. She let out a whimper of fright. The embroiderer knelt and held her in his arms.

"Could this be Lady Yen, your mother?" the town mayor asked.

Dan did not answer; she leaned closer to him and muttered, "Evil man!"

"Is she mad?" the mayor whispered, frowning.

"Quite the opposite," said the embroiderer, standing up and facing his opponent. "She is every bit as sane as you and I, except that she is dying, and she is sometimes delirious. You appear to her as an evil energy. Step back!"

"Come now, sir. You are acting as impulsively as a pregnant woman."

"Now," Dan said. His voice was low and abrasive. "Be gone!"

The mayor spat on the ground. "You wretch!" he thundered. "How dare you provoke me in front of my men? I know why you are here. I have waited many years for this day to come. Clearly you have found the other half of the treasure map. Why else would you come, if not to attempt to salvage your fortune? Without my help, you will never obtain what you are looking for. Trust me, for I know what I am talking about. I myself have been searching for the same object, but the old rascal Toan has been too clever for me. That miserable snake!" He threw a threatening look at Dan. "Do not forget that I am now the mayor. Nothing will leave this town without my consent or my knowledge. If you try to challenge me, I will bring you to ruin."

"Get away from my property," Dan said. The muscles on his back tautened as he struggled for composure. The mayor staggered forward and aimed a punch at Dan's face. To Lady Chin's amazement his fist, instead of smashing into the embroiderer's cheek, was caught in midair by the young man. The guards rushed forward, their guns pointing.

"Do not shoot," the mayor yelled. "I need him alive."

Still holding the mayor's wrist, the embroiderer swung it around with such strength that the man's body was jerked forward. He fell on his knees, thrusting his chest out to accommodate the twisted arm, which was now pressed against the small of his back.

In desperation, the mayor gasped, "Ah, that hurts. Let me go."

Dan gave his wrist another push and released his fingers. Sai fell forward, his face in the grass. He jerked to his feet, stroked his bruised arm, and screamed to his men, "Arrest him!"

Dan took a step back, reaching into his pants pocket. Then he raised his hand, palm facing the team of guards. Inside, dangling at the end of a red ribbon, was the ivory pass that had been given to him by the Queen Mother, Lady Thuc. "In the name of the Imperial Court, I command you to stop," he shouted, thrusting the royal emblem at them. The soldiers halted as if they were seized by an invisible string.

"The palace permit," the mayor cried in recognition. "How did you acquire such an emblem of merit? What is your position in the Imperial City?"

"I am a mandarin in the Ministry of Chancellery," Dan answered. "I am the official embroiderer for His Majesty. Do you think I would be foolish enough to enter this blood-soaked place, knowing the danger that I was going to be facing, without the protection of the Royal Court? I have left a note with a trusted friend, telling the reasons why I have returned to the Cam Le Village. Every afternoon the Meridian Gate closes at precisely six o'clock. If I am not present at that time to resume His Majesty's portrait, my friend will deliver this note to Lady Thuc's attention. You, the Toan family, and your henchmen will be held accountable for my absence. And let me assure you, there is enough evidence in the note to guarantee you a death sentence. I have also requested that the head of this village's mayor, whomever that may be, be speared on a pole before my father's grave. Now, do you really want these guards to seize me?"

The mayor raised a hand and signaled to his men. They fell into two single files, heading toward the entrance.

Lady Chin became aware that she was being lifted. She was so filled with relief that she did not know when she left the grounds of the ruined mansion. The vast blue Heaven that had witnessed the massacre of her loved ones now watched her leave the dark ground.

※

*L*ady Chin was attending her own funeral, or so it seemed.

Her wooden palanquin, lined with pink and purple satin pillows, floated a few inches above an endless golden field where tranquility was the color of ripened corn tassels. Her body, lifeless and disfigured, was covered in several layers of shrouds. At her side walked Dan, as ever a comforting presence. She could see the mayor's face behind the opaque windshield as his car followed her procession. Behind him strode the long lines of soldiers.

At a turn of the road, an ancient banyan tree sprouting twisted tentacles seemed to mimic a woman drying her hair in the wind. In the distance, the tiled rooftop of a temple appeared, its lichen-covered walls blending into the earth. The sound of gongs, the rustle of leaves, the richness of incense smoke, and the rippling cloud of corn pollens combined in an atmosphere of deep calm, as if time were drifting toward a restful emptiness.

Her retinue, like a centipede, crawled into the street where the market was being conducted in busy confusion. She saw the silk vendors' bright ribbons of vermilion and blue and purple, the food stands displaying strings of succulent roasted ducks and chickens and pork, and men and women in tattered clothes staring at her. These were the witnesses to her interment, filling both sides of the street — strange faces carrying flowers, whispering gossip, playing musical instruments, and burning paper money for the afterlife. She searched each and every countenance, looking for the familiar features of someone who might mourn her loss, anyone who would bid farewell to her departing soul.

Then an odd thing happened. Like a flash of lightning slicing a dark sky, an electrifying image shot through her mind. Before this the villagers had seemed ordinary; all their grubby faces contained the same sunburned, inquisitive expression. But among them was a pair of eyes, dark as coal, cavernous as midnight, that penetrated her very soul. The ghosts of her past descended on her in a rush; she saw the dead bodies of her husband and son flung out on the front lawn of the deserted mansion.

She looked again into the face that bore those haunting eyes and waved in vain for the embroiderer, but he was walking ahead of her and failed to notice. She tried to rise; the scene blurred and she shuddered. How could she tell him that she had just looked into the eyes of a murderer?

D an Nguyen halted in his tracks. He, too, had noticed the villager with the piercing eyes. The ragged figure detached itself from the crowd and walked toward him — an androgynous creature, with a hairless skull and face full of scars. Any remnant of beauty was gone. The scars were long and grotesque. It was looking at him and opened its arms. There was something maternal in its gesture, the way it was beckoning to him, as if with longing. Upon careful examination, he could see ample breasts under the dark clothes.

The bearers of the palanquin stopped moving when they saw Dan halt. The crowd whispered — a long rasping sound that swept from one end to the other, the way rain traveled. He followed the woman with his eyes and saw her step into the road. Her arms were stretched outward, her mouth hung open, and her stare seared him with the power of the sun.

She ran toward him, stumbling, yet nothing could stop her headlong dash. From her throat, a loud noise, like the howl of a beaten dog, penetrated the hushed surroundings. Where in his life had he heard such a primitive sound? The emotion it expressed was excruciating, but not one intelligible word was being uttered.

Dan took several steps backward, confused and frightened by the terrible screeching. "Who are you?" he cried, searching her face. There was a trace of the time-teller in her scars, the shaven head, and the look of wild terror . . . Oh, sovereign gods in Heaven, please have mercy . . . he had seen those eyes somewhere. He could see his reflection in them as if looking into a mirror. They were shaped like the wings of a black dragonfly, and the high cheekbones, the oversized teeth — all were familiar.

The woman smiled, even though tears trickled down her rough skin. She grabbed him by the hand, kissed it, and then pressed his fingers against her cheek.

Comprehension washed over him. "Ven?" he muttered. "Is that you?"

She nodded.

From his hips down, the bones melted and he slumped forward. She received him into her bosom as though he were a child.

"The flowers at my father's grave," he said, while she rocked him in her embrace. "It was you that put them there?"

Again she nodded.

Dan could hardly speak. "Your hair, your face, your voice," he said. "What have they done to you?"

She answered him with the devoted, happy whimper of a house pet. Her disfigured face relaxed into an expression of contentment. She kept on touching him, from the side of his forehead to the length of his hair, as though to reassure herself that he was not a dream.

Lady Chin, too, had seen the mesmerizing eyes before. They belonged to the killer in the wanted posters that hung over her bed. For seven long years she had studied the face, the eyes, memorizing the features until they were etched in her mind. For seven wretched years she had searched. And now in this alien territory, when she least expected it, Lady Chin had finally come face to face with her foe.

Staring at Ven, Dan was overcome with shame and horror. Ever since the night of the harvest moon, he had believed that she had given her life to save his. Never did he expect to see her here among the townspeople, disfigured and babbling. He raised her chin with his forefinger, tilting her face toward the sun. She opened her mouth, and he saw the little remaining stump of her tongue.

"Ven," he moaned. "I would give anything to hear you speak again. I curse the cruel wretches who have done this to you. Now your silence will forever guard their vile names."

From behind Dan came a guttural voice. "With your permission, I will talk for her."

Dan turned and saw the time-teller standing at the side of the road, hands folded in front of his chest. There was no slurring in his speech, no stagger in his gait, and no broken bottle in his clenched hand. Even his leathery face was now clean. So much had changed in this village; Dan found himself at a loss for words.

He looked at his wife, then back to Big Con. They could have been twins, with their shaven heads, scars, dark clothing, and air of acquiescence. Dan could not help but wonder if Ven had tried to be the time-teller's mirror image. He wanted to sit and talk with her for hours, hear her melodious voice, absorb her knowledge. With sadness in his heart, he realized he was no longer in the same plane as she. To hear her, he needed an intermediary. Reluctantly, he nodded, and the time-teller stepped forward.

"Ask me anything you want to ask her, Sir Dan," he said.

"Who has harmed you, Ven?" Dan asked.

Ven took a deep breath, squared her shoulders, and looked straight at Dan. Her neck tightened, and her mouth opened, making a loud and continuous "ah" sound.

The time-teller turned to her. Their eyes locked. Then he spoke in a voice that was barely audible. "She says that her tongue was cut out by the hands of that devil Toan."

She whimpered and pounded her chest. Her eyes wore the look of a wounded deer.

"Ven wants to know why you are here," Big Con continued. "She has waited for you, as much for your family's honor as for hers. She adores you and has respected your memory, but many times she was compelled to believe that you were not coming back. What has taken you so long to return? Let her know, at last, that her affliction, which was forced upon her by that monster, is about to be avenged. Tell her that Death has spared your enemy for all these years, only because it is awaiting your judgment."

"If you knew all the prayers I have made to the gods," Dan said, turning to Ven. "If you knew how much I have grieved. In all the years we were together during my childhood, I followed your footsteps, watched you, loved you, and feared you. I did everything that you asked of me. I have contemplated a thousand revenge tactics against him. But when it was time to execute these schemes, I just could not will my hands to strike a blow on the enemy. The reason was neither cowardice nor ignorance. My poor heart's hatred toward him was thwarted by love, a confused, forbidden, hopeless kind of love. However, all of that is about to change. I am now a heartless brigand, ready to renew the vow of vengeance that I made as a young child. For all the lives he has broken, he must pay."

"Why did you not come back sooner?" the time-teller asked, still watching Ven intensely.

Dan extended his hands toward Ven. "I believed you were dead. When I fled the mansion, you had been arrested and were his prisoner. I never thought a madman like Toan would spare your life."

"He did not spare her," Big Con said. "Quite the opposite. She was hung on a post in the middle of a field and left there, bleeding and dying. I rescued her from the claws of Death. And I brought her back." The time-teller related the gruesome details of her torture while his face remained as still as a mask.

"Was it also you," Dan interrupted, "who scarred her face and shaved her head? Was it your plan to permanently damage Ven, so that you can hold on to her forever?"

She shook her head and screeched. Her hands flew up and covered her face. Dan had never seen her act this way — fragile, deeply vulnerable, and undeniably feminine. She seemed ashamed of her damaged face.

The time-teller pulled her into his arms. She pressed against the hollow of his chest, hiding from view. Gently he rocked her, at the same time whispering inaudible phrases that calmed her. The sky was pink from the wicked sun, and the trees surrounding them looked like the shadows of judges, standing over Dan, ready to condemn him. He felt utterly out of place, like an outsider sneaking a peek at an affectionate display through a window, waiting to be caught.

"What are you accusing me of?" said Big Con, speaking over Ven's head. "I have lived to this age, never laying a hand on any woman, let alone one I hold so dear. She destroyed her own face, but that should not surprise you. You, sir, of all people should understand her character. How else could she remain in this village, under the eyes of the watchful guards, among the enemies, without being recognized?" He drew his hand across Ven's scarred cheekbone. "I know this face well, and never for one instant have I ceased to find the beauty in its imperfection, nor could I survive without looking at it first thing every morning." He seemed to stand taller. "I love Ven more than life itself because she, to me, is life. She is everything I have asked the gods for and everything that I, as an educated tutor, deserve. The obstacle to my happiness that I face each day is you. You are married to her, and your ghost has been at our bedside since the day she entered my home."

Dan turned to Ven. She was looking at him through her fingers like a child waiting to be reprimanded. "I understand," he said. "Are you happy, Ven?"

Yes, her eyes seemed to say as she smiled and took her hands away.

"Then, you have my blessing," Dan said. "Enjoy this unity between you and Tutor Con. In the deepest grief and most miserable circumstances, you have managed to find happiness in each other. As a couple, you have vanquished Death. May the gods in Heaven continue to bless your life together as they have done in the past! Live and be content in each other's presence."

Swept by joy, Ven ran to him and seized his hands. "It is time for us to face the enemy," he said to her. "Tell me when you are ready, and we will leave together."

Ven turned around. The time-teller, as if he understood her gesture, cast himself at Dan's feet. His shiny head reflected the golden sunlight. "I thank you with all of my heart. You have liberated us with your generosity. Now I understand why Ven has reserved such a special place in her heart for you, young Master."

Dan bent forward to help the time-teller back on his feet and said, "Tutor Con, you do not need to thank me. I trust your sincerity and character. You have proven to me how much you care for dear Ven. Marry her today if you will, let her become your lawfully wedded wife, protect her, so that she will no longer be alone in the world." His voice was thick with emotion as he continued. "As for me, I have procrastinated long enough. In the name of my ancestors, I must prepare for an appointment with my destiny. But first, there is someone I would like to introduce to you."

Ven's slanted eyes searched his face, waiting.

Dan put his arm around her waist and walked her toward Lady Chin. She examined Ven, paying careful attention to the peasant's shaven head. Not even her most skillful willpower could keep her labored breathing under control. Dan ran to her side and felt her bony hand seize his shoulder.

"You did not warn me," she whispered, looking at Ven in fright. "Even with her scars, I recognized this woman from the wanted poster. But as I listen to her story, I am shocked that she has endured so much pain. Tell me, is she the murderer that we have traveled so far to meet, or is she just a victim of yet another heinous crime?"

"She is my guardian, madam," Dan said with a smile. "She is not the killer of your husband and son, contrary to what you have been told in the past. Like you and I, she has lived for the day she would see revenge and justice, and she is now waiting for judgment to prevail."

Lady Chin leaned forward until her face was inches from his. "Sir Dan, you are indeed a very charming man. I have trusted you this far, and I am willing to trust you until my last breath. Perhaps I am foolish to find you humble and courageous, when in fact your true nature might be greedy and cruel. I urge you, sir, do not deceive this dying woman! She might not be as fragile and helpless as she appears to be. I have been watching you, and I know about the note you left with your friend before we left Hue. I, too, left a note. And the person who is holding your letter also holds mine. That man is my dearest friend, and when the time comes he will not hesitate to carry out my final wish. In this game I do not have much to lose except my life. And as you can see, I have lived long enough. The moment I find out that you are attempting to break your code of honor, which has been the armor that protects you thus far, I promise I will turn you over to the hands of the most vengeful gods. Look above you! There is a Heaven, and it is watching you."

Dan bowed to her. "My life is in your hands, madam. With the witness of Heaven above, I will not deceive you."

"Then," she said, "let us meet the true killer. My time is running out, but I have asked Death to hold back for a little while."

Dan turned to the time-teller and said, "I implore you to tell me what you know about Magistrate Toan, where he is and the size of his team of guards. To enter his territory, I must know his strength."

"He is alone in his mansion," Tutor Con replied. "A short time after the events of the harvest moon, Master Long resigned his position as the town mayor. While his father was at Hue City, reporting the deaths of the minister and his son, Master Long decided to leave with his family. That was the last time the people of Cam Le ever saw or heard of them. The old man returned to an empty house, where he has been waiting for Death ever since."

"Can you, then, be kind enough to lead us there?"

chapter twenty-two

Flames of the Dragon

T hey came to a stop in front of a great house. Although the wall that encircled the prop- erty blocked most of the inside from view, Lady Chin could see the idle destruction of time by looking through the entrance. Before her stood two wooden posts, perhaps once sturdy and grand, but now bent and split open from the dry heat, as though sagging under the weight of the black doors that hung from them.

In the long courtyard, wild grass taller than a man's head veiled a two-story house. Fleeing rodents rustled the overgrown tassels as the humans approached. Lady Chin took in the dusty smell of the house and its gloomy vastness. Who could await Death in this emptiness? Even her apartment of peace, stark and coffinlike though it was, was a haven compared to this place.

Behind them the heavy sound of the mayor's leather shoes thumped closer. Turning, she saw that his car was parked in the shade of an oak tree. His thin lips gashed a crooked smile as he reached inside his crumpled tunic for a handkerchief and used it to wipe his face. "Aye," he said, "no one has walked through this gate since Master Long left his mansion. We all use the back door to visit the old man."

The embroiderer squatted on the step to examine the gates, his back to the mayor. Lady Chin could see the crown of the young man's head on a level with the tips of her toes. "We are going to walk into his house from this front entrance," he said, pushing at the heavy doors to make the opening wider.

He stepped into a grassy yard that nearly swallowed him whole. Lady Chin's bearers followed him. From her elevation she could see the house. Its numerous layers of paint had peeled away; cracks and fissures formed eccentric veins on the walls; trails of dark sap seamed the front surface. The once-red roof had been blanched bone white under the sun; at the same time, the edges of the tiles were encrusted with a residue of brown moss, making them look like teeth that were stained with tobacco.

On the front porch, dead trees in a row of broken vases strained their torturous branches at the guests. Many window shutters and door panels had been stripped from their original positions, leaving behind naked, hollow cavities that gaped like the eyes of a blind man. Shadows hid the interior; even the brightest sun could not dismiss the ancient gloom within. Then, from within this bleak landscape, she heard the faint sound of footsteps.

A woman swept along the hallway, arms extended outward so that her nails scratched the walls, creating an eerie resonance. She thrust her face out from the dark and squinted at the intruders. Lady Chin recognized the woman's housekeeping uniform, a large, loose-fitting blue garment. Her protruding forehead and open mouth gave her the look of a dull child. She stood at the entrance, making no move to come forward.

After a minute, the mayor marched out of rank. The maid shrank back against the wall. "Master Sai —" was all that she could manage.

"How is the old rascal?" Sai asked.

The maid stiffened. Her arm lifted, fingers pointing at the inner room. "Inside," she muttered, "resting."

The mayor strode to the front porch, flanked by two of his men. He adjusted his robe and reached out to pat the maid on her head. She ran back inside, her hands clasped together in front of her chest.

Sai turned and raised his hand to Dan. "It is all right now," he called. "There are no guards in this place. You may enter when you are ready. I'll send some of my men to the market and get you a fresh drink, though I am afraid you may not approve of my gesture. Have you ever had a glass of coconut juice on a hot day such as this one? I have served the same drink to many before you, Sir Dan." He threw his head back and laughed at his own comment.

Lady Chin saw the embroiderer straighten. Throwing a dark look at the mayor, he said, "I don't want your assistance. In fact, I would rather see you leave this place."

Sai stopped laughing. "What is the matter? If I didn't know better, I would think you were frightened at the thought of entering this house. Will you come inside? I cannot blame you if you won't. No, in fact I expect that you are not going to join our little reunion party. But I myself will not leave, not until I find what I have come for." He turned and walked into the adjoining room.

Dan turned to the time-teller. "Where is Song?" he asked.

"She died many years ago," the tutor replied. "They found her body hanging in her room one morning. Some said it was a suicide. Others thought she was murdered."

Ven approached. "You take Ven," the embroiderer said to Con, trying to smile. "I will carry Lady Chin. Let the porters wait here. We are going to meet Magistrate Toan."

⚬≻

*L*ady Chin found herself in the living room of her enemy. It must have been elegant at one time, with its wide floor and high roof. But now rows of ebony pillars and painted black beams framed the dim space. Through her fluttering lashes the ceiling spun gently, and she could see tiny sparkles of stars peering through clusters of fluffy clouds; or was it a random pattern of stains, caused by dampness that had discolored the paint? At the highest point hung three metal poles in an upside-down tripod. Suspended from each rusty, crooked hook was a cluster of oil lanterns; their red bull-eyed flames sputtered ghostly images on the walls.

In the arms of the embroiderer, she lay still. There was an invisible wire running inside her, and her womb felt as though it were being hung at both ends with two iron clothespins and left to dry. The gnawing pain made her visualize the inner world of her body. Slowly, unwillingly, Lady Chin searched inside herself until her eyes met those of the monster that preyed on her flesh — the cancer that would eventually kill her. For a moment she held its steady, burning glare. Then the monster resolved itself into the wrinkled face of an old man, hunched in an armchair ten paces away. A steady, thin, yellow trail of saliva dripped from a corner of his quivering mouth. His fingers wiggled aimlessly. Immediately she knew who he was.

The devil's messenger!

She would never forget a face, especially this man's. He had come into her life one morning and suddenly, with his cold hard presence, made her a widow. The same oversized headdress and loose-fitting garments encased his now shrunken body. But what she locked eyes with made her shudder with fear. The mayor's voice drew her back to her companions.

"I am sorry to tell you this, Sir Dan," Sai said, fixing his eyes on the frail body of Magistrate Toan. "I take full credit for tending the magistrate in these past few years. I have sacrificed everything in my power to keep him alive, in hope that he would disclose to me the secret that I, in all fairness, am entitled to know. Just think, I have spent more than two decades of my life by his side, serving him as a slave and a confidant. I deserve a fair share of compensation for my servitude.

"But look at him! The magistrate is no longer in full possession of his mental faculties. His limbs have become completely useless. He has lost the ability to think or to act appropriately. He is not your enemy any longer. What you see before you is a living corpse, following the same ill fate as the ancient one, his own mother. How can I demand anything from a body with no spirit? I have tried, but no technique could retrieve any meaning out of his behavior. I am hoping that with the combination of our strength and wisdom, you and I can help each other interpret the signs and gestures that the old man may use to convey his thoughts. It is, after all, my last chance to locate the missing map. In return for your cooperation, I am willing to divide the treasure in equal halves once we find it together. And if this wealth was indeed buried by pirates as the old legend says, you, sir, will be one of the two richest men in Hue City."

Dan, his face whitened by the anemic lights, approached the old man. Magistrate Toan sat on a carved mahogany chair in the center of the room, his golden tunic spread around him like a spider's web. Staring as if petrified into the distance, he was animated only by the jerking motions of his hands. The fire in the old man's eyes had died to gray ashes, and he moved his lower jaw in a wobbly, grinding rhythm, as if he were working on a large wad of tobacco. The mighty enemy Dan had envisioned had become as dried-up as the heart of a betel nut. Without turning, he could feel Ven drawing near. Her plain, earthy scent rose above the room's mixture of sandalwood incense and opium smoke. He reached for her hand.

"How did he reach this state?" he asked. His eyes never left the old man's face.

"He made himself that way," the mayor replied. "Too much opium, I am afraid. A French physician I hired two years ago made that diagnosis. He also declared that the magistrate's nervous system was permanently damaged. There isn't much that anyone can do for him. It seems that Heaven has decided to condemn the wicked one for the crimes that he committed."

From the back of the room, the time-teller snickered at Sai's comment. He raised his voice and said, "If that was true, why were you spared? My wife was made a mute by your filthy hands."

At the doorway, the dim-witted maid stopped still, hands over her mouth as if in surprise. The mayor, slowly recovering from the effects of opium, flared his nostrils like an angry bull. He turned his sharpest, most indignant scrutiny at the time-teller, cleared his throat, and spat on the floor. "I only did what I was ordered to do," he said. "I was like the Thunder Spirit. Where the gods send me, that will be the spot I strike."

On a small bench near the magistrate's chair, next to an oil lamp, a copper urn was burning. Through the cracks of its covering, Dan saw strings of incense cloud wafting out, carrying the aroma of sandalwood. The old man's hands, misshapen with arthritis, cut through the sultry darkness, crushing the smoke into particles of dust. Those hands had once held a scimitar . . . the ghost of its blade still seemed to glint in his vacant eyes. Dan remembered the green mound of grass beneath his father's feet and the way it had turned red when the blood poured. He thought of his mother standing by the window of the brothel, selling her body to strangers. He thought of Ven and her silence. Could he . . . would he . . . be the instrument of vengeance for these lost souls and for his own?

The anger in him rose, like the smoke inside the urn. He opened his eyes. Then, before Dan was aware of it, he was grabbing the old man by his bony wrists and forcing them down from their mechanical twitching. The magistrate's wrinkled face was convulsing, but he made no attempt to escape. Dan leaned closer. He could see his reflection in the old man's eyes, a distorted, convex likeness of himself full of hate.

"Are you in there?" he screamed. "Answer me! Why are you so wicked? Why did you take so much pleasure in destroying my family? If you can hear me, explain yourself." His grip tightened on the magistrate, his voice hardened. "I could crush you with my bare hands this instant. Your weak, fragile bones would break just like a young chick. Toan! Anyone in here could kill you. But that won't give me back my parents, and Ven won't get back her power of speech. Crimes will not resolve crimes. I cannot . . . I will not become you." Behind him he heard the mayor's coarse laughter.

He felt a sticky liquid seep onto his hands. Dan uncoiled his fingers and raised them. To his horror he saw blood, thick, dark, and pungent. The old man, free from Dan's hold, jerked his arms in careless abandon, again chasing the tendrils of smoke. His frozen face showed no emotion.

Appalled and frightened, Dan let out a groan. The magistrate's arms jutted from the wide sleeves of his tunic, dotted with liver spots and smeared with blood. Why was the old devil bleeding? His grasp had not broken the skin. At the entrance, the maid was squatting on the ground with her hands wrapped around her head, elbows forward, her buttocks inches from the cement floor. She swayed, making soft moans. Dan unfastened the magistrate's tunic and peeled it open. The old man fell forward, laying his forehead against an armrest.

"No more, please," the maid screeched. "Do not hit the master again! I beg you."

Under the luxurious golden robe, the skin on Toan's back was scarred and broken. The black-and-red marks of whiplashes, some old, others still oozing blood, crossed one another like the lines on a road map. The servant's voice faded into a hoarse whisper.

Dan looked for the mayor. Sai spoke from the darkest part of the room. "I have tried every known method to make him talk. According to the physicians, he is in command of his five senses. He feels every physical stimulus that is inflicted upon him, even though he may not be capable of responding the same way any of us do. I was hoping that I could torture him out of his catatonic state. Certainly the magistrate understands that once he gives up what I am looking for, the torment will end."

Faced with Dan's silence, Sai lost his poise. "Sir Dan, don't you ridicule me with that glare!" he said. "You cannot judge me from where you stand, for I must do what I can to survive. I am not as fortunate as any of you: I am not blessed with a conscience. Poor Dan! Poor Ven! What has become of poor Sai? Did anyone even know him? Is he alive and at peace with himself? I am, as you can see, nameless and forgotten."

Turning to Ven, he raised his voice. "I know about the secret affair between you and Big Con, your cottage in the forest and your frequent trips to the cemetery inside the Nguyen mansion. I have kept an eye on the two of you as long as I have been the town mayor. But have I ever bothered or disturbed your happy nest? My mind has only one priority, and that is to retrieve the buried treasure so that it will comfort me in my final years. If you are tempted to judge me, I urge you to keep your comments to yourselves."

"You don't fool me, Mr. Sai," Dan interrupted. "Ven and Tutor Con are necessary actors in your sad drama. To you, they served as bait to lure me back into this village. That is why you have endured their presence for the past seven years without disturbing them. Now that I am here, my knowledge of the second half of the map won't help you find the treasure without the first half, which is lost along with the magistrate's mind. Be that as it may, it is no reason for you to act so cruelly to him. Remember the laws of consequence dictated by the rule of Karma — in twenty years, any of your men may inflict the same torture on you. Judging from the way that you have taken command of Toan's automobile, his men, and his career, I surmise that you are enjoying his estates and his lands as well. This fortune should be sufficient for you, Mr. Sai, to secure a life of leisure and prosperity." As he spoke, Dan turned to the old man and said, "The magistrate has paid his debt to you, to me, and to society. Let him be! He is now alone in his misery. As for me, I see that my trip home has served its purpose. It is time I should leave this place, go far away, and be free from such bitter memories."

He took Ven's hand and turned. The mayor sauntered forward, blocking Dan's exit.

"You cannot leave, my friend," he said, pushing his hands against Dan's bare chest. "I have pursued the hunt for your father's fortune for so long that I cannot let it escape me again. Give me your map! I deserve the right to possess it even though it is, as you have said, useless. You don't seem to care much for its value. Why not give it to me? I shall keep it as a memento."

Ven swept Sai's hands away from Dan and forced herself between them. Dan touched her shoulders, his face calm under the glow of the oil lanterns above.

"Do not fret, Ven," he said. "Sooner or later the mayor will realize I do not have the map in my possession. It is he who made the assumption that I have what he is looking for."

"But you have spoken as if you know where it is," Sai exclaimed.

"And so I have," replied Dan. "I confess, I have mentioned my knowledge of the second half of the map, but it is not in my care. In fact, I have seen it briefly just once. My poor memory, since then, has forgotten its details."

Sai leaned forward and opened his mouth. "Sir Dan," he breathed, "who has it? I have waited for so long, tell me and I will —" His jaw dropped in the middle of the sentence, and his eyes widened. Somewhere in the dark, the time-teller called out for Dan to be careful. A shadow floated up and crept across the ceiling, sweeping along the beams and columns of the stately house and then spreading out like spilled ink above Dan.

He turned and saw a pair of ancient eyes, aglow in the flickering light, staring at him from a few feet away. For a moment, he could not comprehend what he was seeing. Gradually the face of the old magistrate emerged from the vast form of his body. He was standing. His outstretched arms were raised upward, holding a tilted lantern. Some of the liquid inside its glass case spilled from the neck. The smell of kerosene permeated the sweltering air.

As Dan watched, dumbfounded, the old man sprang toward him, and his hands came down. The flash of fire tore through the darkness, a brilliant meteor. Dan caught the old man's wrists. Ven was coming toward him from the side with her face twisted and her arms raised. With his shoulder, Dan blocked her path.

"Get away, Ven," he said. She fell back, startled. More kerosene spilled, and the flame grew larger, crackling inside the transparent covering.

Magistrate Toan pulled himself closer. His rheumy eyes blinked, as his mouth broadened into an evil smile. "Greetings," he hissed. His guttural voice gurgled with pleasure. "You die . . . today . . . with me! We shall find the treasure together . . . in Hell. But first, your father is looking for his head. Will you help him?" His body shook with laughter. The room shuddered, echoing his lunacy.

Then, without pausing, he uncurled his fingers and the lantern slipped. The flaming wick responded to the rush of air and fluttered like the wing of a bat. Dan jumped back, watching the lamp crash onto the cement floor inches from the old man's feet. The splash of fire burst into hundreds of orange petals.

The old man howled as his robe caught fire. He lurched toward Dan, the long panels of his skirt alive with flames. The blaze gained speed, spreading upward. His kerosene-soaked hands were also blooming with the hungry flames. Dan withdrew farther. The old man bent down and scooped up the burning liquid on the ground. "Come, come," he screamed. "I have waited long for your return. Come play with me!" He hurled balls of fire around the room. Some of the sparks landed on the draperies, quickly burning holes through them. Others faltered as they flew across the room and then subsided. The interior walls came alive, bright with the new source of light, and the heat rose.

"Hurry . . . closer . . . if you want to know where I keep your father's tattoo. I have held my silence too long. Come before it . . . too late." His voice sang above the women's screams.

Ignoring the smoke-filled air, he searched for Dan. The flames multiplied, howling like a typhoon. Each long curtain, each narrow beam, every ornately carved piece of furniture fueled the fire. At the center, his body, a human torch, spewed streaming firecrackers like popping coals from a hot stove.

Dan tripped on the armrest of Lady Chin's chair and fell backward. His head crashed against the concrete floor and blackness covered him like a blanket.

Lady Chin tried to scream a warning to the embroiderer, but the words would not come to her throat. She was too weak; the heat of the fire robbed her of her voice. She saw the old man charge forward. His robe fluttered around him, a vast tidal wave in multicolored rings rising high in order to crash down upon her. The rainbow! She had seen it before; its outlandish charisma had visited her many times, making her swoon with fear. Not this time! She would have allowed the terror to consume her wholly, if only the embroiderer were not slumped at her feet, powerless and in danger.

Finding some remote strength inside her, she drew her knees up. The beast stampeded nearer. Its burning flesh sizzled and ruptured and flared just inches from her face. With all her might she kicked out, watching the sparks scatter as the soles of her shoes came in contact with his chest. The monster lurched backward, paused for a moment, and then resumed his charge. He was now screaming in earnest. Fire burst from his mouth in gusts, as though his lungs were filled with pure petroleum. She kicked again. But somewhere behind her, the scar-faced man was much faster. He bounded forward and buried his fist in the old man's chest, knocking him several steps back and into his chair.

The time-teller lifted Lady Chin in his arms. The old house was burning like a bundle of twigs. Angry red tongues of flame pulsed around the painted ceiling beams, hissing at the frightful scene below. She saw the embroiderer come to his feet with the help of the peasant woman. He touched his head, gasping for air.

Above her the time-teller screamed, "Ven, Dan, let's go! Follow me to the door!" In his arms, she was swung this way and that, while smoke filled her eyes with tears. His mutilated face bent closer to her, whispering inaudible phrases. She closed her eyes. Darkness filled her stinging lids with a soothing calmness, purging the fire away.

＞＜

*S*ai could not restrain himself any longer. The house and his inert prisoner, in a few short instants, had come alive in a simultaneous combustion. All this time, the old man had tricked him into believing his mind was gone. That old devil, that bastard . . . he had always been so clever, so devious. During the most severe punishment, he had just sat there and rolled his eyes back into his head and drooled in a steady stream, never closing his lids or clenching his fists. Except for an occasional tremor and sometimes a faint moan, the old man had never given any sign that he knew what was being done to him. How could he, the mayor, suspect otherwise? And now, in the blaze, the old scoundrel stood erect and triumphant, once again outsmarting Sai, making a fool of him.

"Come closer, if you want to know my secret," Magistrate Toan sang out. His wrinkled skin bubbled like rice paper over live charcoals.

Sai stood in his place, pondering. His men had tried to pull him out of the burning house, but he had shooed them off. How could he leave when the secret was only a few feet away? The fire was a pyramid made of human flesh, and somewhere beyond the intense light lay a fortune, about to be devoured in the hungry flames. *Think, Sai, think!* What would the old man do if he were in this situation? Who knew the master better than the slave after twenty years of devotion? He had to find a way to get into that old brain and retrieve what he wanted. Where would that wily fox hide the map?

"Come, come and play with me, Mouse," the magistrate crooned.

"Ven, Dan, get out! Follow me to the door!" the voice of the time-teller urged.

Sai came closer. The heated air, the smell of burning flesh, the snipping and snapping of fire — it was as if Hell had just opened and the devil was raised from a gap in the ground. Beyond a cloud of smoke, Toan sat on a throne made out of flames. His body was almost nude; a red glow shrouded his dark flesh. Fire was bursting out of his eyes.

"Who are you?" the demon screamed at Sai.

"I am Mouse," he lied, shakily. "Tell me your secret."

The skeleton's arm shot forward. It caught Sai's wrist and held him with unbreakable strength. He cried out as the pain seized him like a thousand piercing knives. From the tips of the old man's other hand, the sandalwood urn flew through the smoky air and hit him squarely in the forehead.

Sai sank to his knees. The chandelier of oil lanterns came crashing down, carrying with it a portion of burning roof. In the quaking turmoil, the mayor sprawled, and the weight of the collapsing world was upon him.

chapter twenty-three

The Silver Anklet

As the afternoon sun pivoted toward the bamboo forest on the far side of the river, a tiny group of people, like a long, dark line of ants, gathered at the dock. Lady Chin knew that her body was with them, but somehow she seemed to be watching from above. In the distance, over the house of Toan, the north wind thrust bleak, ruddy clouds of smoke into the clear sky. The frantic buzzing of the villagers was half-drowned by the strident sound of the emergency drum.

The embroiderer led the procession. His brown chest gleamed under the waning sun, his hair was tangled with soot and charcoal, and his left elbow was seared by four burns, each the size of a copper penny. The long wharf, which usually teemed with vendors, was empty. News of the great fire had halted the entire town's activities and attracted all who were curious to the site of destruction.

The bearers laid Lady Chin's palanquin on the wet soil and turned to the embroiderer, anticipating their wages. He reached deep into his pocket and handed them a stack of silver coins. They thanked him and left.

Cool winds flooded over Lady Chin. She watched herself gasping for air. From behind a thick, invisible wall, the embroiderer called her name. She saw him above her, hands on her cheeks, looking anxiously for her pulse. She could not answer. The new world that she was discovering had no sound.

As she watched, the sky became bluer and clearer. On a long-ago summer day she had flown through the air on a bicycle, happy as a child, while her body melted into thousands of tiny air bubbles, each mirroring her husband's face. She had often thought of the vivid colors she had seen that afternoon — the spectacular green hills, the massive orange sun, the traces of magenta in the sleepy clouds. She never forgot how cheerfully shiny her silver bike was; it had all but twinkled a smile at her for the entire trip. She recalled a single golden dandelion lying in the grass next to her nude body where they had stopped to make love. Long afterward, a yellow petal lingered in her hair like a soft kiss from the earth.

She would never forget the beautiful life she once had!

There were, however, many things she did forget. All of her bad memories in the house of Toan had faded away. Nothing seemed important anymore, just this moment in time. She must do yet one more thing, which prompted her to reenter her withered body and focus on the embroiderer. "Wear this," she whispered, thrusting her son's anklet into Dan's hand. "It will protect you."

She was letting go all the ache and pain in her body, all the weight on her chest. The dandelion was still with her, a simple yet lush fragment of her youth dangling from a river of jet-black, luxurious hair. Her belly was firm and flat, and inside it throbbed the tiny heartbeat of a fetus. Green grass sprouted from the dampened soil; the sun liquefied into a lake of red paint. She gave herself one more chance to do it all over again, and this time it was sheer ecstasy. She could not be sure how it happened, nor did she care. Of all the events that were unfolding around her, one thing was certain: she was not imagining this beauty. It was so real to her that she could feel it with her whole being.

She died, quietly and with exquisite poise.

*A*mong the scattered sampans, Dan spotted his vessel floating off to one side. With the corpse in his arms, as warm as a wadded winter quilt, the tip of her forefinger still hooked in the silver chain on his wrist, he walked into the river until the water was up to his hips. As if in a dream he noted the tide pushing against him. At last he felt the exhaustion from his lack of sleep. But the evening approached. He had to leave this place. The eunuch was waiting for him.

The last bright strokes of September sunlight made his eyes tear. He carried her to the boat, raising his arms high so that the water would not touch her body. One by one the tossing waves lunged against his chest, only to disappear into the silvery sunset.

On the bank, Ven stood unmoving. Her brown skin merged with the bamboo forest. Each time the gentle winds blew, the forest gave up a handful of golden leaves that spattered down on her, floating in midair like paper canoes before the river took them into its bosom. She was staring at his back, and without looking, he knew the look of love and wonder in her eyes. He had not yet bidden her good-bye. The time-teller lingered nearby, holding his silence.

Dan had no idea how to take his leave. The sun descended lower into the west, and the winds grew chillier. When the edge of the plywood gunwale touched his skin, he lifted Lady Chin over the side, then climbed in after her. With infinite gentleness, he laid her down on the deck, her head resting on a bench. The lady-in-waiting looked as if she were watching the sunset through half-shut eyes. He arranged her clothing and folded her hands across her chest. Dan saw Ven walk to the water's edge. For a moment they stood, soaking in the glowing twilight.

"Farewell, Ven!" he called and reached for the oars.

Her grief-stricken shout tore through the silence. She dove in, hands stretched out before her. The river received her embrace, the waves exploding their foamy heads into the cool dusk. The time-teller fell to his knees and leaned forward, clutching his head and rocking himself. His howl, deep and whimpering, echoed hers. Ven turned her head to look back at him, then continued to part the river and propel herself forward.

Dan leaned over the boat's starboard side, reached out, and pulled her toward him. Ven grabbed the wood and lifted herself. The vessel swayed. Her wet clothes clung to her body, dripping water onto the deck.

"What are you doing here, Ven?" he asked. "Your life belongs with him."

She shook her head, her eyes wide. Carefully tiptoeing around the dead body, she backed away from him.

"Listen!" Dan said, reaching to grasp her arm. "Do you not hear him? Big Con is your spouse, and he has saved your life. You have to return to him."

She shook her head, slid her hand into the river, and moved her wet finger across the dry bench. It took her a few attempts to form the message she wanted to tell him. *Help* . . . the phrase read.

"You can write," he said with astonishment. "Tutor Con must have educated you. How remarkable!" He grew worried. "Help? You need help?"

She tapped on her chest, and then pointed at the wobbly scribble on the bench. The word was blurring as it was absorbed into the wood. He leaned over, wrinkled his forehead, and guessed out loud, "You . . . help!" She nodded and caressed his face. He saw the entire river in her eyes, immense and endlessly giving. Behind her, the time-teller had ceased his howling. Clutching the front panels of his shirt, he staggered across the wet sand. His face was drawn, eyes hollow. The panic on his features was deafening.

"You'll help me," Dan repeated.

She nodded.

Pointing a finger at the time-teller, he asked, "Who shall help him? What will happen to the tutor if you leave?"

She blinked, pushing the oars into his hands.

"I understand, Ven," Dan said. "You feel that you must be loyal to me first."

She shook her head in disagreement. Quietly, she put a finger against his lips, as if to stop him from talking. Dan pulled away from her touch.

Big Con chose that moment to spread his arms in her direction and scream, "Come to me, Ven! Come back! If you abandon me, you are abandoning yourself."

She turned her head away. "Go," she slurred at Dan. Her strange voice pushed him back on his seat, and he thrust the oars into the water. Ven huddled across from him, hiding her face.

The time-teller stood frozen under a tamarind tree until their boat was out of sight.

By the time they reached the Truong Tien Bridge the sun was gone. The city was soaked in a faint purple shadow like the inside of a dense mosquito net. Through the twilight, Dan could see the south entrance of the Imperial Palace. Along a small stretch of water a series of sampans was docked. He aimed his boat toward them.

In September, the sky got dark quickly. Above the horizon the stout silhouettes of partridges — the game birds with variegated plumage — circled in the wind, wailing for a safe place to nest. Their predators, the local dogs, crouched in the sand, unmoving except for the fuzzy tips of their tails, as they waited patiently for the flock to veer down. Some of the birds wheeled and soared. Others dove into the water, their little bodies rising and falling on the glistening white-caps like lotus blossoms. Watching them, the dogs growled.

Dan recognized the fragile form of the eunuch standing on a wooden platform that reached out into the water. His face was hidden in the dark. In his hand he held a paper lantern. Its faded light flick-ered in the wind, gradually becoming a bright-red flame as Dan came closer. Behind the old man stood a team of guards, six men in the palace uniform, their metal clubs gleaming in spite of the dimness. In another hour the ledge where they stood would be submerged, denot-ing the time for the closing of the Meridian Gate.

Twenty yards from shore, Dan's oars brushed against the muddy floor of the river. Using his upper-body strength, together with the rising tide, he pushed on the paddles and thrust forward. The vessel ripped into the sludge, landing a few feet from the old man. Ung uttered a high-pitched wail when he saw Lady Chin's rigid corpse.

Dan leaped onto the soggy earth and anchored his skiff to a pole. Ven followed him. With his bare hands, he lifted the vessel out of the water, and left it lying at a slight angle on the soft ground. Silently, he returned onboard for the lady-in-waiting's body, which had grown stiff. During the journey, he had torn a panel of fabric from her outer tunic and draped it over her face. The eunuch stood a few feet away, his eyes on Dan and the corpse in his arms.

"She told me to wait for her here," he said.

"She is gone," answered the young man.

The weather was getting colder. Without a shirt, Dan shivered from the stirring air, and possibly from the contact with his inert burden.

"In that case, it was her wish that I am here to collect her body." The eunuch paused, then added, "She left me careful instructions as to what to do after she passed on." He reached inside his long sleeve to pull out a bamboo cylinder, sealed with wax at each end. "This is her will," he said, breaking the seal to retrieve a small scroll. Turning to his men, he shouted, "Would one of you take delivery of my lady from this young gentleman? You will be rewarded handsomely for your service."

One of the guards moved forward and eased Lady Chin from Dan's embrace. The breeze endeavored to rip the veil from her face; as the soldier pressed her against his chest, it remained over her, fluttering as if she were breathing. With the corpse in his arms, he turned and walked back to his initial spot, a few paces behind the old eunuch. "May I inquire whether any of the instructions pertain to me?" Dan asked.

"You will see soon enough, young Master," Ung replied and unrolled the paper. "Would you prefer for me to read the full content of this note in front of these witnesses? Or should I just tell you in brief what it says, since I have full knowledge of my lady's wishes and commands?"

"You can tell me," Dan said. "I will not contest whatever outcome she has reserved for me, because of my respect for your unblemished reputation and the unique relationship between you and the departed. Furthermore, during the period that I have spent with Lady Chin, especially in the Apartments of Peace, I came to trust her noble-hearted character, her generosity in rendering praise or rewards, and her fairness in retribution."

"Very well then," the eunuch said. "To fulfill her wishes I have brought the matter to the attention of the Queen Mother. Under Her

Majesty's direct order, these soldiers are here to arrest the man who is responsible for the kidnapping and possible manslaughter of one of Her Majesty's highest-ranking ladies-in-waiting."

Ven stepped forward, without realizing that she was now blocking the old man's path to Dan. The eunuch gave her a quick look of surprise before regaining his air of calm assurance.

"I do not understand," said Dan. "Please explain your meaning. Kidnapping! Manslaughter! Sir, I do not challenge the wisdom of the court, but those are serious accusations."

"They are," Ung replied, "plus there are many other charges that I have not mentioned. However, the warrant of the arrest is not meant for you, Sir Nguyen. Even if there were doubts to be raised as to the nature of this crime or the validity of your actions, there must be explicit documents to support or deny these charges. It would be tragic to accuse an innocent, would it not? Lady Chin's last will and testament provides a way for you to prove your purity." He lifted up the note and read loudly, "For Dan Nguyen to verify his innocence, look for my son's silver anklet on his wrist. Without this memento, he shall be tried as a murderer for my death, as well as the deaths of my son and husband. If he can provide such object, I hereby designate him as the new heir of my fortune, which amounts to fifty thousand silver coins. The money is temporarily in the custody of Mr. Dinh Ung. It will serve as the reward for his quest to bring the true killer of my family to justice. When this is done, he will thus accomplish my final wish."

The old man paused, lowering his eyes until they looked directly at Dan's arm. "I recognized Master Bui's good luck charm the moment you came ashore. Congratulations, sir. Not only are you now free, but through the generosity of my mistress, you have an inheritance."

chapter twenty-four

The Road to Nirvana

Dan's living room, a blue rectangle with one window open to the front garden, contained only a few pieces of plain furniture. On the main wall, hanging from the ceiling almost to the floor, was a tapestry embroidered in black silk thread on white canvas, as stark and dramatic as if it had been brushed with coarse strokes of India ink. The room was always dark, and the image was too large for Ven to see it wholly. She had been here for five days, distracting herself from memories of the time-teller by studying the artwork.

At first she had thought it was an old Chinese scroll painting, depicting the evanescent details of life: a bamboo forest, a flock of sparrows, or maybe a misty valley in springtime. However, tonight in the hoary moonlight, as she sat in a chair next to the window, the black dots and lines in the tapestry above her merged into the figure of a young maiden. The girl's hand held an elegant lute. The long, idyllic slopes that Ven had taken for a brook running through groves of bamboo were the girl's dress. And the bamboo leaves were her eyes, seeming to demand a response from inside the room. Ven recognized that face, those long fingers, and the silky black hair that flowed like a watercourse. It was the girl from the house of Toan.

In the center of the room, sitting on a leopard-skin rug, Dan was ruminating over a blank piece of paper. Sketches of discarded brushwork, crumpled into irregular balls, lay scattered on the floor. A finely pointed feather was poised between his fingers; nearby sat a block of ink and a lantern. For hours this evening no sound or movement had come from him. Ven understood his concentration. Once he committed his vision onto paper, there was no turning back. The ink line, once laid down, could never be altered or erased. The moonlight flowed through the slats on the window and slid across him like a striped shirt. She wondered if she should open the shade so he would receive more light.

As she raised her hand toward the wood slats, he surprised her by asking, "Tell me, Ven, are you thinking of the tutor?" A corner of his eyebrow rose. He handed her the pen and said, "Come and sit next to me! Write down your thoughts if you would like to."

From her youth she remembered delicate sheets of paper, covered with black marks, as they passed through the hands of the scholars — friends and acquaintances of her father. The time-teller had taught her the Western letters, scrawling them on the sand with a stick or using a piece of charcoal to mark a board. Never had anyone given her such paper, which had the smell of freshly cut wood. She got up from her seat and received the wet feather with both of her hands, fearful of dropping it on the animal skin.

"Go on," he said.

The tip felt as light as a toothpick in her fingers. Dan put his hand on hers and guided the pen down the paper. She sat awkwardly on the floor beside him, thinking she had never held anything so delicate. She moved the pointed tip of the writing tool, slick with ink. The first mark came, wobbly and graceless, sweeping across the blank page like the path of a scratchy broom.

"That one is not your best stroke," Dan said, pulling back his hand. "Now you try, alone. Forget about the brush and ink when you write. Just picture the letters."

Ven gripped the frail handle more firmly. With a surge of confidence, she began to make small dots and lines by moving her wrist as Dan pinned the paper down with his palms. Like magic the letters took shape, a curve here, a straight line there. To Ven it was as thrilling as the first buds of spring. *"A . . . B . . . C . . ."* Her hand glided across the page. *"D . . . E . . ."*

Next to her, Dan burst out laughing. "The alphabet," he said. "How modest of you. Can you put the letters together to form a word?"

"THE MAP . . ."

His eyebrows furrowed. "What about the map?" he asked in a restrained voice.

Ven unfurled one of the crunched-up wads of paper. Shapes and shadows formed a landscape, similar to the tattoo they had seen on his father's back long ago.

Dan snatched the paper back from her. "This accursed map," he said, smoothing it across his knee. "I have been re-creating it both from memory and from observing its partner on my mother's back. Together they form a diagram that leads to my father's treasure. By studying the riddle written at the bottom of the drawing in the old vernacular language, I guessed part of the secret. But without the first map, it is useless. I plan to embroider it into a tapestry, to teach my children someday about their ancestors' legacy."

"Tell me its secret," she wrote.

"Do you remember the verse on the first map?" he asked.

She nodded. He recited it, and she mouthed the words with him, approving his recollection. "The priests make charms out of nature by aligning the constellations, the sun, and the moon. Then they hold the constellations in their hands, and peering at the sun, they find the road to Nirvana. Many invalids shall be cured at the door.

"I remember what my father said about the riddle," Dan said. "It was a famous poem in the early seventh century describing the Taoist rites in the history of the Sui dynasty. Since my father was a true believer that long life and good fortune could be achieved by magical means — the principles of Taoist philosophy — it is understandable that he chose this verse as the clue to his treasure. Look at the first group of characters: *The priests made charms out of nature by aligning them with the constellations, the sun, and the moon.*" His hand brushed over the red dots on the map that he had drawn. "These drawings are descriptions of nature, and the red marks represent the constellations, the sun, and the moon," he said. "If we superimpose the two maps on top of each other, following the alignment of these dots, I believe we will see the whole picture."

Ven moaned. Her forehead was damp from anticipation as she listened to his voice.

"And the second phrase," he murmured. "*Then, they hold the constellations in their hands, and peering at the sun, they find the road to Nirvana.* This must refer to the way to the hidden treasure. By holding the drawings in the sunlight, we will see this path clearly."

He scratched his head with a sigh. "The last line: *Many invalids shall be cured at the door.* I do not understand the meaning of this sentence, but it sounds like a warning of some sort. Invalids shall be cured — what about healthy people?" He shrugged and tore the picture in half. "Ah, let us not dwell on this matter any longer. It is unfortunate that we only possess a partial diagram. My father has carefully made certain that without one of the two maps, the other would be just a mystery."

"*Make a tapestry,*" she wrote, "*for the Nguyens' legacy.*"

"You approve of this idea?" he asked. "So much blood has been shed, I fear to create another fallacy about the treasure to pass on to the next generation."

She shook her head vigorously. Dan scrutinized her facial expression. She tried to form a smile in response to his glare.

"Dear Ven," he said solemnly, "there is an important question that I must ask. You lived near Magistrate Toan for seven years, so you must understand his strength as well as his limitations. If you wished to take revenge on the old man, you must have had countless opportunities to do so. Yet, you waited for me to return. Why, Ven?"

She looked away. Her smile faded.

"Please do not refuse me the answer — tell me why you spared his life," he said.

She dropped the pen on top of the stack of paper, lifted her hands to her face, and looked at him in silent panic. The bright moon passed through the wooden slats, streaking on both of them. He thrust the brush back into her hand.

With a loud bang, the front door was flung open. Against the dark background of Dan's garden, she saw a round, wrinkled face lit to pastiness by the frail beam of a lantern.

"Do you know, sir," asked the visitor, "that your gate is never bolted? Generally I have to announce myself to the host in order to be led inside, but not at your doorstep."

When Dan saw the intruder, he burst out, "Mr. Ung, come inside where it is warm." Turning to Ven, he said, "Here is a dear friend of poor Lady Chin, Mr. Dinh Ung. You must remember him from the Truong Tien Bridge."

The memory of his presence, along with the palace guards, on the riverbank was still fresh in her mind. She fell to her knees and knocked her head on the wooden floor, inches away from his black velvet slippers. Stealing out from the open tips of the shoes, his toenails were glossy with red paint: his guilty little pleasure. The eunuch gasped at the unexpected display of obeisance. He took a step back, almost tripping on the high threshold, but recovered.

"Raise her, please," he said to Dan. "I am, after all, just a low-ranking eunuch, who does not deserve such reverence."

She felt herself being lifted off the ground. "Do not fret," Dan whispered in her ear. "Mr. Ung is a friend."

He led her back to the chair next to the window. She could feel his fingers wiping the dirt off her forehead. "This is Ven, my guardian and friend," he told the old man.

Ven stiffened as she heard how casually he converted her from his first wife into his custodian. Or was that how he had always viewed her?

What could she expect from him? What could she expect from anyone? A surge of guilt flooded her chest. For the first time since she had left Cam Le, Ven began to understand how her lover, Big Con, must feel. She recalled the muddy pasture by the river, his crouching position, his cries, the way he had grabbed at his head to try to contain his tormented love for her. Big Con was right. By abandoning him — a damaged person — she had abandoned herself. A longing for his presence ate at her like acid. If she could only explain to him why she had come to the city with Dan! But that was impossible; the time-teller was far away, and she was so close to what she wanted to achieve in the citadel.

The old man's voice broke the silence, gliding toward the highest pitch. "I beg the young master's pardon for keeping you waiting the past few days, but the funds deposited by Lady Chin required some legal clearances before I could withdraw them from the treasury. It has all been handled now. I am here to pay out her estate, the sum of fifty thousand silver coins." He reached inside his gray satin robe and, to Dan's surprise, removed a stack of paper. "The money is here, in the form of imperial banknotes. It is a luxury to have such credit and not have to carry so many coins all at once. That is one good thing we have learned from the French. You must see it to believe it."

"I believe you, Mr. Ung," said Dan. "And I am grateful to both Lady Chin and you. I will always remember her for her generosity."

"Then you shall keep this money. It is yours!" He shoved the bank-notes in Dan's hands and turned away.

At the entrance, the eunuch paused and scratched his naked scalp. "There is one other thing," he added. "Before you went away with my lady, you left me a document — your will and testament."

"I remember," said Dan.

"Well, sir." The old man was nervous. "There was also a letter for Lady Tai May, the opera dancer, in case . . . in case . . ."

"In case I did not return," Dan interrupted.

At the sound of the familiar name, Ven went limp inside. How could she be so blind to what was so obvious? The girl's image appeared all over the apartment, in drawings, in the tapestry, every day. She would have confronted him about this deception if she had had a tongue. However, even if she could speak . . . she was now so far removed from his life, it was impossible for her to be authoritative. Her mind echoed, *What happens to those tadpoles that were captured by the goldfish? Will they ever realize their true origin and run away from the captors?* That story was told to her by her mother, who had learned it from her own mother growing up, and that was the only happy ending she knew. Ven felt as though she had run a long-distance race, and while she was still far from the final destination, she had burned up all her fuel. Nevertheless, she couldn't stop now.

"Please, sir." The old man fell upon his knees, clutching Dan's hands. "Forgive me for reading that letter. My curiosity and my loyalty to my lady were so great that I could not help myself. But I swear I would have delivered it to the young miss, if you did not return."

Dan's face twisted in annoyance. "May I please have the letter returned to me?" he asked.

"Indeed," the old man said, wiping his eyes with the hem of his tunic. "I shall deliver it to you tomorrow morning. But I have more to tell you before I leave. Miss Tai May and her troupe will be leaving the citadel tomorrow. The Royal Court has dismissed them from their duties. The emperor replaced them with another group of artists, formed and educated in France. The new performers are widely acclaimed for their acrobatic acts and the tricks they do with trained tigers. From reading your letter, I've learned how important the young lady is to you. I feel compelled to report the news of her departure, so that you can make the necessary arrangements to meet her before it is too late. No longer the emperor's property, she is now a free woman."

"Mr. Ung!" cried Dan. "Can this be true?"

The eunuch got up from his kneeling position and said, "That is what I heard on leaving the Imperial Palace a few hours ago. If you still want me to deliver that note to her, I shall try my best to accommodate your wishes. It is the very least that I can do to regain your friendship."

"Oh!" Dan exclaimed, grabbing the old man in his arms and squeezing him tight. "Thank you, thank you, Mr. Ung! This is wonderful news! You must discard the old letter, and I will compose another to her immediately." He turned his face to Ven so that she could see his smile under the light. "Can you imagine that, Ven?" he said in a triumphant voice. "I have nothing more to ask of Heaven — now that I will see Tai May again. Tomorrow I shall tell her how much I love her and that I will devote myself to her until the day I die. Better yet, I will tell her now, using this pen and paper. I must let her know that my passion for her is still burning brightly, in spite of time and adversities." Turning back to Ung, he said, "Please take a seat, dear Mr. Ung. This will take but a few moments."

He dipped the feather's tip in the inkwell, smoothed out a piece of paper, and began to write. All Ven heard was the steady scratching of the quill on the page, digging at her head like a termite's crunching.

The eunuch inspected his reflection in a mirror that was hung by the door to ward off evil spirits.

Rising from her chair, Ven stood in the moonlight, watching him. She knew at once that it was Heaven's will to place her in this room at this hour, so she could stop his obsession with the girl. Now was her chance. She had to bring a perfect ending to her story, the only way she knew how.

Dan rose gracefully from the floor. In his hand, the sheet of paper was still wet with black ink. He blew at it impatiently. Ven rushed over and snatched the letter from his hand. She must show him that she — his sole custodian — opposed this forbidden union of the two enemy houses. She hid the paper behind her. Dan grabbed her shoulders. She stared in his eyes, just as she had done throughout his childhood, expecting him to surrender to her will. But instead of fear she saw a wall of anger and a blaze of defiance, and for the first time in her relationship with Dan, she had to look away.

"Listen to me, Ven," he said. "I understand how you feel, although I never felt the same way."

You don't know how I feel, she heard herself screaming in her mind. *You do not know how deep my devotion to you is.* He continued. "You are bound to an old belief system, and you follow its rules so blindly that you cannot see the coming of your own doom. Time has changed for the two of us. You must free me to discover life for myself. With you, I have always played the passive role of a voyeur, watching life from a safe distance. You solve every puzzle, every calamity for me. You even came close to dying once to let me live. For such a long time I carried this infection of fear in me, and I have infected everyone I have touched. I cannot do that anymore. I am all grown up, and —"

He burst out in tears. "I don't need you anymore."

His words collapsed upon her like a falling tower. She released her fingers, letting the letter slip away. The eunuch caught it before it hit the floor.

"Go back to Tutor Con, my dearest Ven," Dan said. He put his hand on her shoulder. "I must go and see my mother before the night is over. This unexpected inheritance will help me redeem her freedom. When tomorrow comes, my life will change forever."

*L*eaving Ven behind in his apartment, Dan moved through New Town with the single-mindedness of a stalking panther. Though the streets were alive with noise and motion, he had little awareness of their raucous vitality. A drunken coolie jostled him, but he never faltered, nor did his nose turn away from the smells of rotten fruits, decaying fish, and overflowing sewage. From a dark wall came a voice: "Five pennies to have your fortune told." Ignoring every distraction, he strode to the tea shop on Morin Street.

Crossing into the front parlor, he stopped to catch his breath. The glass wall with its man-made waterfall sent tiny bubbles swimming in the air like silver coins. The light was dimmed to almost black, and the rotating ceiling fans made the room so cool that his skin became covered in gooseflesh. The room was alive with the sounds of customers enjoying the company of the female employees.

Dan walked to the end of the room, where the man with the black beard stood behind the counter. He slammed his fist against the bar's surface with a loud smacking sound to get the bartender's attention.

"Well," the burly man said, looking up and wiping an empty glass with a dirty rag he hooked at the end of his sleeve. "It is you, Dan the farmer. How are you doing this evening? I imagine you are looking for Camille. I'll send for her."

Straddling a barstool, Dan said, "I am here to conduct a business transaction. As you know, up to this time, it has been Camille that I came to see. However, tonight the meeting I am requesting must have your presence as well as hers. I must warn you, it is your signature that I want."

Setting the glass on a rack at his side, the bartender narrowed his eyes. "You wish to speak to me? What sort of business?"

"Tell me, do you possess a bill of ownership for every woman that works for you in this brothel?"

The man bristled. "You are incorrect in using the term 'brothel.' This is the finest tea shop in town. Still, I must confess that I do need to obtain proper police documents and ownership licenses for the girls."

"Aha," Dan said, nodding. "Knowing your strict moral code, I assume that you will not surrender these bills bearing your released signature unless you first receive a substantial sum of money in exchange for them."

There was a moment of silence as the bartender's eyebrows rose. Then he burst out laughing as if Dan had said something funny. "Why?" he asked with sudden friendliness. "Are you trying to negotiate for Camille's freedom? If so, how much are you thinking of?"

He paused and looked up at the sound of a woman's nervous laughter. Under the churning yellow and orange lights, Camille stood wearing an elegant black dress, like a deity of destruction, fragile but ferocious. Her dark eyes shone from her powdered pale face.

"Van Tong," she said, breaking right through their conversation, "you failed to inform me that my customer is here."

She glided to Dan's side. Her hand caressed his collar as she said, "You speak as though you have just stumbled upon a great treasure. Do not disclose to strangers your vital business, since they may cause you more harm than good. Come into my room! We shall talk where no one can hear us."

"No one leaves my station," said the bartender. His massive hand caught Lady Yen's shoulder. "What have you been hiding from me, Camille? I am beginning to think that this young farmer is your new lover. Is this so? I demand a straightforward answer."

Turning to Dan, he said, "Yes, you shall pay me for her freedom — if, as I hope, you have enough silver coins to help me procure a new girl who is blessed with as many talents as she has. If not, I must content myself with Camille. In this business, one cannot afford to be parted easily from such a valuable property."

Camille wrenched away. The tight knot in her hair became undone, and it spilled down her arching back like a school of snakes.

"Take your hand off me," she hissed. "I wish Hell would open this minute and swallow you whole, damnable brute. Do you wish for a straightforward answer? Here it is. This is my son, and whatever cash he brought to this place shall belong to me. You are not my keeper." Her exploding words brought the room to silence.

The bartender raised his brows until the whites of his eyes became opaque. He breathed in her face, "Be careful! You are not being truthful to either of us. Forgive me for being the messenger of bad news. Have you informed your son that I, Van Tong, am your legal husband? Judging from his behavior, I think he was led to believe that you are just one of my whores."

His words stabbed her with enough venom to make her collapse on top of a barstool. In the stillness of the cavernous room, Dan said to her, "Is that true what he said, madam?"

She covered her face in her hands. The bartender cleared his throat and snickered, wagging his fingers. Her silence was enough to confirm Dan's suspicion.

He rose; anger magnified in his voice. "Where is your heart, Mother? You have forsaken me once again! When I was just a child, you chose your life over mine. I came here with the intention of saving your honor, but now I see that even the gods in Heaven could not rescue you. Here is the treasure that you were waiting for." He reached inside his tunic for a banknote and threw it on the counter. "This is a bill that is worth twenty thousand silver coins, intended to procure your freedom. I am turning it over to both of you. I hope you will kill each other over this money. As for you, madam, I shall expect you to keep away from me. And someday when I have children, I shall teach them a new legacy of my ancestors, that I was born under a rock."

He backed away from her, holding the rim of the bar for support. Camille stifled a sob, watching her son stagger to the door.

chapter twenty-five

Clumps of Bindweed

D an sat on his haunches against the cool darkness of the great stone wall overlooking the courtyard that led to the Meridian Gate. He had been sitting in the same huddled position since returning from the tea shop the previous night. Above him an oak tree stretched its brawny branches around a central trunk like the hinged ribs of a parasol.

With his chin resting on his bent knees, Dan watched the night fade into dawn. Beside him a reedy and neglected rosebush held a single blossom. The graceful curve of its stem reminded him of Tai May. To Dan there was no beauty more wonderful than the sight of her in soft white silk garments, and he longed to see her among the crowd of strangers. He wondered how much longer he had to wait.

He was disheartened to see how many people were traveling in and out of this opulent city through the two majestic banks of granite. Rich men and women in silvery rickshas and horse-drawn carriages waved their ivory passes at the guards. Laborers carried bread and cakes and cauldrons of stew meat on their backs to cater the endless feasts inside the city. Once in a while, among the dirty black clothing of the peasants, he caught a glimpse of a sumptuous silk robe, or a belt cut tight at the waist, or a wide pair of trousers, and he jumped up. He craned his neck to follow these faceless visions, only to realize that he was looking at a complete stranger, and he would sigh in disappointment, then begin his search once more.

As the morning passed, the active scene before him became thinner and duller. The sky was a blend of black smoke from a nearby bakery and peach-colored clouds, with a stubborn ray of sunshine breaking through the leaves. Just when he was on the verge of bursting with expectation, he heard a female voice calling his name.

Eagerly he turned toward the noise, but to his great dismay, he saw his mother, standing alone before a carriage on the other side of the main road. Her hair hung in strings, and her large eyes, the color of litchi nuts, were swollen and red-rimmed. She wore no makeup; under the sun her skin was bleached to a much starker shade than he remembered. How had she managed to locate him? He wondered if he had unwittingly given her a clue the night before.

He watched her hobble across the street. One beggar whined at her, asking for a penny; another offered his hand to accompany her. He watched his mother reach in her purse and spray a handful of change at the men as though she were feeding a flock of chickens.

Something had changed. As a child, he had never seen her pay heed to the beggars; her habit was to look through them. Not wanting to confront her, he turned away. Again she called out his name. She swayed toward him on her little feet, a pitiful sight, and he took a bitter satisfaction in her obvious struggle.

"Let me have one more moment of your time," she said through tears that she didn't bother to brush away.

"Whatever you have to say to me," he replied, "please make it quick. I am waiting for someone."

She nodded, leaning against the wall for support. Nearby in the courtyard, a young girl hid her face in a conical hat, the white panels of her robe flapping in the wind. Over the fishmonger's protests, the girl poked her fingers at a basket full of red snappers. Beyond them, he recognized the familiar face of Mr. Ung, who was watching from a distance. In his hands he held a silver bicycle. Dan glared at the old man and frowned. Red-faced, the eunuch turned to the basket of fish, pushed his shoulders back, and tried to initiate a conversation with the vendor.

"For a minute of your time," said his mother, pulling at his sleeve, "I beg you to give me your full attention. This is the last time you will ever see me, so please listen carefully to what I have to say. Give me one final chance to prove my affection to you. Later, when I am gone, respect and pity the memory of this poor woman, because for one shining moment she is giving up her happiness for yours."

Dan looked at his mother with amazement. In her eyes he saw a trace of benevolence that almost melted his heart. "I am listening," he said.

Her mouth lifted in a mournful smile. "Very well. I came here with a purpose, and that is to tell you something you don't know about our little family affairs. For as many years as you have been alive, I have carried deep inside me a great secret. Forgive me, dear son!" She paused, brushing an invisible gnat from her shoulder. "You are not the son of Captain Tat Nguyen. In fact, you do not have any relation to the Nguyen family. Therefore, you are not obligated to take revenge for his death."

His mother's words made the scenery around him sway. The heat flared, and his lungs seemed devoid of air. "Whose son am I then?" Dan asked.

"You were a result of my love affair with the gardener," she said, "whose name I would rather die than speak. Please, do not look upon me as your enemy. You are free, my son! You can love and marry that girl, because you are not her family's enemy. This is my wedding gift to you. In the depth of my shameful and dishonored soul, I beg your forgiveness. And now that I have said what I came to say, I will not take any more of your time. Soon I shall be going to a faraway land, where I will devote the rest of my life to repenting for my sins. After all, the gods are the only ones with power over Earth."

She turned and fumbled along the wall.

"Where are you going?" Dan asked.

Lady Yen hesitated. Dan could not see her face. All he saw was her bent head and the soft mass of her hair, moving like a curtain that hid her features from sight. She reached inside her blouse and, without looking back, pressed the banknote against his chest.

"I almost forgot," she said. "I am giving you back your money so that you can begin a fresh life. Take care of yourself and your new family! Forget me, and instead of pursuing my whereabouts, let me go."

"You are too late, madam. I have already forgiven you. Please stay."

She looked up and smiled. "Then I must definitely leave. If I stay, nothing will remain for us to do but to torture each other with our expectations. Each time I look at you, I will only remember how I have abandoned you. Think of me with good thoughts; that is all I ask."

"But will you not need this money?" he asked.

"Where I am going," she replied, "I will not require any material things."

Dan could see her tears flow again. They were quite different this time — genuine, heartfelt, lacking her usual manipulation and shrewdness. He watched from across the street as the coachman shut the door behind her. She never looked back.

The second time Dan saw his mother walk out of his life, he was smiling. He began to erase her from his memory; bit by bit she was vanishing while his mind became a white canvas once again.

≻⊱

After the carriage disappeared down the road, the eunuch ventured closer. His gloomy face portended bad news. In his hands, the bicycle made a low yet unremitting *tic-tic* sound with its two wheels turning. Beyond the old man's shaven head, a few black herons soared on the wind above the jagged tips of the shining city.

"Master Dan," the old man began, his eyes darting around the market. "You have not returned to your apartment since last night. Your guardian wrote a letter to you before she went back to her village. She insisted that I deliver it to you. Despite her difficulties, she is quite eloquent in expressing herself." He presented a sealed envelope to Dan, and added, "Sometimes I feel like a postal messenger with all of these notes. All I need is a horse to qualify for the position."

He turned unsteadily, and his knee bumped against the bicycle. Like a clever conjurer, he grabbed the steering handle and regained his balance. He wobbled again and touched his leg. "Go ahead," he said. "Read it. Then I will tell you more."

Dan sat on the sidewalk and tore open the envelope. He recognized Ven's handwriting on the delicate paper inside.

My dearest Dan,

Although this letter is being written this evening with the assistance of Mr. Ung, my story actually began in the month of January 1916.

I remember it as clearly as yesterday. On the first dawn after our wedding night, while you, a child of seven, were still asleep in your comfortable bed, I was awakened to make breakfast for the Nguyen family. There, outside the window of the main living room, accompanied by the young maid Song, I saw the shadows of two men leaning over a desk. Being new and strange in unfamiliar territory, my curiosity prompted me to spy on them. Song made a hole in the parchment that sealed the window, and through this opening I saw your father, Captain Nguyen. The other man was Master Long. They were discussing politics.

From their conversation, I learned that your father was an avid supporter of a rebel group whose leader's name was Le Ngung. They called themselves the Antitax Antiforeigners Blood Brotherhood, and your father recruited Master Long to join them in their fight against the influence of the French over Vietnam. I witnessed them swearing a blood oath of loyalty to each other. I developed a tremendous respect for your father, who had undoubtedly proven his courage and passion for his country. Instantly I became his devotee.

As time passed, I continued watching their frequent gatherings. In the middle of March, before your father went to sea, I overheard a plot to help King Duy Tan to escape the palace, and to deliver a large cargo of gunpowder to the Blood Brotherhood's secret hideaway. Your father trusted Master Long. Unfortunately, this traitor deceived him. Captain Nguyen and his crew were placed in chains and led away blindfolded the minute their ship returned to shore.

Dan, you know the rest of the story, from the burning of the mansion to the beheading of your father. In that moment, my whole world was shattered. I endured the cruelty of your household so that some day I could enjoy the rewards of being your first mistress. Because of Toan, I became a beggar instead, and you a slave. Since then, my only reason for survival is to see you take revenge on them. But you failed me.

My dear young Master, there is one more secret I must confess to you. Song could no longer live with the shame and abuse from the old magistrate, so before she killed herself, she stole your father's map from Toan and gave it to me. You once asked me why I did not bring the old man to his demise. By letting him live with the knowledge that he had lost everything, including the buried treasure, I knew he would suffer long and deeply. Greed destroyed him in the end.

When I leave your apartment, I will take with me the drawing of the second half of the map. I will put the two maps together as you explained and find the treasure. I am returning to Tutor Con and maybe together we will build the life I never had with you.

Dan, you will always be my first husband. I shall never forget you.

Ven

Pain cut through him as he came to the last line of the letter. How articulate her thoughts and language were; she never ceased to surprise him. At the same time, he recognized that she was using words to unleash her silent scorn, to prove to him that she always knew more than he did. He once had her, lost her, found her, and now he had lost her again, forever. But she had also granted him freedom, and a new phase of his life was beginning.

"I am so sorry, young Master," the eunuch said. "I have another piece of bad news. This morning I came to find Lady Tai May. Because I had shown her your note the night before and witnessed the delighted expression on her face, I was hoping to gather more information about her departure. But the young lady was gone, together with her troupe. I came in the very nick of time to watch them being escorted out of the palace through the North Gate."

Dan blinked. He was not sure he understood what the eunuch had said. But then it did not matter. Whatever he saw was not true; she had received Dan's letter, and soon she would find him sitting on the sidewalk and waiting for her. His faith in her was strong enough to withstand any test.

"She will come," he muttered. "It may take her some time, but she will find me."

"But sir, you do not understand," the eunuch said, offering his hand. "The young emperor is changing everything. No one knows what he is going to do next. The whole court system looks like it is about to come to an end. There has been so much confusion in the palace. The Queen Mother feared that letting the royal opera performers leave through the Meridian Gate would stir up an undesirable reaction from the people of Hue. That is why they were taken to the other exit. I saw Lady Tai May begging for mercy from one of the guards, but her cries were in vain. You should go inside, young Master. The gate will only remain open for less than another hour."

Dan pushed the old man's hand away.

"Please, sir, I fear that you may be waiting for a hopeless dream."

Dan sprang to his feet. The fire in his eyes must have been scathing, for Ung drew back in fear. In his hands, the bicycle skidded on the gravel. Dan grasped the handlebar and caught the elderly man's bony fingers, clenching them so tightly that the eunuch squealed.

"You must think that I am mad," he said. "Well, you and the rest of the world! You do not know her the way I do. If only you could have seen us as children together. I fell in love the very first time I was brought to her home. I saw her dancing, and I was bought as a slave to bring her happiness. If only you could have heard us exchanging vows under the harvest moon, if only you were the screen that separated us — the hapless embroiderer and the lonely dancer — you would see how deep our love is for each other. Things are not always as they seem, Mr. Ung. Just listen! I wrote to her that I would wait for her here. I can almost feel her presence getting closer, and I will stay on this step until she comes. If I leave, she will never find me."

The old man looked at him as if he were losing his mind. "This bicycle belonged to Lady Chin. Since you are the sole heir of her estate, I have brought it to you." With those words, he propped the bike on its stand and left.

Dan sat back on the ground and inhaled. If he had to be here for another thousand years, he told himself, if he had to turn into a stone grave marker while waiting for her, then so be it. Maybe someday, someone would burn a stick of incense for him.

✕

*I*t was toward the end of the afternoon when Ven arrived at the time-teller's hut. An oak tree reached thick, tattered branches over the cabin, heightening the impression of desolation. The last rays of sun broke through an umbrella of leaves and dappled the thatched roof, and for a moment, it seemed possible to Ven that spring might come again.

The rains of the past couple of days had left the earth muddy. Around the hut a flotsam of broken wine bottles lay scattered over piles of banana peels, clumps of rice, and fish bones. It was obvious that Big Con had gone back to his drinking. The contented home she had left was now a reminder of what his life had once been.

With each step, Ven stirred up a blanket of flies from the garbage-strewn ground. Their buzzing echoed in the silence of the forest. She found the front door, made of bamboo stalks, overgrown with bindweed dotted with tiny violet blossoms.

Slowly she pulled the door to one side and entered. A condensed mist of mustiness and rotten woodchips permeated the interior. Except for a few brittle beams of light peeping though the holes in the roof, the room was in total darkness. She searched the bamboo bench in the corner for the sight of his drunken face, but all she saw was a blanket, folded neatly, just as she had left it. The barrenness of the place made her so restless that she could not remain inside. She went back out to the edge of the forest.

Beyond the trees she could hear the sound of the brook, small and silvery, running in the forest. Above her, the leaves floated through the air like the sampans on the river, and the fading sun was a red, festering volcano, ready to erupt. Her eyes were drawn to a small metal object reflecting the light on the bed of decaying leaves. She knew exactly what it was — his little gong, which he never let out of sight even when he was most intoxicated.

The wind felt cold against her skin. She clutched at her shirt as she took hesitant steps across the soggy loam. Above the heavy odor of decaying plants, Ven detected the stench of urine and vomit. He must still be nearby. She made a series of loud yelps, calling out for him. The echo returned without his reply.

She came to the thick bamboo floor on the bank of the creek. Beside the constant droning of the water current, the woods stood motionless in a brooding silence. She searched for him behind every bush and came up with nothing. She wondered if she should go back to the cabin and wait for him there. But her throat was scratchy and dry. The babble of the stream reminded her that she had not eaten or drunk anything since that morning.

She walked to the edge of the platform and knelt down, scooping up a handful of water and holding it to her face. The coldness seized at her skin. Instantly she saw a red ribbon of blood and stopped in frozen disbelief. Through the slats of the bamboo floor, she saw the body of the time-teller, stretched out in a trough of mud. He lay on his stomach, one side of his face resting in the water. Streams of blood seeped from his throat, wiggling like the tail of a carp.

Ven screamed and plunged into the creek. The water came up to her knees, frightfully cold for autumn. She crawled under the bamboo boardwalk and lifted Big Con with both her hands. His head rolled on the cradle of her arm; his teeth were chattering; his mouth was blue, as though he had just ingested an entire bottle of ink. At the side of his neck, a gaping dark wound slashed deep into his flesh. She touched the cut, trying to close it with her hand. Shakily, she called to him in her foreign, unintelligible voice. The time-teller moaned and opened his eyes.

"You came," he whispered. "My scarecrow." He gasped for air, struggling for consciousness. "I've . . . been waiting for you."

Her tears fell on his wound and trickled down his chest, tiny violet blossoms like the wild weed on the door of his shack.

"Whooo . . . ?" she fought for words, angry at her inability to pronounce the simplest sound.

Even through her tears he could read her. "It does not matter," he rasped. "I was drunk, got in a fight . . . an old enemy . . . my own fault."

He reached for her hand. The ridges on his fingertips were prominent from soaking in the water too long. "Good-bye," he said.

"No! No!" In desperation, she pulled him closer to her chest, hoping the warmth of her body would bring him back to life. But she felt his body growing colder. *Don't go!* her mind screamed to him. *You and I are going to share a great fortune.*

He raised his eyelids one last time to look at her. "I am the time-teller," he said. "I know when it is time . . . especially for me." His head rolled to one side.

Long afterward, Ven remained crouching in the water with his body wrapped in her embrace. She did not see the night falling, but she sensed her body sink into a world of black, or so it seemed. For the first time in her life, Ven was frightened of the dark.

A Taste of Gardenia

*I*t was about six o'clock in the morning. Beyond the south entrance, the Imperial City was submerged in an opalescent darkness. Another night had elapsed, and Dan had not moved from his position.

He could feel dawn stealing into the courtyard. A speck of sunlight, bright as a diamond, slanted through the curve of a palace rooftop to beam down upon him. At the booming of the cannon, the citadel roused.

Dan sat leaning against the stone wall and resting his head in the palms of his hands. He was aware of everything around him, and yet he was aware of nothing; he did not know whether it was a sunny morning or midnight or an interim of time between life and death.

The marketplace began to fill with people. They surrounded him with their loud arguments and their scuffling feet, and the noisy rustling of their coarse garments pulled him away from his quiet sanctuary. A pair of wooden sabots, chaste and elegant in their form, entered his range of vision. Red velvet straps were fastened across the insteps of the owner's petite feet. He was thinking of the scarlet rose petals he had once stitched on white fabric. He detected the sweet fragrance of gardenia, and joy infused his mind.

"I am sorry I could not get here sooner," a soft voice above him breathed.

When he looked up, Dan saw a vision, bathed in the glow of the ruddy, pulsating dawn. The sunlight was behind a human outline, and for an instant, it blinded him. He sat up at once, unable to believe what he was seeing. It was her, Tai May! She seemed to rise out of the glorious sun. His fingers unconsciously pulled at the collar of his tunic, straightening it, and then he smoothed out his hair.

She was smiling. Her jet-black hair, fiery in the sun, framed her small face. At a slight tug of her hand, the hair fell loose over one shoulder. The beauty in that gesture was enough to make his head spin.

"I am not too late, am I?" she said, blushing a little because she was staring straight into his eyes.

"Is it really you?" he asked, touching her neck. Her skin was smooth and soft, and he could feel the pulse of a tiny vein. She leaned closer and placed her lips against his. He could taste the gardenia at the tip of his tongue.

They drew apart, both beaming. The sun was bursting out of the sky and embracing them with its intensity. "Oh, Mouse," she said, "put your arms tight around me so I can feel you."

"I am yours," he replied, holding her firmly. "I will show you how great my love for you is, and how it has deepened through all the years we waited for each other. No one on Earth can pull us apart now. Come with me!" He ran his fingers down her back, and the touch made her shiver even more.

"Where are we going?" she whispered.

"Far from here," he said, reaching for the bicycle. Its silver frame caught the sunlight. As if he were reciting the words to a poem, he said, "As far as this metal horse can take us — to the end of the world."

She felt the steering handle under her palms; it was cool. One of his arms was wrapped around her waist, while the other covered her wrist and wove into her fingers. They were sharing the same saddle. She could feel the roughness of his unshaven chin against the nape of her neck, and inside her something that she had never noticed came alive for the first time. She leaned back into his chest; his muscular legs thrust at her side. She was wrapped inside the rippling body of her lover as the bike crunched the gravel on the road.

"Look, Mouse." She pointed at the single rosebush along the stone wall. "Can you see that last rose of autumn?"

"No, darling," he said, his breath hot against her ear. "It is the first rose of spring."

Author's Note

I was six days old when my grandfather first told me his life stories. I was lying in a small bamboo cradle suspended by ropes from a high wooden beam. From the window, the summer sky shone like an inverted ocean, motionless except for a few distant clouds. Hummingbirds fluttered over the garden fountain, then disappeared into the pomegranate trees.

While the ceiling swayed he would speak to me in a melodic tone, always with the same introduction: "During the winter months, the Perfume River was chilly, especially at dawn." In my recollection, the world of my grandfather was simple, irregular, and deliberately void of anything material. No photo albums or mementos helped illustrate his tales, only his soothing voice, flowing in the river of his memory.

At times, my grandmother would join him. In the background, she would pluck the strings of her lute and sing Vietnamese folk songs. Between the two of them, my childhood was filled with wonder. I could always close my eyes and allow myself to be transported back to a time when my grandfather was a child. While in the rest of the world, children grew up with fairy tales, I lived in my grandfather's stream of consciousness, feasting on his thoughts, feeling his emotions, and absorbing his legacy.

When I was older and able to retain some of the plots, we ventured into our garden. By that time, the trees had been replaced with rose vines on white trellises. The hummingbirds had moved on, and the new tenants were butterflies. No matter what direction I looked, the sky would be drenched in a sea of ocean blue, forever concealing its secrets.

I was at the age when everything seemed complicated, and giving something a name only added to my confusion about its nature. I could not understand why a dog would be called "dog" and a cat "cat." The stories took longer for my grandfather to tell because of my endless questions. But with great patience, he always explained them to me in meticulous detail.

This state of communication between the two of us was heightened as time passed, because of my love for him as a storyteller and also because of his zest for living. I remember the excitement I felt the first time we waited together for the midnight cactus to bloom. I marveled at the sight of the plant's tender buds and the way they reached for the moonlight with long, tapering, and delicate sprouts, uncurling like tendrils of a fern. To purify the air, my grandmother had lit sandalwood bark in a copper urn nearby. Listening to my grandfather, I could almost see the music of his voice swirling in the smoke. But the endless wait was impossible to endure. Before long, I fell asleep on his lap.

Late into the night, I was awakened by a strong scent of perfume. I opened my eyes. The moon seemed to shine through a layer of rice paper. The sandalwood had burned out. We were still in the garden, but now the wind was softer and almost liquid with humidity. At first I thought it was the moon that had the smell like the inside of a temple. But then I saw the blossoms on the cactus. The outer sheaths that had once been pinkish were now red — vermilion — like blood flowing over the white petals. I remember the very moment when the moonlight became a part of the flower's pistils. I watched as the entire tree emitted an iridescent glow. My grandfather was silent. And when the fragrant mist disappeared, all of the white petals withdrew into the plant. The brief courtship between the moon and the flowers was over.

Living with my grandfather, every day was a surprise. I never knew what his next lesson would be. It could be a story he read from an old book, or a tale he told of his own experience, or my likeness that he embroidered in one of his tapestries, or a discussion of the plants and herbs in the garden.

In the morning, he would wake me before the sun rose to go to the pond where the lotus plants thrived. I can still feel the cold sand under my bare feet as I ran a few paces ahead of him, carrying a child-sized teapot. While he collected the morning dew from the lotus leaves, I would hunt for tea that was hidden deep inside the blossoms.

For a long time I didn't know how the tea got there. I imagined that the plants manufactured their own tea, or perhaps it was placed there by a water nymph for the taking. Years later, it dawned on me that my grandmother had been putting the tea leaves inside the lotus buds the night before, so that they could marinate over night. Even after the mystery was solved, the enchantment lingered in me whenever I reminisced on those days. Like a child looking for Easter eggs, I would run from flower to flower, searching for my treasure, disappointed each time I found an empty bloom.

When he had gathered enough water off the leaves, and my little pot was one-third full, we returned home. Outside the kitchen, my grandmother had prepared a terra-cotta stove with burning coals, ready for his ritual. It was his own ceremonious way to pay respect to the higher power of nature. As the water boiled, its steam became a thick mist, erasing all that was real around me. A new setting would emerge, narrated by his voice — a world that had once belonged to him, a world that he now handed over to me. After telling me a story, he would ask me to repeat it over and over again. I did not know whether it was a test to see if I was listening, or his way to keep the past alive.

I asked him, "Who was the beautiful dancer, Tai May?"

"She is here," he replied.

"Really?"

"Yes, only now her name is Grandma."

"What happened to Ven?"

He stirred the fire with a bamboo stick. Sparks of ember crackled. "After she took the maps, she vanished. I never saw her again. Your grandmother and I returned to live in the Cam Le Village. For many years that followed, on the morning of my every birthday, I would wake up to find a small tray of my favorite food on the front stoop of my house."

"Banana custard packed in rice with coconut juice?" I asked.

He smiled. "She was the only person who knew how to prepare it to my liking. This went on for many years, and one day it stopped. I knew then that she had died."

"What about the treasure in the maps?"

"I don't know if Ven ever found it. It didn't matter because I have found my own fortune. It is the family that I have now."

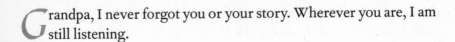

Grandpa, I never forgot you or your story. Wherever you are, I am still listening.

Acknowledgments

In memory of Christine Jampolsky and my grandparents

With heartfelt thanks to Judy Clain, Fiona and Jake Eberts, Michaela Hamilton, Brenda Marsh, Peter Miller, Claire Smith, my brother, Jimmy, and sister, Be Ti

Special thanks to Do Phuong Khanh, Kathleen Bui Mai Khanh, Vu Quang Ninh, Nguyen Xuan Nghia, and Dinh Quang Anh Thai

Additional thanks to Kathy Bishop, cau mo Hoa Buu, Christine Crownin, Doan Thu Doan, Pi Gardner, Michelle Hillman, chu thim Hoc, Bob and Sally Huxley, Tom John, Bill Richards, Camilo Sanchez, Julia Szabo, and Patricia Urevith

And thanks to everyone at Little, Brown; PMA; Corbin and Associates; Little Saigon radio; Viet Tide *newspaper; and Thuy Nga Productions*

Kien Nguyen was born in Nhatrang, South Vietnam, to a Vietnamese mother and an American father. He left Vietnam in 1985 through the United Nations' Orderly Departure Program. After spending time in a refugee camp in the Philippines, Nguyen arrived in the United States. His first book, The Unwanted, *was a memoir about his childhood in Vietnam.*